THE BOOK

a novel

M. CLIFFORD

Also by M. Clifford

PROPAGANDA from the desk of:
Martin Trust - Director of Historic Homeland
Preservation and Restoration

THE MUSE OF EDOUARD MANET

FELINIAN

FERTILE CRESCENT

THE DRACULA INDEX

#WHOISLEROSY

FOR MY FATHER

HE WAS A SPRINKLER FITTER
HE WAS A SIMPLE MAN

TO THOSE FEW HE LOVED MORE THAN HIMSELF,
HE WAS A HERO

COPYRIGHT *2010* BY M. CLIFFORD
COVER ART COPYRIGHT *2015* BY M. CLIFFORD

ALL RIGHTS RESERVED. NO PART OF THIS BOOK MAY BE REPRODUCED
IN ANY FORM OR BY ANY ELECTRONIC OR MECHANICAL MEANS,
INCLUDING INFORMATION STORAGE AND RETRIEVAL SYSTEMS,
WITHOUT PERMISSION IN WRITING FROM THE AUTHOR.

THE EVENTS AND CHARACTERS IN THIS BOOK – EVEN THOSE BASED ON REAL PEOPLE - ARE
FICTIONAL. ANY DIRECT SIMILARITY IS COINCIDENTAL
AND NOT INTENDED BY THE AUTHOR.

Praise and Response

Publishers Weekly calls THE BOOK a "compelling...futuristic novel about a world overrun by 'The Editors' who control society through censorship. While a radical group known as the Free Thinkers attempts to bring down the ruling regime, Holden devises a plan to set the world free and in doing so becomes a radical himself." *Publishers Weekly* found "similarities to Huxley's BRAVE NEW WORLD and Orwell's 1984" concluding that the government-issued digital reading device called The Book "takes the place of Big Brother" which was seen as a "nice twist on the current e-reader trend".

My thanks to the many English teachers across the country who have incorporated this novel into their class curriculum. Your words and stories are encouraging and it has been rewarding to read them all over the past year. As always, my email inbox is open to you and your students. I will always devote myself to the readership of this nation's next generation and I'm glad to see that I have made an impact.

THE BOOK

"The one who tells the stories rules the world."
- Hopi Indian proverb

"Young readers, you whose hearts are open, whose understandings are not yet hardened, and whose feelings are neither exhausted nor encrusted with the world, take from me a better rule than any professors of criticism will teach you. Would you know whether the tendency of a book is good or evil, examine in what state of mind you lay it down. Has it distracted the sense of right and wrong which the Creator has implanted in the human soul? If so – if you have felt that such were the effects it was intended to produce – throw the book into the fire, whatever name it may bear on the cover."
- Southey

"It is sure to be dark if you close your eyes."
- unknown

DON'T READ THE BOOK

Don't read The Book.

That phrase has followed me my entire life.

I was never trained to tell stories. Most people these days aren't born in that percentile. Those who are write passive sonnets about duty, honor and glory to the government. Complacency that breeds. This tale, however, has never been told and you are risking your life by continuing. We, the people, have learned that while there is danger in the printed word, so is there power. In the days of our ancestors, it stirred us to revolution. Words were honored and protected. They were spiritual and rehabilitating. But that was before recycling sustained the world and asphyxiated our minds. For the sake of clarity, I'll save those details for another page.

If you are reading these words from a source other than a bound stack of printed paper, the following pages have been compromised. Including the sentences above, there are a total of 97,777 words in this story. You need to brand this number to your mind. If you reach the end of this book and the number is incorrect, the following pages have been compromised.

M. CLIFFORD

Remember a single word can change the world. You must always keep track of the word count so it won't happen again.

Before we begin, I would like to offer you a guarantee. This *will* be difficult and you will come to a point between paragraphs where you must choose one of two diverging roads – either continue and learn the truth or stop flipping the paper pages, suppress what you have read and tell Robert Frost that *all the difference* can go suck a grenade. Forgive the disjunction and my insensitive language, but I need your undivided attention so it won't happen again. So the people we love most won't die because we tried to fix things too quickly. If we have learned anything from the Editors, it is to be patient. Subtlety is the greatest weapon. Combined with truth, it is an unstoppable force. For that very reason, you are still holding this book. You want to learn the truth. To *read* the truth, unedited. Ex Libris. If you are willing to be patient, I'll need to start from the beginning. Our beginning, at least. That way, despite how desperate things still are, you'll be able to appreciate how far we've come and how bad it was, once upon a time.

I knew him. I am one of the few people, few fortunate people, who can say that. In fact, I loved him before any of this began. When he was a simple-minded journeyman. When he wasn't hated by every single person in the world. No one knew him like I did. If they had, they wouldn't have believed what they were told to believe. I tried to change their minds after he was gone, but people assumed I was disillusioned. Even those who should have known better. But I believed him. I knew he was telling the truth. Even before he told me, I knew that he had discovered something none of us lemmings knew. On that day, in that windowless Chicago bar, the truth of our deception was exposed. Before he knew it, our emancipation rested in his hands.

THE BOOK

He'd say it was the best of times. Holden always did because he loved quoting Dickens. It was the best of times. Of course, by the end of the day it would feel like the opposite, but it was Friday and he was riding the elevated train home from work.

His fingernails were dirty. Of course they were.

He closed his Book and glared down at the notice that slithered across the screen, sealed into the black, leather binding. The words faded away and came back, breathing: *Update in Progress.* With an irritated huff, Holden Clifford glanced up from his seat to watch as everyone on the train closed their Books to search for something beyond the foggy windows. Something in the distortion of rain that could occupy their minds for the next two, exasperating minutes. For Holden, it was his fingernails.

His hands were generally caked in filth throughout the day. Why clean the grease and pipe dope when it would only resurface after lunch? A pant leg ordinarily did the trick until five o'clock, when he could expect the long train ride home. Holden would glide to the sink, tailored in grubby jeans and a torn flannel shirt, and scrub his arms like a cardiologist before surgery. The other sprinkler fitters were used to his ritualistic insanity, but they still poked a joke now and again. Not many water monkeys read novels. Especially pre-digital novels. If sprinkler fitters even used The Book for anything beyond

THE BOOK

studying blueprints, it was for the sports column. What frustrated Holden, as he took the nail file from his shirt pocket to scrape the grime from his forefinger, was that he even noticed his hands at all. He should have been lost in the final chapters of *Edwin Drood*, seeking to understand the lurking mystery. This was the third time in two days the Editors of The Book had interrupted him, and everyone else in the world, with another futile update. Of course, he couldn't complain. The Book was the most significant device to come out of his grandfather's selfish, unwilling generation. He really couldn't complain.

Holden had been born into a world where The Book was a necessity. Everyone on the planet had at least one copy. There were many different versions available with almost infinite design possibilities, including hundreds of applications for deeper study and general convenience. Holden had two copies, but he'd say that, on average, most people had three.

It was understood that The Book was a part of life. The portable reading device was used to learn the alphabet, to study history in school, to develop your career and to eventually retire in your favorite story.

As one global society, they read.

Often.

With his hands as clean as they could be, Holden turned his attention to the sharpened nail on his pointer finger. It was duller than usual. He scraped at it with six long slashes, filing the tip to a fine, angled spear. Outlawing paper made writing utensils pointless and the stylus pen that once came with the touch-sensitive Book was replaced over time by a swirling pointer finger. The lack of a single sharpened fingernail was the scarlet flag of the non-reader and it waved itself to the society of Book lovers. That number was dwindling by the decade.

A rumble coursed through the elevated train. Holden was unsure if it was the decaying wooden tracks below or the impatient excitement of expectant readers. He was annoyed that he'd been interrupted, but the update was necessary. Perhaps a new book had been published today, or the first draft of a story was included in the superfluous addendums that accompanied every purchased novel. Holden didn't need an explanation on the significant conditions surrounding every story to understand its purpose or relevance, but he respected those in the world that did. Two minutes a day was worth the benefit because, like everyone else in the world, Holden Clifford loved The Book.

The screen breathed *Update Complete* and Holden watched as the teenage girl on the seat beside him slipped back into her Book. Her device was blue, with generous detailing of thin, red and white stripes. It had been a popular model ten years ago and was obviously a hand-me-down, but she personalized it by lining the inside cover with a patchwork of neon stickers. On a normal day, Holden would engulf himself greedily in his story and ignore everyone during the train ride, but he couldn't stop staring at her fingers as they swirled along the screen. Two of her dazzlingly gold nails were sharpened points and they danced an elegant minuet to a sonata unheard beyond the tiny, blue buds in her be-jeweled ears. Holden had never seen a ballet, but he imagined that the intoxication would return when watching women dance with such similar grace. She was clearly using the device to talk to a friend and it made Holden wonder about the times when she wasn't talking. What stories filled her Book? Which one did she return to when life was disagreeing with her?

The train jerked to a stop and the doors opened with a familiar chime. The girl growled beside him, closed her Book and ambled off the train with a few others. Holden watched her

THE BOOK

dive for shelter from the rain as the car sealed its doors and rolled on to the next stop.

Seeking to be withdrawn from the rest of the commute, he flipped back the leather binding of his Book and watched as the inside screen flickered away from its black slumber and shifted to green. No, not green. More of an eerie white that pretended to be blameless and clean. There were some who preferred to read from a crisp white background in the comforts of their home computer, but those people weren't true Book lovers. Those with a sharpened pointer finger found the murky green filter soothing and would always prefer to go green even if a white version had been available.

Black text swam to the surface, interrupting his story with the GRATIS PRESS digital newspaper - a bonus for buying the latest edition of The Book. Holden longed to return to his story, but the scrolling headline drew him in. *The Free Thinkers*, terrorists against knowledge and history, had attacked another city.

That afternoon, city politicians mourned a once impeccable monument to twentieth century architecture. At street level, the north face of the Sears Tower had been branded with the emblem of *The Free Thinkers*. Holden swooped his fingernail around the photograph in the article and it enlarged to the width of the screen. Police surrounded the tower's jet black aluminum facing, studying the trivial design. Upon a stately crest was the ornamental script of their motto: THINK AGAIN. Above this, Holden noticed the delicately etched icons of a bow and arrow and a revolver. Although the insignia was exquisitely drawn, the brand scarred the building in a violent technique, eating away at the seamless material.

Holden skimmed the article, but it was the same old news. Nothing much was known about the group other than the obvious; they were a syndicate of anarchists linked to the destruction of major historical monuments and meaningful pieces of our global history. When he reached the bottom of the article, a video began streaming of a man at a press conference. In the top right corner was the graphic of an American flag swimming in windless air beside the words: *Gallantly Streaming*. The man at the press conference behind a podium that carried the seal of the United States was sharp, attractive and, despite a similarity in age, was in an entirely different category than Holden. His name was Martin Trust. As the video continued within the brackets of unprinted text, Trust announced his commission as the head of a new sector of Homeland Security. He continued by affirming that it was the job of the Department of Historic Homeland Preservation and Restoration to protect and rehabilitate the nation's most cherished antiquities. Trust comforted the press by declaring his passion for tracking down *The Free Thinkers* and Holden felt himself nod. He wasn't the type to care much about history, but he also disliked people that rocked the boat.

    Holden was bored with the images of demolished buildings that begged him to read on, so he found the recycling emblem for the Book and swirled his finger around it. The triangled arrows of the icon animated slowly before vanishing in a velvet haze of green. *The Mystery of Edwin Drood* bled back to the screen with an invitation to learn more about the author. He denied the request and sat back in his seat, quickly enveloped in the digital universe of his mind.

Holden stepped off the train, instantly bombarded by a repeat offense of regret. Living eight blocks from the tracks was still a bad idea. He tried to shelter himself under the awnings of shops along Montrose Avenue, but the jog home from the station was muculent and wet. The gravel driveway to his historic, but not preserved, residence was like tar in the downpour that sucked onto his boots from below dark puddles. Gripping his duffle bag, Holden climbed the unbalanced steps to the covered porch, shook himself free from the rain and went inside.

He tugged the cord that hung from the ceiling and a florescent glow reminded him of why he hated living there. *Home again, home again. Jiggety Jig*, Holden thought, as he searched his forever-empty mailbox before heading to the second floor. Every surface in the narrow stairwell was coated in the same thick, mint green paint as the exterior. When he first rented the place, he envisioned the house being dipped in fresh-smelling toothpaste. Unfortunately, the preventative act hadn't killed the moist bacteria or cleared the grime from the corners or overtaken the stench from the many molding crevices. Like most historical buildings, the house where Holden lived was falling apart. It cost too much to restore and it was against the law to tear down. At least the rent was cheap. Holden often dreamed that the house would collapse one winter night under a tide of snow and swallow him while he slept.

The striped bamboo door to his apartment closed with significance. Holden lowered his eyes as he dropped his duffle bag to the floorboards, rolled his shoulders and cracked the top of his spine with a long, exhaled breath. He was home and it was time for the ritual to begin. Leave work at the door, take off the boots and break the seal of a richly deserved, locally brewed beer. *Jiggety Jig.* Yes, his family life was non-existent. But Holden was content with his small story. Most days he strolled directly to his easy chair and picked up where he left off on the train. On special days, he went back to his father's copy of The Book that sat by the window and returned to his favorite story. Today, there was a kink. The phone on the wall was blinking.

Sweaty beer in hand, he closed the fridge and approached the answering machine, already knowing what he was about to hear and already regretting his actions of the past forty minutes. The two messages were from, or about, his two favorite people in the world. Shane and Jane.

Shane was his best friend. In fact, they had the All-American relationship. They grew up in the same neighborhood, dated the same girls, fought over the same girls and spent every moment they could together to this day. Like Holden, Shane worked for General Fire Protection. His message was typical and to the point.

"Meet me at The Library, man. Maybe we can reignite what happened last month with the librarian," Shane's charred, confident voice chuckled before he continued. "I know it's raining, but don't spend the weekend at home, bro. I'm buying and the game starts at six. Don't be late."

He clicked to the next message and looked at his watch, hoping the call would be from Jane. It wasn't. Jane was Holden's eleven-year-old daughter. Their relationship could be summed up in two conflicting words: simple and complicated. They barely saw one another. On the off chance that Holden pulled himself from his nothingness to see her, it was under the discretion of his militant ex-wife, Eve. Jane loved her father, but life kept them separate. That, and Holden's unwavering forgetfulness.

Eve's message was blunt.

"How many times is this going to happen, Hold? You were supposed to pick up Jane an hour ago. What a surprise!" Her stringent, acid-laced tone curdled in his ears. He cracked his beer open. "Why don't you just enjoy that drink I'm sure you're holding and I'll make something up again. I can't watch her sit by the phone waiting for your call. So don't call."

He took a swig from his beer and laughed. Despite being disappointed in himself for abandoning his daughter again, this was the first time in years that Eve hadn't finished a conversation by calling him 'predictably unreliable' or mentioning that pipe fitters shouldn't have pipe dreams they couldn't finish. *Maybe that wasn't a good thing*, Holden thought, as he reached for the picture frame on the shelf beside the phone. The digital frame held thirty pictures from Jane's ninth birthday. Eve looked miserable in every over-exposed shot. What made Holden put it down and reach for his beer was that he realized these were the only photos of Jane in the whole house and they were two years old. He felt so suddenly guilty. What kind of a father didn't have a recent picture of his kid?

In a glance, Holden's reflection in the frame spoke a thousand words. The brown fuzz of his hair was coarse and his long, ragged, unshaven face was four days past socially acceptable. His notched nose, broken by a young Shane during one of their many childish arguments, carried a slight twist that most women found markedly attractive. Eve had been one of those, long ago. Holden stared into his dull brown eyes. Once young and gleaming with lightness and hope, they now drooped from his face, empty. He was thirty-three going on fifty and felt more lost than ever.

Holden eyed the phone's dusty receiver and debated if he should call Jane. With a twisted lip, he ran a hand through his hair, used his middle finger to carry the beer from inside the bottle neck and tugged his duffle bag to the window with the oversized easy chair that beckoned him to relax in its downy, plush embrace. Maybe later he would watch the game. For now, escaping into the written world of his favorite story was an easier way to ignore his inadequacies.

Resting on the windowsill was his father's copy of The Book. It was a first edition, passed down from his grandfather. It had a linen-wrapped, hard cover binding with a thick screen, so that it mimicked a printed book. The antique device reminded him that there had once been a time when people needed an easy transition to such technology. For Holden, there was something romantic about the archaic device. He got settled into the chair and picked up The Book, rubbing the front cover with his thumb. The recycling imprint of the Publishing House was missing from the binding. It hadn't been mandatory at that time. Holden lifted the cover to reveal the darkened screen. By design, current day Books revived themselves when the cover was lifted. With his father's Book he had to press the oval button in the corner to ignite the power. He always found a simple joy in that. The

THE BOOK

worn screen awoke to a plain list of options. Holden felt the thin arrow key on the right side of the device and used it to scroll down to the only author listed.

The name was J.D. Salinger.

The preliminary version of The Book stored an unremarkable one thousand mid-sized novels. That didn't matter to Holden. There was only one story loaded onto the ancient appliance. The same story that had been there when Holden got The Book from their family's estate lawyer. Apparently, it had been his father's favorite novel and the origin of Holden's unique name. After receiving The Book in his father's will, Holden read it repeatedly, hoping to understand some unknown part of the man. Quickly, *The Catcher in the Rye* became the standard; the novel by which he judged all others, and the one he always ran to when there was a need to forget the present. He knew those pixels of narrative like the arrangement of tiny, white hexagon tiles on his monotonous bathroom floor. There was an unyielding order to it all and he found comfort knowing what came next.

Holden switched on the lamp beside his chair and nestled into the worn, single pillow. He sipped gently from his beer and flipped the page, exhaling instantaneous relaxation. And just as he began to read the words he had read so many times before, the screen went from dull green to black. The relic had powered down.

Aggravated, Holden rose from his comfort, snatched the adapter cord from the wall and plugged it into the binding. No light. No response. The battery was acting up again. He closed his eyes to calm himself and gulped a fifth of his beer before grabbing his new copy of The Book from his duffle bag. But when Holden returned to his seat in search of rest, he noticed that the small, rectangular display built into the leather cover above the recycling icon was breathing a phrase that drove him to toss The Book onto the windowsill, reach for his jacket and leave the apartment in heated frustration.

That phrase was: *Update in Progress.*

Cold rain nagged the window of the cab with a constant, maddening rhythm that seemed to disagree with the swiping wipers. Holden watched them glide silently along the glass as the driver clicked her turning signal and pulled over below the elevated tracks of the Uptown train station.

Holden paid the woman and stepped into the irrelevant rain. The red door he had opened and walked through so many times before stood ominous beside the shadow of a nearby alley. For John Q. Passerby, there were no windows to shed light on the character of the business. In fact, the building would have appeared vacant if it weren't for the single neon image of an open book hanging unsteadily over the doorway. Holden shook the water from his coat, scraped it over the rough fuzz of hair on his cold head and ran for the door. He reached the wide, curling handle and saw the thick carving at the center of the rotting wood. His eyes traced the remnants of two words, once engraved in ornate script and framed in baroque molding. It was difficult to discern, but Holden had frequented the bar often enough to know that it read, THE LIBRARY. He tugged the handle and the door gave way, blasting him with a puff of warm, stale air and muffled voices.

Throughout Chicago, boutique bars blinked the corners of many elite intersections while a multitude of sports bars lingered nearby like cockroaches. The Library was one of the oldest bars in the once trendy neighborhood of Uptown that wouldn't fit into a singular category. Decades before the neighborhood was overrun with musicians and artists, the bar had established its presence. Which meant that the crowd was always an older one. That began to change once the owner retired and left the business to his daughter. Marion Tabor, commonly known by regulars as *the librarian*, began hosting music acts and themed sports nights every week until she eventually drew a younger crowd. That group included Holden and Shane, who would have normally avoided such an eccentric venue for controlled inebriation.

The Library got its name from its peculiar and controversial interior design. The windowless walls of the bar were clothed with pages from hundreds of recycled books. The building had broken ground during a vital junction in the history of the world, when the selfish ways of our forefathers were recognized and recycling was evolving into a powerful tool for allowing mother earth to thrive. Laws were being passed and using paper for recreational means was frowned upon, to say the least. Like the few creative minds of that decade, Marion's grandfather searched for an innovative solution to the problem and chose to line the walls of his new bar with pages from recognizable books before recycling them for the sake of the planet. At a time when the words *Reduce*, *Reuse* and *Recycle* were fast becoming the mantra of the intellectual world, such innovative design made The Library a custodian for progress and environmentalism. But sadly, like most novelties, the bar was forgotten and its crumbling, fragile façade soon joined the landscape of deserted, but historically protected, buildings along Wilson Avenue.

Tonight, Holden entered the bar like the rest of those before him. He ignored the yellowing book pages that crusted the walls like rotting fish scales, hung his jacket on one of the tarnished brass hooks near the warm wood bar and searched for his best friend.

"There he is."

The graveled voice came from the thick stone fireplace at the center of the large seating area. Shane was standing on a shelf of stone that circled the base of the column, half obscured by the flat screen television. He adjusted the volume, hopped down and threw an arm around Holden as if they hadn't just spent every moment of the work week together.

"Glad you could make it out, bro!" he barked, tugging his old friend toward their usual booth. His brash attitude lit up the tiny eyes that were ever shadowed under his tattered baseball cap. The Blackhawks jersey he wore hung from his sloping, definitionless shoulders like a red garbage bag. Unlike Holden's sturdy frame, Shane Dagget was as thin as they came and not the least bit aware of his shortcomings. "Thanks for getting all dolled up."

Holden looked down at his raggedy work clothes. He had left the house so quickly, so agitated, that he had forgotten to change. "Didn't realize this was a date," he replied, squeezing into the varnished oak booth.

Shane took the cigarette from behind his ear and sparked his butane lighter. "Sweetheart, I thought Friday was date night."

Holden grinned at his friend's overt eye batting and attempted to pull the cigarette from his hand. "I just got here. Don't get us kicked out."

"Where have you been, Clifford? The ban on smoking was lifted last week," Shane tugged his hand back, pulled a long drag from his cigarette and spat a laugh of smoke at the ceiling. "I swear, bro, I thought you'd be Mickey the Mope all weekend reading that stupid Book of yours." Holden pursed his lips and nodded as a smirk curled the edge of Shane's sly lips. "Don't look now, but Marion's been eyeing you like an empty glass. I told ya. That girl wants what you're sellin'."

Holden stole a glance over his shoulder and pretended to watch the pre-game arguments on the plasma screen before turning back. "She's lookin' at you, Dagget."

"Not a chance, sailor," he smirked, digging in with the nickname Holden would never live down. "I've been your wingman since we turned nineteen." Shane paused to release another haze of glorious smoke, "I know when a girl is checking you out and she is check…ing…you…out."

"Whatever." Holden rolled his flannel sleeves and cracked his back again, trying to gather what crumbs of comfort were available in the cushionless booth.

Shane delighted in another slow drag before tilting his head curiously. "Hey, weren't you supposed to have Jane this weekend?" In a glare of unspoken frustration, Shane knew what had happened. "It's like that, huh? Man." He slid an empty bottle across the table and clinked the glass with the edge of his full one. "A.D.A.D. right?"

Holden nodded sheepishly. "A.D.A.D."

Another Day. Another Dollar. Where the phrase originated from, neither of them knew. They picked it up when they were young and somewhere between summer vacations and joining the pipe fitters union, the saying stuck. Eventually, it became the smartest, most carefree response to any situation in life.

Car breaks down? Another day. Another dollar.

THE BOOK

Got promoted? Another day. Another dollar.

Wife leaves you? Another day. Another dollar.

Brother goes to jail? Another day. Another dollar.

If the situation wasn't a big deal, or they didn't want it to seem like a big deal, they abbreviated. It was hokey and nonsense to them now, but it was how they communicated and it worked.

Shane drank eagerly from the micro-brewed lager and used the back of his hand to wipe the froth from his mouth, already searching for a subject to override the topic of Holden's failed home life. "Numbskull has me pulling doubles tomorrow. I think it's some new building on Wacker."

Holden shrugged, uninterested, before glancing back at the television screen to watch the game begin. The opposing team snatched the puck and Holden stared as they glided delicately across the ice like a flock of geese until one of the men went sprawling into the wall. He was too engulfed in the game to notice Shane beckoning the bartender to their table.

"Think I'm gonna run off to the bathroom or something before your girlfriend gets here. Leave the love birds to the branch, ya know what I'm sayin', bro?"

Yanked quickly back to reality, Holden reached for his friend's jersey. "Come on, don't do me like that. I told you…she just needed a ride back to her apartment. Shane."

Holden collected himself and twisted casually away from the bar to admire the series of book pages that plastered the wall. The gloss that once glued the printed paper to the bar, bonding them together to create a seamless surface, had gradually degraded to a rough, clear texture. The recycled pages were flaking earnestly from the wall. Holden found this a pleasant distraction from the fact that Marion, the librarian, had already strolled up to the booth with her digital notepad in hand looking harmless and polite. He tried not to notice her, but the attempt was a failure from the start.

Marion was beautiful in the sense that she was unattainable and confusing to most of the men that vied constantly for her attention. She had strong features, but her face was still kind and elegant. Holden knew she was special. She had a rare personality and a look that could only be defined as grubby, but gorgeous. To Holden, Marion Tabor was a greasy, bohemian princess. The piece of her he liked best was the delicate Japanese floral tattoos that snuck a glance at him when she leaned to hand over a drink and her short sleeves grew shorter. There was an attraction there. One night it almost led to a *here's my place* kiss. But Holden came with complications and any woman that didn't mind adding complication to her life was someone to avoid. That rationalization was the only thing that kept him grounded when she would look deeply into his eyes or reach across the table to take his glass away.

"Hi Holden. Haven't seen you here in a while."

He turned absent-mindedly toward her as she swept a flirty tangle of dark brown hair over her ears and his breath cut short. "Work has been busy..." he grunted, clearing his throat. "Taking a lot out of me." He tried to keep his cool, but instead his voice hung with passive, synthetic neutrality.

"Yeah. You look tired," she mused, reaching for Shane's empty glass. "What can I get you?"

"Whatever import you have on tap is fine."

Marion swooped her pointer finger over the notepad screen and offered him a soft smile. "Okay. I'll be right back."

Holden flashed an adjourned expression as she returned to the bar and he tilted his head back to the quilt of overlapping pages. Having been so pulled away at home, so drawn out of his story when he needed it most, his eyes instantly scanned the

THE BOOK

pages for some form of fictitious freedom, only to discover that the text on the walls was neither literary nor inviting. Beyond the stacked condiments and laminated lists of drinks were a series of shadowed pages quite mathematic in nature with random equations that made no sense to Holden. He passed over them and many others with a glaze of dull consideration until he noticed something of interest.

He tilted in place to an awkward, acrobatic position in order to view a page behind him from a book entitled *Little Women*. He read the series of words and quickly discovered that nothing on the roughly 5 inch by 8 inch page, which was partially concealed beneath an historical account of the Incan empire, described the size of women, their height, their intellect or anything that would lend substance to the innocuous, yet intriguing, title. The mysterious story bore the signs of pre-digital fiction and it kept him enthralled for the few minutes before the librarian returned.

Marion stepped around the boundaries of the bar and walked the drink to his booth while Holden watched her approach with studying eyes. The amber liquid swayed with her hips and it absorbed him. Its ambient gracefulness recalling a sentence from the page he had just read.

"Why not? I'm neat and cool and comfortable, quite proper for a dusty walk on a warm day."

Much like that language from another time, the approaching beer drew him in. Marion set the drink on the table and Holden nodded a thank you as he happily tipped the cold glass rim toward his welcoming lips.

"So, are you excited about the game?"

"Huh?"

"The game," she repeated, arching her manicured eyebrows. "It's supposed to be a good one."

Small talk? Holden felt suddenly distant and spoke his reply through a dripping sip. "Is it?"

"You feeling all right? You're acting strange."

"Don't I always?" He faked a charming smirk and pointed a thumb at the wall. "Did you know these pages are coming loose?"

"Yeah," Marion nodded, wiping down the scraps of garbage Shane left on the table. "I'd just paint over the whole thing, but then the name of the bar wouldn't make sense, would it?"

Holden snickered. "You'd have to buy new stationary and everything."

"Right," she laughed, brandishing a wide smile. "Stationary."

Instead of leaving, Marion narrowed the space between them and traced a hand across his right arm, pulling aside the fine crop of brown hair. "What is that?" she asked, spotting a blotch of bluish-black ink. "It looks like skin cancer or something."

Holden tugged his arm abruptly, almost too abruptly, away and unrolled his flannel sleeve to cover up his embarrassment. "Yeah, just kids being stupid."

Before Marion could ask, Shane skipped his chicken legs back to the booth, just in time to sit and revel in his friend's discomfort. "Showing off your tattoo there, sailor? Did he tell you it was an anchor or that he got it from his girlfriend in jail?"

Holden shot daggers at Shane Dagget and lowered his head in an understood look of *one more of those and you're going to get it.* Shane tossed up his hands in innocence and puffed, "I wasn't going to tell her that you stopped mid-way because it hurt too much..." A boot crashed into his flimsy ankle and a surge of pain shot through his loose tendons.

"You don't seem the type to give up."

THE BOOK

Holden continued to stare angrily at Shane as he sputtered, "Talk to my ex-wife."

Gently, Marion pulled back Holden's sleeve and edged closer to the half-inch wide, geometric blemish. "It looks like the number four."

"It was supposed to be an anchor but…it hurt. So I stopped. It's my *four*arm." Holden's attempt at a pathetic joke lost its charm on her, or at least he thought it had. Marion didn't laugh; the hand she placed on his shoulder before walking back to the bar was tender and comforting. Shane rose his arms in defense the moment they were alone because it appeared that Holden was about to lay into him. The serendipitous arrival of a phone call gave him an escape from certain punishment.

The tacky ring tone ceased as Shane flicked his phone open and yanked himself away from the booth through a barrage of flying peanuts. Clutching the phone, he laughed in surprise with one of their mutual friends over the fact that Holden had actually shown up. The crowded bar swiftly filled with jeers and jubilation as the score on the screen shifted. Holden listened to the tumult and was glad he could no longer hear Shane's opinion of him, no matter how right it was. He knew he was usually unavailable to his friends on the weekends. He liked it that way. In fact, he was debating an escape that moment so he could return home to where the Book was fully charged and waiting for him.

Home was comfortable. The Book was comfortable. It gave him everything he needed. Friends, like life, were unpredictable. In his stories, he knew what to expect. He understood the characters and they didn't need to understand him. The Book provided him with a life he didn't have the energy to live himself. The digital lines of text scrolling below his eyes gave him adventure and solidarity. Beyond any person, place or thing in existence, he trusted The Book. He trusted those who wrote the stories; that they had his best interests at heart. It was more than he could say for Shane, who stood by the television laughing into the newest smart phone, leaving his best friend to nurse a lukewarm beer. Holden nudged his drink aside, pushed away from the booth and navigated the crowded bar toward the bathroom to release what he could before trying to escape without notice.

When he reached the dark and dingy room, a line of tottering sports fans told Holden that finding a stall was the easier route. He shut the door gladly and completed the deed he came to do. Although Holden was ready to leave (the odor alone was urging him to), he found himself staring at the pages on the wall, yearning to be drawn away from the languid existence, from the emotionless mirth that encompassed him. Something felt wrong about life. There was a creeping distrust that he couldn't quite put his sharpened pointer finger on. Sometimes, even the shadow that followed his feet felt irregular. But there, standing before a cacophony of pages that held order despite the disorder, he was freed from his incarceration of doubt. He lost himself and found himself in the thousands upon thousands of sandy pages and printed words that covered the five square feet of wall space behind the toilet. He scanned them slowly as if searching for truth. Searching for wisdom in a single word.

He saw so many. The word *vertigo*. The word *triumph*. The word *bliss*. The word *infantile*. He saw the words *retraction* and *conglomerate*, *God* and *sacrilegious*. He saw the word, *finality*. He saw the word -

Holden slipped on the floor and caught himself on the toilet paper holder. It tore free from the 100% post-consumer recycled content divider walls. Fragments of the composite plastic material rattled on the floor of the stall and the toilet

THE BOOK

flushed as his shadow passed over the fixture's cyclopean eye. Inebriated men at the urinals were laughing, but he didn't hear them. Holden pushed himself terribly close to the toilet until he could see it again. See the word that had his heart cycling in erratic disagreement. On the haphazard, paper-coated wall he found the word. Beside a modicum of sexually suggestive graffiti art, Holden Clifford had seen his name.

Holden was not a popular name. He could never seem to find it anywhere else in the world. He had only seen his name in digital script, and yet there it was in all its rare splendor. A piece of his favorite story had been pasted to a most inconsequential wall. *The Catcher in the Rye*. When Holden finally found his name again, his heart leapt. He had never seen a page from that book in person. The printed words were like manna to him and he devoured all two-hundred and seventy-seven with fervor. Each line was sheer delight and he read over them again the instant his studying eyes reached the awkward end. After the second read, Holden knew he had to read it again, but not because he was so overjoyed to finally be reading his favorite story from an actual piece of paper, printed with ink and touched by oily fingers. He had to read it again because something about the page was wrong.

Whatever it was, he couldn't define the source. It was like seeing a reflection in rippling water. It was right and at the same time it didn't make sense. Then, in the middle of the third read, it hit him. The entire scene he was reading was new. That was

THE BOOK

why he needed so badly to read it again. It was new to him. There was something new on the page. He couldn't tell if it was a phrase or a paragraph or a word or a sentence. No, it wasn't something that small. It was the majority of it. The majority of the sentences on the wall he had never read before.

One of the overlapping pages was dry and crusted, breaching the excerpt of *The Catcher in the Rye* like a hang nail waiting to be gnawed off. He blew delicately at the overhanging sheet and found enough space between it to know that the page wouldn't be harmed if it peeled free. A crinkling, crackle; a delicate tear; and he could swiftly see the title along the ridge of the page. There was no question now. He was reading from *The Catcher in the Rye*, page two-hundred and forty-seven.

> *they're thinking and all. It really is. I kept trying not to yawn. It wasn't that I was bored or anything – I wasn't – but I was so damn sleepy all of a sudden.*
>
> *"Something else an academic education will do for you. If you go along with it any considerable distance, it'll begin to give you an idea what size mind you have. What it'll fit and, maybe, what it won't. After a while, you'll have an idea what kind of thoughts your particular size mind should be wearing. For one thing, it may save you an extraordinary amount of time trying on ideas that don't suit you, aren't becoming to you. You'll begin to know your true measurements and dress your mind accordingly."*
>
> *Then, all of a sudden, I yawned. What a* rude bastard, *but I couldn't help it!*
>
> *Mr. Antolini just laughed, though. "C'mon, Holden," he said, and got up. "We'll fix up the couch for you."*
>
> *I followed him and he went over to this closet and tried to take down some sheets and blankets and stuff that was*

on the top shelf, but he couldn't do it with this highball glass in his hand. So he drank it and then put the glass down on the floor and then *he took the stuff down. I helped him bring it over to the couch. We both made the bed together. He wasn't too hot at it. He didn't tuck anything in very tight. I didn't care, though. I could've slept standing up I was so tired.*

"How're all your women?"

"They're okay." I was being a lousy conversationalist, but I didn't feel like it.

Holden exhaled a long breath, but he was no less confused. He backed out of the stall and stumbled toward the sink. He saw himself in the mirror, and yet there was a different person standing there. His forehead and eyebrows were knotted into a tangle of curls and wrinkles. His eyes were sharp and stunningly focused. Suddenly nothing else mattered. He didn't know why, but nothing else mattered beyond the words he had just read. The page was prodigious. The very moment he had been thinking of his trust in The Book and faith in what was written between its digital pages, he was besieged by a sense of betrayal. There soon came a hollowness in his chest and Holden knew that none of what was happening would make sense until he could make sense of it all.

He left the bathroom imbalanced; his mind overflowing with indefinable possibilities. He stepped quickly toward the bar where Marion was laughing with a customer, drawing a long draft of vanilla white beer, and shoved his way through the giddy patrons watching the game on a small television that was integrated into the mirror behind her before spitting out to her, "Where did these book pages come from?" She noticed him and her eyes brightened. "Marion, where did these pages come from?"

She handed her customer his drink, pointed to her ear and mouthed the words, *I can't hear you.*

Holden walked around to the side of the bar and ducked below the hinged countertop, joining her near the register. Marion couldn't help blushing in his sudden presence. Holden closed his eyes and leaned close to her ear, repeating, "The pages on the wall...where did they come from?"

Marion shrugged. "I don't know. I'd have to ask my mother. Why?"

"I can't really explain. Find out for me, will ya?" Holden muttered, scurrying back to the legal side of the bar. Marion watched as he fought with his jacket, mumbled crazily to himself and left the bar. Shane looked as confused as she did, but he shook his head and assumed the same. Once again, Holden Clifford had to escape the reality of life.

In truth, the reality of life was becoming frighteningly clear for him. As each moment passed, Holden continued to fear the worst and told himself that what he was imaging was incorrect. What he thought he had just stumbled upon was too implausible to be true. He wouldn't even consider it until he saw the text for himself. It was simply horrific; the connotations behind such a discovery were altogether too frightening to accept. So he took a cab back to his neighborhood, walked slowly through the rain toward his apartment, stumbled absently to the darkened corner where he had left his father's copy of The Book open and plugged in and fell to his knees before the greenish tint of the glowing screen.

With the excerpt from the bar in his mind, Holden scanned to the corresponding page. At once, he noticed it was different. Whatever scene he had read, it wasn't on this page. He scanned two pages forward and two pages backward, and still nothing. For the sake of argument, he scanned back one more page and there it was. Or at least, there part of it was.

He was right. The majority of the scene was missing from The Book. He felt the smart of betrayal and didn't even understand why. There was nothing overtly graphic or politically insensitive or anti-establishment enough to cause alarm to anyone. It didn't seem important enough to be censored. In fact, he had never heard of such censorship. Censorship itself was extinct. He had been raised in a censor-free environment. The only occasion in which things were removed from society was when they could cause actual damage.

Or at least that was what he had been told.

He looked down at the page and realized that if what he was reading was three pages prior to wherever it had originally been, then more than just the scene from the bar had been removed. If that was right, what had it been? A word on each page? A phrase? Perhaps it was something larger. Maybe an entire character had been removed. There was no telling. The truth was, *The Catcher in the Rye* had been altered and the only reason Holden even caught it was because he had known the story well enough to recognize the difference. The question that remained in his heart, as he knelt on the floor of his decaying apartment in the green glow of The Book, hung heavy in his chest and pulled him down toward the digital screen.

What else had been altered?

A shrill noise squawked from the invoice pad as Marion stuffed it into the back of her pants before wiping the sleep from her eyes. As the men continued to unload the shipment from the truck, the sound of clinking beer bottles and the perfume of stale alcohol created a dissonance of sensory overload. They so grabbed her attention that she didn't notice Holden walking up to the truck looking frantic and confused.

"Hi, Hold. What happened to you last night?"

"I need to know where these book pages came from. I...I nee...I need to know. I...you don't understand. I read the entire book last night. I read the whole thing through because I just couldn't believe...myself. I just couldn't believe. So, I read it all the way through. And...I mean...I think I know it by heart enough to notice...if I had the whole book. So, I need to know where the rest of that book is."

"Hang on, tiger," Marion responded in a soothing tone, "Why don't you pick up one of these boxes and help me bring it inside." Holden's erratic breathing pulsed with the bobbing of his head as he bent to lift the case of beer and follow her into the darkened bar. She studied his irregular behavior and hollered back to the truck, "I'll catch up with you guys in a minute."

Without warning, Holden ran straight to the bathroom. Marion couldn't help but laugh. What she liked most about Holden was that he was a mystery she just couldn't seem to solve. He was a different sort of man than she was accustomed to. She could never figure out what he was thinking. Although he was solid and predictable overall, there was a lingering question that always hung behind his eyes - a question she wanted to answer.

Holden glided from the men's bathroom with a torn scrap of paper and slammed it on the cold metal bar. It had come from the wall. Pieces of other books, torn and bent, bordered the single page. "Thanks for destroying my bar. Books don't come too cheap these days. Oh wait, there aren't any more books," she spat sarcastically, reaching for the page. He swiped it back, blinking frantically. She dropped her hands to her sharply curved hips and bit her tongue. "What's going on, wack jack? You're acting crazy."

"I *am going* crazy," he agreed, continuing to blink rapidly. "Do you have a copy of The Book...with you?"

She shrugged absent mindedly and glanced down at the invoice pad the delivery guys were waiting for. "Um...somewhere. Why? I don't really read, Holden."

"Listen. I have a feeling that something terrible is going on all around us and I need you to trust me, okay?"

"You're being a cuckoo bird, but...go ahead."

"I need you to take your Book and search all the pages in this bar. Every single page. Most of the stories are public domain by now, so it should be free. Go to the corresponding page in The Book and check the writing on the wall. See if things match up. I know it sounds crazy, but I'm telling you that this page here,"

THE BOOK

Holden lifted the single sheet he had torn from the bathroom wall, "This is from my favorite book…and it's different."

"What do you mean it's different?"

"It's been edited. The Editors of the Publishing House have deleted things."

"So? Maybe there was some racism in there." Marion chuckled to herself and noticed instantly that Holden wasn't amused. "I doubt this is as big as you're making it. But even if you're right, so what? To be honest, I couldn't care less. So, they deleted some stuff. What's the big deal?"

"What's the big deal? Do you understand the implications of editing without approval? If an original printing is different than what we're reading today, what does that mean? The Book is like…a hundred years old. When did the information change? And why? Who decided that something needed to be altered from the original? And that it was okay to do so…"

"Holden, I care about you. Maybe more than I should. I know it's not a secret. But you're not acting like yourself and it's a little scary. Do you think that maybe you might be getting worked up about something that's not that important?"

Holden exhaled and looked down at the torn page, realizing that she may be right. There were hundreds of reasons why the story could have been edited over time. What if the original copy of the book had been destroyed at some point and this page was from another draft? Maybe descendants of the author had decided to change some things.

"I guess you could be right. I'm sorry I've been acting so…weird. I just…" Holden couldn't find the right way to explain how finding the inaccuracy had made him feel. "It seemed to make the world…understandable."

Marion poured them a couple pints before bringing the invoice pad out to the delivery truck. Holden brewed in his thoughts as they sat silently at the bar for a half hour. He still felt a need to understand what had happened. Something was still incomplete and he was almost positive that if he could read the original manuscript, every question he couldn't put into words would be answered.

"Did you have a chance to talk to your mother last night?"

She nodded through sips. "Could've gone without that. The conversation centered around all the men she's been dating. How they're half her age and yet I can't find a decent man…da…da…da…"

"What about the pages?"

"It was my grandfather's idea, I guess. He found all these books in the attic when he moved here and figured that he should recycle them because it was frowned upon not to. This was before the laws were changed, so everyone was lenient as long as you found a way to use the books for some higher purpose. He used a bunch of them on the walls of the bar. Rest of them he tossed. That's it."

"So there's no more pages left?" Holden muttered, crashing onto the cushion of the bar stool as he realized that he may never fully understand why the page was different. Accepting this reality was going to be hard and if he needed to start accepting it now, he was going to need some air. "Thanks Marion, I'll pay you back for the wall. Can I just hang onto the page for a little while? I don't know…I just feel like I need to…look over it again."

"Whatever klepto," she joked, trying to lighten the mood. "Hey, relax. Things are fine. Okay?" She gave him a hug.

Being that close to her, smelling the scent that was only hers, he was reminded of the night they almost kissed. Feeling too vulnerable, Holden released her early, walked gently back to the

THE BOOK

exit door without saying goodbye and left her standing there, bewildered and bewitched.

Instead of returning home, Holden stepped onto the first bus he saw and found himself riding into the city. The bustling chaos of the weekend morning was soothing and it floated him away from his dramatic over-thinking. He looked out the window and watched as the buildings raced by. Then the park. And then the people. When the bus came to a stop outside the Art Institute, a spark of genius burned his brain and he looked around to find the map for the bus. It was heading toward the Museum of Science and Industry. Precisely where he needed to go.

The only other time Holden had seen a real book, a complete book, intact, it had been beneath a thick layer of glass at the Museum of Science and Industry when he was a teenager. Books had been rare if not completely extinct for over fifty years. The Great Recycling had taken care of that. Holden remembered enjoying the eminence of the book much more than those in his class. Most, if not all, looked upon it with disdain, unable to believe how insensitive to the earth their forefathers had been; raping trees to make paper and using paper to write fluffy fiction. The image of a man reading a book on a park bench, flipping the pages over and over, was akin to a savage Neanderthal tearing the flesh from an animal and devouring it over the sheer face of a cliff. Holden didn't seem to care that mother earth had been raped. He was told to care. He supposed he was supposed to care, but he didn't. If breaking trees down in order to communicate was all they'd had available, with their limited technology, then they did the best with what they had. The stories weren't any different from that time and, in fact, when Holden would read them on his copy of The Book, he preferred reading things that most people wouldn't enjoy. Digital and pre-digital work was easy to transition through because it had the same dull, green background. The same black text. The same simple margins and flickered movement between pages. It was fun reading pre-digital work because those authors hadn't seen his world and he hadn't seen theirs. It was his way to travel through time. To view the past through someone else's written eyes.

Holden left the bus with a bad taste in his mouth and had to spit. *Who had given the Editors of the Publishing House the right to silence someone who couldn't be there to defend their work?* These Editors were cowards, whoever they were. Holden was so worked up about it, he couldn't move from the bus station. He stood outside the pillars of the museum and cracked the knuckles on his right fist. He was determined to find an original copy of the manuscript, *The Catcher in the Rye* by J.D. Salinger. He had to find it. The story seemed to call to him. It beckoned from across fields of pixeled black text and digitized landscapes in thirty-six hues of gray.

In a gust of wind, Holden realized that, for the first time in years, he was no longer lost. How could it be that, in these hours when he was the most misplaced he had been in his entire life, he no longer felt lost? Such emotions were impossible to decipher. It was similar to waking abruptly from a dream. *Who was he, again? Where was he? What time was it? Hell, what day was it?* Regardless of the unanswered questions, he could be sure of one thing – he was awake. The only questions that remained were: what world had Holden been so anxiously sleeping in and what world had he woken into?

The walls in the Hall of Publishing and Media were pristine white and resonating with harmonious jingles that chimed when patrons entered the welcoming alcove. Holden ignored the robotic voice that rang out an invitation from some hidden speaker. His face was blank and his eyes were unblinking as he strode forward, almost floating, with articulated steps that were both precise and resolute. It had been over a decade, but he knew where to go. He ignored groups of children with volumeless voices that marveled over the interactive machinery; he ignored the groups of older students sketching on digital pads and ignored the garish displays that begged him to pause in his journey to reflect on the many items of interest. The display case that held original manuscripts from a pre-digital age was only feet away and he wouldn't allow himself to accept a yield sign of any sort. There was an overwhelming curiosity in him now that begged to be satisfied. No, it wasn't even that simple. Holden felt as if he had some liquid answer lodged in his brain that wouldn't drip from his ear no matter how hard he shook his head or how fiercely he pounded his temple with the butt of his palm. It unhinged him so quickly that it nourished a new need. Holden needed to know if he was willing to dig deep enough into his mind and risk sacrificing himself simply to get the answer out.

He reached the display case.

The display case was empty.

Holden blinked in the stark whiteness of the room and slowed his pace. The case that had once held ten books from his grandfather's generation was empty. A synthetic cloth, cut to the shape of the inner counter, added to protect the spines, still held an imprint from the weight of the delicate artifacts. They had been moved. And recently.

The Catcher in the Rye was not one of the books at the museum; he knew that it wasn't. Holden was hoping, in his desperation, to find some clue as to why the story had been edited or, at the very least, to find information on an establishment that had copies of books for study or view. But all he discovered was nothing. Nothing but glass and fabric and air in an echoey chamber of white walls and parquet floors. Holden turned in place. He twisted his tongue through his lips like a lizard. He had come to an abrupt end in his search and was unable to grasp his next steps. Then he noticed the expression painted on the face of the woman posted firmly in the corner of the room. She was a guard and had apparently found Holden's overt distress amusing.

"Something I can help you with, sir?" the guard asked with a curt smile. Her rude, Chicago twang actually comforted him.

"Yeah, where are the books?"

"I'm sorry?"

"The books. The books from the empty case. The ones that you are no longer guarding." His question seemed obvious. "Wherever they disappeared to, it must have just happened."

The guard released an exasperated breath, rolled her eyes and pulled her walkie-talkie up to her mouth, clicking the button with annoyance. "Jo, I'm in gallery two-oh-nine and I've got someone here asking about these books. You were working here this week. They were moved, right?"

"Yeah, they were moved."

The woman looked at Holden as if that were enough of an answer to appease him. He laughed and kneaded his arms in a rolling gesture as if to say, *And they were moved where?*

The guard clicked the walkie-talkie and asked, "Where were those moved to, Jo?"

After ten seconds of dead air and staring back at one another, Jo, the woman whose nickname he could only assume was short for Joann or Josephine or Jolene, came back. "I wanna say it was that government preservation group, whatever the name is. I think they had to be moved because of all that terrorist stuff going on. Guy thought they might get stolen or something. I guess you can't take chances with those *Free Thinkers* around."

THE BOOK

The guard lowered her walkie-talkie, but Holden was already ambling away, rapt in thought. Before long, he found himself standing outside the museum near the bus stop beside a few other people. His mind was blank. In fact, he was almost angry. It didn't make much sense, but he was angry at Marion. Things, up until yesterday, had been fine. This was, of course, a lie, but it seemed right because life had made sense. Sure it wasn't great; in fact, it had been pretty damn complicated. At least he knew what he knew and going through the motions everyday kept things safe. His routine was solid. But now, even attempting to rekindle that state of mind seemed impossible. It wasn't working because this was huge. No, beyond huge.

Still, hadn't all of it been so odd? Why Holden? How was it possible that this enormous detail about everyday life had lost itself on everyone except him? He wasn't the type of person that thought about deep things or went on long arduous walks to contemplate the circularity of the universe. He was average. Below that, if he could have things his way. Sure, he was a reader - most people were. But beyond The Book, he didn't think much. He watched television and hung out with his guys. The extent of his brain power was tested only with sprinkler fitting. He knew sprinklers. And his daughter, Jane. He knew he loved her. He also knew the names of every player on the Chicago Blackhawks, but that didn't do him much good. And, of course, a point of pride was that he knew the streets. In fact, he could be blindfolded and dropped anywhere in Chicago and would have the ability to pinpoint what intersection he was at, simply through the sounds of the street. Those were the things he knew and he was fine with that. He always felt that most other people, with their dreams and goals, were brought into this world with a much larger mind. His birth category had smaller brains; but since his brain was smaller, he was plum happy that way. He didn't know any better. Life was small. Life was simple. But hey, the guy was happy.

Still, if that was true, if those books and many others – bigger, more substantial books that Holden could never imagine – were edited and altered, how was it that no one else had discovered such irregularities? If stumbling on that single, inaccurate page in Marion's bar meant that he was the first person outside of the Publishing House to know about the differences, what was he supposed to do about that? How could anyone, especially someone like Holden Clifford, react properly when met with such life-altering knowledge?

Without a clue of what to do, Holden trudged onto the bus with the rest of the museum-goers, found a seat and crashed into it. He wasn't surprised to find that nearly every person on the bus had a face that was glowing with dull, green light. Clouds had unfolded across the sky while he was inside the museum and the fact that it was going to rain again made the green lights shine ever brighter on the focused faces of those holding The Book. Even with his reservations and unanswered questions, it was a natural tendency for Holden to reach into his jacket pocket to pull out his copy of the Book. He wanted to resist. To avoid falling back into his old rhythm because something was wrong. But he didn't. He opened the digital reading device and flipped again to *The Catcher in the Rye*. Only this time, he found himself clicking through the many menus of extra notes and details.

There it was. A crisp photograph of the original, printed book. There were many pictures available. He was able to see the front cover, the back, the binding, and even a photograph of the author himself. Naturally, the Publishing House found the most crisp, unblemished images possible. Holden would have preferred something that actually looked real, with creases and stains. Something that didn't looked fabricated and airbrushed

THE BOOK

for optimal pixel value. What he saw made him sad, but mostly for a different reason. Holden realized in that humid, condensed bus that this was likely the closest he would come to seeing his favorite book in person and that the rest of his life would be filled with a forced decision to forget.

The bus came to a stop in Uptown and Holden stepped off with two others – people with a destination in mind that walked briskly toward it because the rain had returned. It was light and blowing pleasantly in the wind, but no less bothersome. Trudging through stagnant puddles on the way back to his apartment, Holden noticed the lights of a few shops along the street. One of the signs was blinking with false intention. The irregular rhythm forced him to stop and take notice. The sign was for an antique store that he had never seen before. A glimmer of hope promptly moved his legs toward the unwelcoming neon. Books were antiques. And it was very possible, although extremely illegal, that the shop owner had books for sale. At this point, Holden would have settled for an idea. A rough idea of where he could find an original manuscript.

Aisles of old furniture and scraps of history snaked through the long shop, dormant in a cracked, translucent skin of dust. The store wore a crisp smell of decay that made Holden recall every time he had been forced to squeeze along the many cramped rafters of a dying city with too many sprinkler heads in

THE BOOK

hand to cover his nose. It was repellent. But, no matter how unbearable, there were some problems in life he just had to accept.

Holden strolled cautiously to the immense oak counter where a skeletal man in a tight, red t-shirt was fiddling with the innards of a prehistoric computer. Three long, beaded necklaces draped his scraggly neck and his poorly-aged face, with oddly dark eyebrows and a handlebar mustache, was warped in concentration. Up close, Holden could see that the man was in his late sixties and was mostly bald except for a tangle of grey hair that swooped the crest of his ears to his neck. Holden knew he should wait until the man was available to answer his question, but he couldn't help himself. He hadn't gotten through five words before the shop owner interrupted him to laugh.

"You're barkin' up the wrong tree, kid," he blurted, scanning Holden with a cagey gaze. "Books are illegal. Book pages are made out of paper which means they are against the Laws of Environmentalism. You ain't gonna find any books here. If you do, point them out to me and I'll have them destroyed."

The man returned to his mound of microchips and circuit boards, leaving Holden aggravated. He normally wasn't spoken to in that way. Most people respected guys with a lot of build and a little patience, especially when they had a confusing tattoo on their arm that could have come from prison. Holden reached into his jacket pocket, took out the page of *The Catcher in the Rye* he had torn from the wall of Marion's bar and slapped it onto the counter.

"Listen, I don't give a dog's tail about your environmentalist viewpoint. I just need to know if you have a copy of this book or know where I can find a copy of this book."

The man looked down at the page, shocked. And for a moment, Holden almost believed he saw a flicker of interest, a spirit of excitement kindled behind the man's eyes before it vanished and Holden was wrenched over the counter like a blanket over a woman's cold shoulders. The man looped his fist in Holden's shirt and yanked him across the counter, toward a half-open door at the back wall, toppling many boxes of impulse items. There was a short flight of curving steps beyond the door and Holden fought to climb them under the man's grip, but tripped on each one except the last.

Holden realized too late that the shop owner with mummified muscles was shockingly strong and was fully against the idea of discussing the topic of illegal, unrecycled books. At the top of the stairs, surrounded by boxes of curious items and a fort of furniture that yearned for its own demise, the man, half Holden's size, charged forward and slammed him against the cracked, plaster wall. He crowded Holden, revealing a face as red as the shirt on his wrinkled back. He was close enough that Holden felt the tickle of the man's beard and could smell whatever sauerkraut delight the shop owner had enjoyed during his lunch break. The pointy odor was the only thing that covered the must of molding antiques and, for a fraction of a moment, it was refreshing.

The man spat a fevered barrage of words. "I told you already, I don't have any books. I don't sell any books. No one does. It's not worth the suffering we would go through. What are you here for? Who sent you here?"

Holden lifted the page he was still holding, stumbling over his tongue as it got in the way of his defense. "I'm just looking for this book. That's all."

"You're lying to me and I'm going to find out who sent you here."

"I'm not lying. I'm serious. I found this page from my favorite story and something wasn't right when I compared it to my Book. I just want to see an original copy." Holden fought the man's grip and it loosened. "Just tell me...do you have a copy of this book? I'll pay anything. I need to read it."

The shop owner apologized with conscious embarrassment. "I am sorry. I'm afraid that I can't help you. For your own sake, I suggest you forget that we ever had this discussion. The world of thought is not safe these days..."

Holden watched as the man's expression gradually shifted to a well-controlled concern. He began studying the area around them, at the many boxes of remarkable items, and seemed suddenly more concerned that he had dragged someone into a space he never wanted anyone to see. Holden didn't care about the contraband or paraphernalia the man was harboring. None of that mattered. It had been a mistake to come into the antique store, and that man, while he may have had a book or two hidden in that back room, did not have *The Catcher in the Rye*.

The long walk through the rain was shameful and when Holden returned to his home, if that was what you called it, he found messages blinking his answering machine again. Talk about antiques, that archaic machine had been getting more use that week than ever!

A short, delightful message from Jane compelled Holden to pick up the phone and call her back. They spoke for a short time about really nothing at all. Pleasant nothings between dad and daughter. When Holden hung up, he listened to the second message, which was far less enjoyable. Numbskull's voice rattled the speaker in eagerness.

"I know you need another day of work like a hog needs a side-saddle, but a job has opened up for tomorrow morning and hey...luck of the draw, right? Side job, so off the books...which means cash, baby. If I don't hear back from you by nine, I'll assume your holiness is going to church instead."

As the message crackled to a finish and beeped its last breath before deletion, Holden's face lit up, and not from the hope of cash in hand. The answer to the question that was picking away at his brain had been on his answering machine the whole time, waiting for him.

He went to his fridge and cracked open a beer, nodding his head in realization. He wouldn't be working a side job tomorrow. Holden had finally figured out where he would be able to find a copy of *The Catcher in the Rye* by J.D. Salinger.

And the drive would take forty-five minutes.

The ladders clanged atop Holden's wide, windowless, semi-white van, jerking the ropes taut as he banked a corner on Sheridan Road and drove further into the forest encroached suburb of Wilmette. He hadn't slept last night. Two things had kept him awake: the lasting, raspy words of the antique shop owner, *the world of thought is not safe these days*, and the message from Numbskull about a side job for cash. Throughout the night Holden had watched as the moon faded and the sun gently rose through the milky bay window in his living room, knowing that he had finally figured out where he could find a copy of his favorite book and that the answers to so many unasked questions were only a wily, lie away.

At the end, when everything would make sense, Holden would recall this day, driving to Wilmette, as the culmination of seemingly unrelated acts that led to his beginning – a curious greed that forced him to accept a side job from an enchantingly worried elderly man named Winston and a lack of social skills that led to the discovery of the page from his favorite book. He thought, of course, that the answers awaiting him that morning would be simple. This was a gross error in expectation.

General Fire Protection had kept Holden constantly busy. His free time was limited because he often worked late into the evening. Even his weekends were detained for emergency calls and random side jobs that were too good to pass up. He made enough money to live well, if he chose to, but he was too cautious to enjoy it. *You never know when Uncle Sam is gonna take a bite out of ya.* It was good to feel a sense of security, no matter how false it was. But with such little free time available, it was better for Holden to turn down side jobs that weren't worth the effort.

For that reason, when he was approached by an elderly man about a side job a year prior during his break at a café in Wilmette, Holden did his best to get rid of him so he could get back to his van and return to work. Fortunately, he hadn't been able to. There was a deceptive persistence in the man who had eagerly introduced himself as Winston. Although his face was innocent and his manner gentle, Winston chose to place his walker fully between Holden and the door. Behind frail, thin glasses were two of the most active eyes Holden had ever seen. While Winston explained that he had seen Holden a few times that week and had noticed the emblem of a sprinkler head on the side of his clunky work van, Holden watched the man's beady, gray eyes analyze his own. It was obvious that there was more happening at that moment than the man led him to believe.

"Well, I'm a wealthy man and I need to protect my house," Winston continued, as he labored to recycle his plastic coffee cup. "I don't move as well as I used to and if a fire erupted somewhere in my home, I fear I would be unable to put it out. The items within it are very precious to me."

The man had one and a half feet in the grave. Holden had to laugh. *You can't take it with you, buddy.*

THE BOOK

He tried to pass Winston onto someone from General Fire, but Winston continued. The man wanted Holden, and no one else, to do the work. When Holden pressed him for an explanation, the man dodged the question with ease. In an effort to end the conversation, Holden finally threw out a disgracefully high quote, assuming that the man would abruptly disengage and allow him to finish his croissant in the van. This was the moment when their conversation became the most memorable. Instead of responding, Winston asked Holden his name. When he replied, the man's tender face brightened and he lost five years of age in a smile before speaking the words Holden would never forget, "Double it and the job is yours." As Holden attempted to regain his composure, the man removed his copy of The Book from a satchel bag and rested the corner against Holden's copy, transferring his contact information to Holden's screen. "I expect you'll be professional," Winston continued, "because I intend to leave this off the books and pay you up front...in cash."

Cash.

It was the only form of paper that was still legal. Really, the only use for paper anymore. All money was composed of synthetic material, but it was the paper element that proved authenticity. With the limitless technological advancements, anyone with a computer could create counterfeit money if it weren't for the integration of paper. Paper was so expensive, especially clean, bleached paper, that it was nearly worth more than the bill itself. Cash was unforgeable. Cash was untraceable. Receiving such an amount for a side job that was completely off the books was nearly impossible to pass up.

Holden slammed on his brakes and the van rocked to an abrupt stop as an over-eager driver tore out of their hidden driveway, yanking him back to the present. Their bumpers stopped inches apart from one another. The owner of the Jaguar ignored his recklessness and headed in the opposite direction without a worry in the world. Holden shook his head clear and took a deep breath before releasing the break and pressing the accelerator, throttling his memory further into the events that had taken place at Winston's home a week after their first meeting.

That day had also been murky. Chicago clouds interrupted the sky with cumulus resentment, as if waiting for the moment to pour out their wet revenge on unsuspecting citizens who were enjoying life too much. When Holden had arrived at Winston's home, the man led him quietly throughout the large estate, pointing out the many locations where he would like added protection. While the estate was luxurious and divided into many bewildering rooms, it was all very typical. That is, until Winston brought him down to the cellar.

From first glance, the cellar appeared to be fitted for a lavish wine collection. The brick ceiling was vaulted and the long walls were lined with empty racks that jutted out at even intervals to create many rows. But something was odd about them. They were shallow, almost too shallow, and seemed impractical for displaying wine. It almost seemed that these little alleyways created by the empty rack system were used to store food or containers of some sort in expectation of an apocalyptic disaster. Whatever the items were that the man had been storing in the cellar prior to Holden's arrival, they had been moved. The entire cellar was bare.

Holden began sketching out a plan for the arrangement of the piping system on his Book with a sharpened fingernail. Winston watched as the sketchy lines quickly transformed to a well-drafted blueprint with dimensions and line weights and interrupted by placing a hand over the screen. "This room is quite unlike any area you have ever worked on before," he said, with unease. "And I find it necessary to request that you triple the average number of sprinkler heads."

Holden grinned at this. He had seen such reactions before from people who were obnoxiously protective of their home, regardless of what he said to set their mind at ease. Although it made logical sense in Winston's mind to cover the basement with an overkill of sprinkler heads, Holden's experience was to always keep the spray radius simple and orderly. Winston's reaction to Holden's grin was unforgettable. The man stated that he wanted saturation; that not a centimeter of space should be dry if a fire began. He then squeezed Holden's hand to punctuate his declaration. Holden remembered that this articulated gesture gave more substance to the discovery he would find later that day, because the items that the shelving had been built for were not as plain as fine wine or containers of food. No, it was something far more precious to the man. Something that could touch water, but not fire.

After the complicated structure of plans had been devised, Winston trudged back up the stairs, leaving Holden in the cellar to map out his array of sprinkler heads. The space was vast and hauntingly empty, like a train station without smoking engines, and Holden had difficulty finding the existing water system. He began his usual reconnaissance mission of following the piping in the ceiling and was soon forced to twist Winston's old appliances from the walls and peek behind closed doors. It was then, when he found a closet with a short door that angled sharply from the handle to the hinge, that he stumbled upon the source of the elderly man's insatiable need for protection.

The space beyond the door was misleading. It resembled a long hallway but it led nowhere and was lit by a single bulb that hung like a specter at the center of the tight space. The wall opposite the door was lined with plastic boxes stacked waist-high and draped in a thick, tangerine tarp. Curious despite his caution, Holden lifted the tarp enough to notice that the first box had a series of names written on it in thick, black lettering. Eleven surnames, to be precise. He remembered these names very clearly because the moment he noticed them, Holden understood why the cellar had been lined with shelving and why Winston had needed to hire a sprinkler fitter surreptitiously to protect it all. The names were: Farrell, Faulkner, Feynman, Fitzgerald, Flynn, Ford, Forster, Fowles, Frazer, Friedman and Fussell. Each name began with the same letter and each name was recognizable. Well, except for one. But that didn't seem to matter. The rest were names of famous authors.

Holden pulled the tarp down and got to work. He finished the job in a remarkable three weeks. It easily could have taken triple the amount of time, but Holden wanted to get out of there as quickly as possible. No matter how much he loved reading, he knew that he shouldn't be associated with someone who was so blatantly disobeying the law. On occasion, he recalled the man and supposed that, at his age, Winston didn't care if he were caught with such an extensive collection and arrested. What was a life sentence to someone with little life remaining?

But now, this day, feeling the weight of the single torn page in the front pocket of his jacket, Holden pulled into the man's long, curving driveway, knowing that somewhere in that hidden closet, there had been a plastic box with surnames that began with the letter 'S'. A box that very likely held a book by J.D. Salinger.

The rain instantly poured down as if, like in his recollection, the clouds were simply waiting to release their penetrating droplets the moment he left the van. Holden ignored the rain and tossed a bag over his shoulder (it held a random assortment of tools that would help him sell the lie) before rushing toward the door with a box of sprinkler heads under his arm.

From outside, the enormous lake-side estate was just as exquisite as he remembered with thick, stone walls topped by a sloping roof line that was shingled with a charming patchiness. Even standing under the eave with its reticent columns and cornice work, Holden knew this man had a wealth he would never attain, even in ten lifetimes. Paper was so rare that for a man to keep such a vast store of books, his wealth was likely without measure. Steadying the box of sprinkler heads against the heavy iron wrench on his belt, Holden approached the door and knocked. After a few moments passed, he realized he wasn't patient enough to wait and rang the doorbell. Just as he depressed the button, Winston poked his head a bit into the side window, wearing a bowtie and a grin. A series of unlocking latches followed and it gave Holden a chance to review what he wanted to say. After an annoying chime was silenced, the door opened and Holden and Winston met once again under the darkness of a cloudy, sleet-streaked day.

"A bit eager, are we? A knock *and* a ring?"

Winston stood uneven in the opening of his front door, sprouting a surprisingly adolescent tuft of hair from the bottom of his boney chin. Behind a new pair of thinly-rimmed glasses, Holden saw the same fiery gaze. The bowtie on Winston's neck spoke of a gallantry long before this digital world, where men looked their best even if they were stewing in their home behind a light, fiberglass walker.

"Good Morning. I don't know if you recognize me, but I installed the sprinkler system in your house."

"Yes," the man nodded with a grin. "Holden. A memorable name." His words and tone were courteous, but his face said differently. A strong suspicion seemed to tighten the skin on his cheeks and his filigree of eyebrow feathers hung drastically lower than Holden remembered. Still, the pale-lipped grin gave Holden hope and he quickly went into the act he had rehearsed during the long drive.

"It's very important for me to keep track of the homes I do work for and I believe that the sprinkler heads I installed here may have been faulty. If it is alright with you, I would like to replace them. Free of charge, of course."

Winston nudged the door a little wider and stared down at the box of sprinkler heads under Holden's arm. Gradually, his eyes rose to mark Holden's face with a deep, inquisitive gaze. "You couldn't come back another day?"

"The structure I installed was a dry system which means that the water only discharges when a fire is present. If you would allow me to do this today, I could be finished before lunch."

Winston scratched the bushel of white hair atop his head, realizing that he was losing whatever game was being played. "Well then, it appears as if I do not have a choice. The protection of this home is paramount to me." Before his next words, a grin tipped from the corners of his mouth and stretched like a stain across the contours of his face. He took Holden by the eyes, skewed his head to the left and said, "I was wondering how long it would take you to come back."

Before a response could come, the elderly man stepped aside and allowed the door to open on the weight of its own hinges. Holden had once more been invited into the perspective of Winston Pratt.

The interior of the immense estate was exactly the same as when Holden had completed the job. The smell of leather and pipe tobacco hung in swags from the heights of darkened rafters; not an off-putting smell, but something that just didn't seem to agree with Holden's nose. The simple decoration, subtle furniture and clean environment were that of someone who had everything and had nothing. It was comfortable, yes, but there was something sad about the estate as well.

By the time Holden closed the door, Winston was halfway to the kitchen. "I was in the midst of brewing a pot of coffee, if you would like some."

"Nope. I'm good," Holden replied, turning his eyes toward the cellar door. "If it's alright with you, I'm gonna jump right in. Get started downstairs."

The man rose a tired hand and waved it flippantly with his back turned, marching his walker toward the kitchen.

Be my guest, it said.

Exactly what Holden wanted to hear.

His greedy footfalls echoed off the crown molding, harmonizing with the creaking tones from uneven floorboards as he moved through the sitting room, foyer and dining room before tracing the narrow runner toward the singular door that he had been envisioning throughout the night. It was positioned to the left of a wide, curving staircase and beckoned for him to open it. He approached the door like a man to a mirage, envisioning everything that could take place the moment he reached it. The dull brass handle was cold and it turned with an unrelenting shuffle to expose a wall of darkness beyond that smelled of something biting and unidentifiable. Holden set that aside for the moment and recalled the light switch to the right of the door before allowing his finger to unearth it in the evocative darkness. It snapped on with little effort and a crackle of electricity released before the cellar stairwell was coated with incandescent splendor.

Holden ground his teeth and turned the corner. Staring down at the unvarnished wood steps, he was almost frightened by the uncertainty of the place in which he was about to enter. Light traced gracefully down the hand rail and the wall to the left guarded Holden's view from what he remembered to be a very open and cavernous cellar. When he reached the bottom of the stairs, the view that met his eyes and the smell that reached his nostrils were altogether astounding. The rows of shelving he had once seen empty were now lined with hundreds upon

THE BOOK

hundreds of books. Lanes of story and fact along a city of so much unrecycled paper. The stripes of tattered bindings stretched along each shelf like a rectangular horizon of dull rainbows. A potent, almost minty, smell caught itself in his nose and it made him want to simultaneously cough and breath deeper. The absolute quiet of the cellar allowed him to wonder for a moment if two of his senses had overpowered the other three. Holding The Book and knowing any story was a double-tap away had been one thing, but seeing them lining the space all around him - a new romantic fascination came over Holden.

In the silence, he noticed, from the sound of his own breathing, that his jaw had slackened, leaving his mouth open and vulnerable. Holden forced himself to abandon his shock for the moment, in fear that Winston would come to the stairs and see him standing there dumbstruck, and unloaded his box of sprinkler heads and tools. He stumbled into the nest of illegal paper and reached for the step ladder Winston had placed at the center of two aisles, no doubt to reach the top tier of shelving, and positioned himself below a pageantry of pipes to begin his fictitious renovations.

Over the course of the next seventy-two seconds, Holden breathed very evenly and allowed his eyes to soundlessly navigate the lines of the nearest shelving unit. He was simply amazed at the number of book spines and how the sheer volume of names embossed upon them with sparkling gold ink had chipped to leave a shadow of authors behind. He hadn't come that morning expecting so much bewilderment. The reason he eventually rested on was the thickness. He had seen only a few books in his life and had never imagined the disturbing thickness of multiple books beside one another. So much information squeezed together in a printed form and yet, so little information taking up so much space. His digitized viewpoint was designed in the web of the internet and the green arms of The Book, where entire encyclopedias of knowledge took up less space than a pair of shoes. And yet, he instantly understood the man's willingness to break so many laws and risk sacrificing his future for such tender obsession. Each one of those books had pages upon pages of shadowed text that, even at that very moment, were sitting stagnant, yearning to be flipped through. Among its dusty volumes, Holden could lock himself away and lose his life with a tome in hand. It was a dream he never knew he had.

A sprinkler head came free of its threading and fell to the ground, waking him swiftly from a dazed sleep. Holden had been unscrewing it, unaware. He stepped down from the ladder and reached for the fallen metal sprocket, but once down there, so near the closest shelf, he felt a duality of strength and sadness take over him and he dropped to his knees. The space around Holden seemed to pulse with an overwhelming power. It was as if the books were alive. And yet, there was a heartbreaking sensation lingering in the dust that reminded Holden of a job he had done a few years back at a small assisted living facility downtown. The two spaces shared the same air, and he knew why. It was the dissonant melody of life ending. Life that was barely holding on in a world that had forsaken it and moved on to something it believed was better.

Holden reached for the closest shelf and caressed the book nearest him. He felt the grain of the linen cover and memorized the sporadic stripes of black and white along the bead of binding, with a sympathetic spirit of guilt. In his jacket was The Book with all its gadgetry and perfection, the device he adored above all others. The Book suddenly seemed so arrogant. With the patience of an art connoisseur, he admired the novel in its entirety, memorizing the finest details, until he moved on to other books nearby. Holden felt a surge of excitement as he saw

THE BOOK

so many names beginning with the same letter. The shelves were in alphabetical order. His eyes scanned the walls until he discovered that in the shadowed corner, where a reading nook had been built with a small desk, couch and reading light, all grounded with a finely woven rug, was where he would find the letter he needed.

The step ladder folded effortlessly and Holden held an ear out for Winston. He remembered how easy it had been, when installing the sprinkler system, to hear the man shuffle his walker along the hardwood floor. For the moment he was safe to approach the shelves and he did so with the fervor of a monk before a row of succulent meat on the forty-first day of a fast. His eyes flickered past each name, trying with difficulty not to stop and admire the collection in his search for the one most important. On a shelf sharing space with books by authors like Salman Rushdie and Edward Said, he found it.

His breath released in a long summer wind and Holden nearly lost his balance as he very carefully traced a finger over the top edge of the paperback book. It was solid, nearly solid, there had been so many pages packed in there. With the gentlest care, he pulled it free from its position on the shelf. It was lighter than it looked, less substantial than it felt. Holden rested the book with a protective hand on the desk beside him before absorbing the cover he had been longing to find on the bus the day prior. It was worn and bent, with more than a few smudges and a blushing ring of dirt along the rim. The capital letter 'D' in Salinger's first initials was nearly smudged down to the white of the background. Droplets of sweat escaped Holden's hair line and soothed the taught wrinkles of skin on his forehead as he pulled free the page from his pocket and rested it beside the book on the writing table. And then, carefully – very carefully –

he lifted the limp cover of *The Catcher in the Rye* and turned the many pieces of paper to page two-hundred and forty-seven.

An overwhelming joy that he had never felt before in his life overcame him as a smile took precedence upon his face. The pages matched. Perfectly. From the first word at the top to the last words at the bottom, they were identical. Holden hadn't realized yet the importance of such a discovery, but it didn't matter. He was right and had found it, against all fear and doubt. And now, with the complete, unedited manuscript at his fingertips he would finally be able to –

"So that's the one, huh?"

Holden awoke from his trance and turned to see Winston standing at the base of the staircase without his walker, wearing a grin that didn't mean to make sense. Holden did his best in the moments available to decipher what the man meant, but was lost in the emotions laced within that grin.

"I...I'm sorry, sir. I couldn't help myself. I noticed these books here and I..."

"Holden, please," Winston complained, shuffling forward. "There is no need to lie, especially when you're holding the book that revealed the lies to you." As he lumbered near, Winston noticed the fragment of crumpled paper beside the book and approached the desk carefully, as if one wrong step could make the page disappear.

Holden thought the man was reaching for it when he passed his arm over the page and gently lifted the book from the desk. His smile shifted, but it remained unclear as he wiped the dust from the stained cover with ethereal delicacy. Holden had never before witnessed a person employ such a gesture with an inanimate object. This man, nearing the close of his life, had a love affair with the items on these shelves that Holden would never understand.

THE BOOK

"*The Catcher in the Rye*, by J.D. Salinger." His shining, false teeth broke through the sly, enigmatic grin. "How amazing…that *this* is the book."

Holden didn't know how to respond, so he stood quietly and allowed Winston to continue.

"Did you know that, at one time, a printed copy of this book could be found in every school, book store, and library in the world? Shame…I don't think many people read this book these days."

"Listen, I didn't mean to…"

"You have a good name, Holden. It makes me think that it called you to this book and the revision you found. Funny that most of this happened because of a name. It's one of the reasons I trusted you with the act of protecting my library," he claimed, with a careworn stare. "The other reason is parked in my driveway."

"My van?"

"I had seen you in the café a number of times that week. On one of these occasions I was privy to an argument between you and another customer over your *willful denigration of the planet*. I doubt you recall it because I would think this argument happens on a regular basis. Your work vehicle is a gas guzzling hybrid."

Holden rolled his eyes. "I know."

"And yet you don't care that this politically incorrect machine on its death bed, with laws against its constant use, may be one of only thirty hybrid vehicles in the city limits…maybe the state."

"Nope."

"And why?"

"Because I don't care."

Winston pulled the novel to his chest and closed his eyes. "Which is precisely why you were the only one I...the only one in so many years, that I felt I could risk inviting into my home."

Holden shrugged. "I don't understand."

"When I see you, young man, I see someone who is willing to stay put when everyone else in the world feels required to move...to disobey the law and do what you want, regardless of the punishment threatened against you. Someone willing to deal with the daily insults and self-righteous glares, simply because it is your right to do what you want. A free-thinking man who persists even if it means he has to run his vehicle on individual quarts of gasoline bought under cover at the back door of a filling station. An anomaly of the socially acceptable."

"It's just a work vehicle, man."

"No," he whispered, with deepest conviction. "No, it is so much more than that. Now, I would love to get into this, but there is no time. We must act quickly."

"What are you talking about?"

"They may already be on their way. So, what I would like, Holden, is for you to take a seat and answer a few questions for me."

"I should probably just get back to what I was doing."

"Holden, don't insult these pages by pretending you're here for work."

The blunt honesty in the man made Holden relinquish himself. With reluctance, he found a comfortable spot on the couch within the dark recesses of the reading nook and waited. Winston neared the desk and looked down at the ragged scrap of frayed paper Holden had ripped from the wall of Marion's bar. He put his weight against the side of the desk and studied the torn edge of the page with a frail finger.

THE BOOK

"Now, I can assume that wherever you got this...the source either has no knowledge of its absence or was fine with you taking it?"

"Yes."

"And to have recognized such a minute difference in the story, you must have read it multiple times. I'm assuming by your name that I am correct."

"It's my favorite story," Holden admitted with pride, unsure of where the man was leading him.

"That is to your benefit. But do not assume your luck will last much longer. For now, I think it's safe to say that they aren't aware of what you've realized."

"Who are you talking about? And why would they care if I found out that a few words were changed in a book?"

"Please, let me finish. Time is crucial." Winston adjusted his eyeglasses and neared closer to the page from the wall of The Library's bathroom. "The first thing I'm going to ask you is very important. Depending on your answer, they may already be on their way." He glanced down at the watch that hung loose on his thin wrist. "Where you came upon this page is important...*very* important. But, for the moment, there are more important things to discuss. What I need to know is, when you went to The Book to judge your discovery against the digital version...did you go directly to the corresponding page or did you use the *Explore* function to perform a search within the entirety of the story?"

"I went to the page and...it was different. Most of what was on the page had been deleted. It doesn't make sense..."

"Right now, it doesn't need to." He waved Holden's concern away with levity. "Might I also assume that you did not search the internet for an explanation of what you discovered?"

"No, actually...I didn't. I really should have."

"More luck, I suppose. The important part in all this is that you *didn't* blindly search for answers," he confirmed, before returning the book to its proper place on the shelf. "If you had, we wouldn't be having this conversation. An average reader skimming to a random page in their favorite book doesn't register as odd behavior and no follow-up searches online means no one is tracking the query about alterations. You're okay so far, but not out of the woods entirely."

"Hold on a second." Holden opened his jacket and pulled The Book out from his pocket. He lifted the leather cover and watched the screen flash to its dull hue of swamp green before Winston leapt over and slammed it to the table with shocking speed.

Winston looked down at his hand as if it had been contaminated by touching The Book, but left it there as he continued. Holden didn't respond. He could see in the man's eyes that something of greater significance was taking place. "I understand your need for answers. I do. But this is a time to be very brief." Winston removed his glasses and replaced them with a different pair before unclipping a very fine screwdriver from his pocket and unscrewing the back of Holden's Book. "You went directly to *The Catcher in the Rye* when you got here, so I can also assume that it's the only story you've found an inconsistency with...and only on that page. Is that true?"

"Yeah."

"And once you noticed the inconsistency, you did your best to track down an original copy of the book, which is how you came to arrive at my doorstep this morning. Because when you were installing my sprinkler system, you recognized, at some point, that I am a man with books."

"Yeah, sorry. I did."

THE BOOK

Winston nodded as he removed the back cover of The Book and rested the device on the table, revealing the network of chips, plates and blinking lights. He turned The Book over in his hands and began reviewing the digital contents before replacing his glasses and walking over to his shelves. Holden watched in expectation as Winston carefully removed a few books from their resting places and stacked them upon his feeble arms, seemingly at random, before limping his way back to the writing desk. "I guess I will take this time then, to thank you for not telling anyone about the enormous secret I am keeping here. This assures me that I can not only trust you, but that I may be able to rely on you in some fashion."

Holden couldn't keep it in any longer. He had to speak up. "Really, sir. I was only…I mean, I just had this need to find out what the difference was and that's it. I know you believe what you say, and that's good and all, but as long as I've earned your trust, I'm glad. Because that means I can ask you what I came here to ask. If I could simply borrow this book, I would be forever grateful. I'm not looking to get involved in anything or put myself at risk here by being…you know…in league with someone who…no offense or anything…" Holden stopped when he noticed the look on Winston's face; it was like a father watching his child attempt to tie a shoelace for the first time.

"Oh, boy. You really have no idea what you've walked into. You found that page. You found one of the last libraries, if not *the* last library in the entire world that isn't controlled by our government. Holden, you *are* at risk." The crackle of his raspy words was like the resounding gong of the Liberty Bell. Holden wanted to protest, but knew the man was right and watched as Winston, very lightly, laid each of the books he had gathered from the shelves at the center of the circular coffee table.

One of the books had a cover that had been taped together and was gripping onto the spine like eight fingers digging for dear life into the fragile dirt of a cliffside. Winston sat on the cushioned chair and beckoned for Holden to take up The Book, as if the man desired not to touch it any more than he had to. Holden did what was asked, completely unaware of what was about to take place, but certain that the lasting memory of the moment would be monumental. As Winston tilted The Book in Holden's grasp, he removed a square chip from the back and rested it onto the table with trembling hands.

"You have eighteen minutes," he said, rising from his seat. He walked across the room and began trudging up the stairs, without another word.

"Eighteen minutes for what?"

A moment later Holden was alone in the cellar before a dismantled digital reading device and five books that he had only read digitally. They were lying flat and unopened, but Holden could see that each of them had dollar bills inside. Some of them were large bills. This completely confused him until he opened the first book to where the bill had been resting. Over the face of the president were details written in a sloppy hand about what had been altered on the page the dollar had bookmarked. Holden could only assume that Winston had chosen these from his collection so that he could look up the corresponding versions in The Book and check the digital printing against the original.

Holden returned the bill to its home and looked over the five titles before reaching for the most perplexing. The book was *Winnie the Pooh* by A. A. Milne. He flipped to the correct marker and moved quickly with The Book to find the corresponding page. Before searching for the inconsistency, he read the note on

THE BOOK

the twenty dollar bill that was marking the alteration. In scratchy red handwriting was a simple, yet profound, statement:

"One word can change the world."

The difference between the written copy and the digital was one word. Nothing extravagant or even legitimate. Just a single word that had been replaced with another. Holden couldn't make sense of it. He shook his head, closed the children's story unhurriedly and moved on to the next. It was a murder mystery novel; wherein many of the pages were lined with dollar bills. Apparently it had been heavily altered. Holden discovered, after only a few pages, that this had been for one reason alone: each of the alterations was the same. A singular revision ran the course of the story. For some unknown reason, the murderer was given a different first name.

Thus far, everything he had discovered was pointless and unpurposeful. He had been expecting obvious changes and deductions, but he closed each book more confused than before.

The third book, *Of Human Bondage* by W. Somerset Maugham, was, surprisingly, the novel in bondage. Holden carefully lifted the tape-coated cover and noticed, with excitement, that it had multiple entries. Each time he looked them up in The Book a phrase had either been altered or removed. On one page, an entire paragraph that seemed garish and unnecessary had been added and then he reached a section where an entire page had been removed - page three-hundred and ninety-nine.

"I'm a failure," he murmured, "I'm unfit for the brutality of the struggle of life. All I can do is to stand aside and let

the vulgar throng hustle by in their pursuit of the good things."

He gave you the impression that to fail was a more delicate, a more exquisite thing, than to succeed. He insinuated that his aloofness was due to distaste for all that was common and low. He talked beautifully of Plato.

"I should have thought you'd got through with Plato by now," said Philip impatiently.

"Would you?" he asked, raising his eyebrows.

He was not inclined to pursue the subject. He had discovered of late the effective dignity of silence.

"I don't see the use of reading the same thing over and over again," said Philip. "That's only a laborious form of idleness."

"But are you under the impression that you have so great a mind that you can understand the most profound writer at a first reading?"

I don't want to understand him, I'm not a critic. I'm not interested in him for his sake but for mine."

"Why'd you read then?"

"Partly for pleasure, because it's a habit and I'm just as uncomfortable if I don't read as if I don't smoke, and partly to know myself. When I read a book I seem to read it with my eyes only, but now and then I come across a passage, perhaps only a phrase, which has a meaning for me, and it becomes part of me; I've got out of the book all that's any use to me, and I can't get anything more if I read it a dozen times. You see, it seems to me, one's like a closed bud, and most of what one reads and does has no effect at all; but there are certain things that have a particular significance for one, and they open a petal; and the petals open one by one; and at last the flower is there."

THE BOOK

> *Philip was not satisfied with his metaphor, but he did not know how else to explain a thing which he felt and yet was not clear about.*
>
> *"You want to do things, you want to become things," said Hayward, with a shrug of the shoulders. "It's so vulgar."*

The page that had been virtually ripped out of the digital version was startling to read. Holden didn't know why, but it almost seemed as if the entry had been removed because it encouraged self-awareness. *What sort of person would want to delete something so personal?*

In the next book, the note upon the five dollar bill described that the entire ending after that point had been removed and completely rewritten. Holden couldn't believe it. He had just read that book a month prior and he had to take the fifth and final book, *Remembrance of Things Past* by a man named Marcel Proust, which had a fur of money fluttering from its spine, and set it aside in order to fulfill his need to learn how the fourth story was supposed to end. Even then, his joy was stunted because he read everything except the final paragraphs. The moment he turned the page to devour them, Winston shuffled hurriedly down the stairs with an eye on his watch.

Far more energized, the elderly librarian strode fearlessly to the table, snatched The Book from Holden's grip and returned the chip to the rear control panel before crashing into his oversized chair, gasping desperately for breath. Apparently eighteen minutes had just ended.

As Winston delicately refastened the back cover, Holden sat in a stunned paralytic state, unable to move in the knowledge that was slapping him in the face. Winston returned The Book to Holden, pushed the five stories aside and said, "I know you have a million questions, but I'm only going to answer a few of them...and in the order of my choosing. Let me preface this by confirming what you have just realized. What I just made you realize." He slowly interlocked his arthritic fingers and rested them on the tightly buttoned vest that seemed to hold his organs in place. "The discovery you found in J.D. Salinger's book was not a one page mistake. It wasn't even a one book mistake. What you have stumbled onto is an atrocious reality...a mistake in every book. I chose books from *your* device at random to prove that the truth you found is universal."

"Wait a minute." Holden sat forward, mashing his eyelids tightly as if that would pull the thought quicker to his trembling lips. "You're telling me that all books...*every single book ever written* has been altered in some form or another?"

"Yes. A very crucial fact that I could only illustrate through someone else's words."

"No." Holden stood from his seat and crept past the table. "That's not true. I don't believe you. There's no way you could know that."

Winston adjusted himself on the chair so that he could cross his legs. It took him quite a while to get comfortable and in the silence of that long minute Holden was forced to linger on his final statement. When Winston came to a place where he was willing to speak again, his words were simple. "Indeed, I cannot prove that every book ever written has been altered, but what I can do is base my judgment on the fact that every book I own or have seen in person has been altered, which leads me to believe that the books beyond this rarely vast library have been altered as well."

"Even if you're right, it doesn't make sense," Holden argued, his voice echoing loudly in the brick-lined cellar. "Why is this happening?"

THE BOOK

"I don't know. I'm sure that somewhere in the past people knew why these pages were being adjusted, why things had to be changed, but we don't know anymore. There's no telling why they're doing it. All we can glean from this is that we are forced to live without the knowledge of our own imprisonment. We willingly accept it, in fact, the moment a new edition of The Book goes on sale. The sad reality, Holden, is that we are all too stupid to know that we are being controlled, word by word, and, once realizing this, we would rather return to our stupidity because what we have stumbled onto is not a glorious endeavor toward a life of truth and peace, but a life of fear. And a short one at that."

"But it's all so wrong. What gives someone the right to censor people that way?" Holden barked, angry at Winston's straightforward attitude. "How can you be so casual about this? The Editors of the Publishing House have stolen our freedom of speech."

"Quite untrue. Don't you understand? It's not us, Holden. It's our forefathers and their characters that have had their voices removed. You have accidentally stumbled upon one of the most tragic conspiracies of all time. The taming of all mankind through addition and subtraction. The only reason I'm opening you up to the entirety of it is because you need to realize that life will be very frustrating from this point forward because there is nothing, *absolutely nothing* that you will be able to do to stop it."

Silence caved in the walls and brought a deafening pressure to Holden's ears. An hour ago, he had been a pipe fitter in search of a few answers on his day off. What was he now? In what sort of deep horror did he now find himself swimming? For a time that felt far longer than it was in reality, Holden stared at his copy of The Book. It was so new, the cover still shined and carried the crisp musk of fresh leather. He had been so proud to have it with him every day. What a part of life it had been. And what was it, really? After today, the man Holden had been, with a simple mind and a small life, would be gone. There was no going back from this.

Holden turned to Winston and searched for something to break the silence before the sound of him getting sick all over the man's adorable reading room would do the job for him. He reached down for The Book and turned it over in his hands.

"Why did you take this apart before I started looking through my stories for inconsistencies?"

Before responding, Winston cleared his throat and uncrossed his legs. "Every Book is installed with two tracking systems. One global. One internal. If you would've performed an *Explore* search through these five books for the words that were missing or jumped directly to pages that have a record of being altered, you would have been flagged, tracked, captured and recycled."

"Sorry? What do you mean *recycled*?"

Winston looked up at the brick-vaulted ceiling and adjusted his glasses. "Why don't we save that for another day."

"Whatever. Just tell me then…that chip you took out of my Book made them unable to know what's going on?"

"Precisely. Let me elaborate. This planet is completely networked, even over our oceans and deserts, but there are still untracked dead zones. Although they are extremely small, the Publishing House expects to deal with them once in a golden moon. If a Book on their network loses contact with the server, they allow eighteen minutes before reconnection. At that time, the user is guaranteed to pass over the minuscule dead zone. But, because the probability of any Book going off-line twice is so minute, really a mathematical improbability, that was the first and only time your Book can be taken off the grid. Otherwise, they will assume that you are manipulating the system. See, you can't even imagine how lucky you are Holden. Most people who reach this information as you have make the very large mistake of combing the entire Book, going onto the internet and searching for similar incidents, or requesting information directly from the Publishing House on why things would have been edited in such a way. That's why you have never heard about this. Those unfortunate people have been removed from society."

"Wait a minute. So you're telling me that if I searched my Book over and over for…"

"Yes."

Holden tore from the cellar at a subsonic speed and Winston did everything he could to catch up. "Where are you going? There is so much more you need to know before you go out on your own with this knowledge." By the time Winston had reached the top of the stairs, Holden was already in his van trying to get it started. Winston reached for his overcoat and cane, slipped on his house shoes and walked out into the driveway. "You told someone, didn't you?"

He slammed his fists on the steering wheel and turned the key again, hoping for ignition. "Yeah. Where I found this page," Holden spat, as the man hobbled to the driver's side window. "It was from a bar. The walls are coated in pages like this. Right now, she's probably searching every book she can to find the differences."

"Mister Clifford." The engine turned over and Winston reached through the window to take him by the shirt. "This will be hard to hear…but she's gone. Believe me and forget what you want to do right now. She's already gone."

"What?" Holden erupted with incredulity, tearing himself free.

"An hour's time is more than enough. There's no way she could get more than that before they would flag it as suspicious activity and take her."

"No. I won't believe that. I know I still have time."

"You don't have to believe the truth for it to be right."

"Well, I'm going whether they have taken her or not."

He cranked the gear shift and the van rumbled ten feet in reverse.

"Holden...wait." Winston called, out of breath as he skipped after the van. "You're going to leave and there's nothing I can do about that. But...there is more we have to discuss. You're not ready yet. Please, you must return. We have to finish this discussion."

"I will."

"Go then, but take this with you. If you do succeed and she is still alive...if you can, at all, get more of the pages." His face was tight with determination, his words aggressive and direct as he pointed his free hand at Holden. "You *MUST* do it. Those words are more valuable than you...or I...or this woman. Please, get as many of them as you can, because if it isn't already, that place will be in ashes by nightfall!"

Holden turned the wheel, put the car in drive and flicked on the windshield wipers. He knew, and could clearly see, that he had put a lot of pressure on this elderly man who was not expecting the fallout from such a bomb. Holden had come to his house hoping to find relief, expecting some joy by seeing his favorite book in person and perhaps building a relationship with a man that knew more about books than he did. But, at that moment, Holden Clifford wished he hadn't discovered the extent of it all because a deep regret for what he had brought on Marion was taking over his mind. If Winston was right, Marion was in terrible trouble and he hoped to God that he could reach her in time before it was too late.

As the van careened down the slick driveway, Winston's lips lowered to a frown. The cold rain pelted the glasses on his face. "Be careful, Holden. They are always two steps ahead," he whispered as he watched the van disappear. "And they know more than you think."

For thirty-seven minutes, Holden drove.

Fourteen of those thirty-seven, he felt he couldn't breath. He was so unable to get a handle on the moment that, like the tires on the rain-drenched expressway, seemed almost too slippery to grasp onto. Marion was gone? How could that man, that covert criminal, have the nerve to look Holden in the eye and act as if her life meant nothing? It was true that Holden didn't have feelings for Marion beyond the physical, but she was a person and if there was at all some way that he could save her from whatever this was, whoever *they* were, he would do his best.

Recycled.

He couldn't get that word out of his head.

What would they do to her?

The only wind of hope he could find as he glided into the city was in the way he had tried to recruit her help. Holden knew he had looked insane the day earlier. Maybe he had sounded crazy enough for her to have simply ignored him. Any other idea that came to relieve his anxiety was unlikely. He hoped that something had gone wrong at the bar. That the electricity had

THE BOOK

gone out because she had forgotten to pay the bill. That a keg had exploded. That a bar fight sent her to the hospital. Hell, he'd take a robbery at that point. Anything that would force her not to consider his ranting request. Anything to keep her from scanning The Book for the many pages on the walls.

As the van veered through traffic and he parked illegally outside the door of The Library, Holden could see at once that that something was wrong. The neon sign above the door was off. Marion usually opened early on Sundays; people needed a place to drink and enjoy their sports. But, as Holden wiped the condensation from the windshield with the back of his sleeve, he noticed one of the regulars at the darkened, red door, covering his head from the tenacious rain with one hand and tugging wildly at the handle with the other. It was locked. With no windows looking in, Holden imagined the worst. Instead of thinking out a logical way to confront the possible problem, Holden acted on pure, destructive instinct. He hastily pulled back into traffic before cutting dangerously into the shadows of the narrow alley that traced its way to the rear of the bar.

Holden couldn't remember much before he heard the door to The Library slam to a close behind him. The impact of what he saw at that moment made the moments prior irrelevant. He remembered the door of the van slamming, the cool rain water on his face and crashing the rear door to the bar open as if he were a drunk, scrounging for booze. But the shock of so many lights amid such silence overtook his ability to retain inconsequential details.

The appeal of The Library was that it was usually rather dark. Most of the ambient light came from television screens or the few oil lamps on the walls that thrived off of clean, repurposed oil. It provided its customers with a dark and private atmosphere where they could drink the liquid that their liver hated most without consequence. Standing at the rear door, bracing his eyes from the abrasive light streaming from the main seating area, Holden felt himself pulled to the conclusion of his life. He was staring at the light at the end of the tunnel that was created by mangy bathroom doors, empty kegs and beer boxes.

Droplets of rainwater followed along the contours of Holden's ear and he heard a rustling. Immediately his mind allowed images of terrible things to flash in the bright white of the light beyond and he rushed forward to see the truth. It wasn't until he saw Marion beside a series of work lights, huddled coolly on the floor with her back to him that he was able to breathe. His worst fears had been wrong. For now.

"Marion," Holden gasped, scanning the room in disbelieving shock. She didn't turn and he was glad because he needed a moment to gather the information that was bombarding his eyes.

The three walls that wrapped the bar had been ravaged by a sharpened object. Its jagged edge left gouges and canyons in the bludgeoned, red wood paneling that had been hiding beneath yellowing scraps of paper, leaving the walls to resemble the fang-torn flesh of an animal attack. All around him, the floor was littered with scraps of paper. Corners and strips that were worth thousands of dollars. But there were no full sheets. With Winston's cautious words in his mind, Holden looked beyond what Marion had done and called out to her again. That time, she hopped in place. Her legs uncrossed and she rolled to her right carrying the appearance of an Unfortunate. Like so many Unfortunates, *homeless people* to the minds of another time, Marion's eyes were glazed in shock and her loose posture made her appear more disturbed than confused by whomever was greeting her. He dared to charge toward her and lowered himself to her level, hoping to pull her from the trance she was in.

THE BOOK

"Marion, what happened to you?"

"Holden. Oh, I'm so glad it's you," she cheered tiredly before wrapping her arms around him, only to release them just as quickly. "You were right. I've been checking everything. So many of these pages..." She held up a scattered pile of paper fragments and waved them absently in the air. Pieces fluttered freely from her grip as she lifted her other hand. It was an old edition of The Book and it was attached to a long, green extension cord. "It's a word, right? Sometimes it's just a word. And what's the big deal about a word, right? But other times...other times, it's big stuff. I mean, BIG stuff. And I've been trying to figure out why. I mean, why would they do this? Whoever is in charge...why would they change...this...paragraph. Out of everything, why this? And then...a whole character is gone. This book here," Marion announced, scrambling for a few pages that rested on the fireplace, "This book is completely missing and...and...I can't even find *this* author anywhere. And on this page, it was a scene where a married couple were *sharing a memory. What's wrong with sharing a memory?*"

As she continued spouting her conclusion and interpretations of the pages that had surrounded her life, Holden saw in her eyes the same tenor of desperation and fear that he felt, only at a higher pitch. The only examples that had been revealed to him were chosen by Winston or found on the page of *The Catcher in the Rye* that started it all. What sort of monumental alterations had Marion discovered in the dark silence of the bar? What words carved from the wall had brought such fright?

CAND...Curklunk.

They reeled and stared wide-eyed at the front door. At some point during the night Marion had tipped over the immense coat rack to stop anyone from coming in. Whoever was at the door, rapped their knuckles a few times against the worn wood before trying the handle again. *CAND...Curklunk.*

"Marion, we have to get out of here."

"What?"

She tilted her head and looked at Holden as if he hadn't been beside her that whole time. Her blue eyes were distant as they trailed back to the page at her feet, the one she had been studying with feverish attention when he had come into the room. Holden watched as Marion absently returned to the party-of-one she had been attending, cross-legged on a wrinkled rug of paper that would look obscene to any other eyes but his. Next to them, perched delicately against the wall of booths, were eight large, black garbage bags, overflowing with paper feathers of history. Seeing them through the strings of hair that hung beside her face, Holden was beginning to understand a bit of the insatiable journey Marion had been on since last he'd seen her. Guilt throttled him for the awful things that coursed through her mind, of which he could only imagine.

CAND...Curklunk.

His eyes darted back to the door and he reached for her arm. "Marion, you have to wake up from this. We are leaving. If there is anything here at the bar that you want to see again, you need to get it now. Please."

"Why?"

"That could be them right now, trying to get in."

"Who?"

"Listen to me. Whoever altered these books...they had a reason. And it's my guess that they don't want anyone to find out. I can't get into it all. Just trust me...we have to go."

For a moment, her face resisted. Her mouth hung open with unspoken questions, but the grip Holden locked on her arm made her slacken. "There is something. It's just beyond the bar. I'll get it and we can go."

Holden was prepared to skate across the shards of paper into the alley and get the van running when he remembered what Winston had said about the page Holden brought to the house. He spun on his heels, snatched two of the eight garbage bags filled with recycled book pages and skipped toward the door. He heard Marion rattling through a few drawers and then she was on his heels, holding the door open for him. Holden side-stepped the two bags of priceless paper through the back entrance and moved to the side door of the van. It slid open with a comforting screech that made him think of crisp mornings, warm cigarette smoke and aisles of oil-slickened pipe waiting to be installed. Memories of a much smaller life.

He twirled the bags closed and tossed them carelessly into the rear of the van before yanking the door shut. A few of the pages that had fluttered out as he walked them to the truck were resting on the filthy asphalt. The edges, once glazed in low VOC polyurethane, now softened in the wetness of the gentle rain. Marion reached down to pick one up and Holden shoved her into the passenger seat before nearly vaulting over the hood. Marion wanted to gripe, but she bent to his will, knowing that Holden was moving quickly for a reason. The van door slammed with importance. Holden cranked the key and clamped fiercely to the steering wheel. The alley was a one way street and he knew that if he didn't hurry, they may be stuck dealing with the person who saw fit to wrench on the door despite the deadbolt.

The mufflerless van lurched onward to the end of the alley. Without letting up on the gas, he jerked the wheel to the left and narrowly missed the sharp edge of a thickly bricked apartment building. Something heavy crashed behind him, metal on metal, but he wouldn't dare check the back of the van. The buckets of built-in shelving were growing light in the folly of his reckless driving and he could hear the metal knuckles of many little pieces rolling along the plywood floor. They were half a block away from the gridlock of freedom when he noticed that Marion was holding her Book with an arrested grip. Without a word, he rolled down his window, tore it from her hand, and whipped it with all his strength against the rough, aged brick of the building. There was a spark and a shattering of material, followed by a pinched scream that escaped the passenger seat.

"Holden!" she exclaimed, "Why did you do that? I've had that Book my whole life."

He forced the wheel to the right. "There is a GPS device located in the back. They're probably tracking you and we cannot be followed by these people. I'm sorry."

Marion didn't respond.

Thinking quickly, Holden dodged a few cars, drove a few blocks down the next street and pulled into another forlorn alleyway. It was dark and unsuspecting, and it gave him a chance to stop his heart from beating itself to death. He was hardly ever forced to elude anyone, let alone anything he couldn't see. Although it was against his instincts, Holden assumed that stopping somewhere nearby the last known location of a wanted felon, if that's what Marion was now, would be an unexpected move.

The van idled noisily in the falling rain. Holden closed his eyes and gripped the steering wheel with unanticipated force. Knowing that Marion was watching him, reserved in fear, he pushed his head back into the cracked pleather seat, took a deep breath and spoke his words plainly and evenly, hoping that the manufactured courage in his voice would seem genuine.

"That may not have been them at the door," he began. "You may not be in as much immediate danger as I thought. But, for the sake of argument, we need to assume the worst. The bar is gone…and you can't go back to your apartment again. If there's something important to you there, tell me what it is and I'll go back and get it. But you need to tell me in the next fifteen seconds. Because if there is nothing important enough for me to risk my life, we need to…"

"My diary." Marion said without hesitation. "I've had it forever. My mother gave it to me and…it has my whole childhood. If there's one thing I can't live without, it's that. Please."

Holden sniffed. He nodded.

He loosened the tension in his eyelids and turned up the defrost to clear the fog that was either covering his vision or the windshield.

He glanced over at Marion and said, "You'll need to stay in the van."

She agreed.

He put the van in gear and headed in the direction of her apartment.

He had been to her apartment before. It was on a night when he and Shane had been at a popular north side restaurant celebrating the birthday of a mutual friend. They were lost in an immense dining room, mingling through a large group of Library regulars, when Marion pulled Holden aside and asked if he could drive her home. She had forgotten her present. They wouldn't be missed, and knowing that she lived on Belmont, he was sure to find a much needed pack of cigarettes. Of course, that was before he had quit smoking for his daughter's sake. Now, with all the stress that The Book had brought on, he thanked God *that* monkey was no longer digging its nails in his back. But because Shane had nabbed his last smoke that night, he had agreed to drive her and they snuck out with another party.

The thing Holden remembered most about her apartment was that it hadn't looked at all like he'd expected. When she opened the door and let him in he noticed that the interior was subtle and calm, orderly and clean. For the first time, he saw her differently. If he had walked in to find three cats lounging about, incense burning on the television from the mouth of some angry, clay figurine and sheer orange fabric hanging between open doorways, he wouldn't have thought twice. But the sight of such a fresh apartment gave Marion a new, unexpected dimension that made him notice her. So when she offered him a drink, his guard was down and he accepted (he was used to ordering drinks from her anyway). When she turned on the light to the kitchen, his mind awoke and he retracted.

A drink? No problem. If it was just a free drink, that would have been great. But, what Marion was offering had been: *A drink...and.*

It wasn't that he didn't find her attractive. It was that fear had overtaken him. Fear of *what*, he didn't know. Fear of relationships? Maybe. Commitment? Hell, he screwed that up with Eve. Fear of women? Hello Freud. Fear of love? Yeah, maybe. What he realized, as they drew close to one another in her entryway without much space for Marion to put on her jacket while reaching for an umbrella (It was raining again. Why was it always raining?), was that it had been her lips. For some reason, he had a fear of her lips, as if kissing her would draw him deeply into some form of unrestrained existence. It was a mysterious feeling and there was no reason for it. Marion had never given off the impression that she could sustain such power over Holden. But the thought frightened him all the same because he knew he would succumb to it.

The van jostled to the right as Holden turned the wheel powerfully to the left, banking around a parked car in the lot across the street from her building. He rolled into the nearest spot and killed the engine. The continuous chatter of rain kept their eyes darting about and Holden had to take a few calm breaths before turning to her.

"Alright Marion, I probably don't have too much time, so I need to know where your diary is, exactly."

"It's on my bedside table and looks identical to my Book, if you can remember what it looked like. It came as a companion to The Book when I got it on my eighth birthday."

Holden drooped his head and looked down. "I'm sorry I broke your Book, Marion. And no...I don't remember what it looked like." She nodded and held up her hands, as if modeling the shape would somehow help him imagine the device.

"It's dark green and orange with some thin, metal details. Like geometric shapes and things, I don't know. There isn't much on the table so it should be easy to find."

Holden cranked the thick handle to the door and it swung open in the wind, scratching the car beside him. That didn't matter. He tugged his jacket against his neck in preparation for the rain and heard the jingling of Marion's keys. She had pulled them from her pocket and held them out for him. When their hands met, Marion reached across the wheel and grabbed the scruff of his neck, pulling him close to kiss him with all the shivering spirit she had. The kiss between them was fleeting and simple, but it spoke of her undying trust for Holden and the volumes of dread they both shared in that moment, completely unsure of the profoundness into which they were embarking.

"I have to go Marion." he said, when she pulled back, embarrassed.

"I know. I'm just afraid I'll never see you again." She leaned toward the window. "It's stupid."

"I'll be right back." Holden glinted a delicate smile and closed the van door. He grabbed onto the truss work that was latched to the top of his van, hopped onto the thick, driver's side tire and unfastened the rope that clung to the longest ladder. He pulled it free, threaded his arm through the middle rung and hoisted the ladder onto his shoulder before striding boldly toward the

THE BOOK

polished surface of the steel structure that was her apartment building.

The only information that Holden had to go off of was what Winston had fed him that morning. Any fear that gathered in his chest and moved his legs, fear that caused his heart to dash with dread, was born from the sense that they were in danger. Holden felt that the information he was holding, including the bags of pages in the van, were extremely important and hauntingly dangerous. If what Winston said was correct, he couldn't assume he was safe. There were layers here. Layers of danger, where one element could be more dangerous than another and he was choosing, rather foolishly, to walk further into it once again. Willingly. By returning to the bar, he risked. By taking Marion and the garbage bags, he risked. And now, by going into her apartment, he risked. *But wasn't Marion his responsibility? She was innocent in this. He* ripped the page off the wall; *he* learned the truth; *he* sought out the museum exhibit, the antique dealer and eventually Winston; she was innocent in this and he couldn't allow her to suffer over his lust for the truth. He wouldn't allow her to be harmed over his need for answers to questions that should have been left alone. The least he could do for ruining her life was attempt to retrieve her diary.

Thankfully, his fear was overpowering and it often forced him to think creatively. He assumed that, by entering her building as a common worker, someone with a job to do, he wouldn't be bothered. What kind of guy would carry an enormous ladder into a building when he needed to look inconsequential or would need a quick getaway? He hoped that this attitude would give him looks of disregard if anyone involved with The Book were waiting for her to come home. Walking around with a badge of blamelessness was always a safer route.

As he entered her building, climbed the quiet stairs to her floor and walked down the empty hallway to her apartment, his mind began its cycling re-evaluation. *When he pulled up to The Library, hadn't one of the regulars been yanking on the door?* Maybe it had been the same guy later, just searching for a drink to drown his Sunday sorrows. *What if all this had been the ravings of a senile old man? What if they were fine? What if a lot of people were aware of the edits in The Book?* Holden considered that maybe there had been a clear explanation online and if he had only taken a moment to review his curiosities on the internet, he would have found that they were perfectly safe. That this was a government sanctioned, socially accepted detail that he had stumbled onto and overreacted about; and some elderly man's conspiracy theory made him yank Marion out of the business she had destroyed over some perplexing anxiety. It could have all been for nothing.

This attitude sustained Holden and strengthened him as he reached for her keys and drew close to the door to her apartment.

One of the interesting details about Marion's building was that there were short, rectangular windows above each door that could be propped open a few inches to allow air to circulate. At times, it made the hallways stink of many different scents that should never circulate, but it remained an interesting architectural detail and Marion, it seemed, was one of the few people that took advantage of the window. It was by that small detail, that Holden was saved.

As he neared the door with the ladder balanced evenly on his shoulder, he stopped. There were noises. Faint, suspicious noises that could have been anything. If the window above her door had been closed, Holden would have ignored the noises and unlocked the deadbolt. With it open, he could tell that they were

THE BOOK

coming from her apartment. There was a scratching. A shuffling. Then footsteps followed by the cracking sound of a plastic bag being whipped open in hollow, suspicious air.

There were people inside her apartment and he was standing at the door, holding her keys. Holden quickly realized how foolish and dangerous it had been to go into that building. To think, for even a moment, that he was safe enough to risk entering her apartment. He holstered the keys and walked silently back to the staircase, being careful not to knock the walls with the ladder. He didn't look back, didn't act out of the ordinary and didn't rush. He calmly returned to the lower level and exited the building, as if nothing had happened. Winston had been right. Marion's simple act of searching The Book to confirm the writing on the pages from her walls had launched a chain of events that caused men to conceal themselves inside her apartment and search through her stuff. It made him appreciate how right he was to race back and rescue her, despite success being unlikely. If he hadn't, she may have already been inside one of those bags that had been whipped frivolously open.

Holden could see through the rain and passing cars that Marion was sitting calmly in the front seat. Her eyes were closed and her hands were pressed together, as if she were praying. And he was right. She had been praying. In fact, it was the most intense time with God she had ever experienced. But once she heard him reattaching the ladder to the roof, Marion swung her hands to the sides of the vinyl seat and gripped tight, staring intensely at the driver's side window. He had come back quickly and she was certain of the reason – Holden had found her diary on the bedside table without a problem. When he opened the door looking frightened, his hair and shirt soaked from the rain, and tossed his jacket to her saying, "Cover up your face," Marion guessed she was wrong.

Holden started the car and put it in reverse, waiting to move until she was completely covered. "What am I doing Holden? Why do I have to hide?"

"There are men in your apartment and, more than likely, they'll review the traffic cameras out here at some point. We cannot have them trace you back to me because...right now I think my apartment is the only place we can go."

Marion agreed with a frightened nod and pulled Holden's thick work jacket over her head, all strong self-confident sprit within her stripped away. Holden couldn't believe, as he drove calmly out of the parking lot and in the direction of Ashland Avenue (*Home again, home again. Jiggety Jig*), that the actions of only a handful of hours could have altered their lives so dramatically. With life changing so fast, he was almost unable to imagine tomorrow or the next day or a week in the future. Marion couldn't stay in his apartment without eventually being linked to him. And how long could Holden go before they, the men with the plastic bags, started combing secretively through *his* apartment. His small story, his small life, had become so suddenly immense.

And as Holden drove his van through the dismal, dreary street, he felt as if a wide, effervescent green light was radiating from his van, pulsing a warning in the rain to those who would be looking.

Alert: those within the green light know the truth.
Here's where you can find them.

A thin needle of pain bore its way into Holden's neck, stirring him from a dreamless sleep. Without opening his eyes, he pushed himself to a sitting position and hung his head over his knees. Normally his neck and back accepted the discomfort of the couch, but with all he had gone through in twenty-four hours, even his body seemed unsure of itself. The boards beneath Holden's bare feet knocked and groaned as he stood and walked to the toilet, trying to be as silent as possible. The door to his bedroom was half open, but he waited to peek in until he was finished with his morning duties. Marion was resting over the covers of his bed, the picture of tranquility, and Holden closed the door. Better if she were asleep while he determined what to do with her.

He dragged his feet toward the bay window where he normally sat to read each morning before work and felt his ritual calling to him in the item that sometimes gleamed in the morning sun. *Not today, though. Weather sucked.*

The Book was tilted out toward him, looking innocent and full of knowledge. It pulsed a beacon of desire and Holden smiled in fear at the device's uncanny ability to draw him in like the landing lights of a runway despite the horrible truth he had learned. Holden glided toward it, inch by inch, until The Book was just below his hand. He flicked out his pointer finger and allowed the sharpened nail to trace the lines in the leather cover, almost helpless against its power over him. It was wrong, Holden knew that now, but he couldn't help himself. For so long The Book had been his salvation against the monotony of life, an object of harmony in a world of uproarious boredom. The habit of losing himself in its pixels when life grew difficult was so ingrained in Holden that he found himself lifting the lie machine and flipping back the thin cover.

From the center of the dark screen, the recycling icon bled forward in the brightest green, sparkling and intense. It welcomed him with the gentlest animation and Holden fell further as the arrows followed one another on their triangular path. It throbbed as the darkened background turned the white of stagnant water and the recycling symbol faded away in a haze of greenish brown. The GRATIS PRESS digital newspaper arrived at the center of the screen and Holden awoke fully in the shock of what he saw on the front page. For no reason other than the bold black text of the headline, he hurried to his bedroom door to check on Marion before discarding The Book on his entryway table and racing to the television in the kitchen. On the plasma screen was a photograph of Marion. Holden glanced into the living room before raising the volume enough to make out what the news anchors were saying. The man's cyborgian face read the news alert with a cold, expressionless tone. Holden inclined his ear closer to the speaker to hear it more clearly.

"...to the ground late last night. An icon of a generation long past that was struck down too close to home. The flames over The Library burned until two o'clock this morning when the

THE BOOK

Chicago Fire Department was finally able to gain control over the inferno. Marion Tabor, the proprietor, is now wanted for suspicion of terrorist activities linked to the anarchist group *The Free Thinkers*. If you have any information on her whereabouts or can provide assistance to the government in any way, please contact the number listed below."

Holden blinked. It was much worse than he'd thought. He fought the urge to turn the television off and throw it out the window, leaning closer instead. The newscasters broke to banter about how sad it was that these terrorists could be lurking anywhere and that this historical monument, this watchtower of environmentalism in the city, was now gone. All those wonderful walls, covered in book pages, were all burned in the fire. Their disingenuous feelings made him sick.

An image of the charred and blackened bar came to the screen. The sidewalk, lined with police tape, was covered in shadowed flashes of the flames from the night's blaze. Holden couldn't believe what he was seeing. The Library was gone, and so perfectly. Not a brick on the businesses nearby, or a board on the elevated tracks above, had been harmed.

Old images of the interior fluttered to the screen, showing Marion's grandfather shaking hands with the Mayor of Chicago. Another showed a billiard room that had eventually been replaced by handicap accessible bathrooms. The mug shot of Marion shrank to the bottom of the screen beside a phone number in bright white text. After adding that her picture and the information on how to contact the authorities would be up on the screen throughout the duration of the broadcast day, the newscasters moved on to the topic of a festival in Old Town. Holden backed away from the television, knowing exactly what the broadcast meant – it would be that much harder to get around with Marion. She would be added to some *Most Wanted* list that covered every major news outlet in the world. Marion Tabor, the innocent woman in his bedroom, was now a wanted felon. A terrorist, apparently, to society with a face that would be published generously on the waves of the ever-ebbing internet.

Holden turned the television off, knowing their options were limited. He went to the refrigerator to pour a glass of orange juice and, after seeing her in the living room, spilled half the bottle on the floor. Marion was sitting on the chair in the bay window, holding his leather Book. Her face was drawn and out of place, with eyes that dragged, tired and confused. She was reading the article. And from her expression, the typed version was more detailed than the televised version. After cleaning up the floor, Holden poured two glasses from the rest of the orange juice and tiptoed into the living room, so as not to startle her, wishing he hadn't left The Book open on the table.

Marion wouldn't look up at him. She was a part of the article now and she wouldn't allow herself to leave until she finished reading. Holden rested the glass on the window ledge and returned to the awkward discomfort of the couch. When she was done, Marion closed the cover and rested The Book silently on the window ledge. She looked out the window, through streaks of rain water that created asymmetrical patterns on the glass, and studied the life below. Children racing to school. People walking their dogs under multi-colored umbrellas. A jet plane cutting its way through ever-angry clouds. Holden didn't need to ask Marion to know what she was feeling. Her freedom was gone. It was gone and, more than likely, forever.

"Marion. I know this has gotta be hard for you and I wish there was something I could say that could give you a sense of peace, but the fact is...we need to get out of here. Only the people who have seen or read the news this morning will be looking for you. I wish we could take a few days to mull things over, but you're too exposed being here in the city and the time to leave is now." Holden could see that Marion was ready to talk, so he took a nervous sip of his drink, rested it on the coffee table and waited.

"Holden," Marion whispered, still staring out the window. "My life is over. There's nothing I can do to defend myself. These people are...so powerful. This whole thing is so much larger than...I don't think there is anything I can do except hide and live...long enough until they eventually catch me." Her head tilted to her chest and Holden rose to place a hand on her shoulder.

"I'm sorry about the bar, Marion. I know how much that meant to you and your family."

Marion shrugged off his tenderness and turned to face him. "What have you gotten me into, Holden? I have nowhere to go."

He frowned and sat on the footstool beside her. "I think I need to take you to the man who started all of this. He may welcome you in, based on the circumstances. His home is large. And he lives far enough away from the city that...you know. I just have to tell work that I'll be late."

There were some intense emotions in the room, but Marion turned back to the window, rolled her shoulders and nodded, not wanting to appear weak in front of him anymore.

By the time Holden walked over to the phone and left a message for Numbskull, Marion had already packed what little she'd brought with and they were soon outside the door to his apartment, sneaking around corners. Thankfully Holden had parked near the back entrance. He had assumed they may need to avoid contact with the two other people renting space in the minty-fresh house. Holden opened the rear doors of the van, moved some debris aside and reversed it toward the back entrance. Other than sitting on the last remaining pieces of the bar in black garbage bags, there wasn't much for Marion, in terms of comfort. But she climbed into the back without complaint and closed the doors.

As Holden turned the key and they drove off toward Wilmette, unseen by the eyes of the public, Marion had already accepted a horrifying truth. For the rest of her life, she would never again step foot within the city limits of Chicago.

And she was right.

12

The cold rain returned, insistent on soaking the Second City. It had been weeks of inclement weather, but finally, along Chicago's sinful fringe, the clouds were breaking to extend a hand of photosynthetic peace. Marion poked her head out nervously from between the front seats to see the first sliver of blue sky in a lifetime. As they wove the snaking streets of Wilmette, that fragile moment of sunshine brightened her despair. The greens of the trees shone more saturated against the dark gray clouds. The multitude of branches and limbs flickered the light of life onto the glistening ladders and waterlogged windshield of the environmentally-impolite van. Kneeling uncomfortably on the filthy plywood floor, dreading the prospect of hiding away for the rest of her life, Marion was unexpectedly serene. The setting of where she would live now blessed her with a few crumbs of hope.

When the van slowed, Holden pointed toward the large Tudor estate, shocking Marion by its enormity. As they drew near, she could see that the home stepped back an acre from the main road. Pebbles knocked the side of the van as Holden navigated them along the curling path that cut through the pristine yard. Marion stared out her window at the mammoth oak trees that speckled the lawn's thick green blades with intention. To her, it was as if the trees were so free that they could uproot and mingle where they pleased, as long as they shaded the leaded glass windows. Holden was already mumbling through the pitch he would deliver to Winston as he parked the van where it had been a day earlier and hopped out.

"Holden," Marion began, as he wrenched the handle to the rusty side door, "How do you know you can trust this guy?"

He reached out for Marion and eased her gently to the gravel driveway. "I guess….it's because he trusted me first." She forced herself to nod in agreement as he dragged the garbage bags from the van. "I know you're scared. I am too. But I promise I'll keep you safe." Holden turned to face her with an assuring grin. "This is much bigger than the both of us. I don't know what we can do at this point. We need someone with answers."

"How does he know so much?"

Holden slid the door closed and stared at rain-smattered gravel. "I have no idea."

They shared an expression of strength and approached the door of the estate, gripping the tightly compacted garbage bags of old book pages. Within moments of their knocking, Winston was at the door, greeting his guests as if he had been waiting for them.

"Holden, I'm glad to see you again. And Marion…" his aged voice seemed to ask, "It's a pleasure." He held up his hand as they entered, halting her obvious question, "Yes, I know your name. I *do* own a television."

"I was going to call. But I…well…"

"I'm certain you have an entertaining story waiting in the wings for me." Winston closed his gray eyes and nodded. When

THE BOOK

he opened them again, there was a glint of admiration in them. The man was impressed. Holden had achieved far more than Winston had expected he could, and it gave him hope. "Might I borrow him, dear?"

Marion shrugged and looked to Holden for confirmation. "Yeah, I guess."

"We'll only be a moment."

Winston took Holden by the arm and walked him into the sitting room off the foyer. Winston skidded his walker to a stop beside the piano. "I know why you brought her here, but what do you expect will happen? They will find her. There's nothing you can do to stop them."

"I know, but she needs help and it's my fault. For some reason, you're the only one in the world who knows anything about this."

"Let's hope that's not true," Winston whispered, pausing as he glanced back at Marion. She was perched quietly, like a lost puppy – innocent, hungry and wet from the rain. "You have courage Holden, but please tell me you weren't stupid enough to bring her Book with you."

"No. We ditched it right away."

Winston bobbed his boney head, stroked the flock of hair on his chin and took a seat at the piano bench. "I've been watching the news all day. It's too bad that the whole bar burned down. All those innocent pages..."

Marion couldn't wait by the door another moment. She raced into the room with the two bags and took Winston by the hand, pleading, "I'm sorry. I don't know you. But I have nowhere else to go and I need to understand why these lies are being spread about me when I've done nothing wrong."

A small giggle escaped the many lines of Winston's tightened lips as he ignored the bags and gave her his attention. "You have done nothing wrong, my dear. You have done everything right. And, I must say, it would be nice to have a female presence in this house. It has been a long time. And I have many, many rooms for you to choose from. You know...I love gardening," he added, pointing to a beveled window beyond the dining room. Through the prism of glass, it revealed a breathtaking back yard with rolling foliage and manicured hedges leading off toward Lake Michigan, placid in the drizzling distance. "I never seem to know what to do with the vegetables once they're grown. If you're willing to give them a proper death in the kitchen, slice us up a nice salad now and again, I think we have a deal."

"Oh, Sir. That would be fantastic."

"Sir!" the elderly man spat, in mock aggravation. "*Sir* is my father. Call me Winston."

"Thank you, Winston."

"So tell me...what do we have here? I must know, because...as you will certainly discover, my patience is rivaled only by my child-like attention span." Winston inquired, as his gaze traveled to the two garbage bags. Confused but interested, he shuffled his walker to the right and propped himself up dexterously to admire them.

"Hopefully this will grease the pan a bit."

Winston fondled the many strands of goat hair on his chin. "Am I to assume then that you brought me the neighbor's refuse in exchange for harboring this woman?" he queried, shooting his right eye up to Holden.

Marion lifted the bag and let it drop to the wood floor, allowing the crinkling sound of leaves to resonate in the piano's hollow chamber. "This is what's left."

As realization set in, the wrinkles on Winston's face were intensified with sharp definition and his eyebrows stood at attention. He scrambled for the twisted top of the bag and instantly released an exhalation of intense joy, like a child on Christmas morning. *"You have a page from this book!?* Oh...my goodness...oh..." He very carefully lifted a single page from the bag and rested it on the polished piano, switching between eyeglasses for a closer look.

Holden used this distraction as an opportunity to escape. He put his arm around Marion and said, "I need to run, but I'll be back by three. You gonna be alright?" She nodded. "Winston, you have my cell number, right? Winston?"

"Yes...yes...I may be old, but I'm not deaf. We'll be fine." He waved Holden away in surprising adolescence while he regained his focus on the page in front of him. His tired eyes were more alive than they had been in years, scanning every letter in obvious delight.

Holden stood at the large oak door, granted Marion a simple grin and left the house. He knew he was leaving her in complete distress, but Numbskull had called on his way to Wilmette and told him to return to a job he had completed a few months earlier. Nothing serious. One of the apprentices would be there to do the work. All Holden had to do was supervise, instruct and switch out a few sprinkler heads. Thankfully, all the materials he needed for the job were in his van and he wouldn't have to return to the city.

At the end of it all, the work day was much easier than usual. Beyond discovering a single book page in the rear of the van from a story entitled *Jurassic Park* by a man named Michael Crichton, which he quickly stashed into his pocket before the apprentice noticed, the normal drudgery of working in horrible weather was a bit of a relief. Going through the motions of carrying greasy pipe, walking through a busy job site, dealing with clients, eating lunch and feeling the cold surety of his wrench as he tightened sprinkler heads allowed Holden's heart to slow and his mind to regain function. He was so tired and so tense with everything that had happened that consistent manual labor had become the perfect way for him to gather back what little of himself remained. An unforeseen blessing was that the apprentice hadn't known Marion, like most of the other men at General Fire, so Holden wasn't forced to talk about how she had turned against her country or why she had burned The Library down. That hour was coming like an owl to the night, but at least he knew he was safe for the day.

By the time Holden made it back to Winston's home, he was refreshed and determined to learn precisely how deep the alterations in The Book went. Questions raked his mind during the drive as each mile brought him closer to his answers. Winston knew more than Holden could guess and this made him certain that by the end of the evening, this enormous life changing event would be explained. It had to be explained. Imagining the next twenty-four hours without understanding seemed impossible. He simply could not exist under the weight of such confusion.

When no one answered at Winston's estate, he instantly expected the worst and opened the door. The ground floor, while decadent in its decoration, was totally empty. Eventually, Holden found Winston in the cellar, sitting in the reading nook beside a pile of the tiniest slivers of paper. The elderly man was spellbound in an innocent focus, very carefully separating the pages from the garbage bags and using whatever wisdom he had to devise some sort of plan for archiving them. On the cellar floor were rows of many crusty pages, ordered, it seemed, by title. Most of the thin stacks were one page thick, but a few had ten to fifteen pages.

THE BOOK

Winston wouldn't allow his eyes to move from the scraps below him to address the man standing quietly at the foot of the stairs. "Is it three o'clock already?"

"Actually, it's five."

"Wonderful," he breathed, wrapped in smiles and satiated by long lost words. "Wonderful. I haven't been this excited in years." He tried to get up and a wince twisted his face.

"Man, you don't need to get up."

"No. I do," he groaned. "No circulation to these puppies and I'm done for."

"Where's Marion? I didn't see her upstairs."

"She has been resting since you brought her here. We were speaking on the couch in the great room one minute, and the next...it was lights out. To be completely honest, I was glad to see it. I've been looking forward to going through these bags. But, not to worry, I have been checking on her every hour or so. Her mind must have been exhausted. Makes sense, I suppose." Winston gazed down at the cellar floor and to all the tousled paper Marion had peeled from the walls of her family business.

"It must be from the shock of what she discovered while looking up all these pages on The Book."

Life returned to Winston like rowdy horses through the starting gate and he raised his arms in triumph. "Oh, and what pages, Holden. What pages! Marion's grandfather was an oracle. It was as if his accidental arrangement of these pages was done intentionally to showcase the most controversial work of all."

"Marion will be glad to hear that. At least something good could come out of this."

"Oh, it is wonderful. I cannot explain to you just how wonderful yet, but you should be able to tell by my attitude that this is a find indeed. So many books, Holden. So many books gone. What you see here, in this cellar...all these shelves stocked with literature...this is quite unnatural. My knowledge comes from a high source and I can tell you for certain that libraries of this caliber don't exist anymore. They simply don't."

"How do you know all this?" Holden asked, still wearing his work boots and jacket. "Honestly, that is the one thing I'm still in the dark about. Where is all your information coming from? I mean...you're making me feel trapped...making Marion feel trapped...and I guess I just need some answers. I don't sit well when things aren't explained enough to me."

"Right you are," Winston agreed, stepping out from the reading nook. "I have neglected you in my haste to devour these works of art. I must remind myself that not everyone is like me and stewing on such bold information, especially when it's new, is a difficult one." He waddled forward and placed a hand on Holden's shoulder to steady himself and apologize. "Forgive me. I've known about these errors since I was a young man. I would explain things to you now, but Marion has risked much and is as deep in the dark as any. First, let us wake her. And then dinner. No doubt she needs to eat. Answers will come, Holden. Tonight, you will understand everything. Now, be a good man and hand me my cane."

When Marion woke, she was relieved to see Holden on the couch beside her and wrapped herself around his neck. Her dreams had only increased the buoyancy of the building stress. Any calmness she exhibited had come from her enthusiasm over the details of the Pratt family estate. As Winston prepared their dinner, she took Holden by the arm and led him throughout the labyrinth of rooms. Holden recognized the hallways and much of the meticulously carved woodwork, but almost everything else seemed new to him. When he had installed the sprinkler system, Winston had most of the antique furnishings and paintings removed or covered in plastic so that nothing would get damaged. Now, walking through the house as a guest, with all the many detailed items displayed and free to the elements, it was quite amazing to absorb it all.

The numerous bedrooms were designed with an individual taste and walking past their doors was like silently stepping through a house museum with the red velvet ropes removed. Eras of furniture and accessories from the early 19th century to their own greeted their eyes in a pristine, dust-free display. The only room unlike the rest was Winston's. His bedroom was a mismatched collection of different styles, with bright colored furniture, animal print window coverings and post modern sculpture. But no matter how riotous the cacophony of color, print and shape had been to their eyes, none of this gathered their attention. What made them stop and accept that the bedroom had been Winston's was the many books he had scattered throughout the space, like laundry in the room of a teenager. There were books on his bedside table; books on his sleek, black *Voido* rocking chair; books on his dresser and leaning against his lamp; books displayed proudly beside framed photographs and on shelves beside random items that no man would normally romanticize. The most beautiful of all was a single book filled with ten dollar bills that was encased in glass beside the cigar store statue of an over-dramatized Native American chief.

Holden edged into the room to see the book more closely. The dull brown cover had a blackened, print block image of a man standing over an open coffin with a lantern. It was curiously eerie. Although the rest of the cover was terribly worn, the structure held so strongly that the pages seemed almost unable to be torn from their binding. This seemingly precious book had the appearance of one that had been read often, and yet, Holden wondered if Winston even liked the story, since it was the only book in the house he couldn't read. It made them wonder if Winston had meant to protect the book for a specific reason or to highlight it as a constant reminder of some larger purpose they would never comprehend. Holden and Marion attempted to garner some answers from the title, but it only confused them further.

The title of the book was *Mr. Weston's Good Wine* and it was written by someone named T.F. Powys.

THE BOOK

The rest of the second floor was divided into smaller reading rooms and short flights of stairs leading to even more reading rooms with books scattered on tables and shelves. After showing Holden the terrace and the conservatory, Marion brought him back to the room where she had been resting. It was the area of the estate that she most enjoyed. The great room. With its high ceilings and dark oak rafters that stood boldly upon the flattest white plaster, it provided the perfect shelter in a shelterless world. Her favorite detail was the thick stone wall that stretched to the chunky triangle support beam above. Carved into the stone was a craggy hearth with an immense railroad beam mantle, all darkened from years of warm fireside nights of reading and relaxation. Despite Marion's utter fear of the outside world, she truly loved Winston's home. If this was her jail, what a jail it would be.

When Winston finished cooking, they ate in the dining room, surrounded by conversations that were taking place in marvelous works of art. Painted people sitting in chairs across from one another, men and women eating a luncheon on the grass. Holden wasn't a man of art, all those swaths of oil and varnish were a mystery to him, but he assumed that with the man's wealth, the paintings hung around the table were priceless. And yet, they were beautiful to gaze at and, for Holden, it was a night of new experiences and stories yet to come.

Winston knew he had been testing their patience by choosing dinner as the time to discuss how Holden rescued Marion, gathered the remaining bags of pages and escaped from the city, but he couldn't stop himself. At times, Marion had to remind the man to eat because he was so enraptured by the courage Holden had exhibited during the night. It recalled to Winston the long dormant character traits of his own and exposed what he had believed was no longer present in the hearts of other story-lovers. He listened and ate with a constant, fancified smile.

When the deluxe dining experience of black cod and asparagus was finished they returned to the great room where, in the gloom of the consistent irritating rain, Winston asked Holden to start a fire and they sat around the gargantuan hearth drinking coffee and smoking – Winston with his pipe, Marion with her filter-free, thin-fabric cigarettes, and Holden, since he had recently quit, with nothing. The agitated sense of wishing he had a cigarette made Holden curb his manners and chuck his patience into the fire with the logs.

"Winston, I've been waiting a long time and I feel like I..."

"I know, Holden," he responded in serene relaxation, "Ask me your first question."

"Good. What I want to know is simple. What should I do now? Because from what I've gathered...it's all controlled. Apparently, someone knows everything we do with The Book. Everyday it updates with new ways to suppress...something. Anyone who discovers the truth is seized. And Marion is stuck here for the rest of her life. The rest of *your* life, I guess. So, what should I do now? What can we do with all this information?"

His reply was just as simple and he made it through many puffs of his tortoise shell pipe.

"Nothing."

"What?"

"Nothing, son. There is nothing you can do or should do."

Holden sat with his back to the growing fire and stared off into the dim light of his shadow. He had been expecting a solution. "How can I respond to that? You've given us a nice evening, but there's so much hopelessness, man. How do you expect us to deal with such a harsh reality?"

THE BOOK

"Just as I have. Through enjoying what elements of life they don't have control over."

"The government can't just do this," Holden declared to the gentle smoke at their faces. "Society won't allow it if we go out and tell people."

"I agree, Holden...but that time has passed. Maybe if we had caught the revisions within a few years, when independent publishers were still printing paper copies, when mankind still had a romantic obsession with the printed word. Maybe then we could have had a chance. But not now. Not after The Great Recycling."

Marion swiveled on the leather couch to look at Winston. "Can't you consider it for a moment, though? How could we convince people that they aren't reading the truth?"

"That's a good question. How do you convince the entire population of the world that the device they trust more than any other, the mechanized manuscript of propaganda they willingly enjoy on a daily basis, is false? Tell me, Holden. In fact, you don't even have to answer this question. Have you been tempted to re-open The Book? Have you found yourself wanting to believe in it again, despite all I have told you and what you have been shown in the last twenty-four hours?" Winston paused to pack more tobacco into his pipe. "There are reasons we trust what we read, regardless of the source. And there are reasons we exist in a world that still shackles itself to The Book."

Holden furled the skin on his nose as he looked down on Winston for the first time with disappointment. "I think you're wrong. I think you're a frightened old man who knows the truth, but hides away in his castle of books when the rest of the suffering world needs to read them. Well, I'm not hiding away. And you can't stop me from telling people."

"Holden," Marion booed, attempting to correct his rudeness.

Winston seemed unaffected by the outburst, almost accustomed to such a response. After allowing Holden a chance to catch his breath and cool down, he replied. "You may be too young to remember this...well, I know you're too young to remember the event, but I believe they may have been trying to erase this story from our memories as well. Thankfully, some things are a little harder to delete than others, but I guess we'll find out. Do you recall the story of the British Prince?"

Holden shook his head and shrugged indifferently. Marion was nodding. "Yeah, there was some failed assassination on Prince John like fifty years ago or something."

Winston cleared his throat as the rain began to fall harder and louder on the roof. The window panes around them were like the rocks below a waterfall, splashed and drenched in perpetual water, and it was difficult to hear his timid voice through the downpour. "That's correct. I was your age when that happened. The man behind it all was named Dennis Wayne Conrad. He infiltrated Buckingham Palace in London with the sole task of capturing Prince John. The standoff was long, I believe. I would later find out that this was the intention. Conrad wanted that day to last as long as possible and for his deed to achieve the most media attention it could. The sheer planning that went into it is mind-boggling. He had entire sections of Buckingham Palace quarantined. It was obvious that the man had been part of a much larger team. And yet, like so many other times in our history, it appeared, to the public eye, to be one man with a grudge."

"But he failed," Marion protested, "They shot him from the window."

"Yes. He failed, but not in the way you imagine. At the end of many hours, Conrad brought the prince to the window and spouted off a statement that grew more famous than 'Sic Semper

THE BOOK

Tyrannis'. Standing in the windows of the White Drawing Room, he exclaimed...*To breathe is to live, but to write unimpeded is to breathe eternal.*"

"That's beautiful." Holden said, relishing the old language.

"More than you realize. More than any of us realized."

Marion was bobbing the cigarette in her hand, looking confused. "See, I knew the story of Prince John from school, but...this is the first time I've ever heard about him standing at the window and speaking."

"Then his failure, as you say, is complete," Winston rose from his seat to stoke the fire and remained standing for the rest of the story. The shadows cast from the flickering flames created a moving statue of boldness that seemed to speak of the spirit inside Winston rather than the haggard old man hunched before them. "After his declaration, he allowed the prince to dodge away from the window. In the moments following, Conrad was shot and killed. What no one understood was that Conrad had gone there with the intention of being killed."

"What?" Holden asked, scooting closer to Marion along the shag rug. "Why would he go through all that trouble just to die?"

"Because of words," Winston answered with simple pride. "Conrad was quoting a line from the novel *The Valiance of Raphael Petitto*. Have you heard of it?" They both shook their heads. "In the story, which took place in the 16th century, Raphael was part of a rebellion of commoners under the oppression of a prince in the King's absence. The people of the town were surrounding the castle, restless and enslaved. Bent on revolution, Raphael Petitto infiltrated the castle surreptitiously and captured the prince. He then brought the frightened little man to the window, where all the commoners could see, before bellowing out his legendary phrase. Almost immediately an arrow runs him through and he plummets to his death. But, seeing this, the people of the town rise up and overthrow the kingdom." Winston paused. "I can tell by the look on your faces that it still doesn't make sense. That's because I'm leaving out a key detail. In the story, when Raphael brings the prince to the window, he cries out...*To breathe is to live, but to act unimpeded is to breathe eternal.*"

"You said *to write* before," Marion exclaimed. "To *write* unimpeded is to breathe eternal."

"Correct. Although Raphael died in the story, he succeeded in defeating the powers that were enslaving them all. Conrad had hoped his death at the window would spur on the same revolution. Clearly it did not." Winston struck a match along the stone wall and brought the flame to his pipe. "This makes sense when you take time to understand the common folk. They were so enlivened by Petitto's courage and angered by his death that they stormed the castle. Never before had they realized that their sheer numbers could easily overtake any government fortification. Dennis Wayne Conrad went to London with the goal of getting the rest of the world to realize the same thing. He willingly sacrificed himself for the sake of this." Winston took a book from the end table and held it high in the random luminance of the fire.

"Only the commoners didn't react," Marion finished with a grim expression.

"Exactly. Our ability to understand what happened and to spread the word to one another had been stunted...quickly confused by the government-sanctioned media. None of us knew that he wasn't going there to assassinate an innocent prince. That he was going there to die in the hope of making people realize that what they were reading was a lie. To free the world from The Book. Soon after, as was just displayed by you Marion, his courageous words were lost upon society."

THE BOOK

In the pleasant crackling of the fireplace and the sober reality of someone else's failure to stop The Book, Holden started shaking his head in confusion. "But someone must have known what he was doing. Known the quote from that story and realized what he was trying to say. Someone must have done something."

"Yes. There were people who understood and, unfortunately...they were dealt with before they could organize."

"What do you mean?" Marion asked, needing an answer.

"Well-read people who caught the source of the line before the media started pretending it wasn't spoken, went directly to their Books and searched for the story. Those who did were quickly tracked by the Publishing House and...without knowing what happened after that, I can only tell you what I was told. They were recycled."

Holden lost his balance and threw an elbow into the couch to steady himself. This was too much for him to take and he found himself eyeing the leftovers of Marion's cigarette in Winston's designer ashtray. Instead of breaking his vow to never smoke again he asked the question that was gnawing on his mind. "How could you possibly know all of this?"

Winston slid his hands to his knees and sat on the stone bench before the fire, a drawn expression on his face as he remembered things dear to his heart. "My mother. They worked together."

"With Conrad?" Marion confirmed, as she pulled her legs up to the couch and sat on them in sudden interest. "You're kidding. She knew him?"

"Where did they work?" Holden asked, feeling that this was the most crucial element of the story.

As the thunder tumbled over the drenched world beyond the windows. Winston replied, "My mother, like Conrad, was one of twenty Editors for the Publishing House."

"Your mother edited The Book?" Holden confirmed in shocked disgust.

"Yes, sadly. It was her job to erase information from valuable novels and update The Book with the corrections. Dennis Wayne Conrad was so discrete in his plan that my mother had never heard a whisper of what was going to happen. When Conrad was missing from work, she assumed he had quit. And after the news storm hit, it started to make sense. She looked back at her interactions with Conrad over the past few years and recalled instances where he may have been trying to recruit her through random chit-chat. But my mother was smart. She always played it safe and never gave any inclination that she thought things were wrong. She simply did her job, kept her judgments to herself and came home. It was a good job with excellent benefits. To my mother, the safety of our family was paramount, but the events that took place with Conrad were simply too much for her. I came home one day from work and found her on this very couch, crying her eyes out. And it was that day...a Thursday, I believe...when I came to learn about The Book and what my mother had done for a living."

Winston paused, unexpectedly emotional, and Marion stood to put an arm around him. Holden went to the closet off the kitchen where he knew Winston kept his liquor and returned with a bottle of twenty-year-old whiskey and three glasses.

"That must have been hard for you."

"Yes, but not anymore," Winston replied, taking the glass with thanks and sipping from it happily. He knew they were confused by the glisten in his eyes. "I just miss my mother."

THE BOOK

When Marion felt enough time had passed, she asked, "So, is that where all these books came from? The Publishing House?"

"No. I suppose I should explain that." He finished his drink and Holden poured him another as they found new seats around the shimmering glass of Winston's *Noguchi* coffee table. "As the both of you, I grew up in a digital world. This home and everything in it is the result of greed in my family. My father was a reader, and while I would like to say that my collection of books were saved for their content and merit, the truth is that they were saved for their value. My father went to his death bed unaware of our government's control over The Book. Before he passed away, he told me about the boxes of books he had hidden away. My inheritance. See, when The Great Recycling was taking place, my family decided that they would keep their collection in the hopes that the laws would be overturned one day and their unlawful library could be sold at a premium. Those books avoided destruction for selfish greed. Nothing more. Our joy and our future, born through the expectation of outrageous profit. How funny."

"So what happened?" Holden asked, sipping his whiskey. "You started reading them all?"

"No. I only saw them as my retirement and kept them hidden, even from my mother. And on that day, when I found her weeping and she confessed everything to me...I did the same." Winston stood, took a framed photograph from the mantle and handed it to Marion.

"This is your mother? She was beautiful."

Winston smiled as he continued. "She kept repeating that she was going to quit. My mother was so ashamed of what she did for a living and wanted to tell others. That was when I told her about the secret collection of books my father had kept. That night, we left the house together and dug them up, right where my father had told me they were. We pulled up so many waterproof boxes, there were almost too many to count. It was a night I knew I would never forget...and I haven't. Covered in mud and carting a van full of illegal material back to our home, my mother and I made a silent pact that we would do something to fight back. We knew there was nothing we could do to stop the government ourselves. Conrad had gone to such extreme lengths and yet he had failed...but we knew we had to do something. We decided that she would stay at her job and gather as much information as she could until the day she retired. Throughout that time, we built the library you saw downstairs and read every single book that my father and his father and his father and his father had collected."

"Every book?" Holden asked, surprised.

"We read every book...together. And each time we began a new story, my mother would gain access to the master files at work and search the contents for recorded alterations. Since money was the only item the guards didn't check when she exited the building, she would write out the revisions on dollar bills using makeup as ink, then put them back in her purse. And, as you saw, sometimes all she had was a hundred dollar bill. But the information she gathered was always worth the money. We were marking these books for the sake of the future. At the same time, she began to keep a digital log book here at the house. Each day she came home from work, my mother would list out everything she had been forced to change. She memorized book pages and entire strings of words, just to record them into the log book without knowing at all how future generations would use them."

"That's how you knew to remove the chip from the back of my book."

THE BOOK

"That's right, Holden. And when she retired, our link to information ceased. We realized that there was no use trying to stop anything and spent most of our time reading. When my mother passed, this was some years back, I resolved to fix things myself, if I could. I didn't get very far before a group of people disappeared. The only reason I escaped intact was because I had spent quite a long time prior to that developing an alias for myself. I spent a fortune and no less than a decade of my life, and succeeded in barely denting the issue. All this effort makes me certain enough to say, as I stand before you, that all the feelings you have will pass. Over time, despite how depressing the reality is, that fact remains true. There is nothing we can do to stop them. You must bear your fate and enjoy what life you have left. Enjoy this world. Enjoy each other. This is a harsh reality, but it is the one we were born into. Accept it. We do not have a choice."

Holden glanced over at Marion and she was nodding with admission. Unable to dam the waters of his own disappointment, he rose from his seat. "I'm gonna head out. I got work tomorrow."

"Holden, I didn't mean to upset you."

"Nah...forget it, man. This is messed up, though. You know that, right? I don't mean to be rude, but I can't sit here and listen to this. You can't expect me to just roll over and give up before we've even started."

"Of course, Holden."

"I know I'm being a jerk...I just...I've gotta go home."

"Let us walk you out, at the very least."

Holden agreed and waited by the front door, pacing in uncontrolled aggravation. Winston took his time. Once he reached the foyer, he turned and headed toward the cellar. Marion looked at Holden and put her arms around him again. He knew in his heart that he should comfort her, to leave her with something affirming and hopeful, but he was just too frustrated and selfish. It wasn't his job to take care of Marion. It was his job to take care of himself. And right now he felt that someone, somewhere, was doing a number on him and he just couldn't have that.

He released his hug abruptly and stepped back. "Marion, watch out for this guy. I know he's got a good head on his shoulders, but something isn't sitting right."

"I'll be fine, Holden," she said. "Will you come here tomorrow?"

"Yeah, I'll stop over after work. We're gonna figure everything out, okay?" Marion nodded, holding her emotions behind moist, tired eyes. Still stewing in disbelief, her whole body appeared exhausted and overwhelmed.

When Winston returned to the top of the stairs, he was holding a book. Marion assumed he would want privacy, so she hugged Holden once more and went to the dining room to clean up their dinner. Winston shuffled to the door and gently handed his guest a paperback book. But before Holden could read the title, a hand speckled in age spots flapped onto the cover.

"I knew," his tired voice began, "when I first saw you in a café one spring morning that our meeting was destined."

"Is that right?" Holden asked, mockingly.

"Yes. See, at birth…I too was named after quite a famous literary character, of whom I was supposed to emulate."

"Is that character from the book you're giving me, here?"

Winston removed his hand and Holden could see the title. "No…no. I'm afraid that book would be a little big for you at this point." He could see his words were insulting, but he didn't care because they were true. And truth was hurtful nowadays. "You need to slow down. And you also need to be reminded of our

THE BOOK

freedoms and how easily they can be taken away. To learn of the inevitability of certain things. The book you're holding was written quite a long time ago. But the story within its pages will resonate with the situation at hand and, strangely enough, with you and your profession."

Holden glanced down at the intriguing cover to see a man standing in an awkward, yet triumphant position. He was made of paper and there were flames coming off of his arms and his legs in striking shades, matching the title that blazed across the top. The book was called *Fahrenheit 451* and had been written by a man named Ray Bradbury.

"It looks interesting," Holden began, wishing the man had brought him *The Catcher in the Rye* instead. Winston knew he wanted to borrow it.

"What is most interesting is that you can't find this story on The Book. It was completely banned about sixty years ago. Along with other priceless novels, the government destroyed the only remaining copy en route to The Library of Congress. They used a mock data corruption at the Publishing House to completely remove the story from The Book. Not something that happens often."

"Why would they erase the whole thing?"

"You'll see," Winston said, with a smirk. He glimpsed as a new fascination came over Holden and it was a delight to witness. "Have you ever read a book like this before? From a bound stack of printed paper?"

"No. I haven't."

"Well, enjoy it. The experience is a unique one. I look forward to hearing your thoughts." Winston smiled and adjusted his weight on the cane he had been using that evening. "I know how hard this must be for you Holden. Just realize that, for right now, we have one another and we can get through this time together. You are quite strong. Your heart. Your will. Might I ask a personal question?"

"Shoot."

"Do you believe in God?"

Holden was taken for a ride on that one. He wasn't sure how to answer. "Umm...I don't know what I believe."

"Well, I do. Age does that to a person. I believe in God and I also believe he has brought you into my life for a purpose. And I believe that purpose involves books like the one you are holding. I commend your ability to fight me on this. It's a breath of fresh air. There is so much going on here Holden...things that will be revealed to you over time. But for now, I will leave you to your life. I look forward to speaking with you again."

"Yeah. I told Marion that I'll stop by tomorrow. Take care of her, alright?"

"Certainly. Good night to you."

"Night."

With that, Holden left. He returned to his van and to his simple life, only this time holding the full, unedited manuscript of an original book that the government didn't want him to read. Holden was suddenly delighted to be leaving early because tonight he would allow that book to take him away from everything. He was going to devour every page, leap into the chapters and discover all that they could reveal to him.

Holden drove to work the next morning more tired and more alive than he had ever been in his life. The clouds beyond the city were murky and the sky as foreboding as ever, but he couldn't care less. He stuck true to his decision and read *Fahrenheit 451* in its entirety. Beginning to glorious end. Paper page after paper page. Cover to brittle cover. After completing the book, he reviewed it again, leafing through each chapter in search of something that would explain the many feelings running through him. It would make him late for work again. Two days in a row was a red flag, but it didn't seem to matter to Holden. This was bigger. He needed to find whatever elements had been in the story that made him feel so free.

At the end, he couldn't nail it down to a specific chapter or page and was left with a disturbingly new feeling. As he changed into his work clothes, Holden had felt an overwhelming surety that the story he had just finished wasn't controlled by anyone. It gave him a sense of strength and freedom that he had never before experienced and had not expected. A euphoric feeling that lasted the short drive to work. Never in his life had Holden felt so simultaneously frightened, that at any corner he could be taken by some government agent, and at the same time feel as if no one could control him. As if he were boundless on a calm sea.

Yearning to return to Winston's home to discuss the book, Holden fought the urge that morning to call-in sick to work and peeked at his duffle bag. He had been too frightened to leave the book at home, so he carefully wrapped it in a change of clothes and laid it delicately in his bag beside his lunch. It was a terrible risk, but it was one he had to take. If his landlord discovered the novel in his apartment, Holden would find himself in the same sinking boat as Marion. As long as he had a genuine book in his possession, it would have to stay on him.

The small parking lot beside General Fire Protection was unusually full, with several black Lincoln town cars crowding the loading dock. It was odd to find anyone else there in the morning because their first task was always loading up their vans with precut pipe and parts. Holden brushed it off, glad that no one had parked in his space. He turned the keys and dropped them into the grime-coated cup holder, reached for his duffle bag with satisfaction and closed the door to find Shane walking in a sprint toward his van, looking absurdly frightened. Before Holden could even question his appearance or wonder why his friend had been waiting for his arrival, one word escaped Shane's lips. A single word that chilled Holden's bones to the marrow, freezing and killing every fractured fragment of freedom he had just been experiencing.

"Run."

Holden stepped back unexpectedly and bumped his shoulder into the large side-view mirror. With a pinched whisper, he responded, "What?"

Shane's eyes were wide with an unspoken terror. "Run," he breathed, with far more emphasis. "There are people here

THE BOOK

looking for you. They were here when I showed up, talking to Numbskull." He swallowed. His eyes darted feverishly to his right. "Government, I think. I don't know what you did, man. But you gotta get outta here. They've been asking a lot of questions about you and Marion. How ever you got involved in her burning down the bar...don't say a word. I don't like the look of this."

Holden glanced back at the Lincoln town cars blocking the dock and said, "It's too late. Forget it. What I need for you to do right now is take this bag." Shane tried to protest, but Holden stopped him by shoving the duffle bag into his arms. "Take this. Don't ask any questions. Don't open it. Pretend it's yours. I need you to do this for me. If you don't, then...you may never see me again."

"Yeah...fine. Okay."

As the drooping duffle bag with the controversial book was transferred between best friends, the side door to General Fire Protection opened with a squeal of dented metal and three men walked out into the tender swath of rain. All three had short, blond hair cropped along the sides of their heads, delicately outlining their ears. Their green eyes were the same shade as their matching, striped ties. They were striking to behold. Not just in looks. It was in the seamless integration of their movement – as if they were some sort of animatronic robots seeking out terrorists for the government. Holden could not begin to imagine just how much they knew. He thought all his tracks had been covered, so there must have been another reason. The best solution he could invent, in the flickering milliseconds, was to play dumb. He laughed absently at Shane, scratched his buzzed head and strutted toward the door, carefree. He almost made it.

"Holden Clifford?" one of the men inquired in a cool, electric tone.

He turned with a lighthearted smirk. "Have been and always will be. What can I do for you guys?"

"We are Agents from the United States Publishing House and we would like for you to come with us."

"Whoa," he responded in mock surprise. "Shane, you hear that? I'm gonna be published! Nice try, fellas. I got work to do and you can tell Numbskull to cut the crap. My book never left the 'idea' stage. My hero's a sprinkler fitter for Pete's sake."

One of them flashed a badge so quickly that Holden was beginning to think they actually *were* robots. A different man stepped forward and spoke, with a blunt, mechanical impatience. "We assume, like most people, you have an honorable reputation here at your job that you would prefer to uphold. Please do not force us to make this..." he paused to choose the last word carefully, "...dishonorable."

Holden blithely tossed his arms up. "Well, I don't know what this is about, but you gotta do whatcha gotta do, right? Everyone's got a boss. I hope you talked to mine, 'cause I'm not gonna get in trouble here." In their silence, Holden felt a deepness of disparity. Although he needed to be assured, he wouldn't dare consider turning to look back at Shane in fear that they would notice. If they grew curious and searched through that duffle bag, he was as good as recycled. Whatever that meant.

Holden followed them toward the idling town cars with a singular string of hope pulling him closer. The truth was, these men had come to his workplace. It must have meant that they didn't know everything. It had to. If they had known everything, they could have easily come to his home that morning to collect him. It must have meant that they didn't know everything.

THE BOOK

Repeating that phrase to himself was the only thing that gave Holden strength enough to slip into the back seat of the car and not stare desperately out the tinted windows as they drove away without speaking a word.

His gut reaction to the entire scenario was typical: take out the guy in the back seat any way he could, then take out the driver and get out of town faster than Harry's ghost can say "Cubs win." He ignored his gut and chose instead to keep up the pretense of a stereotypical meat-head, water monkey that only cared about money, sports, food, women and sleep (and in that order) as he nestled comfortably into the perfectly detailed rear seat of the town car toward wherever they were taking him.

Most of the silent drive was crowded with stress, helped along by the two black Lincolns that bookended his own. To break the tension, Holden told a dirty joke from Shane's file of the filthiest, in attempt to see the reaction it would bring to one of the androidian Agents. As he expected, the man didn't react. Rather, he remained cold and emotionless, bolted to his seat. Stationary in standby mode.

As fate would have it, the Lincoln town cars parked in the immeasurably empty lot beside Lincoln Park. In perfect unison, the Agents emptied from the dark automobiles and unfurled their darker umbrellas. The rain was falling harder again, full and intense, and Holden waited for one of the men to open the door for him. They didn't. They stood outside in the rain without talking, waiting for Holden to leave the car himself. He felt awkward and unsure of what was happening, but was certain he had to keep up the pretense that he had done nothing wrong in order to get out of the situation alive. He opened the car door and stepped bravely into the falling rain, realizing that none of the surrounding Agents would be handing him an umbrella, and cracked a curious smirk. The rain didn't faze him.

He was used to working in rough conditions. But as he was led into the Lincoln Park Zoo, Holden understood how intimidating this would be for someone who was unaccustomed to weathering a downpour. He stole a glance over his shoulder to see that two of the Agents were staying behind to keep an eye on things.

As they approached the empty zoo that remained open to the public despite the rain, Holden imagined some secret headquarters below the shallow, recreational pond where the plastic swan pedal boats swam empty, unaware of the hidden control center. The zoo had a haunting, unoccupied feeling and Holden continued to follow. It was as if they were trespassing on a day when nuclear testing was being done on the animals. The bomb dropped when he noticed the single umbrella at the bottom of a short hill and the man that was standing in front of the zebra habitat. He recognized the man instantly from the article he had read on the train only days before. The man, staring lazily at the two zebras below a green umbrella, was the head of a new division of Homeland Security. Historic Homeland Preservation and Restoration, from what Holden could remember. He recalled the man's name just as easily. It was memorable.

As Holden squinted through the rain and approached Martin Trust, he noticed that the director's face was distant and preoccupied. Without looking at the four agents that had delivered Holden, Trust nodded and the robotic men retracted one hundred feet to a four-pronged perimeter. Holden shrugged and turned to look at the zebras, without a clue of what was happening, and more than slightly disturbed by the fact that none of them were speaking,. They huddled from the rain under an outcropping of manufactured rock and he watched as their legs stumbled in the clumping mud.

THE BOOK

He couldn't run. Holden accepted that gem of a detail the moment the men, who were clearly working for more than one government Agency, had pulled him from work. It was obvious that he was in it now. And deep. Why else would he be chaperoned to the zoo for a surreptitious meeting in the rain? Waiting in the irreducible silence, Holden understood that he was in more danger than he could imagine.

"I enjoy the zoo," the director began with odd authenticity. Holden didn't know at all how to respond. He nodded and hoped his sentiment could remain unspoken. After an unyielding minute passed, he knew he was playing a silent game of chicken. One of them would blink first and something told Holden to stay quiet. It took another full minute for Martin Trust to break the silence.

"I know you," the man said, turning delicately in Holden's direction without allowing their eyes to meet, "Do you know me?"

All Holden could do, all he knew to do, was play dumb. "Yeah, man. Your picture was in the paper the other day. You're like...with the government or something. Didn't read it. I'm not political. Anyway...what am I doing here?" he laughed, "I got bills to pay, bro. Gotta get back to work." Holden prayed his dull-witted impersonation of Shane would not read as fake as it felt during the delivery.

The man pursed his lips and nodded very slowly, so slowly that it seemed as if his head wasn't moving. Instead of answering, he stepped closer to the railing of the habitat below. "Do you know what I love about these zebras, Mister Clifford?"

Holden shrugged. "Their stripes?"

The man breathed a laugh before continuing. "I've been brought here for the weekend to handle the terrorism on the Sears Tower and I have visited this zoo many times. What I noticed, as the weather shifted, was how the zebras, these majestic animals, interacted with one another and with the people who watched them. When it began to rain and people left the zoo and they were alone, they changed. They *changed*, Mister Clifford. They were thinking."

Holden stepped closer to the concave environment that, while completely fabricated and built to make the animals feel comfortable, only appeared false and manufactured from his perspective. The two animals were huddled beside one another, neck to neck, in an effort to stay warm in the driest corner.

"I guess I never knew zebras did that."

"I don't pretend to affix this trait on the species; rather, it's just a feeling. While I'm here, when a lot of people are around and they are being watched, they seem to enjoy life. To enjoy being...zebras. And yet, on a day like today, when no one is in the park and it's raining and they have to cower into the corner for shelter, I look beyond their eyes and I can see more. Today, they are looking at me and looking at you and they see our freedom. They look at their fences. They remember that they don't want to be fenced. Like the color of their stripes, life is very black and white today. They want to be free and are, at this very moment, contemplating how they can be so. But that will change." As he continued, the tenor in his voice harmonized with the chorus of the falling rain. "When all the people come back with the sun, the caged animals forget their troubled time and will, once again, enjoy being zebras." Trust paused to step closer to the railing, reticent in his cold and studying gaze. His voice was a heated whisper. "But I fight to believe it. Because I wonder, for a moment, if they are only playing at appearances, hoping that the zookeeper doesn't become suspicious of them. Because what they are doing, what they are *actually* doing is biding their time. They are memorizing traffic patterns, learning the system and developing a plan so that when the rain returns...and no one is watching...they can escape. But Mister Clifford," the director broke, keeping his eyes hidden as he reached out to grip the cold railing. "You and I both know that the zebras aren't going to escape. It doesn't matter how much they scheme. Captivity is as much a part of their life as the cold water that won't stop falling." He shook the railing so vigorously that his wedding ring rattled the glistening metal. Holden glanced down at the noise and saw that the nail on the man's pointer finger had been sharpened to a fine spear. This elected official, despite appearances, was a reader.

"Well," Holden began, hoping to break the tension. "They just look cold to me."

The director nodded and spoke in a dry, omnipotent tone. "Walk with me."

Holden blinked in the rain as it poured a continuous shower onto his face. He wanted to wipe the excess away, but he felt that the pointless action would read as weak. An announcement that he wasn't able to handle the pressure of the moment. If he wanted to get through this alive, Holden knew he had to keep up the pretense that he was doing just fine and simply wanted to get back to work. Walking steadily beside the director, he wondered if his choice to not clear the moistness from his cheeks was his final act of freedom. The thought gave Holden a little joy as he weathered the storm.

They continued their wordless walk as if there were some destination in mind beyond the sprinkling of old trees. The minutes dragged on like months. Alone in the empty park, where no one could hear him if he cried for help, a disheartening hollow submerged itself in Holden's chest. It only grew worse as they came to a stop near a statue of a man sitting on a tree trunk, holding a book that was painted in a drippy, green patina. The expression on the man's face was withdrawn and unsure, as if he couldn't understand why the words he was reading seemed different.

"Mister Clifford, have you ever heard of this man?" the director asked, admiring the statue.

Holden inspected the inscription and read it aloud. "Hans Christen Anderson...*I never knew ye*," he joked, trying desperately to release the tension. "Should I know this dude?"

Again the director remained silent, as if running through the remaining conversation before speaking a word. "He was an author. Mostly fables for children. Fairy tales. Mind you, this was before The Book was published."

Holden nodded, uncaring. "Got it. Was he from Chicago or something?"

"This statue pays tribute to his accomplishments in the art of literature and was erected in his honor. One story he wrote is of particular interest to me. *The Steadfast Tin Soldier*. Have you heard of it?"

"Nope," Holden spouted quickly, getting a better read on the man. The director was just as good at playing dumb. A question about an author and now a question about a story. The Agents wouldn't have brought him to the park without searching his reading history on The Book. The director knew exactly what Holden liked to read and fairy tales weren't on the list.

"It's a rather short story about a small tin soldier with only one leg and how he fell in love with another toy. A paper ballerina, posed in an arabesque."

"Arab what?" he interrupted, sounding as ignorant as possible.

"It is a dance position where the ballerina is bending on one leg." The director studied the statue with striking appreciation. "Every minute he watched her and every minute his obsession with her grew stronger, until one day a goblin approached the tin soldier and warned him not to fall in love with the paper ballerina. He told him that there would be consequences. But the tin soldier ignored the goblin and continued to admire the paper ballerina, which eventually leads to him being dropped out the windowsill, down a gutter and swallowed by a fish."

"The end. That's depressing."

"Oh, no. It's not finished. This is where the moral reveals itself. The fish was caught, brought back to the house and ripped open, his guts spilling from between torn scales, and low and behold...out pops our little toy soldier. Once returned to his home, the tin soldier is reunited with his paper love. Most critics agree that this is where the tragedy of the story turns. I disagree. A rambunctious boy under the influence of the goblin decided to throw the soldier into the fire, where he began to melt with his eyes fixed on the ballerina. As the blaze ate away at his body, a gust of wind pulled the ballerina into the inferno where they were united in its unforgiving flame. The next day, the maid discovered the remains of the soldier and was amazed to find that it had melted into the shape of a heart."

"That's actually kind of beautiful," Holden admitted, testing the waters.

His response made the director stop in his tracks. His jaw locked and he began walking away toward the parking lot. "Marion Tabor." The director said her name with such arctic liquidity that his voice traced a chill along Holden's eardrum. "We are aware that you two know each other and I assume you have seen the news."

Holden responded robotically. "Yeah. Shame. I loved The Library, man."

"I would like to express my regret that I didn't clearly explain why I brought you here this morning." He stopped to swat aggressively at a flock of gnats that were following them, growling mid-thought. "But I strive to get a feel for people these days and avoid my natural tendency of, well, shooting from the hip. See, Miss Tabor is deeply involved with *The Free Thinkers*. I'm assuming you've heard of them."

Holden hesitated in his response and prayed that his emotions weren't giving him away. "Freaks, man. Terrorists. Whatever they're doing...it's messed up."

They reached the short tunnel that connected the stone walkway in the park to the empty parking lot and it was there that the director halted to ask Holden a final question before allowing him some minimal shelter from the rain. "Mister Clifford. Is there anything...anything at all that you would like to tell me about Miss Tabor? Keep in mind that we may already know."

Those final words resonated from the moss laden stone of the tunnel's vaulted ceiling and it made Holden, with his hands firmly in his pockets, grip the meat of his thighs. "Sorry, bro. Wish I could help you out."

Still keeping his gaze fixed on the path in front of him, the director nodded before breaking out with an overwhelmingly bright smile. "Well, we are simply conducting a few interviews with those closest to her and we got your name from her diary. Seems you made more than a few appearances to catch the attention of our team."

"Hey, we can't help it if the ladies like us. Am I right?"

Once more, Martin Trust was absent of all reaction. They entered the tunnel. "This group, *The Free Thinkers*, they are a danger to society. All they care about is the destruction of what we hold most dear." The director stepped from the shelter of the tunnel and stopped to look at a tree in the unwavering awareness of the rain. He soaked up every line and crinkle, admiring the ants that crawled along its sweating skin before moving on toward the parking lot.

When they reached the two idling automobiles that remained as black as the night is dark, he asked one final question before lowering his umbrella. "The moral. Do you know what it is?"

"From the tin soldier story? Uhm...I don't know. It seemed like a *love will overcome* kinda thing."

The director stepped toward the nearest town car and opened the rear door patiently. "I find it interesting, Mister Clifford, how you interpret such a tragedy. Because I've always seen it as more of a cautionary tale." Finally they locked eyes, his piercing green shade overpowering the muddiness of Holden's dull brown. "Listen to someone who knows more than you do and stop falling in love with paper."

His words lingered in the falling rain like the burnished circle of white on a retina when someone is stupid enough to look directly at the sun. Holden couldn't concentrate on anything longer than a millisecond; he was so overwhelmed by what he was experiencing. The director's words seemed to follow his every thought. They wouldn't leave him. The skin on Holden's neck tightened in the fright of them as the man retracted his umbrella and stepped lightly into the warmth of the car.

The door closed and Holden was left to stand in the parking lot without a ride home, shaking in his work boots. Despite the strength and courage he normally wielded in situations like this, Holden wanted to make a joke; to keep things lighthearted and relaxed, because his entire being was cuffed in fright.

The cars pulled ever so slowly from their spaces and drove away. He stood in the park, another statue, knowing that every move he made from then on would leave a trace in the grass behind. Life, it seemed, was about to get much more difficult and he just couldn't rationalize why they had let him go.

Jiggety Jig.

The cab driver dropped Holden at the door of the squat, square building of General Fire Protection. He stepped out, comfortable again in the rain. Everyone was gone on their assignments for the day, but Numbskull was waiting for him. The enormous man with the tinny, effervescent voice, stood by the receptionist's desk, unable to resist asking the questions that had been racing through his numb skull since the men had come to question his fitters.

"*Free Thinkers*, huh? Man! Can't believe that girl was a terrorist. She ever give you an idea that she was a terrorist, man? I tell ya, we've got more terrorists in this world than Carter's got pills."

Whatever that means, Holden thought as he walked past. He stopped at a box of green shop towels, pulled a few from the slot and dried himself off as best he could.

"So, talk ya' sad sack. What did they do?"

"Just took me for a walk."

THE BOOK

"Walk, my rear end," Numbskull's womanly voice shrieked at the comment that only he found hilarious. "I bet they told you not to tell anyone. Whatever. I get it, man. Just back to work, right?"

"That's right."

"It's kinda weird that all this would happen today, because the job I'm sending you to has a similar flare." Holden could tell in a glance, through the fluttering of thin, green fabric, that Numbskull wasn't about to elaborate. He dropped the shop towels in the recycling bin. "I need you to meet Jensen on Rush. Cakewalk, really. Just change out a standpipe."

"Yeah, alright."

"Call me when it's done, ya *Free Thinkin'* ape."

Numbskull assumed that he wasn't in the mood to talk, but in reality Holden was trying to calm his nerves.

It was as if the director knew, like he knew that Holden had found an enormous library and had just spent the night reading a book that technically didn't exist. *And Shane still had it*, Holden recalled. *Fahrenheit 451*. What was he going to do about that? And what would Shane do if he looked in the bag? They were probably monitoring Holden's phone, so he couldn't rightly call Shane to arrange a pickup. He would have to just wait until they stumbled into one another. He wasn't good with waiting.

From the stoplight on Rush, Holden could spot the building. It was a newer one. A flashy, glass edifice that touched the clouds with the trademark of some new, indolent architect. General Fire had finished the job six months back and changing out the standpipes didn't make a whole lot of sense. But he did what he was told to do. Jensen, the guy barking on the other end of the walkie-talkie as Holden parked the van and entered the rear of the building, worked as a liaison between the fire department and the pipe fitters. They met at the shaft of the main elevator bay where the man was shutting down the water supply to the building. Jensen was wafer thin and his little bug eyes popped from the drawn skin of his skull like a rotting cadaver. Holden was glad General didn't use the man very often because he had a face that lodged itself in your brain and waited until you slept to eek out and frighten you. Funny thing was, Jensen had the disposition of an ice cream vendor and he was ever the ruin of first impressions.

"Holden, right?" Jensen confirmed, with a charming smile. He wiped his hand and extended it through the open elevator doors. Holden shook it firmly, wondering if he may accidentally break a few tiny bones in the man's delicate wrist.

"The standpipe is outside. I'll keep going here. I've already loosened the bolts for you. Change it out, holler back and I'll turn the water on. Easy peasy." Holden nodded as the man upheld his joyful character by bobbing his fearsome noggin as he spoke. "This is one of those political jobs. We've gotta finish, lickety split."

Holden had no idea what the cherry-topped creep meant, but shrugged his shoulders and got to work. Finding his way back outside, he scanned the sparkling exterior until he noticed what Numbskull had meant by *a similar flare*. Branded into the side of the flawless building, partially obscured by the bright, silver standpipe, was the emblem of *The Free Thinkers*. The area had been partitioned from the rest of the sidewalk with police tape and an officer was standing nearby, keeping a surprisingly sharp watch on the scene. Apparently the fabled terrorist faction wanted to leave their mark on new architecture as well. Holden bent down, threw his weight below the plastic tape and lined himself up with the standpipe. The end of an arrow with its ornately drawn feathers flashed across the words: General Fire.

THE BOOK

Whatever machine they used to brand the buildings, it seemed to carve its molten design into the surface.

The standpipe was heavy and expensive, so Holden took his time removing it. He set the piece on the ground and was ready to pull the new one from its plastic container and thin, cellophane blanket, but he couldn't help staring at the emblem emblazoned on the building.

Whoever controlled The Book had decided to link Marion with this anarchist movement. And according to the director's demeanor during their walk, it wasn't a fictitious group. Holden studied the emblem. There was some thought in his mind that he followed, but couldn't quite catch, like chasing a feather in the wind. Then it came to him. This was the answer. The way they could fight back. This group probably knew about The Book. Hell, maybe that's what they were all about. This had to be an answer, if not *the* answer.

A squawk erupted from the walkie. "What's the problem?"

"Uh…" Holden stumbled, shaking his head back to reality, "Nothing. It's a little stuck."

"Just wail on the mother and it should loosen up," the ice cream vendor responded through the radio's fuzzy speaker.

As Holden replaced the ruined standpipe he felt a sense of purpose, once again. He may not need to live in fear the rest of his life. The answer he was searching for had come to find him. The new standpipe and its shiny bronze surface gleamed like the broken tusks of some golden idol and he kneeled before its supernal brilliance. He gazed up at the ornamental words *Think Again* and felt a swell of relief. They weren't alone. There was something they could do.

Winston Pratt seemed to think no one else had been gathering to stop The Book. That no one else was trying to find a solution to the subtle mind control that was being updated daily.

The Free Thinkers must have known about the editing process. Their name was a declaration of that very fact. Even their crest reassured him. The axis created between the revolver and the arrow had to symbolize the connection between the story of Raphael Petitto and the assassination attempt of Dennis Wayne Conrad. They knew about The Book. Why else would Marion and The Library be associated with such a group? Although they were branding buildings and destroying monuments to architectural history, at the heart of *The Free Thinkers* must have been a passion to overthrow the Publishing House.

Holden glanced once more at the scarred script of their motto and nodded. He was certain of it now. They were the answer and he needed to find them.

For hours, Holden worked in a daze as he planned the particulars of finding the group. But no matter what angle he came from, he kept returning to the same question: How could he succeed where the government had failed? Finding and joining their cause would be much more difficult than simply deciding to do so. Although they were apparently vast in number, Holden couldn't simply contact them.

What were the mechanics of joining an anarchist collective? he thought, while tightening a patched coupling to the joint of an oversized pipe.

As he bounced from job to job, he imagined their purpose in choosing to brand the buildings with such violence and a far simpler reason began to present itself. Branding the buildings appeared on the surface as a way to defile the architecture, but what if they were really advertisements? It made sense, didn't it? How else would a secret group recruit new members to their cause?

On his return to General Fire he stopped back at the building off Rush to inspect the brand. Something would be there - an address or a phone number entwining the details like vines across a trellis. From the road, he could see that the plastic police tape had been removed and that the granite had been ground back to reveal a stain of honed stone above the gleaming bronze standpipe. Although the brand had been erased, the corner was unguarded. Holden parked his van at the loading dock and jogged around the building to have a closer look.

It was raining again.

Or was it still?

He wasn't sure if it had ever stopped.

Standing before the standpipe, he collected the water from his jacket and rubbed his hand along the smooth, open pores of the peppered gray granite. Like an ancient, architectural secret, the dry crest of *The Free Thinkers* gradually revealed itself in the swath of his dripping hand. He uncovered as much of it as he could before stopping to stare deeply at its details, losing himself in its lines and folds. But it was a lost cause. After all that energy, nothing was there. At least nothing that his eyes or his limited intelligence could see.

Frustrated, Holden kicked the wall and limped away swearing. He thought he had found the answer, but there was nothing he could do with it. *Now what?* The construction crews erased most of the imprint of their brand from the stone and he couldn't rightly search the web for a detail of their seal. *So what else is there?* In the flash of sudden rainfall, he realized what he could do and returned swiftly to his soiled, sustainably-insolent, hybrid van.

He reached the Sears Tower before he had mentally walked through his exact reason for being there. From what he recalled of the article with Martin Trust, *The Free Thinkers* had branded their crest into the darkened steel of the building. Beyond lacquering the façade in some acid wash, there wasn't much to be done in such a short time - which meant that the artistic work of *The Free Thinkers* should still be visible to John Q. Passerby. And it was.

"Hey Mister...twenty?"

Holden shielded his eyes from the rain to look down. A beached whale of a man was smoushed into the corner of the building holding out a warped, plastic cup from a fast food restaurant. He hadn't been out of the van for more than a minute and already Holden was being baited by a begging Unfortunate. The man (if you could call him a man), who was lounging directly under the wrinkled wounds of the brand that Holden came to study, held out his plastic cup and shook its contents loudly. "Can you spare a twenty?"

"What?" Holden couldn't believe his ears. "No. What happened to asking for change, man?"

The Unfortunate adjusted his gargantuan frame and rolled from the corner, covering his shorn head with the shards of a broken umbrella. He inspected Holden with awkward intention before falling back and muttering, "A twenty is change for a fifty."

"Leave me alone, please."

"At least I got your attention, right?"

Holden shook his head, rose a hand to cover his eyes and leaned forward to study the brand, looking for some secret detail in the growing darkness of the cloud-coated sky. The slices and gashes that had been created in the stone of the other building looked like molten wax upon the tower's black steel, hardened in its syrupy state. Holden lowered his hand and stepped back. Unless he could find another building where the text could be clearly visible, there was nothing he could safely do to find the group.

Failure. Again.

THE BOOK

"I'm hungry, man," the Unfortunate grumbled, shuffling in place. When Holden didn't answer, the whale of a man grew more restless and soon splashes of wild mutterings began spouting from his blowhole. "What are you standing here for? Are you spying on me? Get out of here. Get away from me!"

Holden ducked as a plastic crate was launched powerfully at his head. Without bothering to respond (willfully engaging with an Unfortunate was like trying to reason with an alley cat that doesn't cover its feces), Holden left the sidewalk and returned to his van, depressed and slighted by a barrage of judgment from a drifter that seemed oddly well-fed.

Holden wove into traffic, arguing with himself. What did he expect to find? Some secret passageway to a ruined corner of the city where writers lived in hiding behind a fortification of books that somehow avoided the churning machine of The Great Recycling? There was nothing special in the branded image and he needed to recognize that. Glancing down at his watch, he realized that he was supposed to be dropping in on Marion and Winston. But with the day he was having, and the fact that his every move was likely being monitored by Martin Trust and Agents of The Publishing House, going home to hit the hay seemed like a smarter move.

The next day Holden was in his element, or at least it appeared that way. He worked meticulously on each individual task he was called to accomplish. Removing leaking couplings, cutting and threading new pipe, adjusting fittings, spinning the main valves off and on like a gyroscopic top, replacing ancient sprinkler heads with the newest and shiniest models and, all the while, ignoring the self-righteous indignation from the upright society of Chicago's gold coast about how his van was butchering and stealing the sacred virginity of the earth. He was focused more that day than he had been in years, because he wasn't thinking about the Blackhawks or his daughter or the novel he was excited to get back to during lunch. Holden was *thinking again*. His irrepressible thoughts circumnavigated the illusive terrorism of *The Free Thinkers*.

Regardless of what his hands were doing or how unsuccessful he had been at tracking them down, his mind continued to imagine what the group would be like. He romanticized them living in an old, abandoned library in the deserted suburbs to the south. He heard them spouting quotes from Shakespeare before diving from the side of a building. He saw passionate chases on freight trains and helicopter crashes. Courage and love and retribution. The only reason Holden stopped thinking about them was because he found himself in the parking lot of General Fire Protection with the van idling. He was done for the day.

As he muscled the remnants of pipe from a renovated building into the shop and dumped them onto the recycling pile, Holden found himself faced with the fact that the work day was over and he still didn't know how to make contact with *The Free Thinkers*. The only solution that seemed at all promising was to circle the city to study each of the brands and hope that something interesting would link them. Some clue that could tell him what to do next. The idea wasn't a pearl, but it was something. Naturally, the brands would have all been removed or erased by the government – so, really, there was nothing to do but think about the arrangement of them and which buildings were chosen, hoping that a connection could be made.

On the way to the locker room, Holden recalled the locations he had heard of or seen throughout the last few years and was busy creating a mental map of the city when all thoughts of *The Free Thinkers* left him for the first time in thirty hours. Shane was standing motionless in the aisle of lockers, his skinny fist gripping the straps of Holden's brown duffle bag.

It had been quite obvious that his best friend in the world, the only person he had ever really trusted, had been avoiding him. Shane had come in an hour early that morning and it was the first time in years that he hadn't sent Holden a pointless text or called him with a filthy joke. *But it made sense, didn't it?* Shane didn't know, didn't want to know, why Agents were asking questions. Terrorism was hitting too close to home and, just like Holden, Shane avoided trouble like fish to a sand box.

So he did what was right. Holden left the puck with Shane's goalie. Rather than address the fact that his duffle bag was in the room, he walked to his locker and took his time with the padlock. The very moment it opened, Shane was beside him with the bag. He tossed it against the back of the locker and swung the door shut.

"I don't know what you're a part of, but I just want to tell you right now that I don't want to be a part of it." His voice was charged and his face showed a surprising degree of emotion that neither of them had ever seen in Shane before. "I know you, Holden. And I know the way you think. Do not include me in whatever is going on. Okay?"

"Bro, what are you talking about?"

"Don't act stupid," he spat, stepping close. He lowered his shoulders, readying himself to fight. "That stuff with Marion and those guys that came by...I can't be involved in any of that, alright?"

"Did you look in the bag?"

Shane spun away, noticeably conflicted, and bent to tie his shoe.

"Another day. Another dollar. Right?"

Without reply, Shane stood straight and walked to the door of the locker room. Holden called after him, but the door swung closed and the silence of his friend's absent response mingled with the noxious scent of perspiration to create an aura that was disheartening and deeply lonely.

What was that all about?

Shane's reaction took Holden by surprise. It was completely unexpected. It had been years since his friend had come at him like that. And there was more behind his words than something as simple as fear. Shane didn't like bad attention, but he was fearless in the eyes of battle. This was a side of Shane that Holden had never seen and it scared him. Everything normal in his world was changing so rapidly. Things were getting out of hand and he couldn't regain his grip.

And then there was the bag.

Holden's greed for its contents pushed thoughts of his only confidant in life aside. He unlatched the flimsy metal door and stared into the back of his locker. With a delicate hand, he reached into the dark void and thumbed the zipper head before pulling it back along the seam. His eyes rummaged through the contents until he saw the cover of the book Winston had imparted to him. The man made of paper was still on fire and the pages within carried the same rustled, well-read appearance. He released the breath he had been holding and drew the zipper closed. Although his friendship was in jeopardy, the book he had entrusted to Shane was safe.

To keep up appearances, Holden completed his regimen by scrubbing his hands vigorously in the sink before leaving with his leather-bound Book in hand. He wanted everyone around him to know that life for Holden Clifford, no matter how unhinged in reality, hadn't changed in the slightest.

THE BOOK

Amid the flurry of commuters hiding from the obnoxious and redundant downpour, he stepped onto the elevated train as he always had before the truth was exposed, sat in a quiet corner and found himself gripping his Book with eagerness. All around him passengers were swirling their pointed fingers in the green glow of bondage and Holden found himself longing to open his own. The warm leather felt so right in his hands. The hidden words invited him to partake and, before the next stop, Holden was searching its contents for the right story to alleviate his many disappointments.

The train completed a full circuit of the city and Holden stayed on, scanning names of authors and titles of books with a ravenous craving. But not one, not a single one, seemed to have enough flavor to slake the hunger within. That is, until The Book decided for him. Without his control, the screen darkened and bled back through the green pond scum to offer a suggestion.

Having trouble deciding? Why not try:
THE DAY OF THE TRIFFIDS *by John Wyndham*
Click here to download.
This story was chosen for you by the Publishing House, based on your own, unique reading record.

The temptation to click the glowing line below the title was more than he could have imagined. He knew it was wrong when he decided to download the book. He knew it was wrong to start reading it. But it took him three full pages to realize why he wouldn't stop. To fight against the Publishing House was pointless. What could someone like him really do to stop them? Returning to his simple life was easy. There was no thought in the option. All he had to do was read. He loved to read. And then he remembered Marion and how she was still at Winston's home, waiting. Wondering why he hadn't come back to check on her like he promised. With her face upon his mind once more, Holden closed the cover to The Book and shoved it into his duffle bag before looking out the window.

The sight that met his eyes changed everything.

Scrawled into the glass of the windowpane beside him, inches from his face that whole time, was the emblem of *The Free Thinkers*. His mind quickly retracted from where it had been and he suddenly felt so very stupid. The Book was a lie. The Book was filled with lies and he had gone back to it. Although his daydreaming about *The Free Thinkers* made the work day go faster and brought him no closer to discovering how to find them, at least they were real. They were truth.

Holden got off the train and grabbed a taxi with a simple decision at his core. He was going to seek out the only location in the city where a historic landmark had been branded and the emblem had never been removed. It was there he knew he would find his answer. And it was there that he did.

It had been one of the first ornaments of architecture and one of the first monuments in Chicago marred by the work of *The Free Thinkers*. Eager to keep his actions clandestine, Holden coasted safely between buildings in the back of a taxi, beyond the radar of watchful eyes, until they reached the corner of State and Washington.

The Reliance Building stood as a testimony of faith from a time when the world hadn't fully trusted its architects. The building had been launched to mass fear because the windows, quite small in comparison to today's modern glass facades, had been too large for the people of that time. So much fear eventually gave the building clout and it became an enticement to the daring. Because of its avant garde nature, a rich appreciation grew for the structure in the years to come until it was eventually granted landmark status and adored by the city.

The architects of *The Free Thinkers* had a different view of the building. They decided that it was the perfect structure to receive their very first brand of molten graffiti. And it was burned on the one spot the landmark committees would be unable to remove. The extinct rectangular tiles of polished white clay that lined the building were now interrupted above the State Street entrance with a small version of the soon-to-be-well-known emblem. At the time of its origination, the crest, with its arrow and revolver crossing over the puzzling words of *Think Again*, was odd and the newspapers were baffled. For months, journalists asked themselves where it had come from and what, if anything, was its purpose. As he walked down the street toward the building, seeing the rain splash against the windows that had been so infamous in the past, something told Holden that he would find himself at the end of the day with the exact same question burning his mind.

But then something *unfortunate* happened. Mister Twenty Dollar Bill.

The tremendously tall, rotund oaf from the Sears Tower was now camped out along the side of the Reliance Building, rattling a glass jar of coins at innocent people on their way home from work. This shrine to all that was still wrong with the world noticed Holden at the same time and puffed out his cheeks, adjusting his monumental weight on the plastic milk crate that was straining to keep its shape below his wide girth. Holden almost didn't want to cross the street and force another confrontation just to inspect the emblem, but he had come all that way and there were few options left.

He approached the building from across the street and gazed up at the crest that was, once again, positioned directly above where the large man was stationed. In the brighter light, Holden could see that the man was a heavily tattooed Polynesian whose shaven head looked a little clean for an Unfortunate. Holden neared the glass and looked up at the emblem, but he couldn't avoid the dark eyes that were burning into him. In a fleeting look, Holden glanced down and it was just enough time.

THE BOOK

"Can you spare a twenty?"

Holden laughed. That guy was pretty insistent. He looked him in the eyes and, in the lighter drizzle of the day, was able to see something else in them that hadn't been there the night before. Or at least something he'd been unable to see in the dusk. "I'm a vet and I'm selling ribbons." The whale-like man pointed to the light green ribbon on the lapel of his tattered jacket and then down to a coffee can beside him that was filled with them. "You got a twenty? Want to buy a ribbon?"

He saw it again. Something in the man's eyes made Holden believe that he was saying something entirely different. Against his better judgment, he reached into his back pocket and took out his wallet. "Yeah," Holden replied, taking out a twenty dollar bill. The man reached for it slowly, never removing his steadfast gaze. After placing the crisp bill into his shirt pocket, he unpinned a ribbon from the inside of his jacket and lowered his eyes before handing it over.

"Tonight," he whispered. "Eight o'clock."

Stunned, Holden tightened his grip on the ribbon and said, "Okay."

"I'm about to react in a...uhm...*unusual* way."

Suddenly the large man's demeanor changed and he threw his entire jar of coins at Holden. The thick glass grazed his arm and shattered on the sidewalk with a triumphant crash. He rose like a giant over the crowd and began spouting random complaints and gibberish with a snarled, insane expression that frightened everyone outside the famous building. A wide-berthed grin lightened his face maddeningly and Holden had to remind himself that this was some sort of act before jogging to freedom like everyone else on the street. A faint thrill chased his shadow and a block away he slowed to glance back at the man who was swiping the shards of glass from his scattered change.

He looked psychotic as he flailed his arms about and then things magically began to make sense. Holden surmised that the only way such a group could recruit new members was to place beacons around the city and station someone near the beacon to guide the boats to shore.

He had done it. He had found *The Free Thinkers*.

With the smooth texture of the silky ribbon between his fingers, Holden felt his heart race. He needed to look at it without anyone seeing. Halfway down the block, he dodged a cavalcade of pedestrians and hid in the wide loading dock of Marshall Field's before retracting his fingers and looking down into his palm. The green tone of the ribbon was bold against the gloomy background of dirty concrete. Four words were stitched with black thread into the silk. Holden smirked as he quickly understood where he needed to go. On one of the ribbon's crisscrossed wings were the words, *The Spire*; on the other were the words, *Top Floor*.

This was the first night in many that would see Holden wearing a sport coat. It was one of his father's humdrum hand-me-downs and smelled a bit musty, but Holden wore it on special occasions and he felt the night called for a bit of poise. Of course, he had forgotten to shave. Along with the accompanying rain and smattering of wetness on his shortly cropped hair, Holden knew that, to these people, he would likely resemble a greasy raccoon scurrying around their legendary building for scraps of food. Granted, he had been given the invitation by an Unfortunate who stank and dressed far below par, so it was quite possible that he would find himself to be the only clean ball on the golf course.

Shoving the silken ribbon into his jacket pocket, Holden tilted his head toward the rain to follow the winding lines of the building to the topmost floor. The structure was otherworldly. The Calatrava Spire corkscrewed into the violet clouds like some mechanical edifice that controlled the weather one rotation at a time. Holden paused in the drizzle because he felt he should offer the building some note of respect before entering its holistic lobby. Once inside, he was instantly drawn to the back of the structure. Beside the north elevators was a full height mirror that spanned the decadence of space. Holden wiped some of the moisture from his sport coat and adjusted his appearance in the polished mirror before pressing the elevator button.

The journey to the top floor was long. A few people joined him along the way and each of them left before he reached the top. As he watched the numbers grow higher, Holden felt the elevator was reminding him that each floor they passed was another chance to bail. Each was a freedom untaken. He was haunted by the elevator's continual chime because of a singular worry that had plagued him since the moment he received the ribbon. He could be walking directly into a government run militia meant to smoke out those interested in taking down The Book. Passing every floor was a risk.

Still, Holden was a believer. Along the rim of Lake Michigan, at the highest point for blocks around, with the most stunning views that he had only seen while dangerously straddling ceiling joists in the wind, were all the answers. After that night, all his anxiety would cease. Everything would be resolved. He was a believer. Had to be.

When the elevator reached its destination, the doors opened to the immediate and surprising sound of joie de vivre. Large groups of people were laughing and drinking and sitting and flirting and listening to the quiet digital music that felt altogether abnormal and left Holden completely dislocated. He felt for the ribbon in his pocket to determine if he had read it correctly when a woman came to the elevator doors and hastily removed his jacket without explanation. The doors began to close. Holden stepped off and walked after the woman to find her sprucing up his coat. Unable to mentally accept all that was happening around him, Holden stared at the woman as she diligently toweled the moisture from the mostly-nylon fabric. The dark hair that had been slicked down to the contours of her head was bound into a tight braid that traced her spine along her black, open-back gown. Holden was entranced by her thick, unmoving braid because it latched onto her skin as if it were attached to her vertebrae like some exoskeletal accessory. He tried to protest, but was too overtaken by the sheer chaos around him to even open his mouth. Once she returned his jacket, Holden felt more than underdressed. What he had walked in on was so much less of a gathering of anarchists and terrorists and people bent on secretive governmental overthrow and so much more of a dinner party for the upper echelon, midwestern socialite. Actually, there were a few people he recognized. A famous architect, an author that he knew had hailed from Chicago, an actor and a few men and women that he was certain were politicians.

Was this it? Holden thought. *Could this actually be what he was looking for?* If this were an outlet for change, why had he, a lowly pipe fitter who had come from nothing, been invited?

The moment the thought arrived, the enormous man that had given him the invitation, the man who Holden had deemed unworthy to speak to or even look at on the sidewalk of the Sears Tower, approached with a smirk. And he was dressed to the nines.

"I'm glad you could come," he said, his deep voice regal.

"Thanks. Sorry I never introduced myself. My name is Holden."

"Holden, the name's Moby," the man said, grabbing his hand with a solid stocky grip. "But you can…call me Ishmael."

Nervous, Holden laughed unnecessarily loud and stifled himself quickly. Moby got a kick out of this response and released his hand with a smirk. He reached into his jacket pocket and removed a crisp twenty dollar bill. "Welcome to *The Free Thinkers.*"

Holden couldn't hide the grin on his face as he took back the money. This was really it. He couldn't believe it.

As he stepped past the entryway, Holden was amazed at the space before him. Stretching out, covering the entire floor, was a wide room that extended to the wrapping corkscrew of windows. At the eastern end of the open room, with an awe-invoking view of the fog-lined lake, was a sunken oval seating area with a white, patent leather couch that ringed the circumference. The polished surface that was broken only by a short series of concrete steps grabbed his attention because it seemed to faintly reflect the life of the room around it.

There had to have been sixty people there, dressed elegantly and carrying on giddy conversations. The temperature of it all was electrifying, but somewhat irregular. Wrong, even. Choosing to remain within himself, safe behind a thin glass of sparkling water, Holden continued to study his surroundings. To the left of the sleek, open kitchen and oddly visible bedroom, with a bed that seemed to hover above its hidden base, was a slab of slate on legs with fire spilling from a square that wasn't quite centered. Mirrored, on the opposite end of the room, was a table of turquoise glass. It rose four inches from its rough wooden feet and had a movement that bewildered Holden until he was standing beside it. The glass was hollow and within it swam a multitude of minuscule fish. Already, this evening had shown him so many things he had never seen and revealed a world he was never meant to enjoy.

Over the course of an hour, Holden mingled around intellectual conversations and introduced himself to many people who were more than entertained by his profession. A few times he heard, *I wonder how we're going to use you.* And

THE BOOK

other times he heard, *we certainly are taking in all different types these days, aren't we?* He was too excited by being there to recognize their comments as insulting. Everything that night was complimentary, especially to his eyes.

The luxurious furniture pieces, the shallow wading pool near the bathroom, the built-in art piece of thick, marbleized metal ribbons that took up far too much real estate, and the exquisite light fixtures that hung sporadically near the darkened ceiling like stars in 3D. Even the smells were heady and laced with enticement. The drinks and hors d'oeuvres being passed tasted so fantastic that, in a double bite, Holden forgot all the stress he had been feeling. He imagined Winston and Marion sitting by the fireplace playing chess and wished they could experience the satisfaction and rapid (albeit, unauthentic) acceptance that he felt from such higher class people. Purpose and success played like music and he had finally joined the song. What they were up against in The Book was a power unseen and unquantifiable, but there were people in that room that carried an entirely different power.

More comfortable, despite his shabby outfit, Holden gladly replaced his water for a glass of wine from one of the women walking around the room with the same sleek, black hair and opalescent face, just as the man that Holden had recognized as a famous architect raised his hand and ushered for everyone to gather around the seating area.

He stepped down into the oval pit and stood at the center atop an artistically woven detail of their famous emblem. Its prominent lines stood strikingly dark against the white rug and appeared to give the man a heightened stature of importance.

As the architect began speaking, Holden was immediately calmed by the man's dulcet, soothing tone. "I would like to welcome everyone," he began, through his thin, wilted beard, "to the seventy-second meeting of the Chicago branch of *The Free Thinkers*." A concord of clapping fringed the group and Holden sipped gratefully from his wine. "Let us ring in the new season by declaring our code of statutes to our most welcomed guests and newest members."

In eerie unison, the group began announcing their beliefs in a low, chewing monotone. *"To remove all limitations on our creativity by allowing one another a chance to rebuild what has once been. To form a new intellectual freedom over the next century by regressing society to a time when we didn't have all the answers. When our fate was challenged because the computer didn't find our mate. When our faith was challenged because we hadn't found the cure. When our minds were challenged because our problems hadn't already been answered. When our purpose was challenged because we didn't have a god. We will bring freedom to thoughts. We will think again! We will think again!"*

In the sudden, esoteric silence, the architect unwrapped a stick of gum, popped it coolly into his mouth and continued from behind a carefree, cosmopolitan chuckle. "So, let's talk phase four. What do the next six months look like?"

Most of what was brought up throughout the next forty-five minutes was a cornucopia of bogus nonsense that ended on someone's suggestion to try and disassemble the internet for a week. Others said it couldn't be done, but their arrogant leader came up with a plan in half a minute that everyone supported and that seemed too ambitious to be possible. The man enjoyed imagining how society would react when boredom was forced upon them. When their television shows, movies and sports were unviewable. When their contact with others was limited to physical interaction. Could a week alone spur on a new renaissance of ideas? He heralded the possibilities and his followers swooned.

THE BOOK

When all the pomp and speeches had ended and the lemmings scattered excitedly, Holden remained in the same place, unable to move – a mechanical piping system with locked joints, his ungalvanized mind rusting in the foiled acceptance of where he was and what *The Free Thinkers* were really about.

Holden had been wrong.

They had been the exact opposite of what he needed them to be. All he believed and hoped for had been a lie. *The Free Thinkers* were completely misguided, and yet exactly who they meant themselves to be. The newspapers were right. *The Free Thinkers* actually believed what everyone thought they believed.

Holden furled his eyebrows and cocked his head as he prepared himself for what was about to happen. Downing a glass of wine, he charged the architect as the man was completing a fanciful tale of how he had found his sunglasses at a shop in Haiti. "Excuse me, but you didn't mention The Book or the Publishing House. I assume that's part of your deal, right?"

The man eyed Holden's sport coat and pursed his lips before tilting his head back over his shoulder in a moment of perplexing ecstasy. "Oh, what I wouldn't give to be an Editor. How I would caress the delete key every day. Magical."

"Are you joking?" Holden asked, stumbling back as if repulsed by the man's breath. "They're erasing our history, bro. You don't think that's messed up?"

"If only," he booed, fluttering the fur of his salt and pepper beard. "Young man, that is a rumor started by people like us. People who want to start over. Think again!"

"But, I thought…"

"Apparently you didn't. Take for instance, this chair." The man vaulted adroitly from the sunken seating area and grabbed an antique wooden chair from his office. Its dimpled leather cushion reflected the flickering fire as the man brought it to the slate table. "This is an original Eames, circa nineteen fifty-one."

Holden could hear a sudden eagerness in the fraction of whispers around the room. Everyone gradually began to turn and watch the action play out, which told Holden that the man's haughty speech had been given before. "Now, there must be...what...thirty of these in the world?" He took the piece of furniture and toppled it gleefully onto the table where it was quickly charred in the flames. With a laugh that tinged the edge of his words, the man turned back to Holden and continued his speech while the wood sputtered and crackled amid the thunder of applause. "Boop. Gone. Just like that. If all of these were destroyed and all the information and images of it were removed from the internet...well..." He waited, but Holden didn't respond. "Don't you understand? Eventually, someone can be creative enough to design this chair again. See, we live in a world where there are no new musicians. No new artists. No new designers. No new thinkers."

"Of course there are," Holden disagreed. A multitude of digital magazines were advertised in The Book every day, with some new flashy face on the cover beside a lofty heading of how they were revolutionizing their industry. But the people in the room, all the stylish people with their neon drinks and puffed-up expressions, were laughing. *What did that mean? Had the man been right?*

As the laughter subsided, the architect reached for a glass of apricot wine. "Forgive our response. I understand that, if you are new, my words could come as somewhat of a shock. But what are words, really? I'm no big thinker. Even someone with half a brain can see that the only thing new about these *revolutionaries* is that they look different than those they are copying. Sorry...emulating." A snicker coursed through the group and he fingered some quotation marks posthumously in the air around his head.

"There is nothing left to learn. The new and avant garde are simply regurgitation. And puke stinks! We have reached the limit of our ability to be creative. God isn't making any new colors and we gotta start over. Thankfully, most of the people in this room," he paused, glinting a grin as he snapped his gum, "are well-to-do enough to make a difference. I can buy a rare work of art and destroy it. If I want to. I could buy the rights to every song by The Beatles and destroy the original recordings and corrupt each and every digital file. But that won't kill their music. A hundred years in the future, the band will re-emerge in some new form and create a revolution of songs that have never been heard. Our children will thank us. Our children's children will thank us."

A smart-looking woman raised her glass pronouncing, "The next Beethoven will thank us."

"Yes! Let's give mankind a chance to be creative again! To *THINK* again!"

Holden remained still, powerless against the uprising of applause. After a respectful bow, the architect chief of their terrorist tribe motioned for Holden to come closer. They shared a heartless handshake and the man leaned in to whisper, "You'll come around, soldier. We all have. This movement is happening whether you want it to or not."

The clapping fluttered to silence as those who were eager to watch history burn huddled around the fire like Neanderthals reveling over the shredded carcass of a beast their leader had devoured. And Holden felt so suddenly sad. This was the exact opposite of what he had expected. He was assuming the news reports were wrong, but they weren't. Everything these people were about...it was only to destroy. If they had it their way, they would destroy all the books ever written. Delete enough words at random until all semblance of structure and sense and poetry was stripped away, dulled down to a level of stupidity that would force humanity to thirst and cry out for something new and creative. People like this praised the invention of the typewriter that led to the computer keyboard that led to editless texting and editable encyclopedias. They encouraged internet 'bogs' and self-published drivel from make-believe minds. They praised the dishonor of words and disrespected the courage of history and accomplishment. These were things their ancestors had worked hard for and this rabble of overconfident egotists wanted to start over. To regress us back to a time before such wonderful triumphs existed. To unplug civilization and reboot before considering the loss. They *were* terrorists. And their viewpoint was a terror altogether too overwhelming for him to accept.

Small seating areas were being filled and Holden eventually found himself standing alone. He was offered a glass of expensive vodka and he turned it down. He was offered to pick an appetizer from a tray of oddly shaped cheeses and he took one simply so the person would walk away. He bit into it, hopeless. No one around him cared at all about The Book or about breaking the government control. Holden watched as the architect began throwing other priceless pieces onto the alter of fire and it made him instantly ill, as if the small cheese pyramid in his mouth was coated in a thin, hairy mold. He needed to leave. He couldn't stomach another second in that building.

A piece of him, the piece that daydreamed about their group during work, wanted to proclaim a passage from something by Charles Dickens (or, better yet, Victor Hugo) in the hope that it would spur them on to a new thinking. He wanted to convince them that what they believed was foolish. Instead, he turned his

THE BOOK

back on the members of *The Free Thinkers* and searched gladly for the elevator. Real substance from a classic story would be lost upon their feeble, delusional minds.

"Leaving early, friend?" Holden twisted to find Moby, the enormous man that had recruited him from the sidewalk, leaning casually against the wall beside a crystal coat rack. "Listen, I know they're a bit eccentric, but...it's my job to screen people when they want to leave."

"Good luck," Holden spat. "This is a joke. I don't want any part of it."

"I can tell. But I wouldn't be doing my job if I didn't try to convince you to stick around."

"Well, I'm not going to."

"Why?"

Holden spun, shocked by what he was hearing and came at the man who was three times his size with nothing less than enmity. "Seriously? Were you here? Did you see everything that just happened? I mean...how could anyone believe this extremist garbage?"

Moby shrugged and pointed a humungous thumb over his shoulder. "There are definitely a couple of crazies in there, but their heart is in the right place. I guess I just don't like being controlled, is all." Moby pushed the elevator button and waited by the door with Holden as the mingling minions behind them cackled at a a vinyl record being tossed onto the fire. "You know...you're the first person in years to catch the reference to my name. You must read The Book a lot. These people don't read. At least not fiction."

The elevator doors opened and Holden chuffed, "Isn't everything in The Book fiction..."

"Did you just say what I think you said?" Moby stepped in front of the elevator door, his immense frame taking up nearly the entire width of space, dwarfing Holden who generally stood high among his friends. He glanced over his shoulder momentarily before shoving Holden into the elevator and allowing the doors to close. In the small chamber, the man seemed larger than ever and Holden was regretting his choice to get angry. But the man's chestnut face was suddenly glazed with a new buttery color. Behind a sanguine expression and an aristocratic tone, Moby spoke three words that capsized Holden's desire to escape.

"To write unimpeded..."

"...is to breath eternal."

Holden heard himself finishing the sentence without realizing he had responded.

"I can't believe it," Moby stammered, his pale eyes moist. "You?"

"So you guys *do* understand what's happened to The Book?"

The elevator doors opened on another floor and Moby blocked the entrance so no one could get on and interrupt them. They needed to be alone. The moment the doors closed, the giant of a man turned a child in the face of such overwhelming excitement. "I've been waiting for someone like you for over two years."

"What? Someone like me?"

"My uncle told me it was being controlled. Told me about the prince. He was right, wasn't he? Man! The Book *is* being controlled." Moby didn't wait for Holden to answer. He wove his gargantuan arms wildly and blurted out his wishes, regardless of if they were wanted. "Whatever you're doing...I'm in. Sign me up."

"Hang on a second. What about *The Free Thinkers*?"

"I've told them about the editing. They don't seem to care. Or don't believe me. You don't understand...I've stuck around this whole time waiting for the day someone like you would show up. Two years, Holden. You have to let me come with you."

Gnawing on his tongue as the elevator chimed each passing floor, he reached for Moby's jacket and took the man's cell phone from his inside pocket. Although Holden had no clue where it would lead him, he typed out Winston's address. "Meet me here tomorrow. I...don't really know...I mean...I have a few ideas about what we can do with the library in the cellar...but we should probably regroup with the others."

"There are others? Great!" The elevator doors opened and a team of people carrying grimy reusable bags filled with fresh groceries crowded in around them. Holden squeezed through as Moby waved goodbye with a utopian smile that spread broadly along the plains of his sandalwood skin. "I should head back upstairs, Holden. I'll see you tomorrow."

"Tomorrow."

Holden Clifford swallowed with difficulty as the polished elevator doors closed. He was back in the decadent lobby. This time, much less excited about the rest of his life. He had discovered an ally in the most unlikely of places and yet it left him feeling alone. Destitute. Discouraged. Wasn't *he* supposed to be the one joining a group of others? There were no others, were there? What he found was a group of misguided rich people with nothing to do but turn destruction and chaos into the newest art form. It was over. If there was to be a group out there that could make a difference, a group that would exist to break the lies, Holden would have to start that group himself.

The following day, Holden thoroughly reviled his work routine. He could no longer daydream about *The Free Thinkers* and Shane was avoiding him with a fierce dedication. He tried his best to get a grip on his state of mind, but it slipped away from him. During those hours it was trained to chug robotically along. Whether he wanted to be or not, Holden was a small, mechanical ape whose only job was to crash two cymbals together in a continuous rhythm. But at three o'clock, when the sprocket at his back had wound down, he scrubbed his hands to keep up appearances that reading The Book was his only concern and left the warehouse of General Fire in a surprisingly chipper mood. That reason was one hundred and sixty-five pages long.

At every stoplight on the road to Wilmette, Holden glanced secretively down at the open copy of *Fahrenheit 451* that Winston had lent him. He wanted to arrive with a few lines memorized to test the old man's ability to recall it word for word, which had been the claim. It was thrilling to read in the open, but at every intersection Holden was stirred awake by the

THE BOOK

earsplitting honk of those aggravated behind him. Each time he would glance up, Holden found an insistent green eye shining down on his van, detecting his every move, and it made him slam on the gas to get away from its curious gaze.

The persistence of the green light, watching him as he passed each set of its ocular traffic managers, brought to mind a memorable passage from a book he had read recently by a man named F. Scott Fitzgerald. The book's title eluded him, but he knew the character's name was somehow involved and that, when seeing the title on his Book for the first time, Holden had been expecting to read a story about a magician.

> *"Gatsby believed in the green light, the orgiastic future that year by year recedes before us. It eluded us then, but that's no matter - tomorrow we will run faster, stretch our arms farther...and one fine morning -"*

Holden knew that his shade of green was quite different from that of Mister Gatsby. Holden's light was evil. As he eluded his light at each intersection, the green eye was moving faster and stretching out farther for him. Because, for miles and miles and miles, perhaps across the county, he was the only person with a paper bound book concealed under a filthy jacket on his passenger seat. The fear was great, but Holden was greater and he wouldn't allow his fear to devastate him. So, as he drove on, he simply prayed to catch the next stoplight.

Reading without The Book was an unexplainable joy. He found himself enamored with the simple act of it. How he would delicately run a finger along the trace of a single page, slipping it gently behind its chalky pelt as he waited to finish the words that had been stamped delicately onto the priceless surface. How he would pull a finger down toward the spine, ever so carefully tugging, like a breath of wind, until the single page flipped to the other side, joining the multitude of pages that had been given the same delicate caress. Moving, without choice, from the land of the unread pages to the land of the read. It was an act he had never before experienced and once again, it brought such a romance to reading that he had never thought was possible.

How the color of the pages called to him. From each of the many subtle blemishes on their blonde skin, he seemed to feel every person that had read that story before him. As if some of their soul had been what soiled the page.

Winston.

Winston's father.

His grandfather.

Perhaps the man he had purchased it from.

That man's wife.

That wife's sister-in-law.

Her mother.

Her mother's cousin.

The shop owner who ran the used book store that had perused the stories he had recently purchased during the passing of a few dollars.

The roommate that sold it to the bookstore when he had finished reading.

And then, the original owner of whom the book loved most. The person who had seen it on a shelf and had chosen it from a stack of so many other identical copies.

Holden imagined such a thing and the thought itself felt unwelcome in his small mind. A stack of clean books that lined a shelf in a shop that smelled fresh with the freedom that each patron took for granted. That book must have felt so true in the owner's hands as they brought it excitedly to the check-out counter before taking it for its first walk. Carefully, they drew

THE BOOK

back the cover, only enough to keep it from closing. Eventually, a thick canyon of a wrinkle tore at the spine where the cover had been yanked to the back by an irresponsible reader. But that didn't matter. That was the life of the book. It had been born without a crease; without a stain. And now, in the hands of a man who was bound by law to destroy it, the book was a beautiful canvas of lines, creases, tears and age spots. It was worn, but wonderful. Its unique scent, unlike any other in the world, caught in his nose and resonated there like a winter wind. The story had its own story of the hands who exchanged it and the books it shared shelves with. This was the air that Holden breathed - this euphoric bliss that swam with the stench of oily rags and greasy pipe in the driver's seat of his work van. These were the delicate thoughts he yearned to protect when his brakes squealed in front of Winston's home and he was faced with the debate of whether or not to drive away in fear and never ever come back.

Parked near the front door, where Holden often left his van, was a polished black sedan that shone in the sprinkling of rain that seemed to christen the car with elegance. Its twin, silver rims, like sparkling irises, shone back at him through the tousling mists, reminding him that some of the most beautiful creatures were also some of the most deadly. Holden left the idling van in drive, almost certain that he had just ruined Marion's and Winston's lives by being overeager in handing out their address.

But couldn't it be Moby? They could be inside right now, waiting for him to show up. Moby could have already convinced Winston that their future war against The Book would succeed. They could be laughing and smoking and drinking and reveling in plans that Holden dreamt were being written by someone, somewhere.

But then, it might not be Moby.

And how cowardly was Holden?

Good question.

How cowardly would he be if he allowed his mind to believe the car was not the property of some enormous, tattooed man and he chose to drive off? Would someone see that as selfish if he chose the safer route? If he chose freedom? They could be waiting to take him away. Holden was already on the radar of the Publishing House. He thought it over for second, but it was a waste of a good second. There was no other option. If the owner of the black sedan (that continued to stare and stare and stare) had somehow gotten Winston's address through other means, then he was already caught and his choice to retreat from the driveway would only buy him enough time for a last meal. Holden did what he thought made the most logical sense. He pulled into Winston's driveway, parked beside the black car and got out of his van, holding the book Winston had entrusted to him with pride.

The front door was open.

The thought of turning around was strong and beginning to overtake him, but Holden wouldn't allow it. His decision had been to go forward. So he opened the door fully and listened. From the foyer he could hear argumentative voices coming from the music room. As Holden approached the wide oak doors, he hoped that the discussion was one of men debating the history of literature and the future freedoms of its writers. Instead, he found Winston gripping his walker in one hand and poking Moby in the chest with one long, shabby finger.

Moby saw Holden enter the room and tossed out a tree trunk of an arm as if to say, *Help me out here, man.*

"Winston. Please...please..." Holden pleaded, jogging over to them.

THE BOOK

"I told this young man that there is nothing going on here. You tell him, Holden. You tell him that there is nothing going on here."

"Winston, I invited him."

"I know you did. But there is nothing going on here." he repeated, his voice tired and raspy. When Moby turned to lean his nervous weight against the grand piano, Winston shot a glare of warning at Holden. They were supposed to be in agreement.

The situation could have been worse, but not by much. Moby took this opportunity to step back, actually afraid of the feisty little man, and Holden explained. "Winston, I've been trying to find other people that could help and I ended up getting invited to..."

"I know what you did, or at least I have an idea of what you did, and I'm not very pleased. That brute told me he was from *The Free Thinkers* and that's all a man my age needs to hear. Now get out!"

"This can all be explained if you would just..."

Moby stepped forward to interrupt them with the most peculiar question. "Do you have *Leaves of Grass* by Walt Whitman?"

Winston's ears piqued with his interest. "No. No, young man. I don't. What made you think I did?"

"Holden told me that you had a library here and I just...needed to know if you had that collection in your...collection. He's my favorite poet and I was wondering if there were things..."

"Missing?"

"Right. If you had a copy I'd be able to find out."

"Well," Winston began, in a much lighter mood, "I do not own a copy, although that would be a treat. However, while I'm not certain what edition they're from, Marion brought me a few pages from that book."

"That woman from the news?" Moby asked, having recognized her when he arrived.

Winston nodded and arched an eyebrow. "I suppose we could give those a look…if you'd like. Do you have a copy of The Book with you?"

"I do. Yeah." From his jacket, Moby pulled the thinnest version of the reading device either of them had ever seen.

Winston grinned at the difference of stature between man and his Book as he said, "Well, I'm not promising anything, but we can have a look in the cellar. In fact, if you'd like, I can take you through the same explanation I gave Holden."

"That would be really great. Thanks."

"So, you're aware of the alterations in The Book?"

"Yes. In fact, my uncle was part of a group that tried to destroy the Publishing House."

"Really?" Holden asked, turning to Winston. "Didn't your group try the same thing?"

"Where is your uncle now?" the elderly man asked, slowly.

Moby turned his head to the ceiling and counted the years. "He just left. There one day…gone the next. Gotta be going on twenty years now."

Winston tipped dizzily to the right and attempted to regain his unbalanced footing before dropping into a thickly cushioned chair. Holden rushed forward, but he was pushed away. "Might I ask," Winston inquired, clearing his throat before finishing. "Is your surname Van Dinh?" Moby nodded slowly. "As in, Skip Van Dinh?"

"You were part of my uncle's group?" he mumbled, aghast. "What happened to him?"

THE BOOK

"Young man, I was the leader of your uncle's group. And of his whereabouts, I only wish I knew." Winston's entire demeanor shifted in an instant and it frightened Holden before he understood that it was a good thing. The elderly man was nodding. Over and over, he continued to nod as the men stared back in patient curiosity. When he chose to reveal what his mind had decided, Winston's words were crisp and lingered long in their ears. "Kismet. All of us. All of this. Your uncle was a key member of my group. A group that I believe now may have been the only surviving witnesses to the slavery we're still facing. Then, one average day, they vanished. I've been on my own the rest of so many years, with the knowledge that I may be the only holder of this terrible secret."

He nodded again and rose, without the aid of his walker. "I will take you downstairs. We will look through your Book. When the two of us are finished, the four of us are going to discuss things. Never before have I felt such a pull from fate. From God. Everything that has taken place to get us here, was supposed to happen so we could meet under these circumstances and under the leadership of someone far stronger than I." Gingerly, the elderly man turned to Holden who listened to these enamored words with disbelief. Moby was nodding in agreement. Before Holden could dispute their opinion of him, Winston was leading Moby toward the cellar.

"Follow me, big fella." At the stairs, Winston turned back to whisper a final message to Holden. "I was upset with you when he arrived...but then he introduced himself. Anyone who quotes Herman Melville is a friend of mine. I will add though, a heads up would have been nice." He poked Holden with a long, stingy finger before pointing in the direction from where they had come. "Marion is waiting for you. Go say hello."

Holden watched the unlikely duo walk away before he returned to the foyer. Marion was in the kitchen unpacking a table lined with canvas grocery bags and when she noticed him, she quickly towed her hair behind her ears and adjusted the dress that looked uncomfortable on someone like her. The dress hung from her shoulders by two delicate straps and draped flawlessly over her downy skin. The colors were pulled from the floral Japanese tattoos that traced up her left arm and it made Marion look radiant and fresh. Her shoulder-swept hair was light and pulled off her forehead, cropping the bold, attractive features that Holden usually avoided. The reason why, he couldn't grasp at the moment. He supposed that with nothing else to do all day in such odd confinement, Marion had decided to make herself look beautiful.

Her first words when they released their long hug were, "I'm reading *Big as Life* by E.L. Doctorow." She pointed to the coffee table where the lively-covered book was resting. "Winston is taking me through the entire library, story by story. Telling me exactly what I need to read. The first ones are the ones I have to read before I die, apparently." Marion giggled foolishly and covered her mouth. As she managed her embarrassing facial expressions, Marion noticed his eyes and realized how much she had missed him. He looked older to her now. His face was drawn and exhausted. She could sense the weight he was carrying as he muscled out a smile.

"He gave me *Fahrenheit 451*. You have to read it, Marion. It is the most perfect book. It explains so much of how we feel, I think. In a different way, though. I mean...it's different." He struggled to explain his emotions behind the experience he had been having with the book, but was unable to. "When I read from paper, it's...it's as if I'm finally...I don't know. It's almost like the words on the page make me feel..."

THE BOOK

"Free," Marion finished. "That's what I felt. Like, for the first time ever, the story I read was perfect, just the way it was. There was no need to change it. No one had ever changed it or found anything wrong with it. It was finished. I guess I felt that way because I knew it hadn't been changed, but..."

"It's like there was only one author." The words finally came and they were confirmed in Marion's eyes. "Nowhere in the story did it feel like someone else picked up a pen and started writing."

Holden listened as Marion spoke about her book and a thin smile traced along his face. The moment she noticed, Marion stopped mid-sentence, shook her head and said, "You've been here for almost a half hour and you still haven't told me what happened to you. You never came back."

"Well, I left and went home to read *Fahrenheit 451*," Holden confessed, scratching his fuzzy crop of hair. "After that, it was just life as usual."

Marion looked past Holden to the main staircase, where the cellar door beneath the steps was left open. "And that gargantuan man?"

Holden bobbed his head, still shocked by the news. "Turns out he's related to one of Winston's old crew."

"Well, based on recent events, I'm hoping you're going to clarify that whole thing," she smirked, and pulled a case of beer from one of the bags on the table. "For now, what can I get you to drink?"

"Oh, Marion. You know exactly how to get me talking."

A dinner of fine food and well-aged wine could have had the ability to compete with conversations around the dining room, but that proved to be the opposite for the four of them that evening. Nestled around Winston's colonial oak dining table, they listened as Holden retraced his story from the past few days and nothing was more shocking to them than the words he exchanged with Martin Trust. Feathers were being ruffled and the danger of being discovered was very real. Marion could have gone without hearing the news that her diary, with all its personal details, was the key to tracking Holden down. On more than one occasion, she dropped her fork in embarrassment and it clinked loudly in the compact dining room. On the opposite end of the table, Winston couldn't have been more excited. He drank every word with sips of wine, feeling quite certain that success was only a few decisions away.

After they ate, the four of them journeyed to the elongated back yard and eventually found themselves walking along Winston's large deck that stretched like an arm into the lake. A small gazebo capped the end of the dock and they sat

THE BOOK

underneath it, upon moist cast-iron furniture, and opened a waterproof chest of games that hadn't been stirred in a decade. Winston carefully removed a wooden box from the chest and lifted the lid to reveal a set of jade chess pieces. They were faultless and intricately carved in the shape of samurai warriors. He arranged them blissfully on the small table at the center.

Delicate drippings of rain fell from all sides of the gutterless gazebo and it gave them a sense of security, as if an unseen shield surrounded them. They could speak freely, without being heard. Content in the moment, Winston packed his pipe and Marion exchanged cigarettes with Moby. Holden searched his pockets for a stick of gum, but couldn't find any. Thankfully, he had brought another bottle of wine and four glasses.

Moby lifted the thin, fabric cigarette to his mouth and lit it slowly as he looked out on the rain-puckered lake, feeling completely satisfied for the first time in years. He had been taken through a mind-altering journey in the cellar and he finally felt like he was a part of something right. Of course, the situation was helped by the fact that they were sitting in a tall gazebo that had been attached to an immense house. He was a large man in a medium-sized world and the home of Winston Pratt was right up his alley. Feeling free to say what was on his mind, Moby explained his purpose in reaching out to *The Free Thinkers* and how, over time, he had revolutionized their recruitment system. Branding city buildings with their ornamental crest had been his idea, along with many others. They weren't sure yet how they could use a mind like his, but were excited to have him, nevertheless.

As Winston and Marion began what could be a very long game of chess, they laughed through puffs of smoke at Moby's account of how he dressed up as an Unfortunate every day, donning the mask of delirium and the outfit of disgust in the pursuit of truth and revolution. Apparently, few people had reached the doors of the Spire through his hand stitched ribbons, but the group found his tactics quite useful. He elaborated on the type of parties Holden walked in on and described the agenda of *The Free Thinkers*. It was very different than his own, and yet Moby was glad to be a part of it when he had been because it brought him to Holden. The seriousness of that insight moved the conversation to the contentious when Winston sat back from the chess board and added his two cents.

"Moby, I think I can state for the others that we are glad to have you. In the sitting room, I said that we were meant to come together. I still believe that. We are meant to do something. I just don't know what that something will be. The facts haven't changed. As your uncle could attest, having disappeared in our attempt to destroy the Publishing House, there isn't much we can do. Not only do they track our every move, waiting to find someone smart enough to develop a plan and the abilities to achieve its end, but they have measures in place to protect themselves if they cannot find that person. There is much I know about the way they run their House...but that was forty years ago. The possibilities of success may have disappeared with your uncle."

Moby adjusted his weight on the thick wooden bench and doused his drooping cigarette in the rainwater that was collecting on the ledge behind him. "Forgive me Winston, if what I'm about to say comes across as rude," he hummed politely, "but I think you're being too pessimistic. my perspective on this is quite different. When my uncle vanished, none of my family believed what he had said about our minds being controlled by The Book. No one listened. No one believed. Except me. As I grew older, I sought a way to fight an injustice that everyone around me thought was a fairy tale. But I still carried the torch. I had faith in my uncle's words because I could see the truth in his eyes. And today, as you sit here and say that success may have disappeared forty years ago, I am literally breathing in the moments of my own testimony that this struggle to find the truth was not in vain. When Holden arrived at our meeting, he was the homecoming of hope. I couldn't sleep last night because I realized that I wasn't the only one. I know it may not seem real to you now, Winston, but this is going to work. Because I still believe. I know there is something epic waiting for us."

In the wake of those words, Holden and Moby launched ideas back and forth only to have Winston dismiss them easily with well-supported points. As each promising idea was upset by a simple, governmental security measure, the conversation grew heated until Marion, assisted by Winston's inability to play the game with focus, shocked the gazebo by removing one of his major pieces with a meager pawn.

Silence sliced like a tide against the sand and only the sounds of falling rain dancing on the lake could be heard until Marion retracted her smile and spoke, looking radiant as her surprisingly logical mind joined the discussion. "You guys are thinking too big. It was a mistake to try and dismantle the Publishing House. Really, what good can a small band of revolutionaries do? Even with the right resources, a few people cannot take down The Book. It's just impossible. A pawn," she chimed, holding up the jade samurai she had just dethroned, "is incapable of taking out a king. No matter how well planned the strategy, its strength fails. But a legion of pawns moving together across the board, each with their own well-placed attacks…

"With one mind," Moby agreed. "Working in unison."

Winston removed his glasses, took a handkerchief from his jacket pocket and wiped a tear from his eye. "My mother. I think she would have been classified as a knight. She was very well placed and very powerful. As was Conrad."

"Yeah, but your mother only had you," Holden mused, fixing his gaze upon the chess board. "Conrad obviously had others. Enough to get him where he needed to be. Buckingham Palace is not accessible to pawns. Problem is, and forgive the mixed-metaphor, but the guy's solution was a Hail Mary pass. I don't mean to knock his courage, but it was too risky. He made a big move hoping it would work, but not enough people caught the reference."

Marion lowered Winston's chess piece, nodding. "Holden's right. We need to learn from the Editors of The Book and take tiny steps. Make patient, simple moves across a chess board, until we've won. Some of the pages I took down from the bar had only one word altered on the page. One word...added or changed or removed. Who would suspect a single word could change anything?"

Moby suppressed a snicker of understanding. "Subtlety," he agreed, reaching across the board to snag a cigarette from Marion's pack. "Like *The Free Thinkers*. Man, were they ever confused in their beliefs. And yeah, they had too many mislaid plans, but the one thing they had going for them was subtlety. We branded the buildings with nothing more than a picture and then we waited. People believed what they wanted and eventually reached out to us. We never actively recruited anyone."

"But I don't know if that was good either," Holden complained, wishing he had a natural-fiber, fabric cigarette of his own to smoke. "As someone who was reaching out, I can tell you that there were flaws. There is no way you could have known how successful active recruitment would have been. None of us knew how large you were. And all I got to see was the Chicago branch."

A smile twisted Moby's immense jaw as the flame of Marion's lighter licked the end of his cigarette. "I knew I'd have to tell you this at some point. Usually we have more people at those meetings, very important people, but really...there aren't any other branches."

"That's ridiculous," Holden snapped, now fully disappointed with *The Free Thinkers*. "That was everyone? Serious? What bull!"

"No, that's amazing," Winston beamed. "By the way they were vilified in the paper, I thought there were thousands of them across the country. I mean, this is not a bad way to go about things." He abandoned their game and began shuffling pieces around the board, his frail fingers moving steadily like so many motorized bones. "If we're going to do this right, it will take dedication and careful decision making. And we can't do it without some rooks. Some bishops...maybe even a queen some day."

"We'll need to judge our opponent's moves and have a counter attack ready before they make them."

"Good point, Marion," Winston agreed, suddenly somber. As he continued, his attitude shifted and his words were slow and precisely spoken. "Yes, this is a good idea. The first one I think I could actually stand behind. But there are two very hard truths you need to hear. The first is that if this works, and it may work, I guarantee you it will not happen during my lifetime. You need to accept that it may not even happen during your own. More importantly, and this is the more difficult fact to accept...but the game cannot be effective and we cannot win if we aren't willing to make sacrifices."

At those words, a chilling wind rustled through the gazebo, lifting the board a few centimeters and tousling the smaller pieces to their knees. "This fight is very real and there will be a point when hard decisions will need to be made. We will, most assuredly, lose a pawn or two in pursuit of the greater good." Not a word was spoken as they rested on the seriousness of his words. "I hope those moves will be made when I am no longer on the chess board. When victory is close. But knowing that you are all so dedicated to the fight, it gives me hope that one day we could win. There are many layers to this and our government's operation is so much bigger than any one of us could imagine, but I am excited. This is the most active my brain has been in years."

He laughed and puffed from his pipe before adjusting his bowtie as an act of resetting his composure. "You three can count on me to do everything in my power to support this. This home is no longer mine. This is our home. And all the resources I have. My books are our books. And they belong to other people too. Those people don't know it yet, but they're going to be part of our group. Like Moby before he met you, Holden. If we are going to make our group larger, we have to be slow and we need to reach out to those we trust. *Truly* and *deeply* trust. I cannot stress that point enough.

"From there, they will have others that they can trust. And so on, until such a time that we can begin developing a more formal plan of attack. Some of our best moves, when I was working with your uncle," Winston paused, paying respect in a breath of silence, "were made when we could all come together and have many minds focusing on the same singular task. I tell you, there are more ideas out there than the four of us could ever imagine and we need to find those minds. If we are steadfast, forthright with one another and focused, I believe we may actually have a shot. I am a tired man and my voice is growing weak in my old age, but together we will strike fear into the hearts of the Publishing House with a voice that has never been heard. A voice that will ring out and last the ages."

Each of them left the gazebo that night with a plan of who they were going to reach. Moby couldn't wait to contact a husband and wife from *The Free Thinkers*. They were the only two who showed any interest in what he said about The Book and he trusted them fully. Like Holden, they found little in much of what was said during those meetings and had stopped attending a few months back. Moby was certain that they would give themselves freely to the cause.

Winston planned to reach out to the antique dealer Holden had had an altercation with in search of his favorite book. From the man's reaction to Holden's persistence and with the illusive back room he seemed anxious to keep secret, Winston was positive that the man had books and knew exactly what he needed to say to reach him.

For her own safety and for the safety of the group, Marion would not attempt to reach anyone by phone or mail or anything that could track the government back to Winston's home. Her family, and those of her friends she trusted, could not get involved on any level. She had to remain neutral in this stage no matter how hard it would be. Instead, Marion devoted herself to Holden.

As Winston brought Moby to his car, she urged Holden to follow her to the room she called *home*. It was on the opposite side of the house and had been one of the more spacious of Winston's guest rooms. Holden didn't know what to expect by her eagerness to lead him there. He assumed she wanted to be alone. To talk about her feelings, whatever those may be, and he couldn't help but adore her for it. In the face of such adversity, Marion was still thinking of her heart.

Holden missed the mark on her motives, but not by much. Marion had an uncanny ability to anticipate, to the letter, the actions of others and she saw a profound struggle brewing in Holden. She truly viewed him as their leader and could see all the heartache and pain he would be forced to witness by having that role thrust upon him. When she led him by the arm to her bedroom, and eventually to the comfortable chair by the window, she had a very specific gift in mind to give him. Marion walked to the antique vanity, sat at the low-backed seat and opened one of the thin, rectangular drawers that lined its face. It glided forward with a smooth drag. Marion removed a single, small item, closed the drawer and walked back to sit on the floor in front of Holden.

"I know who you trust more than anyone. And I know it's going to be hard to reach out to him," she said, gazing tenderly into his eyes. "I thought you might need something to remind you of what we talked about tonight."

Gently, she reached for Holden's hand and took his pointer finger in her own. In her other hand, she lifted the item she had removed from the vanity drawer and brought it to his finger. With a single, quick snip, Marion clipped his sharpened fingernail. The one he, and so many others, used to navigate the unruly seas of The Book. She kissed the bridge of his knuckles and sat back, eyes moist. And with a soft whisper, Marion gripped his hand and immersed herself in his eyes. "Don't forget, Holden. Don't forget what you're fighting for."

He looked down at his nail, its ridge dirty, but smooth, and accepted his fate for the first time. "I won't."

The opportunity for Holden to reach out to the one person in the world he trusted more than any other arose nearly a week after their decision to start a grass roots movement. The reason it had taken so long was because his best friend was still avoiding him. Shane Dagget was as good as invisible. He came in to work early. He left late. And with seniority over Holden, if Numbskull gave him the option, Shane always chose to work with someone else. But when four of them were assigned at random to install a full system on a new high-rise in the loop, the moment Holden had been waiting for presented itself. There was nowhere that Shane could run.

The majority of the rain-drenched day was spent on a concrete slab thirty stories in the air. The men of General Fire were stationed near the open, glassless windows and were forced to work under a constant swath of moist air. They slaved in silence. Holden spent each of those grueling hours deciding what he would say to Shane the moment he could get him alone. On occasion, Shane noticed his friend making eye contact and continued to look away, almost consciously keeping thirty feet of empty space between them at all times. For Holden, under the weight of four lengthy, iron pipes, struggling each minute to remain steady on a fourteen-foot ladder, the more confusing pieces started falling into place. There was only one reason he could come up with for why his friend would be acting that way - he had seen the book.

Holden was sure of it. At some point during the night, Shane had opened the duffle bag and seen the illegal, printed book among his things. It was the only explanation.

This reaction wasn't new. In fact, it was one of Shane's classic maneuvers. He was in *Protection Mode*. He focused solely on his work and nothing more. He had probably even stopped following the Blackhawks. When tragedy struck his life, Shane tended to shut down. It wasn't that he got depressed or overwrought with grief. It was simply that Shane didn't have the capacity to figure out what to do next.

Nothing new. It always took Shane longer to figure things out. Twice as long as it took Holden. As teenagers, when they would start a feral, fist-flinging, rolling in the yard argument, Holden would be over it by the end of the day. It took Shane weeks to work through all his emotions. He wasn't trying to find the last word to set Holden straight and wasn't even really angry. It was just that his mind was a funnel and it took a while for any issue to circle its way through to the bottom where the drain could allow it a chance to escape. The distance and the disregard made sense. Shane had seen the book and he was contemplating what to do about it.

With this as a real possibility, Holden gained more confidence. When they broke for lunch, he made a move. As Shane passed the group, Holden grabbed him by the arm and whispered, "Stay behind. We have to talk." Shane yanked himself away, but Holden could sense that he wouldn't go far. Once their

THE BOOK

fellow pipe fitters left the cold slab of concrete and had taken the elevator down, the two of them were alone and Shane instantly drew his shoulders back. A moment later he raised his arms in defense.

"Where did that book come from?" he blurted, curling his lips. "I looked it up. It doesn't exist."

"Uhm..."

Holden didn't know what to say. He was expecting to be in control of the conversation and had already been forced to take a knee. Rather than complain about the fact that he could have faced jail time by having an unrecycled book in his possession, Shane's curiosity about the book threw Holden off his game.

"It doesn't exist anywhere. This guy...Ray Bradbury...he's written some other things, but nothing called *Fahrenheit 451*. What are you involved with, man?" he asked, fuming as he paced the unfinished room. When Holden didn't respond, he stepped closer.

Expecting Shane to start sweeping his fists, he responded, "I got that book from a friend, okay?"

"From Marion? Are you hiding her out, bro? She's wanted. And not even by the police. By like...big people. And I stuck my neck out on the line for you without realizing what was in that bag. I'm not stupid, Holden. I know what you're going to try to do and I'm not getting involved. If one freakin' word comes out where I think you're gonna try and get me involved...I will throw you over the side of this building. Do not involve me. I mean it!"

It was finally clear. Holden realized the truth in that last twist of phrase and was surprised that he hadn't figured it out earlier. Shane was not playing offense. He was playing defense. Holden tried to stop the smile that arched at the corner of his mouth as he said the words, but couldn't help himself.

"You read it. Didn't you...?" Shane looked away. "You read the book."

"Yeah, so what. I read the whole dang thing. Doesn't matter. I was just curious. I've never even seen a book before and I needed to know why my best friend would *risk his life* to keep it. And then...I saw that the guy was a firefighter. You know how much I wanted to be a fire fighter. But it was messed up, bro. Burnin' books. People dying." Shane stopped to regain his frustration. It was Holden's fault that he felt whatever it was that he felt, and he needed to point his anger back at the one responsible. "Are you and Marion involved in some anarchist thing now, bro?"

"That's kind of a big question and...there's a big answer for it," Holden admitted, since what they were starting *would* be considered anarchy.

"None of that matters. Why you gotta rock the boat, man? Everything we did and all the things we planned for our lives...you wrecked it. You changed. You're not the same guy. And...I just...."

Shane released a visceral howl and it shook a tremendous guilt through Holden. His friend was right. He had changed. He wasn't the same person. And he never would be again. Shane looked so dramatically dismayed, pacing near the horizontal strip of open sky and Holden could size him up in a second. Shane was mourning the loss of his best friend. Yes, he had been affected by what he read in *Fahrenheit 451*, likely more than Holden realized, but the main reason Shane had been so upset was because he knew that their friendship would never get back to the way it used to be.

There was a history there. Both of them had lost their parents before they could legally drink the sorrow away and once the funeral march ended, Shane had been left with no one.

His older brother moved away. His sister got married and moved away. The only person Shane could count on was Holden, his best friend from across the street. It had been that way ever since. And now, there was a battle raging inside him that could go either way. Shane would join the group in an instant, regardless of what they believed, if it meant that he could reunite with his best friend. But the other side of him was putting up a fight. He didn't like feeling those emotions. They scared him because they made Shane realize how much their relationship meant to him. He would give up any of his freedoms to keep it safe or to regain something that resembled what it once was.

When he was finished pacing, Shane spoke with forced satisfaction. "I'm going to lunch, Holden. And I'm done talking about this. Maybe done talking to you. That's if you're even around tomorrow."

"Dagget," Holden argued, feeling his friend slip away. "Wait. We've seen each other through everything, man. Can't you trust me on this? Will you at least give me a chance to..."

Shane was already in Holden's face, gripping his shirt and whispering ferociously, "Don't think for an instant that I won't turn you in if they ask me! 'Cause guess what brother, Shane Dagget fixes himself first!"

Shane shoved himself away and, at those words, walked past the elevator and down the railingless concrete cube that held a multitude of diamond-plated emergency stairs. With each echoing reverberation, Holden felt their friendship, the closest relationship in his life, crumbling to nothing. He wanted to holler out to Shane. He even pulled out his phone to call him in a last desperate attempt to get him back, but it didn't work. He heard Shane's phone rattling near a pile of black pipe that was waiting to be fastened to the ceiling. He'd left it at the job site on purpose.

Rather than leave a message, Holden picked up his best friend's phone and typed Winston's address onto the screen before closing it and leaving work early. He didn't care about the consequences. Moby and Winston were so excited to bring new people in and Holden dreamed of Shane standing beside him, sharing his passion for the freedoms of future generations. But they were different people. A limiting fact he had been forced to realize so many times before. No matter how well they got along, they saw the world through different eyes. Holden was powerless. No matter what logic he could develop to convince people of the truth, he could never force people to care about The Book.

Weeks passed in the life of Holden Clifford like the trailing emissions of a classic, American-made automobile. The earth was still polluted and everything was accelerating. The three of them had reached out to those they wanted to bring into the fold and although Holden had been unsuccessful, the same could not be said of the other two. The husband and wife Moby had recruited, the former members of *The Free Thinkers*, were so eager to join that they began dropping by Winston's on a regular basis. Their names were Jeff and Abby Johnson and they were a much needed ingredient.

Marion was relieved to have another woman at the house and Winston found Jeff to be a better match for him intellectually. The conversations they struck under the rain-soaked gazebo gave peace to the others because they noticed a positive shift in the wise man's demeanor. As he had done before, Winston brought them separately to the cellar, removed the chip from the back of their Book and walked them through eighteen minutes of their favorite stories. After which, he brought them to the sitting room where they clipped their fingernail and listened to the sacrifices Dennis Wayne Conrad, Winston's mother, Moby's uncle and the rest of his former group had made. Winston felt that reliving these stories was a crucial element of inducting new members into their group. People needed to know the road they were on and how it could diverge to another. They needed to understand the risks and to accept them.

Each time Winston told these tragic stories, he became more comfortable as a storyteller, which seemed to bring the group unexpected warmth. Storytelling quickly became the way they relaxed. The moment that Abby discovered her favorite story along the shelves in the cellar, *Peter Pan* by J.M. Barrie, Winston encouraged her to read it aloud to everyone during the course of a few quiet, but damp, evenings. The consensus between each of their favorite lines rested on something Abby read in the final chapter.

> *"Wendy was grown up. You need not be sorry for her. She was one of the kind that likes to grow up. In the end she grew up of her own free will a day quicker than other girls. All the boys were grown up and done for by this time; so it's scarcely worth while saying anything more about them."*

Wanting to be around in case Jeff and Abby stopped by, Moby had started coming to the house early every day and leaving well into the night. So often, in fact, that Winston suggested he move into one of the many spare bedrooms. Although Moby tried to protest, Winston found a room that was large enough for such a giant and, within days, the former Unfortunate sold his condo, all his belongings and took up permanent residence on the estate. This was also nice for Marion because she was no longer the only one responsible for keeping an eye on Winston. While she cherished spending all her time with the elderly man, a little relief pitching went a long way.

With each passing, cloud-enclosed day, Holden grew more embarrassed that he had been unable to succeed with Shane. He considered who else he trusted and could reach out to, but his ex-wife was the only one to make the list. Of course, it didn't take him long to develop arguments against that option. Eve was more than temperamental and had an ability to lose her hearing whenever she was around her ex-husband. It was a hard pill to swallow, but Holden knew that if their group was to become a success, he'd need to get beyond whatever had been keeping him from reaching out.

On his own, Winston had done a superb job. After a week and a half of meeting as a six-person group, the thin, bearded man with the bright red t-shirt who had launched Holden with ease to the back room of his antique shop, arrived at Winston's door, serene and eager to pass along his sensible, surprisingly academic expertise to the other six. The home-made necklaces that festooned the man's wrinkled throat held their attention as they listened to his opinion of how the world of science had been distorted since the origination of the Publishing House. The antique dealer was aware of the general alteration in novels, but was unaware of the connection between Conrad and the Prince and he allowed Winston the opportunity to take him through the entrance ritual.

With earnest, Winston brought him down to the cellar and, after eighteen minutes, they shared a meal in private. The following day, the man returned with five plastic bins filled to the lid with fifty-seven books that he had been hoarding for most of his life. Special books he vowed never to sell. Stacked precariously on each of these were smaller containers overflowing with half-torn stories he had discovered behind the drawers of antique dressers and single pages that he had found lining the insides of ruined suitcases. Winston and the antique dealer, Ephraim Wheeler, were like two giddy gardeners among a patch of ideas and they spent hours in the cellar getting their hands dirty discussing books and reveling in one another's collections. Along with his wife Lolita and young son Ronnie, Ephraim moved from their apartment and into one of Winston's dual-suite bedrooms. It was an adjustment for sure, but to have a rascally eight-year-old scurrying around and creating havoc was an unforeseen breath of fresh air. It had been ages since Winston's house had been full and he was thrilled to watch life running through the halls. His sanctuary of thoughts and paper was a home again.

Storage was an issue that they could see coming from far off, so Moby took it upon himself to begin rummaging through the contents of Winston's garage. In the process, he discovered the bin of items Winston's mother had stored since leaving the Publishing House. Inside were three wide screens carrying the recycling icon of The Book and a framed metal sign with dark green text. The sign read:

Editors found with written material or records of editing will be recycled.

When Moby brought this to Winston, a laugh escaped his lined lips. The three screens were digital log books that his mother had kept and recorded in while working for the Publishing House. Each day she had come home from work, they spent an hour typing out exactly what she had edited, added or deleted. The sign was something she had stolen as a joke that was both apt because the records were in her head, and foreboding, because it reminded her each day what awaited those who were caught keeping track. As a group of eight, they decided that the digital records were just as important as the original texts themselves because they could be used to convince others of the truth if a specific edition was missing from their underground library.

While the group may have been growing, its leader was still having difficulty accepting the dynamic. One un-sunny afternoon, Holden dropped in after work to find Marion waiting to ask him if he would start spending the night. He insisted he couldn't and blamed it on an early start in the morning, but she wasn't buying it. Marion channeled her disappointment by pressing him on his necessity to continue working when they needed him at the house. So much was going on while he was straddling joists and crawling through truss work and the group was desperate for his opinion. Holden tried to explain himself, but what Marion didn't understand was that during such synchronized turmoil, he needed part of his life to keep its rituals. He knew it made sense to move from his minty-fresh (*home again, home again*) house, based on mileage alone, but in the end, Holden felt that he was merely unable to release the part of his day that was most secure.

There were a lot of reasons beyond his need for stability. Although the group considered him to be their leader, part of Holden still wanted to be the minion for someone else's group, while the other part was unable to fully trust the group he had started himself. It wasn't that he didn't believe in the group; it was that he found himself frightened by the stories Winston would tell about Moby's uncle and their friends and how they had all simply vanished one day. Winston's group had always met at the same place. They planned the plan and went through the motions without a worry. A week away from delivering a swift kick to the pants of the Publishing House, Winston had chosen to bring food to their meeting and ended up arriving to "base camp" a little late. Luckily late. Whatever had happened, everyone in his group had been taken, including Moby's uncle. Winston had been spared purely by the fact that his stomach was rumbling. Whoever spilled the beans didn't wait around for him to show up. It was hard for the man to go on living after that, knowing that his friends had disappeared from the group he started, but with this new group's progress and passion, he seemed to be healing. Whereas Holden was fast becoming less confident. He couldn't stop picturing the scene of Winston walking in to find everyone he cared about and trusted gone. It made him realize that he never wanted to be one of the *gone*. He wanted to be the one walking through the door. Visiting. Moving into Winston's home was choosing a side that he wasn't ready yet to accept. That would change over time as his courage grew. He knew that it would. But it was still early and things were moving quickly and Holden didn't like when things moved quickly.

Another un-sunny afternoon, Holden made it back to Winston's house to find the seven other members of their group in a heated discussion over an item Moby had been working on secretively in the garage. When they noticed Holden's arrival, they allowed Moby a chance to showcase his newfangled mechanism. They watched with pride as Holden approached the kitchen table where they had been circled and enjoyed the look on his face as he noticed that his very large and clever friend had created another branding machine.

Its body was small and made of tough, blackened steel. It was attached to a nylon harness system that was teeming with wires and switches. On the rectangular branding surface were a series of sharp metal letters, carved backwards and spelling four words:

Don't Read The Book.

Moby spoke before Holden could have the chance.

"The branding machine I built for *The Free Thinkers* was difficult to transport and we were constantly forced to strike at night, so no one would see. This machine is light. It has a handheld, portable design and all the mechanics are hidden in the shoulder straps. Obviously, I'll clean it up. Pretty nice, huh? We don't have to be as cautious. I can brand a building in the middle of a crowd."

All Holden could do was smile as he listened to the group chatter on about how smart it was to start branding buildings themselves. It made sense. If the eight of them wouldn't be able to gather new members they could trust, at least people would start questioning what they read in The Book. Moby explained his plans to add imagery or a specific quote from one of their favorite books, but they thought better of it. *Don't Read The Book* was more than enough to get people to start talking and Holden could attest to the fact that, at the very least, the workmen having to remove the brand would take notice.

From outward appearances, it seemed that their group was doing well, but Holden knew as he watched Moby, upon Winston's suggestion, branding their phrase into the thick stone of the fireplace to tumultuous applause, that they were just a bunch of dreamers. Readers with imaginations so entertained by the idea of revolution that they were dumb enough to think success was possible. Nearly all of their time was spent working toward a future that only their children would see. A dream that even little, rambunctious Ronnie could outlive.

Marion was the only one who could see the skepticism behind Holden's enthusiasm because as each of them stared at the smoking stone and the angled blackened words, her eyes were on him. She knew the struggle within Holden and could see it on his wrinkled brow, but she kept it to herself and offered him a simple smile instead when their eyes met.

The next week passed and the sun was still missing. Sure, it was beginning to get on their nerves, but the group rationalized it as a healthy thing. The lack of sunshine, open flowers and tweeting birdies reminded them that they were living in storm season. Even Mother Nature, that supercilious skirt, wasn't about to pretend that things were going the way she had planned. And it was on one of the more thunderous of days, when Holden had felt the most uncertain of himself as their leader, that Shane showed up at the door.

In the great room, Holden had been reading a children's story to Ronnie entitled *Alice's Adventures in Wonderland* by a man named Lewis Carroll. He stood atop a wide, leather ottoman to add a sense of magnitude to the task and attempted to capture the essence of the wildly odd, but enjoyable tale. He read the story with silly voices and Ronnie's attention was latched from the overstuffed couch while Marion looked on from the window seat.

"'Oh, you're sure to do that,' said the Cat, 'if you only walk long enough.' Alice felt that this could not be denied, so she tried another question. 'What sort of people live around here?' 'In that direction,' the Cat said, waiving its right paw round, 'lives a Hatter; and in that direction,' waving the other paw, 'lives a March Hare. Visit either you like; they're both mad.' 'But I don't want to go among mad people,' Alice remarked. 'Oh, you can't help that,' said the Cat. 'We're all mad here. I'm mad. You're mad,'" Holden paused as he heard a knock at the door. Winston left the kitchen to answer it and Marion scurried away from the windows. There was no telling who was at the door, why they had come and if they would recognize Marion from the news. This was the first time any of them had had a guest arrive unannounced and they had to be cautious and assess the risk before reacting. Ronnie squirmed in his seat, so Holden finished the paragraph with a watchful eye on the foyer. *"How do you know I'm mad?' said Alice. 'You must be,' said the Cat, 'or else you wouldn't have come here.'"*

Holden closed the book and stumbled off the ottoman, blinking his eyes like the rapid wings of a butterfly in unspeakable disbelief. Dragging his feet skittishly across the marble tiles of the foyer was his best friend. Shane didn't turn or give attention to anyone in the house. He simply followed Winston toward the cellar door.

Marion turned to Holden, her lips pressed together in a smile of unreserved joy. Holden handed the book on to Ronnie with care and soon found himself jogging to the foyer. At the cellar door Shane turned to glance back at him before heading down the stairs.

Zeal.

Enchantment.

Unobtainable Relief.

The flurry of emotion hurricaned Holden as he skipped excitedly to the door where Winston threw out a hand to stop him. He peaked blissfully around the frame without restraint to watch as his best friend was introduced to the smells and sights below. Winston tugged intensely on Holden's shirt and he turned to discover that he was not about to be included.

"Holden, your friend needs to do this alone."

"But I can..."

"This one is for me." Winston's eyes were sharp and prickled and they told Holden to let it go. So he did. Out of respect. Begrudgingly.

Holden walked backward toward the foyer and watched the cellar door close. He stood there for three minutes before joining Marion in the sitting room where they sat beside one another on the piano bench and listened for the door to open again. The whole time, Holden stared at the floorboards as if studying the life lines that were drawn across their polished surface. Marion stared instead at Holden, her eyes warm and affectionate. She wanted to grip his hand and tell him to be patient; to remind him that Shane had taken the difficult first step; to encourage him. Instead, she kept her hands in her lap and they remained as silent as silence would allow.

Fifteen minutes had passed. Then the big eighteen. And then thirty.

Forty-eight minutes after the cellar door closed, it opened again. Holden sat up from the piano bench, but didn't rise; Marion had stood for him. She took a handful of tentative steps toward the hallway before they heard Shane draw a slight cough and approach the foyer. They held their breath as they saw him walk steadily to the front door. Before he reached for the tarnished handle, he tilted his head toward the sitting room and paused, bringing one hundred unanswered questions to Holden's lips. But he continued sitting and he continued staring. After Shane was gone, and the rest of the house started asking who the man was, Holden launched himself from the piano bench to watch his friend's truck as it backed into the street below the constant oppression of clouds. Marion was there to offer him a comforting glance, but Holden ignored her and marched angrily to the cellar, where he found Winston holding a book by Virginia Wolf called *The Waves*. He dismissed its

THE BOOK

interesting cover art, stopped speculating on how the book could have related to his best friend and started to berate the elderly man who was shelving it prudently away.

"I'm his best friend. I'm the only person he has in this horrible world. I should have been involved in this! If you wanted me to stay quiet, you could have at least given me the courtesy of watching him go through this. He's the most important person in the world to me. You didn't even give me the chance, man! I know this is your house and I want to respect you, but you aren't my father. You aren't my boss. You're not even the leader of this group!" Winston adjusted his dainty glasses and turned toward Holden, giving him the respect to finish. "Who knows, bro. You might have said something wrong down here. Someone like you could *never* understand Shane. You probably just screwed this whole thing up."

"That's possible, Holden. Your friend discovered more than one deplorable thing in this cellar. He may never come back, it's true." Winston removed his handkerchief to wipe the bead of fretful sweat from his delicate hair line before continuing. "But that is his choice. And he will make his own decision, just like the rest of us. The one thing our group is trying to preserve is our ability to choose to read what we want and then choose if we agree with it or not, without being told that we should. Out of anything here, that fact should be the most important to you."

"You don't get what I'm saying. I understand that you want to do this...*ceremony* with everyone. I get it. Take them down here go through your whole spiel like you did with me. But it was wrong of you to cut me out of this, Winston. I don't care what you think he needed to hear. Shane is a different type of guy than you...and I could have at least interpreted things. Worded things differently, so he would understand."

"Holden. I will only speak once more and then we are through talking about this. Agreed?" He waited for Holden to nod before finding a comfortable place to sit within the dim reading nook. "You don't give Shane enough credit. He is stronger than you think. But where he may be lacking in wisdom, he makes up for in his passion and dedication to you. To your friendship. What a heart your friend has. You say you know him better than I do, and that is irrefutable, but if you knew him as well as you say you do, you wouldn't be upset with me right now. You would know that Shane needed to figure this out on his own. And that he would need to hear the truth from someone that wasn't you."

Winston's words were an arrow in Holden's chest. He was right. What Holden thought didn't matter. Shane was what mattered and Holden was acting like a child that couldn't share. He wanted to control the fate of his best friend, when that was a lesson each of them had already learned. Maybe the most important lesson thus far. Their fates rested in their own hands.

All he could do was hope that Shane's fate would bring him back.

And soon.

The small band of bibliophiles had made some interesting headway. It took three weeks, but once Moby had finished building a series of branding machines, the group separated in order to enact a multi-pronged assault on the Publishing House. They divided into three teams: Moby and Holden, Jeff and Abby, and Ephraim and Lolita. In the name of truth, they left Marion home with Winston and Ronnie and traveled to three major areas of the United States.

Moby and Holden were gone for the longest. They spent a week in New York where they branded the rooftop deck of the Empire State Building, a flashing, led-coated building in Times Square, the wall of a popular subway station, the side of a ritzy, East End condominium and, Holden's favorite of all the locations, the oversized sculpture in Central Park which displayed characters from the book *Alice's Adventures in Wonderland*. Along with a few other random locations, they thought this diversified their paraphernalia across the city. They only hoped during the tight flight home (human whales weren't the best travel-pals) that the other groups had been able to inflict as much truth-laden damage.

Jeff and Abby were perfectly successful in Los Angeles and Las Vegas while Ephraim and his wife hit Dallas with an all-night desecration tour one day and then stopped in Miami the next day for round two. It was a courageous move, they knew, but each of them realized that hitting different states on the same weekend would leave open the speculation to their numbers and they wanted people to start talking. Who would believe that the word could get out in such a way with only eight people responsible?

Winston, needing to be on the front lines in some capacity, chose to brand one of the south side elevated train stations, to keep the brand away from home, and then topped the weekend off by hitting the Sears Tower a few feet from the emblem of *The Free Thinkers*. Alone, among so many people younger than him, the adventure downtown was the highlight of the decade for Winston. And although they didn't want to come right out and associate themselves with *The Free Thinkers*, Winston thought that, in terms of publicity, it was a good move. And he was right.

When Holden and Moby returned, carrying the names of seven people Moby had met while impersonating an Unfortunate, they watched the news broadcasts as the government attempted to cover up the story of The Book by claiming that similar phrases had been stamped in other cities, including *Read The Book* and *Your Mom Reads The Book*.

It only made them laugh. Nothing the Publishing House could do to stop the word from spreading mattered. People were talking and it was smart to branch themselves out – which had been Jeff's idea. He determined that the outbreak of brands across the country during the same weekend helped them in two distinct ways: it brought a higher sense of pandemonium to those who wanted to protect the secret and it provided protection to the true location of their group. If their branding campaign was limited to the Chicagoland area, it would only be a matter of time before they were pinned down. Now, with questions out there on where the hub could be located, Moby could continue recruiting safely downtown.

After witnessing this good news, and hearing about everyone's separate adventures, Holden and Moby were on such a high that they began developing a plan to brand the famous, stainless steel bean sculpture that perched itself, ever watchful of the city, on the crest of Millennium Park. As a hotspot for Unfortunates, they agreed that it should happen soon.

And there had been more good news. In their absence, Marion, still embarrassed that she hadn't taken more pages from the bar, had followed up on one of Lolita's ideas to start generating a list of where more books could be found. Lolita and Ephraim believed that the library would eventually grow even larger and started work on a card catalog, made of leaves and bark (Ronnie called it *God's Paper*). The argument was posed that the most important thing they could do for the cause was build their collection. Lolita suggested that they should find a wall somewhere in the house where they could keep a list. That way it could be visible at all times and would remain on the forefront of their strategy. So Marion brought it upon herself, with Winston's permission, to use the ladder Moby found in the garage to write the first three ideas they had drafted near the rafters of the high-ceilinged great room. The text, made of homemade ink, was large enough that they could see it from the couch and small enough that they could spend years writing and still leave room on the wall. It was a marvel to look upon and each of them felt that Winston's home was quickly becoming the epicenter of all things free speech.

The most surprising news had been that, while Holden was in New York, Shane had been back to the house multiple times. From what Marion had seen, he would come by, sit with Winston for a while, take a book and leave. On other days, she would wake up to hear him banging away in the cellar, building better shelving. Next day, she would be out for a walk and find him hacking away in the old servant quarters, remodeling the space for some future, yet-to-be-known, tenants. It was odd, but it was his way of helping. His way of being a part of the team, without having to acknowledge Holden, just yet. There was quite a bit Shane needed to work through on his own and Holden would give him the space. It was typical, small life thinking, but sometimes swinging a hammer was the best way for a man to sort through his difficulties.

Holden knew there was a much longer road for Shane than the one he was traveling. And while he was impatient for that road to come near his own, he was forced to remind himself again that they were different people and that they may never come to the same place at the same time. But still, a great weight was lifted from his rejection-fraught shoulders. Shane knew the truth. He believed what Winston told him and he would be a part of their group, on his own terms.

Witnessing even a slight amount of success, Holden decided he could take on the world. It was time to talk to his ex-wife.

Holden stood in the slick driveway that used to be his, debating if the house his wife was trying to steal, the one he was staring at, could still, on some technical level, be called his home; taking into account that the property was still in his name, most of the furniture (the good stuff he hadn't been allowed to take) was his and it was where his only offspring prayed her bedtime prayers and drifted off to delicate dreams. Spotting the curling, floral fabric that laced the front window, he made the distinction; flat screen placement or no, that house was no longer his.

But he was far from upset. In fact, Holden could have left his van downtown that afternoon because he was flying through the murky clouds on a natural high. That afternoon Moby had allowed him to brand the bean.

The plan was easy. They needed to attack the park around midday, when it was bustling with tourists and lunch breakers. Even with the lurking Unfortunates, too many people still needed a photograph on their cell phone of their best friend in front of the bean's polished, steel bosom. People provided cover and cover provided a safe escape. After meeting up with his partner in crime, Moby Van Dinh, the tattooed whale who was now a dear friend, Holden strapped into the makeshift branding suit under the solitude of the pavilion bathrooms during a quiet, afternoon concert in the park. It was a quick process, especially after having worn it so often in New York, but Holden took his time. Branding the bean was an experience he wanted to cherish.

The machinery hung loose on his shoulders, like the holsters of a six-shooter from a time only movies could tell. It was light weight, but awkward. The bulk of the mechanics were hidden beneath his clothes, slung precariously over both kidneys, and the arrangement of wires that coursed up his shoulder and down his long sleeve shirt gave him a tickle that he needed to resist. The time for accidental giggles ended the moment he slipped the fingerless glove over his right hand. The branding iron, with the imprint of *Don't Read The Book*, was stitched into the fabric and it clasped itself easily to the inside of his palm. It was the smartest and most prudent way to exist in an unbranded world one second and a branded world the next.

After gearing up, they took their time perusing the park before mingling with the other tourists toward the bean. Moby was a hard one to miss, so he did his best to crouch whenever possible. Once beneath the silvery surface, Holden switched the power on from a button they had clipped to his belt loop. The charge had begun. Holden could feel a thrilling, electrified warmth in his palm as they carefully chose the perfect location. The spot that would forever be stained with their motto. Once they agreed with a discreet nod, Holden leaned into the cold steel and pressed his palm to its shell.

Hearing a gentle twang of anger as the molecules of the famous sculpture were forever altered was exhilarating. Holden switched the power off immediately before pressing a secondary button to activate the cooling system. As their plan suggested, Moby lifted an old digital camera and nudged his leader to a stereotypical tourist spot beside the now-blemished skin of the bean. With a ridiculous grin, Holden posed and Moby took a photograph like any other, average, run-of-the-mill, three-hundred pound sightseer.

They were gone before the flash faded from the sunless sky. Halfway down the steps, surrounded by flowers and excited patrons, over the din of delicate orchestrations that streamed from the band shell beyond, they could hear someone crying out that they had discovered another brand. The men reached the sidewalk hearing people shouting, *"Don't Read The Book!"*

The delicate trills of that music still resonated in Holden's mind as he strolled confidently to his ex-wife's door and knocked with a triumphant surety. As he waited, imagining how awkward their conversation would be, he realized that he was still wearing the glove. In all the excitement, he had forgotten to remove the branding machine. Spotting her shadow on the glass, he decided that he would have to play it cooler than he had planned.

Eve came to the door amid a tumult of raspy barking. She had gotten a dog. *New things do happen,* he supposed. As she silenced the animal, Holden could see her face through the window and he felt a surprising blend of unexpected memories and emotion.

She didn't look beautiful today. Probably because she was at home, alone. Beauty wasn't what satisfied him. In the moments before she recognized who was at the door, before her usual annoyance contorted her casual features to an attitude of disgust and irritation, Eve's face was warm and relaxed. It reminded him of the good times they shared when they were young –

before bills and car problems and doctors and daughters. He missed that Eve. The one that loved him and wanted to be loved by him. But it changed. Of course it did. The new Eve came back when she saw that Holden was the one who had come knocking. And in that moment, holding one of the three log books that contained years of editing notes from the Publishing House, Holden nurtured a single hope: that his ex-wife would allow him into the house.

Gripping back the dog, Eve opened the front door without unlocking the screen. "What do you want, Holden?" she barked through the glass.

He laughed in surprise. "Uh...to see you. To see my daughter. Can you let me in, Eve?"

His reaction was a lie. He expected this. Actually, Holden expected worse. He had been more than distant lately, nearly unreachable for weeks. Eve had left him numerous messages, threatening to file for custody, and he never called her back. He wanted to, but he didn't really know what to say. When she unlocked the screen door and returned to wherever she had come from, apparently telling him it was alright to come on in, he released a yawn of relief.

Home again, home again.

Jiggety Jig.

"Thanks for the warm welcome," he said sarcastically, entering the place that he had once called home.

Standing in the entry way, he couldn't stop scratching the back of his head. The place looked great. It was clean and organized. The furniture that he had gotten from his cousin's condo actually looked new. Eve's entire life seemed to be more in order since they'd split. Even with a humongous, overly-friendly dog that pawed at his pant leg, the smell and presence of freshly laid, lush, white carpeting made him look at his ex-wife differently. He even removed his shoes.

Where has this woman been my whole life? he thought, stating the long-established mantra of the divorcé.

After the dog was harnessed and he was standing alone in the living room with Eve, her jet black hair shining, her round face softer than he had ever seen it, her body trim and healthy, Holden walked slyly around the couch to search for evidence of his daughter. He normally found it in the form of shoes or tousled bags, but nothing was there.

"Where's our daughter?"

Eve laughed. "So predictably unreliable."

There it is, he mused.

"Jane's on her way home, Holden. She left school less than five minutes ago. You would know that if you ever paid any attention to her. What are you coming around here for, anyway?" Her voice was thick with attitude and although he knew he deserved it, there was a part of him that was glad he didn't have to hear such disappointment every day. "I hope you didn't come here thinking you're taking her for the week. I'm filing for custody. I told you that."

"I know you did."

"You look terrible," she griped. "What's happened to you?"

Holden continued to gaze around the room as if his eleven-year-old daughter hadn't been at school. He forgot how hard it was to talk to Eve, especially when she looked at him as if he were the stupidest ape on the planet. When he glanced up to speak, he saw it on her face, plain as day. The look he hated. "Well, I was hoping to talk to both of you about this. There has been a new development in my life. It's kind of a big deal and...uh..."

"What in all of God's green goodness...?" Eve's face drew back to the expression of a woman walking toward a train wreck, viewing the carnage and the rubble with revulsion. He had been expecting her usual look with pinches of disbelief, disregard and disappointment blended in and poured out through half a grin, under wrinkled eyebrows, but this was unexpected. It was at that point that Holden realized he had been speaking with cordiality and gesturing with open arms. Because he was nervous, the branding iron was exposed.

"*You* did that? It's all over the news. A bunch of different buildings across the country have that stamp. You're a part of that? You're a terrorist? And the bean? Were you involved in that too? We took pictures there on our wedding day!"

"This...uh...I did not want it to start this way."

The door opened. The dog erupted in excitement and Eve caught the animal mid-stride, yanking him back by the collar.

"Dad!" Jane hollered, dropping her bag and racing up to her father. He gave her the tightest hug he could without harming her and lifted his daughter into the air, being careful to guard her from the branding iron that was cupped in his hand. "Are you staying? Are you staying?" Her legs fluttered up in newfound contentment.

He nestled his nose in her cheek and kissed her. "Yeah, honey. I'm going to be here for a while, I think."

"Jane," Eve blurted, chewing on her tongue. "Get your stuff and go to your room. Your dad and I need to talk."

It hadn't been that long since her father had left and Jane knew what that voice meant. She wanted to gripe about it, but she also knew what action would follow if she didn't listen and obey. So Jane smiled up at her father and lifted her bags from the floor. "Don't leave without telling me, okay?"

THE BOOK

"I won't, sweetheart," he said, noticing the sheer innocence in her eyes.

His daughter had grown up so fast. He wished he could slow things down and just enjoy her. He wanted to sit beside her on the couch and mumble about many unimportant things, but Eve's discomfort reminded him of why he had come. So, with apology, he let her go. The moment Jane was out of earshot, Eve clamped her teeth down on her tongue, took three long strides up to Holden and jabbed a finger into his gut.

"What are you up to?" she growled, unfairly. "Whatever it is, don't you dare bring it into this house. That girl trusts you. She believes in you. There is so much I would just *love* to tell her about who you really are, but I'm allowing her to see you as a responsible man, no matter how make-believe it is. Do not make that for nothing and do not make me regret it."

"Eve, listen. What I'm a part of...it's huge. What I've seen and realized over the past few weeks..." He reached for her hand, but she drew it back. He had forgotten about the branding iron again. He had also forgotten that divorced couples don't hold hands. "I've brought this log book here to show you. You're favorite book is still *The Patchwork Girl of Oz* by Baum, right?"

"What? What does that have to do with –"

"Just answer the question."

"Sure," she replied, adjusting her composure at the distressing reminder that he still knew so many of her most intimate secrets. Eve didn't like realizing that, while she could erase him as much as possible from her future, he would always be a crucial piece of her past. "Of course it is, Holden."

"Well, think back to the brand you saw on the news," he began, on his way to the kitchen counter where he powered up the ancient log book. "What saying did we brand into the building?"

"*Don't Read The Book,*" she recalled. "Makes no sense."

"Wait, let me explain." He spun the screen and waved her over. "This is a digital log I...got...from an Editor of The Publishing House."

"Editors? What are you talking about?."

"A lot is going on and those details don't matter. I want to read you something, okay? Will you let me read you something?"

"Fine," she huffed reluctantly, pulling up one of her taller stools as he struggled to navigate the log book without a sharpened fingernail.

Holden stared into Eve's wide-arcing eyes and waited for her fullest attention. After making the decision to reach out to her, he had searched the logs for any alterations Winston's mother had made to Eve's favorite book. What he found was surprising.

"Here we go. *'January fifteenth. Harold asked me to search the contents of another book by Lyman Frank Baum, THE PATCHWORK GIRL OF OZ. Reason was more obscure than last time. Instructed to remove all references to character named Hip Hopper denoting himself as a 'Champion'. Articles removed from pages 267 to 291, including chapter title from page 17. Red was recruited to assist in removal of the word 'Champion' from decorative chapter art drawn at the start of chapter 21 on page 267. Project scheduled for completion by January seventeenth. Sample recorded from personal collection. Click here for sample.'*"

"Holden, what is this?"

"Let me get through a little more," he urged, before continuing. "*'July the twenty-fourth. Returning to PATCHWORK GIRL by L. Frank Baum. Ann O. consulted on addition of green as main color in self-description provided by Patchwork Girl on line four of page 69. Sample recorded from personal collection. Click here for sample.*

THE BOOK

"'January fifteenth. Revisiting PATCHWORK by Baum one year after initial alterations. Red recruited once more to augment illustration art from page 107. Supplement circular sketchy representations of the ground surrounding the tree beside cobbled path to resemble the vertical words NO JURISDICTION. Project schedule for completion by February the first. Original page scanned from personal collection. Click here for original.

"'May. One too many edits to dictate. Will be concise and detail structure and purpose of augmentations versus content of THE PATCHWORK GIRL OF OZ by L. Frank Baum. The entire setting of the story from pages...'"

Holden felt a tender hand on his knee and he glanced up from the screen of the log book to find Eve looking frightened and confused. Without a word, she urged Holden to stop.

"Just one more. It's long, but I think it will make everything come together for you." Eve bit her bottom lip. She pulled her hand from his knee and looked away. Holden continued. "'August thirtieth. Sudden drastic edit of THE PATCHWORK GIRL OF OZ by Lyman Frank Baum after six-year hiatus. Completely unexplained deletion of chapter ending between pages 198-201 as well as references to laws of fictitious world being declared as 'Foolish' from pages 229 and 230. Ann O. sub-contracted to generate smooth transition between words. Project scheduled for immediate action. Sample recorded from personal collection. Click here for sample.'"

Holden tapped the screen, heard the hesitation in Eve's breathing and read the sample passage that Winston's mother had recorded.

"'Ojo was much astonished, for not only was this unlike any prison he had ever heard of, but he was being treated more as a guest than a criminal. There were many windows and they had no locks. There were three doors to the room and none were bolted.

He cautiously opened one of the doors and found it led into a hallway. But he had no intention of trying to escape. If his jailor was willing to trust him in this way he would not betray her trust, and moreover a hot supper was being prepared for him and his prison was very pleasant and comfortable. So he took a book from the case and sat down in a big chair to look at the pictures.

This amused him until the woman came in with a large tray and spread a cloth on one of the tables. Then she arranged his supper, which proved the most varied and delicious meal Ojo had ever eaten in his life.

Tollydiggle sat near him while he ate, sewing on some fancy work she held in her lap. When he had finished she cleared the table and then read to him a story from one of the books.

'Is this really a prison?' he asked, when she had finished reading.

'Indeed it is,' she replied. 'It is the only prison in the Land of Oz.'

'And am I a prisoner?'

'Bless the child! Of course.'

'Then why is the prison so fine, and why are you so kind to me?' he earnestly asked.

Tollydiggle seemed surprised by the question, but she presently answered:

'We consider a prisoner unfortunate. He is unfortunate in two ways – because he has done something wrong and because he is deprived of his liberty. Therefore we should treat him kindly, because of his misfortune, for otherwise he would become hard and bitter and would not be sorry he had done wrong. Ozma thinks that one who has committed a fault did so because he was not strong and brave. When that is accomplished he is no longer a prisoner, but a good and loyal citizen and everyone is glad that he is now strong enough to resist doing wrong. You see, it is kindness *that makes one strong and brave; and so we are kind to our prisoners.'*

Ojo thought this over very carefully. 'I had an idea,' said he, 'that prisoners were always treated harshly, to punish them.'

'That would be dreadful!' cried Tollydiggle. 'Isn't one punished enough in knowing he has done wrong? Don't you wish, Ojo, with all your heart, that you had not been disobedient and broken the Law of Oz?'

'I – I hate to be different from other people,' he admitted.

'Yes; one likes to be respected as highly as his neighbors are,' said the woman. 'When you are tried and found guilty, you will be obliged to make amends, in some way. I don't know just what Ozma will do to you, because this is the first time one of us has broken a Law, but you may be sure she will be just and merciful. Here in the Emerald City people are too happy and contented ever to do wrong; but perhaps you came from some faraway corner of our land, and having no love for Ozma carelessly broke one of her Laws.'

'Yes,' said Ojo, 'I've lived all my life in the heart of a lonely forest, where I saw no one but dear Unc. Nunkie.'

'I thought so,' said Tollydiggle. 'But now we have talked enough, so let us play a game until bedtime.'"

Holden switched the log book off and stood from the table to get a drink of water. He opened the cabinet where the glasses used to be and found it stocked with cans of soup and vegetables. Allowing Eve a chance to process what just happened, he walked the square of his old kitchen in search of the glasses and eventually discovered them in the cabinet above the sink.

"What," Eve attempted, over the splash of tap water. "What are you telling me? The Publishing House is changing the stories without telling us?" Holden sipped from his glass, nodding. "But why?"

"Why do you think, Eve?"

She knew why, but she didn't want to say. From the moment Holden walked into her house, she had been off guard. In fact, she had been folding laundry when the doorbell rang. Eve hadn't been expecting such mind-shifting knowledge and especially to come from him. The man standing in front of her, the one with concern on his face that looked too happy to be worried, was not the same man she had married. He was different. He was confident.

Holden set down his glass, looked back and, for the first time in years, saw the Eve he knew as a child. Soft, precious, gracious and kind hearted, but most of all, fragile. The news he had just delivered had launched her mind into a realm it was never prepared to go, and it frightened her. But, at the same time, he saw the new Eve. The one that plotted and contemplated. The one that was able to get half of his paycheck and possibly sole custody of their daughter. As each second passed, she was taking steps to protect herself. He could see the battle behind her ebony lashes and hazel eyes. She was already compromising. Telling herself that she shouldn't believe because believing meant change and change wasn't always a good thing.

I mean, look around, Eve, she was thinking. *You just got your life back in order. The carpet guy just finished three days ago.*

Holden knew Eve had been wondering what would happen if she listened any further. He was wondering the same thing. How would her life be altered if he read another passage? Would she be able to stop from caring? Would she unknowingly welcome the change that would kill the *new* Eve? This was precisely the thought that forced her to place her hand on Holden's knee. She couldn't allow herself to hear any more.

THE BOOK

This was an important moment in her life. Holden saw the moment in drips of seconds and he knew exactly what to say.

He took a breath before beginning.

"Eve, do you remember when we were dating...when you first told me about what had happened to your grandmother? Do you remember where we were that day and how...?"

The phone rang.

Eve, limp and vulnerable, didn't hear it until the second ring. Then, as if her heart were suddenly pierced with a syringe of adrenaline, she fell from the stool, pivoted on her heels and dove for the rattling cell phone. In one long word, she spat, *"Sorry-Holden-I-have-to-take-this."*

Holden relaxed his shoulders. He smiled. It hadn't taken long to break through the ice, to breach its hard, cold exterior, and he was proud for making himself susceptible enough to failure. Watching Eve skip into the next room, he pictured her and Jane at Winston's and, for a moment, felt a tinge of guilt. How would Marion feel? What would this do to his relationship with her? Not that they were in a relationship, because they weren't, but there had been something going on between them, hadn't there? How would they relate to one another with his ex-wife in the same room? Marion couldn't leave. And if Eve were suddenly over all the time, how would Marion feel? Oh, but Jane. If he could see Jane everyday, how special everything would be.

Knowing she was only a staircase away, Holden left the room to find his daughter, gripping the log book with confidence. He navigated the hallways and up the stairs to the one room he had missed more than any other; but when he reached the threshold, he felt as if he'd been in a coma for the past four years. Everything had changed. Her bedroom was different. The furniture, the paint on the walls, the animals on the bed. Different without Dad. He wondered what choices Jane had made on her own and which ones Eve had orchestrated. *What else could he expect? He never comes over anymore.*

When he came to pick up Jane (when he remembered to pick her up) he pulled his van into the driveway and waited. Normally, Eve dropped her off at the toothpaste house he called home. Whenever she was over, he made the bed for her and placed out the one stuffed animal he had bought at a filling station so she could have a friend to sleep next to. But, without fail, they always ended up in the living room – him in his easy chair, her on the couch and the stuffed animal somewhere amongst the folds of her blanket. Jane would have preferred the comforts of his bed to the coils of his couch, but she never wanted to leave his side. He hoped that love of Daddy would never fade, but her bedroom was telling him different. It was the room of a young girl on the way to young womanhood.

Holden was suddenly longing for the days and hours he had missed out on. How he wanted those back. How he would change things if he could.

Jane caught him in the corner of her eye. She pulled her headphones from her ears and spun, her cropped curly hair bouncing as she shined a bright smile and leapt out of her desk chair to hug him once more. "Daddy, I didn't hear you. Why were you waiting at the door? You could have come in."

"Well..." he said, kissing the crown of her bushy head. To his nose, which often carried the stench of pipe dope laced with threading grease, she still smelled like a newborn. "I didn't want to interrupt you."

"Oh, Daddy. You can be so silly sometimes."

"You working on something there?"

"For school," she answered pleasantly. "Come see."

She reached for his hand and he gave her the left, awkwardly. Although the branding iron had cooled rapidly after shutdown

THE BOOK

hours prior, he didn't want to take any chances with his baby. Jane led him to her new desk (it had the wear and tear of a few years which meant that it was only new to him - another reminder of how much he had missed), and showed him pictures that she had drawn with her digital sketch book. Intricate sketches of animals with bodies that swirled into lines and odd three-dimensional shapes. She forced him to admire each one independently and put him on the spot to hear his artistic assessment. Every time that he said, *"How pretty,"* she would interrupt him with a tilted head of disappointment. Holden just adored the way she would say, *"Dad,"* by breaking the name down in two, distinct vocal registers. *Da-ad* was a rollercoaster drop from high to low. After such drama, he would then, of course, over-elaborate until she rolled her eyes, shook her head and scrolled on to the next picture.

When they were finished studying her newest drawings, Jane tugged him over to her bed where he had left the digital log book and pulled her backpack up to his lap. He admired the many patches that danced irregularly along the straps and between the zippers as she scrounged for something important to show him. His smile faded when he saw what it was. Jane took out a very compact, very sleek version of The Book. His joyous occasion with his daughter suddenly became a stark, hope-drifting nightmare as Holden was gifted with an evocatively honest realization. Jane was still reading The Book. Of course she was. Every day at school.

Holden watched as she flipped it open without fear and, with a sharpened pointer finger, swirled rapidly through the menus on the ever-bland screen. There were swoops, taps, double taps and then, as if by magic, a story by Charles Dickens was upon them. And Jane, his trusting, pure, faithful daughter, was telling him all about the characters that he knew so very well.

"I know how much you love Dickens, Dad," she piped, rolling through the chapters.

"Yeah," he said, slowly accepting the sorrow of what was before him. *He did love Dickens, right? Or was it Ann O. the Editor's best friend that he liked?* Maybe his favorite lines had simply been nothing more than her subcontracted transitions. He didn't love the words of Charles Dickens. He loved The Book's abridged interpretation of Charles Dickens. He loved only what they wanted him to love. Holden stopped listening to her questions in the shock of such a thought. Jane noticed when he stopped commenting. Then she saw that his fingernail wasn't as sharpened as it normally had been and went to inspect it. That was when it happened. The catalyst that brought on the most memorable moment in the rest of his daughter's life.

The screen went dark.

The recycling icon of The Book appeared for a moment, animating, until it dissolved peacefully and the words *Update in Progress* swam in pixels to the screen in a plain script. Holden's jaw slackened and he reached for The Book while his daughter muttered, "Awhh, I hate it when this happens. It's like all the time now, right? That must annoy you, Daddy." Jane's eyes trailed down to his finger again. It hadn't been left unsharpened. His fingernail had been clipped. Retracted back to the level of the others. Her father was wearing a declaration of the non-reader. "I know how much you love The Book."

Jane watched as his face slowly tightened, his teeth grinding below clenched lips, his eyebrows knitting above the bridge of his once-busted nose. His grip on her Book grew so frighteningly strong that his knuckles were whitening. In the calmest manner imaginable, Holden drawled, "Where does your mother keep her copies of The Book?"

"Dad? Are you okay?"

THE BOOK

"Jane. Answer me," he said, his voice like steel in the quiet of the room.

"There's two in the table beside her bed. And there's another one that she tried to throw away last year. I think it's the one you gave her, but...I took it out of the garbage. I'm sorry." Based on the look in her father's eyes, a look she had never seen before that frightened years from her life, Jane rambled off its location, along with the question she needed an answer to, in a single, hasty word. *"It's-in-my-closet-on-top-of-my-sweater-why-is-everything-okay?"*

"No, Jane. Everything is not okay."

Holden rose like a machine from the edge of her tiny bed with a single task to achieve before self-destruction. Without considering the delicacy of sliding doors, he tore them open and began rummaging wildly through her closet. The image of him wrenching sweaters off their shelves and shirts from their hangers welded itself to her mind, where it found a place to hide forever.

"Have I done something wrong, Daddy?"

"No," he wheezed, finding the Book he had purchased for Eve on their first anniversary. He tossed it into the hallway, dropped to his knees and took Jane's face in his left hand, repeating, "No, sweetheart. You haven't done anything wrong. Daddy just needs to do this right now."

Ravenous with the desire to destroy all the Books he could find, Holden sped into Eve's bedroom and tore open her side table. He would not allow such blatant mind control to rest within thirty feet of his daughter ever again. He found the other two quickly and returned to the hallway for the third, where he stood at the top of the stairs, searching blankly for a solution. He took Jane's Book from her hands as his eyes darted in every direction.

It couldn't be water. Water simply wouldn't do the trick anymore. Most hand held computers had an internal, waterproof sheet and drainage system to protect the logic board, hard disk and other components. Everyone knew that. Even if that system was compromised, Eve could easily have the device fixed. And it would take too long to smash them. She could already be off the phone.

"Microwave!" Holden announced, like a mad scientist at the birth of a haunting invention. He raced down the stairs with Jane at his heels and into the kitchen where he tossed the books onto the countertop, yanked open the microwave and threw them onto the lid of a defrosting casserole. The sound of them clanging and clattering against the inside made Eve race into the kitchen with the cell phone at her ear.

"Holden! What are you doing?"

"These Books are controlling you, Eve. You can't have them in the house anymore." He punched the keys for maximum power and pressed start. The reaction between the screens was instantaneous. Sparks scattered from behind the small window. A puff of smoke broke through the hinge of the closest spine. There came a random series of pops and suddenly flames were billowing from each of the plastic corners. Within seconds, the entire microwave was a cloud of brackish smoke and light from angry flames of neon green.

Eve dropped her phone and propelled herself toward the microwave. "Jane get out of here! Your father's going insane."

She began to cry. "Daddy?"

He turned and lowered himself to her level. "Everything's fine now, sweetie," Holden whispered, as Eve erupted at the disarray, grabbed what was left of his water glass and launched it onto the molten remains. The liquid succeeded in dousing the flames, but the puff of acrid stink it sent to her face also met the smoke detector in the hall.

"What have you done?" she asked over the shrill scream of the alarm. "That was my mother's Book, you jerk! I can't believe you just did that!"

Holden grasped his daughter's shoulders and leaned forward, locking himself in her eyes as he prepared to speak slowly and intentionally. Things were about to change. Eve was going to make him leave and he wouldn't know when the next chance to tell his daughter about the Book would come. But as he prepared to explain everything as simply as he could, a noise came from the driveway. Doors were closing. Multiple doors. He peeked over at Eve and her face shifted. A small laugh escaped her mouth. And then she shrugged.

"What did you do, Eve?" Holden asked, fully aware that she had been downstairs, alone, for a long time. Slowly, he stood, his cautious, unblinking eyes judging her tightened body language. He pulled from it many familiar truths before asking the obvious. "Who did you call?"

A knock came at the front door. The simple confession of its aggressiveness confirmed all that she had done.

"You know...I...when you first started talking to me, you made a little bit of sense, but Holden, this is scary what you've done. And...you know what? You're...you're scaring me."

"Eve," Holden began, his face stripped of emotion in such immediate surprise. "You just killed me." The unmasked honesty of his words disturbed her and, seeing a different man standing in her living room than the one she had married, Eve felt certain that he was telling the truth. "Do you realize what you have just done? To me. To yourself. To *our daughter?* Do you have *any idea what you've just done?*"

"Yeah, I know what I've done," she replied stubbornly.

"No, Eve. Truth is you'll never know. In your wildest dreams you could never understand the depth of it."

Now, faced with the dark visage of inevitability, the simple pipe fitter was poetic.

Holden lowered himself to his daughter for the third time. She was shaking with dread. As voices came to the door, he found, deep within himself, a calmness that was foreign to her and he brushed the fingers of his left hand over her ear. The people at the door were wrenching on the handle of the screen and Holden was grateful for unconscious deeds. He had been so used to locking the screen when he lived there, that the involuntary action had bought him some time. Well, it bought him half a minute.

Holden took a breath, locked himself in his daughter's eyes again and said, "I love you, Jane. Whatever they say about me...don't believe it. It's all lies. Don't read The Book, Jane. It's being controlled."

The door broke open.

Holden saw, from the corner of his teary vision, three men wearing dark suits and green striped ties with blonde, delicately cropped hair. Their sharp, green eyes locked onto him and one of the robotic men smiled and said, "If it isn't the Tin Soldier."

He had seconds. Pieces of seconds.

"Don't listen to them, Jane," he said, standing with awkward abruptness as the men approached. She nodded and Eve yanked her to the kitchen. "Whatever they say about your father, don't listen to them."

"I won't, Daddy." Jane blinked, tears streaming in bullets from her eyes.

"Look at me, Jane," he cried, "I want to tell you everything is going to be alright. For you and your friends...and your friend's families...but I can't..."

THE BOOK

Holden felt the grip of many arms as the men seized him by the shoulders. Jane shrieked and Eve clamored to shield her daughter's eyes. Holden struggled against their grip like an untamed tiger. Under their sudden weight, while they grappled for a piece of Holden they could restrain, he turned to see Eve's face and the immediate regret that rested there. She was frightened. She was guilty. What was happening in her home, in her living room, was wrong. But there was nothing she could do to stop it at that point. Those men hadn't come to take her husband away for questioning. They were fighting him. By calling the police, she had done something horribly wrong and, as she watched them struggle to take him to the ground, Eve already knew that Holden was right. She would never see him again.

One of the larger men let go of Holden's arm to reach one of his legs and, in the process, accidentally switched on the branding machine. There was no noise or light to indicate that it had happened. Holden knew because he felt his palm growing warm. As another man, a mass of neckless meat, strolled casually into the room holding a stun gun, Holden reacted in the only way that made sense. He loosened his right shoulder, swung his palm at the man and it caught him directly in the face.

There was a guttural wail. The man jackknifed away with a hand clutched to his smoking face The others, entirely confused by what had happened during the struggle, loosened their grip and Holden pushed himself free. Eve had done the same with Jane and the young girl ran. At that moment, all her eleven-year-old mind understood was that she wanted to lock herself onto her father, hoping that the presence of a little girl would make the bad men leave him alone. That they would see her crying, hear her plea and leave. What did happen was altogether different.

As Jane rushed forward, one of the men shoved her powerfully into the dumpy couch. Holden retaliated with mad rage, kicking the man in the stomach and bashing his jaw to fragments with a sturdy left hook. After hearing one of their own screaming a high-pitched alien squeal of utterly agonizing pain, two other Agents had entered the house. When they saw their comrade on the floor gripping his face, the cyborgian men joined the others in an attempt to lock Holden in place. The Agents strode boldly across the carpeting, their faces maddening and their shoes working traces of filth into the fresh, white fibers.

In a last ditch effort, Holden flailed, kicked and wriggled in place, knowing the fight that was coming. He used his weight to take two of them down, but there were three more grappling for his limbs. He was so aggressive and too focused on taking it to them in a desperate attempt to get away, too lost in the hope of freedom, that he didn't notice where his right arm was swinging.

Jane hadn't seen it coming either.

She didn't know what her father had in his hand. She had seen him hit the man that was still squirming on the floor in pain, but hadn't tried to understand. That man, whose tie was ribboned through his shivering fingers, had been holding his face and she knew he was hurt. But when her father's struggling arm swung and caught her across the chest, all Jane knew was the sting. The pain as his palm collided with her before she was launched into the coffee table, her nylon t-shirt melted to her skin.

Things were moving so quickly. Holden didn't know who he had hit. His strategy was to swing at everything and hope for the best. But when he heard the sound that escaped his daughter's lips, he turned and screamed.

"Jane! No! *NO!*"

THE BOOK

His eyes gushed with tears, the instant he saw that innocent face staring back at him with eyes that only asked why, as pain she had never imagined launched itself into her chest and wouldn't go away no matter how hard she focused or how loud she cried out or how insanely she writhed.

Holden knew the man had risen from the floor, but he wasn't looking and he didn't care. The neckless Agent with burns across his face was approaching with a wail in his voice that was louder than the smoke alarm and wilder still than the dog that howled in the next room, but all Holden heard was his daughter as she scratched violently at her shirt. When the man came close, Holden could hear the sound of his teeth gnashing in vengeance, he could see the stun gun in the man's hand and closed his eyes, welcoming the sweet shock of unconsciousness. For, in the volts it would bring, he would not have to hear the pain he had inflicted on his daughter.

Ever again.

Holden couldn't remember why his face was so cold. How often did he forget things? He felt so stupid. It was like every day he was forgetting something new. Where could he go from here? Vitamins. He never took his vitamins. Maybe if someone came out with a beer that was infused with vitamins. But then, that didn't explain why his face was so cold, did it? Numb almost. As he pushed himself up to settle his sleepy mind, an image of Jane's face –

Holden thunderbolted to an upright stance, locked his knees and yanked his eyes open with a voice-cracking shriek. A sudden dizziness overtook him and he lost his balance. He tried to remain standing, but his shoes were missing and he fell back to where he had been sitting. Laying. A dull gong of cold metal and a tiny scratch swept the room around him as he pushed himself up, blinking every millisecond to adjust his eyes to the brightness.

His shoes. Where were his shoes?
Eve's carpet was new. He took them off at the door.
If his shoes were there, where was he?

THE BOOK

He was in a room. A large, white-walled room with no windows, standing on a lush, loop pile green carpet that resembled a lawn of grass below a ceiling painted in sky blue. He couldn't recall how he had gotten there and, from the way his vision was swimming, assumed that he had been drugged. Despite his complete dislocation, he felt eerily comfortable. At peace. There were no clouds painted in blurry cotton balls of white or hokey drawings of trees on the walls, but he wasn't stupid. Holden knew that the materials and colors chosen throughout the room, even down to the brown metal bench he had slept upon, were all chosen for the specific task of keeping the room's occupants calm. This realization quickly increased his tension.

Why did he need to be calm?

Holden rolled his shoulders. He was sore all throughout his body and he was wearing the same clothes he had worn when he arrived at Eve's. Although he was lighter now, wasn't he...? Yes, the shoes. But, more importantly, the branding machine had been removed along with his wallet and watch. Even the change from his pockets was missing. He was left in a mysterious indoor park with nothing but the clothes on his back, with socks that had holes in the toes. Holden cracked his neck and stood up to look around the room for some identification of where he was, steadying himself as the dizziness returned. Those men who had taken him were Agents from the Publishing House, he knew that. At least that was how they had described themselves before taking him for a stroll through Lincoln Park on an oh-so-sunny day.

Thanks again for the umbrella, guys. First you try to kill me with a cold and then...this. Whatever this is.

Along the shortest wall, there was a rectangular window as tall as him that didn't reach the ground. It stepped out from the flat, white surface with a smooth, metal edge that beveled toward a vibrantly glossy, black-green glass. It seemed to hang like a bedroom mirror and as Holden approached it, he could see his reflection in the darkness. He touched the smooth surface lightly and the window awoke. The black-green glass morphed to the most peaceful white. Holden stepped back a few paces and noticed as the recycling icon of the Publishing House gently broke through the white like a rising bubble in a bottle of milk. The curved, brown arrows that coiled in a triangle wove like silent, hungry snakes, bound for eternity to chase one another's tails. Noiseless and slow, they followed the one before them.

Holden believed, at that moment, that if he continued to watch the icon weaving on the milky screen, he would be drawn into it. Before long he would be a different person. He would be one of The Book's foremost defenders. One of its abdicators, leading the cheering section for technology and convenience. All this was in his head, of course (of course), but wasn't that where the triangle of arrows was attempting to bore its way into?

Standing before the black-green glass, gazing strangely into its depths, Holden felt at once that if he was in that space, that outdoor room, for more than an hour, staring at that stupid icon, he would lose himself in anger and break the glass with his elbow. Maybe his head. Whatever would stop the spinning. Because it seemed to laugh at him. It seemed to stand before him, crisp behind its unblemished frame in that clean, vacuumed environment, laughing the words: REDUCE REUSE RECYCLE.

REDUCE REUSE RECYCLE.
RECYCLE.
RECYCLE.
RECYCLE.

THE BOOK

RECYCLE

M. CLIFFORD

RECYCLE
RECYCLE

THE BOOK

RECYCLE RECYCLE
RECYCLE
RECYCLE

RECYCLE
RECYCLE RECYCLE RECYCLE RECYCLE
RECYCLE RECYCLE
RECYCLE
RECYCLE

THE BOOK

RECYCLE RECYCLE
RECYCLE RECYCLE
RECYCLE RECYCLE
RECYCLE

RECYCLE recycle RECYCLE REDUCE REUSE RECYCLE RECYCLE
RECYCLE RECYCLE

THE BOOK

RECYCLE RECYCLE RECYCLE RECYCLE RECYCLE RECYCLE RECYCLE RECYCLE YOUR PAPER BOOKS RECYCLE RECYCLE RECYCLE RECYCLE RECYCLE RECYCLE RECYCLE RECYCLE RECYCLE RECYCLE RECYCLE RECYCLE RECYCLE RECYCLE
RECYCLE RECYCLE RECYCLE RECYCLE RECYCLE RECYCLE
RECYCLE RECYCLE RECYCLE RECYCLE RECYCLE RECYCLE
RECYCLE RECYCLE RECYCLE RECYCLE RECYCLE RECYCLE
RECYCLE RECYCLE RECYCLE RECYCLE RECYCLE RECYCLE
RECYCLE RECYCLE RECYCLE RECYCLE RECYCLE RECYCLE
RECYCLE RECYCLE RECYCLE RECYCLE RECYCLE RECYCLE
RECYCLE RECYCLE RECYCLE RECYCLE RECYCLE RECYCLE
RECYCLE RECYCLE RECYCLE RECYCLE RECYCLE RECYCLE
RECYCLE RECYCLE RECYCLE RECYCLE RECYCLE RECYCLE
RECYCLE RECYCLE RECYCLE RECYCLE RECYCLE RECYCLE
RECYCLE MOTHER EARTH NEEDS YOU TO RECYCLE RECYCLE RECYCLE RECYCLE RECYCLE RECYCLE RECYCLE RECYCLE
RECYCLE RECYCLE RECYCLE RECYCLE RECYCLE RECYCLE
RECYCLE RECYCLE RECYCLE RECYCLE RECYCLE RECYCLE
RECYCLE RECYCLE RECYCLE RECYCLE RECYCLE RECYCLE
RECYCLE RECYCLE RECYCLE RECYCLE RECYCLE RECYCLE
RECYCLE RECYCLE RECYCLE RECYCLE RECYCLE RECYCLE
RECYCLE RECYCLE recycle RECYCLE RECYCLE RECYCLE
RECYCLE RECYCLE RECYCLE RECYCLE RECYCLE RECYCLE
RECYCLE RECYCLE RECYCLE recycle RECYCLE RECYCLE
RECYCLE RECYCLE RECYCLE RECYCLE RECYCLE RECYCLE
RECYCLE RECYCLE RECYCLE REDUCE REUSE RECYCLE RECYCLE
RECYCLE RECYCLE RECYCLE RECYCLE RECYCLE RECYCLE
RECYCLE RECYCLE RECYCLE RECYCLE RECYCLE RECYCLE
RECYCLE RECYCLE RECYCLE RECYCLE RECYCLE RECYCLE
RECYCLE RECYCLE RECYCLE RECYCLE RECYCLE RECYCLE

RECYCLE RECYCLE RECYCLE RECYCLE RECYCLE RECYCLE
RECYCLE RECYCLE recycle RECYCLE RECYCLE RECYCLE
RECYCLE RECYCLE RECYCLE RECYCLE RECYCLE RECYCLE
RECYCLE RECYCLE RECYCLE RECYCLE RECYCLE RECYCLE
RECYCLE RECYCLE RECYCLE RECYCLE RECYCLE RECYCLE
RECYCLE REDUCE REUSE RECYCLE RECYCLE
RECYCLE RECYCLE RECYCLE RECYCLE RECYCLE RECYCLE
RECYCLE RECYCLE RECYCLE RECYCLE RECYCLE RECYCLE
RECYCLE RECYCLE RECYCLE RECYCLE RECYCLE RECYCLE
RECYCLE RECYCLE RECYCLE RECYCLE RECYCLE RECYCLE
RECYCLE RECYCLE RECYCLE RECYCLE RECYCLE RECYCLE
RECYCLE RECYCLE RECYCLE RECYCLE RECYCLE recycle
RECYCLE RECYCLE RECYCLE RECYCLE RECYCLE RECYCLE
RECYCLE RECYCLE RECYCLE RECYCLE RECYCLE RECYCLE
RECYCLE RECYCLE RECYCLE RECYCLE RECYCLE RECYCLE
RECYCLE RECYCLE RECYCLE RECYCLE RECYCLE RECYCLE
RECYCLE RECYCLE RECYCLE
RECYCLE RECYCLE RECYCLE RECYCLE RECYCLE RECYCLE
RECYCLE RECYCLE RECYCLE RECYCLE RECYCLE RECYCLE
RECYCLE RECYCLE RECYCLE RECYCLE RECYCLE RECYCLE
RECYCLE RECYCLE RECYCLE RECYCLE RECYCLE RECYCLE
RECYCLE RECYCLE RECYCLE RECYCLE RECYCLE RECYCLE
RECYCLE RECYCLE RECYCLE RECYCLE RECYCLE RECYCLE
RECYCLE RECYCLE RECYCLE RECYCLE recycle RECYCLE
RECYCLE RECYCLE RECYCLE reuse RECYCLE RECYCLE
RECYCLE RECYCLE reduce RECYCLE RECYCLE RECYCLE
RECYCLE RECYCLE RECYCLE reuse RECYCLE RECYCLE
RECYCLE RECYCLE RECYCLE RECYCLE recycle RECYCLE
RECYCLE RECYCLE RECYCLE read RECYCLE RECYCLE
RECYCLE RECYCLE reduce RECYCLE RECYCLE RECYCLE
RECYCLE RECYCLE RECYCLE reuse RECYCLE RECYCLE
RECYCLE RECYCLE RECYCLE RECYCLE read RECYCLE

THE BOOK

RECYCLE RECYCLE RECYCLE RECYCLE RECYCLE RECYCLE
RECYCLE RECYCLE RECYCLE RECYCLE RECYCLE RECYCLE
RECYCLE READ RECYCLE RECYCLE RECYCLE RECYCLE
RECYCLE RECYCLE RECYCLE RECYCLE RECYCLE RECYCLE
RECYCLE RECYCLE RECYCLE RECYCLE RECYCLE RECYCLE
RECYCLE RECYCLE RECYCLE RECYCLE RECYCLE RECYCLE
RECYCLE RECYCLE RECYCLE REREAD RECYCLE RECYCLE
RECYCLE RECYCLE RECYCLE RECYCLE RECYCLE RECYCLE
RECYCLE RECYCLE RECYCLE RECYCLE RECYCLE RECYCLE
RECYCLE RECYCLE RECYCLE RECYCLE RECYCLE RECYCLE
RECYCLE RECYCLE RECYCLE RECYCLE RECYCLE RECYCLE
RECYCLE RECYCLE RECYCLE RECYCLE RECYCLE RECYCLE
RECYCLE RECYCLE RECYCLE RECYCLE RECYCLE RECYCLE
RECYCLE RECYCLE RECYCLE RECYCLE RECYCLE RECYCLE
RECYCLE RECYCLE recycle RECYCLE RECYCLE RECYCLE
RECYCLE RECYCLE RECYCLE RECYCLE RECYCLE RECYCLE
RECYCLE RECYCLE RECYCLE RECYCLE RECYCLE RECYCLE
RECYCLE RECYCLE RECYCLE RECYCLE RECYCLE RECYCLE
RECYCLE RECYCLE RECYCLE REDUCE REUSE RECYCLE
RECYCLE RECYCLE RECYCLE RECYCLE RECYCLE RECYCLE
RECYCLE RECYCLE RECYCLE RECYCLE RECYCLE RECYCLE
RECYCLE RECYCLE RECYCLE RECYCLE RECYCLE RECYCLE
RECYCLE RECYCLE RECYCLE RECYCLE RECYCLE RECYCLE
RECYCLE RECYCLE RECYCLE RECYCLE RECYCLE RECYCLE
RECYCLE DON'T WASTE YOUR RESOURCES RECYCLE RECYCLE
RECYCLE RECYCLE RECYCLE RECYCLE RECYCLE RECYCLE
RECYCLE RECYCLE RECYCLE RECYCLE RECYCLE RECYCLE
RECYCLE RECYCLE RECYCLE RECYCLE RECYCLE RECYCLE
RECYCLE RECYCLE RECYCLE RECYCLE RECYCLE RECYCLE
RECYCLE RECYCLE RECYCLE RECYCLE RECYCLE RECYCLE
RECYCLE RECYCLE RECYCLE RECYCLE RECYCLE RECYCLE

RECYCLE RECYCLE RECYCLE RECYCLE RECYCLE RECYCLE
RECYCLE RECYCLE RECYCLE RECYCLE RECYCLE RECYCLE
IT'S UP TO YOU TO RECYCLE RECYCLE RECYCLE RECYCLE
RECYCLE RECYCLE RECYCLE RECYCLE RECYCLE RECYCLE
RECYCLE RECYCLE RECYCLE RECYCLE RECYCLE RECYCLE
RECYCLE RECYCLE RECYCLE RECYCLE RECYCLE RECYCLE
RECYCLE RECYCLE RECYCLE RECYCLE RECYCLE RECYCLE
RECYCLE RECYCLE RECYCLE RECYCLE RECYCLE RECYCLE
RECYCLE RECYCLE RECYCLE RECYCLE RECYCLE RECYCLE
RECYCLE RECYCLE RECYCLE RECYCLE RECYCLE RECYCLE
REDUCE REUSE RECYCLE RECYCLE RECYCLE RECYCLE
RECYCLE RECYCLE RECYCLE RECYCLE RECYCLE RECYCLE
RECYCLE RECYCLE RECYCLE RECYCLE RECYCLE RECYCLE
RECYCLE RECYCLE REDUCE RECYCLE RECYCLE RECYCLE
RECYCLE RECYCLE RECYCLE RECYCLE RECYCLE RECYCLE
RECYCLE RECYCLE RECYCLE RECYCLE RECYCLE RECYCLE
RECYCLE RECYCLE RECYCLE RECYCLE RECYCLE RECYCLE
RECYCLE
RECYCLE
RECYCLE
RECYCLE
RECYCLE
RECYCLE
RECYCLE
RECYCLE
RECYCLE
RECYCLE
RECYCLE
RECYCLE
RECYCLE
RECYCLE

THE BOOK

RECYCLE
RECYCLE
RECYCLE
RECYCLE
RECYCLE
RECYCLE
   RECYCLE
   RECYCLE RECYCLE RECYCLE RECYCLE RECYCLE RECYCLE RECYCLE
RECYCLE
RECYCLE
RECYCLE
RECYCLE
RECYCLE RECYCLE
RECYCLE RECYCLE RECYCLE
RECYCLE RECYCLE RECYCLE RECYCLE
RECYCLE RECYCLE RECYCLE RECYCLE RECYCLE
RECYCLE RECYCLE RECYCLE RECYCLE RECYCLE RECYCLE RECYCLE RECYCLE RECYCLE
RECYCLE
RECYCLE RECYCLE REUSE RECYCLE RECYCLE RECYCLE
RECYCLE RECYCLE RECYCLE RECYCLE RECYCLE RECYCLE RECYCLE DON'T FORGET TO RECYCLE RECYCLE RECYCLE
RECYCLE RECYCLE RECYCLE RECYCLE RECYCLE RECYCLE
RECYCLE RECYCLE RECYCLE RECYCLE RECYCLE REUSE REDUCE

It was a bright, cold day in recycle and the icon was spinning thirteen.

Holden pulled his hands over his widened eyes and turned himself away from the computerized window. Eventually, when he felt he had regained some control over his mind, he allowed himself to remove his hands and admit the rest of the room.

There was an area where the carpet stopped, which he hadn't noticed before, where a smooth, brown, rubbery surface began. Upon it was a desk made of clear, green acrylic material that cantilevered asymmetrically from a single, giant leg that stamped into the brown rubber like the tree trunk of some recycled, extraterrestrial forest. Behind the desk was a simple, stainless steel chair, polished to a mirror finish. Holden looked down at it and saw his reflection again, dislocated and disjointed in its curves. He wasn't looking good, that was for sure. There was a patch of blood on his forehead and a line of dried blood that ran down across his nose. He touched it and a tender pulse rattled his skull. Holden leaned closer to the chair, spit onto his shirt sleeve and wiped the crusted blood from his skin until only a faint scratch snaked along his brow.

He stood in the recurring dizziness and looked down at the desk to find his name atop a digital screen that was incorporated into the clear, green material and only visible from that particular, perpendicular perspective. Below Holden's name was his most recent driver's license picture, his job history, grades in middle school and a family photo of him with Eve and Jane. Beside this was a list of ten people that were, according to the screen, his *likely cohorts*. One of these names, Marion Tabor, was highlighted. All the others, thankfully, were people that knew nothing of their group and the thought relaxed him. But only slightly. More interesting than the list was a series of three letters, capitalized and circled profusely: L.O.C. He didn't know what they meant. There was no L or O in his name and he assumed it was a sort of ranking system for people captured in the room with the revolving symbol. Following the series of three letters was the number one, underlined with three dark, digital slashes.

Holden stepped back from the table and assessed his situation as if he'd just arrived at a job site without a floor plan. There were two things about that scenario that he knew for sure. He knew his time was short and he knew that he would very likely, at any moment, be living out the experience of those that disappeared from Winston's group. Which was why, for the sake of acting out with whatever form of freedom he still had, Holden sat in the chair and threw his legs up on the table, hands locked behind his head. His toes poked from the worn socks on his shoeless feet. Wherever he was, it didn't matter. He closed his eyes as if it were a bright summer's day and he was sitting on the front porch of his grandmother's country home beside a sweaty glass of lemonade that was gradually becoming diluted by the melting ice. Of course, in that reality he was wearing shoes.

When he opened his eyes to find that the spinning, recycling icon had been watching him from across the room, Holden turned his gaze toward the ceiling where he noticed, to his delight (as it usually had), a complete fire sprinkler system. Eight blunt sprockets, spaced an equal distance apart, broke through the delicate blue surface like space ships preparing to douse the earth below with some sort of mind controlling, gelatinous ooze. In actuality, it was a simple thing. Just sprinkler heads arranged in one of many rooms in order to protect the building and whatever was inside from an accidental fire. But the sprinklers brought Holden a different sense of peace than what the luscious green carpet and finely chosen color scheme could ever provide. It was even better than the calm, soothing, gently-swooping eye of the recycling icon that –

REDUCE

beckoned him –

REUSE

to look in and –

RECYCLE

– lose himself.

The fire sprinklers bookmarked Holden to reality. And it was something, he assumed, that his jailers hadn't expected. The surprising fact was that this gave him hope. These people had underestimated him. They didn't realize that, by seeing a finished job, when the unblemished drywall had been cut precisely to fit the outer ring with its polished, metal finish, they would lose control over him. The protective, yet orderly, organization of sprinkler heads brought him joy. The job was done. Even though it wasn't his job, seeing someone else's work gave him the euphoric sense of checking the clock and seeing that it was time to go home. The work day was finished and he was allowed to spend the rest of the day any way he pleased.

The freedom of that feeling numbed the matter of his brains they were trying to reach, but in his mind Holden knew that the work day wasn't finished. A lot of people were counting on him and unless the government leaked the news of his capture to the newspapers and media (which they wouldn't because...who *really* was he, anyway?), he would end up like all the others in Winston's group. One of the vanished. One of the *gone*. It reminded Holden of *Peter Pan*, Abby's favorite story. The one she read aloud to the group. The quote that came to mind was the last line from chapter eight.

"To die would be an awfully big adventure."

The immediate guilt that surged to Holden's heart was surprisingly weakening. He had let the group down. He wished he had done more. Been more. Been more patient. Especially with Eve. He should have taken more time to ensure his protection if there were signs he couldn't trust her. Now, there was no telling what the group would do or how the loss of their leader would affect things. And what about Marion? He had gotten her involved in it all and left her there to deal with the rest of her isolated life alone. He was stunned by how much he missed her. There were feelings there. He finally accepted it. It was the reason he kept dragging Shane back to her bar. Of course, that didn't matter now. He'd seen them all for the last time. And Jane. Oh, Jane. He couldn't allow himself to think of her. To see her face in his mind as she screamed and clawed at her ruined, forever ruined, chest. No, he wouldn't. He would rather stare into that recycling symbol and lose his mind before going to that place.

Holden released his entwining fingers and rubbed his left hand feverishly against the fuzzy fur of his head before dropping his patchy, cold feet from the table. He stood and paced the room. Once. Then twice. Three times. And just as he was ready to launch himself full speed at the window that continued to laugh at him –

REDUCE REUSE RECYCLE

REDUCE

REUSE

RECYCLE

– the door opened.

For some reason, Holden hadn't noticed the door. Of course, it noticed him; it had been there the whole time. Molding. Doorknob. Hinges. Threshold. A gap on all sides that cut a black line into the seamless white walls. Perhaps he had been too absorbed in the inevitability of his capture to truly accept the possibility of escape. But hadn't he also missed the rubber floor? What about the desk? He hadn't seen that either. But there was a door now, cracked open, as real as his nose is crooked. Before it opened completely, Holden thought it would be a smart move to scan the rest of the room to see if he had missed anything else.

He hadn't. No windows. No cameras. Just the door.

When it swung open from the stark white walls in a full arc, a man stepped into the room wearing a casual expression, a gray blazer and a black turtleneck. Holden couldn't believe his eyes (mostly because they had lied to him already), but the man who entered the room was none other than Martin Trust, the director of Historic Homeland Preservation and Restoration. He supposed that he should have been expecting him, but he was still shaken. Suddenly, Holden thought of that little tin soldier who ignored the advice of a goblin and died because he fell in love with paper.

THE BOOK

Trust closed the door with a little more effort than what seemed necessary, kept his hand upon the handle as it rested in the closed position and, almost wholly unaware of Holden's presence, turned to approach the desk. Holden glanced uneasily around the room to check again for other doors and noticed how the image of the recycling icon had morphed into the seal of the Department of Homeland Security. The man adjusted a few things on the desk's digital screen and then, very simply, he stood and waited.

After ten seconds, he tilted his head up to his guest and said, "Mister Clifford, please have a seat." His voice was frigid and oddly professional, as if Holden had stopped in to fill out a questionnaire for a free copy of The Book.

The polished, stainless steel seat, which Holden thought was left for someone of importance, had actually been meant for him. And once he was situated, it finally made sense why the computer screen that was built into the clear, green desktop had only been visible form a perpendicular angle – he was about to be questioned without seeing the questions. Martin Trust gazed down at Holden with an arrogant smile that spoke of many predetermined judgments. He released three short ticks and, in the stillness that followed, Holden pictured a school teacher shaking his head in reprimand at a student who hadn't brought their stylus pen to class.

Tisk, tisk tisk, Mister Clifford. You started your own anarchist movement.

"So..." Holden breathed, "what's the process man? Let's get this going. If I'm done, I'm done. Let's do it."

"Well, you are not lacking in impatience, Holden. May I call you Holden, for the sake of this discussion?"

"Uh..." He paused for an unnecessarily long minute, as if not actually choosing sarcasm as a response. "No," he decided, smartly. Holden wondered if he had just witnessed his final act of rebellion.

"Very well," the director said, nodding his squared jaw. "Mister Clifford. I believe we may have gotten off on the wrong foot. See, the job that has been placed upon me is one of protection. It is important for me, as the head of a division of Homeland Security –" He pronounced *Homeland* as if it were two separate, unequal words and gave each a formidable weight as he released them from his plump-lipped mouth. "– that I ensure those above me that this country, if not this world, is protected. Its values protected. Its," he delayed, "...interests. I'll see if I can explain it with an age-old metaphor. Our government, along with the Publishing House, is a well-oiled machine. You, Mister Clifford, are a wrench that someone, somewhere, at some time, dropped into that machine. My job is simple. I get rid of the wrench before it can do any further damage and then, from that point on, it's all preventative maintenance. I find the other persons responsible for causing the problem and simply ensure that they will never cause problems again. Sometimes, to amuse myself with irony, I drop the wrench on them."

The man's calm, effortless description made the roots of Holden's teeth curl. He swallowed and tried not to look as frightened as he felt inside, but the gesture (as Winston would say) carried less water than a wicker basket.

"I can tell by your expression, Mister Clifford, that what I'm saying doesn't sit comfortably. Well, to be honest, it doesn't matter at this point. The only thing you have going for you," he drawled, putting his hands behind his back as he paced the room in a relaxed, regulatory rhythm, "is that we have a plan you can be involved in...involuntarily though it may be." Trust leaned toward the bench where Holden had awoken moments ago and removed a piece of hair that floated along its cold, metal surface.

THE BOOK

He flaked it from his fingers. "You should be relieved, Mister Clifford. You have been obtained at quite an opportune time. See, most people who come into this room are given few options. I'm sure you've heard the stories, but, to offer you a blurb, our judge and jury are very swift in their declaration of guilty. These days, it's more of an *automatic* thing. But, that's neither here nor there. Doesn't apply to you. And while you may be guilty in every single sense of the word, the task we require of you may change that. Especially in the eyes of history and in the *Free Thinking* group that is currently vilifying our country."

"Get to the point," Holden complained, staring rudely at death, impatient for the restful slash of its sharpened sickle.

The director pursed his lips, stepped onto the rubber floor and placed a hand on the desk. "I feel this could be better explained if I showed you instead of told you. This is a bit unorthodox, but if we're being honest, I've found that I actually enjoy walking with you."

The man turned suddenly and approached the door that had been invisible prior to his arrival. He knocked three times and, like Dorothy clicking her heels, salvation presented itself. Holden stood from his seat and followed, uncertain of where the Wizard's balloon would take him, but glad to be heading anywhere other than the room of fake environments that seemed to bore a hole in his soft, little mind.

It took less than a minute for Holden to be amazed at the Kansas beyond the door. He was in an office. There were people bustling about, holding portfolios and sack lunches, talking on cell phones and tittering away on their handheld computers. Holden watched the activity around him with his mouth swinging low. The director walked him to an open lobby with windows looking down into an even larger lobby that held a feathery steel sculpture where a few worker bees were buzzing.

The shimmering, white marble floors and security guards made Holden realize that he had actually been in a typical office building. There were people circling in and out of the rotating glass doors and he wondered if they were on their way to work, heading out for a meeting over lunch or going golfing. There was an eerie realism to it and Holden seemed to stick out, dressed in his blue-collar jeans and work shirt (the one that actually had a blue collar) and shoeless feet that needed new socks, like a handwritten book in a digital world.

That reality gave him no sense of comfort. What he wanted, what he longed for, as he glimpsed a sliver of sunlight through the lobby windows, was a single panoramic view that could show him the sky, all bluish and real. He had been so thwarted lately with clouds and gloom that just a rectangle of real sky would warm his heart.

Holden's attention was yanked away as Martin Trust ushered him from the windows to lead him on a tour of the building. It felt surprisingly bizarre because it was as if he weren't some hostile prisoner of war, detained against his will among the digital files. Stumbling behind the director, tired, beaten and poorly dressed, he resembled an unemployed Unfortunate who had dropped by for a visit to guilt his more successful brother into getting him a job in the mail room.

He was like the younger brother. The little brother.

"The Publishing House is broken into three floors. You can see this clearly through the elevators in the atrium. Don't you love how they glisten in the light? Real crystal." Holden peeked around the corner and saw the large, well-lit seating area beside three glass elevators that brought employees to the two floors above them. It seemed a bit garish and unnecessary, but who was a prisoner to judge? Stretching to the highest point, below a multi-faceted glass roof, was an abominable, green wall that

THE BOOK

seemed to change its own hue in the shaft of light that cut through the office spaces above. Their affect on the remaining architecture provided Holden with an accurate assessment of how important the Publishing House was to the building.

"The first floor is the Department of Reduction. On this level, you'll find the offices of our Editors. We don't have many, but their job is to reduce the information in The Book that goes against what we call *The Current Purpose*. Next level you'll find the Department of Reusage, where we store a digital copy of all the adjustments we have made over time, in case a real copy is leaked by some pesky, unlawful group, present party included, or if another unpredictable problem arises where we would need to go back to the exact original. We have a record of everything we have ever altered and can, rather easily, make that happen in a simple, one-minute-forty-seven-second update. Then, above that, on the third floor, is the Department of Recycling. Where we recycle."

That final, very simple sentence hung in the air around them like a cloud of so many souls, floating in the unwelcome din of purgatory. Without further explanation, the director of Historic Homeland Preservation and Restoration led Holden into the sitting room and toward the sun-kissed elevators. No one was watching them. No one cared who he was or why he was there. Holden felt his eyes scanning the room as if yearning for some sort of escape that his mind hadn't been developing.

Where were they going? Was the man actually going to walk him on his own to the level of Recycling, whatever that meant? Was he actually making the cold, shoeless stroll right now to everlasting post-life? He needed to get straight with God and, like, now. And what about these people? Were they so used to seeing a man walking toward certain recyclement that it didn't cause them to stir from their sack lunches and personalized website updates?

'Twelve noon and another dead man walking. Me, I'm just riding that trusty escalator called Monday to the bottom and it's slow as hell.'

Holden's frantic panting stuttered as he pictured Jane again, fatherless and struggling through life, unable to get the guidance she always wanted and scrambling to find it in other ways without realizing how it was gradually destroying her life beyond repair. He pictured their cause crumbling, as fear was born like a cancer in the group, until they disbanded and hid inside themselves only to find their hand, years later, with a sharpened nail on the pointer finger. He thought of Marion. Lost, with no one there to help her get through. Winston, sad and descending. And poor, Unfortunate Moby. Hope had been reborn in Holden and now it was nowhere to be found. Everything he had done was for nothing.

But Martin Trust hadn't stopped at the elevators. Holden just realized. The director was leading him down a separate hallway, past a cafeteria and into a quarantined field of cubicles that was surprisingly ordinary.

Men and women passed Martin Trust saying, *"Hello"* and *"Afternoon, Director"*.

The man replied each time with the oddest sentiment, *"Good to see you smiling again."*

At one point, Trust even poked one of the men that was walking by holding a digital folder, and stopped to joke about some recent football game and how the man owed him twenty bucks. It was so disturbing and fake and altogether unbelievable. These people were ruining mankind one word at a time, with a smile on their face and egg salad on their breath. And then, Holden remembered the room he had found himself in only moments before and knew that there was a deep psychological control in the silent solitude of that building, among the desolate aisles of padded cubicle walls, and felt sorry for them.

Near one of the more organized cubicles, the director stopped, turned to face a frosted, green glass door along the wall and began punching a code into its unnumbered keypad. The woman in the cubicle smiled graciously at the director and Holden noticed that, for the slightest of seconds, her eyes faltered. In that millisecond of wavering, Holden wished that he could be free to call Winston. To tell him that he had found a counterpart to his mother: a well-placed knight among the editing staff. Holden witnessed in a glance that this woman either did not like what she was being forced to do or wasn't comfortable around Martin Trust, which meant that she didn't believe in him. He could have done something with that before. But not now. Not as he was being led into this room. *Whatever this room was.* The only thought that granted Holden any degree of liberation was that he was still on the first floor, in the Department of Reduction.

"There we are," the director proclaimed, as three notes of confirmation chirped from the keypad. The frosted glass door separated from the wall with a hissing of pressure. The director swung it open and walked merrily through.

Holden was met with surprise, once again.

It was just a conference room.

Another sleek, green acrylic table spanned the space, twelve feet long with nine thin, leather task chairs that swiveled, spun, and rolled on hidden casters. The floor was composed of some foreign, jet black material. It was seamless, unidentifiable and its shiny onyx wrapped the walls of the room, almost overbearing in its immeasurable darkness. And it would have been, if it weren't for the wide ribbon of dark mahogany that ringed the floor from the wall to the ceiling, where it gradually estranged itself and hung a foot below the can lights. The room was exquisite, but what really captured Holden's eye was outside the room – the scene beyond the single panoramic window. The sky was bright blue, the grass outside was green and luscious and all the buildings were the purest white he had ever seen.

All the buildings were white?

Holden tripped over a task chair and lurched toward the window, amazed at what he was really looking at. In the distance he could see pillars and columns of bleached white, domed rooftops that peaked over one another and hid behind trees, and an obelisk of colorless stone rising tall above the skyline. He was in Washington DC. The Agents had taken him from his ex-wife's home in the suburbs of Chicago and had brought him to the nation's capital.

Martin rolled out the ninth chair at the head of the table and beckoned for Holden to sit. The director stood beside the onyx wall and slipped his hands delicately into the pockets of his slacks, gazing with admiration at the capital buildings. A full minute later, he released a gentle sound of elation before inhaling a long sip of air through his nose. Pleased with the moment, he removed his left hand from his pocket and pointed at the remarkably immaculate city.

"Holden, have you ever just stood and looked at it all? Sure, there are a lot of decisions made here. Elected officials shaping our world. People we trust and place our hope in, all out and about fixing things we could never understand. But have you ever just looked at the city itself? How it's so clean and safe. It invites trust. No, that's not what it does. It *commands* trust." A grin of honest respect glazed over the man's face. "Do you understand what I'm saying?"

Holden remained seated and remained silent. He was unable to formulate any response at the moment and felt that quiet and

THE BOOK

reserved was the only option available for someone in his situation and possibly the only thing he could still control.

"Did you know," the director mused, "that when The Book was first published, the digital copies were much like this scene? The Book was released in only three colors: the purest white, a lofty sky blue and green, like the trustworthy grass below our feet. Commanded respect through color. How ingenious is that?" With no response, the director continued with an unforeseen question. "Holden, have you heard of a story called *The Thirteenth Tale* by Diane Setterfield? It's pre-digital and we had it destroyed, so I'm assuming you haven't. But have you?" Holden kept silent. "Before I became the director of a new division of Homeland Security, I had an...interesting job here at the Publishing House. I often quoted two passages from this story to people in situations similar to yours." He cleared his throat and began.

> *"There is something about words. In expert hands, manipulated deftly, they take you prisoner. Wind themselves around your limbs like spider silk, and when you are so enthralled you cannot move, they pierce your skin, enter your blood, numb your thoughts. Inside you they work their magic."*

Again, he cleared his throat before quoting a passage of that banned book from memory.

> *"My gripe is not with lovers of truth but with truth herself. What succor, what consolation is there in truth, compared to a story? What good is truth, at midnight, in the dark, when the wind is roaring like a bear in the chimney? When the lightning strikes shadows on the*

bedroom wall and the rain taps at the window with its long fingernails? No. When fear and cold make a statue of you in your bed, don't expect hard-boned and fleshless truth to come running to your aid. What you need are the plump comforts of a story. The soothing, rocking safety of a lie."

"Unedited, those quotes," Trust remarked with pride. He exhaled a deep breath of tranquility. "The first provides a truth of who we are and what we are capable of and then its supporting quote reveals the importance of listening to lies. Don't you see, Mister Clifford? This is actually what people want. What *man* wants. Maybe what you are fighting against isn't really all that bad."

Holden was minutes, maybe seconds from his certain recyclement, and yet here this man stood, praising a system that his group had developed a hatred for. A system that robbed his daughter of her beauty and Marion of her heritage and reputation and Moby of a relationship with his uncle. He wanted to speak out and tell the director that he wasn't buying the garbage he was selling, but it wasn't worth it. Holden was conserving his energy by keeping the lights off. Something told him that he would need it later. When he could find a way out of there.

In the immobility of those few seconds, when only the breeze of cool air being exhaled through the mahogany vents could be heard, Holden was thinking. There were two possible reasons why he had been allowed to stroll about the building without a leash and he was determined to figure out which one was right. Martin Trust had either been too confident in Holden's inability to escape or, as he had felt in the room when he found peace in the arrangement of sprinkler heads, they had underestimated him. Or both.

THE BOOK

So, what could he do? If Holden was right and they had misjudged him to some degree, he needed to set aside his thoughts of guilt and remorse to make room for something he wasn't accustomed to – strategy. Trust was clearly trying to sway him into viewing The Book as a gift to society and Holden still didn't understand why. Regardless, he needed to respond. It was all Holden could do at that moment. And if he needed to say something, why not tell the man what he wanted to hear? Against the natural tendencies of every cell in his body, Holden did the opposite of what was expected. He stood from his seat, approached the window and copied the director's gestures by placing a hand in his pocket. Beside one of the more powerful leaders in the free world, Holden stood at the glass and looked out admiringly on the nation's capital. Trust had been right. The buildings were exquisite. And clean. And they commanded a certain respect from him. But standing in the truth of it didn't change a thing. Holden needed to buy some time before the gavel came swinging down.

"So," he began, trying to keep his eyes from the director so they wouldn't give him away, "What is it you want me to do? I'm a man of little talent, but I mean, I'm not dumb...you guys could have taken care of me by now, so I figure...you obviously chose me for a reason. You stand here, acting like you're just a regular guy, but I know how this works. You took me against my will in front of my kid, and she got hurt in the process. I'll do whatever I gotta do, just as long as you leave her out of it. Capiche? We both know you had my number in the park and decided to let me go. So, let's get on with the show and you tell me what role I'm playing."

Holden surprised himself. Although he could see that the director was staring at him, he wouldn't allow himself to turn. Trust was smart and Holden couldn't let any part of his face give him away. Problem was, he hadn't expected the Director's response and could've never expected what would be asked of him.

"Well, Mister Clifford," he repeated again, reminding Holden that, at one point, there had been hostility between them, "we at the Publishing House work on a hundred year plan. You have arrived serendipitously at the culmination of one plan and the beginning of another. We see quite a purpose for you. Plain and simple, we have a need. And I see in you a way to fill that need." Trust began to grin sharply. It left an odd anticipation between words, hanging like dust on a shaft of sunlight. "You are going to be known by everyone in the entire world."

"What?" Holden questioned without thinking. He nearly had to force his head from spinning, so his eyes would remain looking out the window. "Why would people know me?"

Martin Trust pointed to the building on their right, the one closest to the window. It was wide and white, long and short, and topped with a green roof along the edge and a squat dome at the center. Holden had recognized it, but didn't know the building's name. "What you see there is the last library in existence. The Library of Congress. And you, Mister Clifford, will demolish that building and every last book within its walls."

Holden swallowed and raised a hand to rub an itch that didn't exist from his nose. Nervous ticks in the midst of unimaginable horror. He contemplated smashing out the window and leaping from the building to get away, but the fall would break his legs. "Why are you telling me this? Why not just force me to do it?"

"Because we know it's the right thing to do and we want to give you the option of going out for the right reasons."

"But it won't work. People need to know that originals exist somewhere."

THE BOOK

"You're precisely right, Holden," Trust agreed, expecting a more explosive reaction. "There are thousands of books left unchecked in the world, mind you that number dwindles by the day, and even when we come and take them from the house next door, watchful neighbors accept it because they know there are still books out there. They accept the depravity of a world without paper because there is one copy of every book that has ever been written in that building. Right there. Seven hundred feet away. And...how horrible that you, the leader of *The Free Thinkers*, chose to destroy the only ones that we were keeping safe."

Holden broke eye contact with the window and faced him, unable to withhold himself in such delirium. "*The Free Thinkers*? Why are you associating me with them? Those guys don't care about The Book."

The director grinned and tapped Holden on the shoulder. "Oh, we're well aware. We've been watching them for a while now. Yes, we know you went to the meeting. See, that's why we chose you, Holden. Why I chose you. I know you have passion. You aren't a lemming like all the others, following blindly into a mine field. *The Free Thinkers* are helpless drones. Everything they have done we have allowed. And when we want to orchestrate a move of our own," he pointed to the Library of Congress, "we simply blame it on them. Which, in the end, they take credit for. Happily."

"Like Marion and the bar," Holden added, finally understanding.

"Ah, *The Library*." Trust breathed a laugh. "Clever name."

Holden was still unsure about how to escape, so he stole more time with a notion that seemed obvious. "Can you give me a second to process this? I mean, this is huge. And I get it. If I'm not with ya', I'm against ya'. I guess I just feel like something still isn't making sense. There has to be more to this than just getting rid of a few nail-biting thrillers."

Martin Trust chewed on the thought for a bit as Holden punctuated his control of the conversation by taking a seat at the other end of the table, the one furthest from the door.

"After the Library is gone? Sure. Our next move is to destroy a building that we say is the Publishing House. Then we take The Book offline for a few weeks. When it comes back, there's a whole new format. And whoopsie...there are things missing. We make some swift cuts and then blame it on the terrorists...err...you. Entire books can finally be destroyed. Partials corrupted. Normally, in this instance we would go to our store of originals..."

"But I've destroyed them all," Holden concluded, kicking up his legs and resting them on the slick green surface of the table so he could appear relaxed as he continued to formulate his escape between words. His peek-a-boo toes hurt the illustration. "Sounds like you've really thought this through. But I think you're lying."

"I'm sorry?"

Holden couldn't tell if the director was offended when he tilted his head and smirked, or if he was amused that the lowly sprinkler fitter from the north side of Chicago had figured out their plan.

"That's not why you're doing this. I mean, don't get me wrong...makes sense why you would, but I think there's an even bigger purpose." It came to him as he said it and he couldn't believe his own voice. "You want to destroy other documents. The important ones. Government stuff."

A grin formed on the face of Martin Trust as wide as a zebra's stripes are long. "Well, I would be lying if I didn't say that would be a pleasant fallout. And Martin Trust doesn't lie. Yes, we mourn our literature. Our historic accounts of war and glory. But when we replace this country's most cherished documents and records, declarations and proclamations with holographic images...well, it gives mourning a whole new meaning, doesn't it?"

Holden looked at the keypad on the door. He scanned for anything of interest on Trust's belt. Anything that could help him escape. He had to keep the conversation going. "Nothing could stop you from creating an entirely new government."

"Not next year, no. Not even thirty years from now," Trust admitted, throwing up his hands with a smile that still eked toward his ears. "But, remember, we follow a hundred year plan." He approached Holden's chair and ushered him back to the window. "We were hoping you would want to be a part of this on your own after learning how important it is to the survival of our country. And yet, Mister Clifford...I know what you're thinking..." Nearly to the window, Holden froze, his muscles clenched in the fright of Martin's words. "And you're wrong. It isn't about control. It's about peace. Holden, you would be playing one of the largest roles in reestablishing peace in our world. I know...I know...*But-at-what-cost?*" He shrugged off the sentiment. "Think of how sustainable our world is today. Waking up in this veneer of environmentalism is like sitting down for a good meal where every day is a delicious bite. But you can't make a great steak without killing the cow, Holden. There have always been side-effects and negative repercussions to the recycling movement, but wasn't a utopia worth it? With this, destroying that building, we would have peace. For the first time ever...a world without war and tragedy. Isn't such a thing worth a little freedom being stripped away?"

Holden tried to get his mind back on task, to try and escape the man's mental clutches, but he was stuck in the mud of it. He couldn't move past what Trust had been saying. It made sense, all of a sudden. Wars have been raging throughout history and shouldn't he do anything in his power to stop the killing? To stop the unlawfulness that had somehow been helped by destroying books? Shouldn't he care more about that than about some make-believe girl named Lucy who got lost in a wardrobe?

Amid his obvious uncertainty, Trust prodded even deeper into Holden's mind. "Do you recognize the structure across the yard on our left? That's the Capitol Building. Interesting detail, when the dome was under construction, with girders poking out and looking like a broken bottle, Abraham Lincoln, our greatest president, stood beneath it and gave his inaugural address to a country that was completely divided. The man had to wear a disguise on his way there just to avoid assassination. Less than a month later, the Civil War began and our country bled its brothers and sisters dry for the rest of his term. He was killed two weeks after his second inaugural. Shame. But do you know what that man is most remembered for today?"

"Obvious. He got rid of slavery, man. That was huge." The director's ever-present grin was making Holden uncomfortable.

"That's right. The Emancipation Proclamation."

To Holden's astonishment, Trust left the window and walked back to the door. He punched a code rapidly into the keypad and the door released from the wall with the same pressurized hiss. Holden fought to get a read on the code, but it was too far away. As Trust asked the woman in the first cubicle for help, Holden thought desperately for a solution to get out of that room. But he couldn't. He simply could not stop returning to what Trust had been saying about recycling. It was making too much sense and Holden had to get away from it. He needed to find something that could pull him out of that head space. Something that could bring him back. Something that –

THE BOOK

He found it. Salvation in the simplest form, once again.

Before Holden could act, before he could set his escape in motion, Trust was back in the room holding a copy of an Editor's Book. "I'm going to read you an excerpt, *unedited*, from a famous letter written by Abraham Lincoln to the editor of the *New York Tribune*." He marched pompously to the window and tilted The Book toward Holden, so he could read the words himself.

> *"As to the policy I 'seem to be pursuing' as you say, I have not meant to leave anyone in doubt. I would save the Union. I would save it the shortest way under the Constitution. The sooner the national authority can be restored; the nearer the Union will be 'the Union as it was.' If there be those who would not save the Union, unless they could at the same time save slavery, I do not agree with them. If there be those who would not save the Union unless they could at the same time destroy slavery, I do not agree with them. My paramount object in this struggle is to save the Union, and is not either to save or to destroy slavery. If I could save the Union without freeing any slave, I would do it, and if I could save it by freeing all the slaves I would do it; and if I could save it by freeing some and leaving others alone I would also do that. What I do about slavery, and the colored race, I do because it helps to save the Union..."*

If Holden hadn't already developed a solution for escape, he may not have been able to resist following the will of the Publishing House, simply by hearing those unedited words. Words from a former president who was still heralded as the savior of the slaves – when, in actuality, his purpose in doing so was to return peace to his country. Just peace, with or without free will.

"Don't you see, Holden? Even the man who abolished slavery said he would keep it if it meant peace! The cost of enslaving others is great and tragic and real, but the reward, Holden. The reward is everlasting. And it would be for you, too."

"That's not true. Everyone in the world would hate me," Holden muttered, feeling a swell of debate in his mind about whether to proceed with his plan.

"Sure, they will hate you now. People hated Lincoln. But who controls history? Who determines the ones that have statues erected in their honor? Immortality, Holden." The grin on the director's face was demented and strange. Like a vampire, debating the siring of his victim during the moments of hunger instead of ripping their throat away in a single rapturous bite. "Do this for us, and you are immortal. A hero to the generations of the future. History books will enthrone you and your grave stone will be the largest in the country."

Holden looked out the window. He hid his reaction and stared at the building. The Library of Congress. He could feel the strings that were slowly attaching themselves to his little puppet arms and the honest truth became clear. They were going to do it regardless. Whether he agreed or not, they were going to blow up that building.

Did he want to leave? To escape? Of course. But even after getting back to Chicago there would be nothing he could do to stop them. What other options did he have? Either get on board and set sail under the flag of the enemy (who kinda made sense), or go home and stay on the sinking ship and watch the enemy sail away, regardless of your involvement. At the same time, Holden felt resistance. How could he, in his right mind, participate in such an act? Destroy all the books in the world, including the ones he now held so dear. The last remaining copies. Sure, they had a library in Winston's basement, but that was it. Once the Library of Congress was destroyed and The Book was altered to remove thousands, they were gone forever and what were the odds that Winston would be able to find enough sources to compile an original? Holden knew he didn't have time to decide. If he said yes, he would die a terrorist and play a crucial role in the largest catastrophe in the history of the world. If he escaped, he could find a way to get the word out. Maybe even save a book or two. But there was a whole recycle bin full of *What If*'s in that plan. If he said no, the discussion was done. Today. Now. And if his escape plan didn't pan out, he was only two floors below meeting his maker. Holden could go to the pearly gates, drink a beer with Peter and feel right as rain because he didn't contribute to the slavery of the world.

And then he thought back to the room and to the sprinkler heads. They hadn't expected that. The director had planned for everything. He wanted Holden to start losing his mind in that room and then feel more discomfort as he was walked through their offices. He was never supposed to stay in that room. Trust wanted to sell Holden on participating in this self-destructive kamikaze act (which, by the way, only included posthumous fame on the earth and no forty virgins in some alternate heavenscape). Without coming right out and saying it, the director had told Holden, *"Die...or do it and die, and we won't kill anybody else."* Lots of really great options there.

But – *BUT* they had underestimated him.

That room with the grass carpeting and sky blue ceiling was meant to chill him out while, at all times, constructed with the strict intent of causing dislocation and a heightened sense of lingering doom. Marinating the steak before the flame. But they didn't know Holden as well as they thought they did. They underestimated his ability to find peace and security in a simple sprinkler head. It reminded Holden of his escape plan. Really, it was always the sprinkler heads. Sure, how they looked against the ceiling and the emotions they stirred within him, the simple joys of the journeyman, the water monkey who no one expected would be hanging out with one of the more powerful men in the world. But it was always the sprinkler head. And it was always supposed to be Holden. Because only he would know how to escape.

Done. He was ready.

"Sounds good," Holden replied, patting Martin Trust on the back. "When do we get started?"

"Uh..." the director laughed, shocked by the ease of his submission. "I suppose what we should do first is film a scene of you near a bookshelf that resembles one in the main reading room of the Library and then we'll have –"

An odd, face-splitting grin stretched Holden's lips and the director of Historic Homeland Preservation and Restoration stopped speaking to smile in return. His grin was stupid and curious. He had no idea that behind Holden's smile was a decision to kick the wind out of the director's chest, bring the man to his knees and lodge a fist into the crook of his boxy jaw. In the revelry of it, Holden tightened his grip and nodded his head, turning to look at the director one last time.

Lights out, zebra man.

His knee swung up in the single, most powerful gesture he had ever conjured and crashed like lighting into the soft tissue of the director's unready abdomen. The man's radiant eyes bulged from his sockets and he crumbled to the glimmering, onyx floor in unexpected pain and disbelief. He hadn't been there for more than a second before the wind from Holden's tightened left fist fluttered his blond hair as the sprinkler fitter's knuckles came crashing into the man's square jar, hammering him powerfully to the ground.

Holden bounced in place for a moment as Martin Trust landed shoulder first into the smooth black surface of the floor, kicking one of the chairs out from below the table. Holden knew there wasn't much time. There could be cameras anywhere. He yanked the shoes from the director's feet, cranked them down over his own, pulled the expensive jacket off the man's shoulders and slipped awkwardly into it. The director's feet were too small and his arms had no definition. Holden's bulky frame tightened the jacket's tailored seams as he launched himself onto the green acrylic table that cracked under his weight.

This is gonna hurt.

He took a moment to breathe before pulverizing his right fist, the one he spared in the struggle, directly into one of the sprinkler heads, breaking it free from its threaded home and launching it into the wooden strip on the wall. It nicked the mahogany with a crack and Holden leapt down from the table as silently as he could. So far, everything was going according to plan. He would only have to wait a minute. The longest minute of his life.

What Holden had figured out, as he stood staring at the lemmings that walked stupidly across the lawns of the nation's capital, was that the company who had sprinkled the building would have likely installed a dry pipe fire sprinkler system. Government buildings, especially one so invested in technology, would need surety and fortification and those making the decisions realized that the probability of computer damage was too high to leave water in the pipes at all times. Only the presence of a fire would release the water and the delay was worth avoiding accidents. Yes, Holden was their prisoner. Yes, he was not nearly as intelligent as the man that cleaned their toilets. But Holden Clifford was the only person in that building who understood fire sprinklers and he knew that deliberate sabotage to the sprinkler head created accidental discharge. Accidental discharge meant that all fire protection methods in the building were activated. Which also meant that, for the necessity of egress, every single door, even of the frosted green and invisible variety, would unlock regardless of safety protocols. Details only a sprinkler fitter would know.

And it was now, as Holden wiped the blood that trickled freely from the lacerations on his fist, that he waited for the water to come, for the alarm to resound and for the glass door to release its bated breath of freedom. Within seconds, Holden Clifford would not have to face the certainty of yes or no. He could simply walk out the building.

A hiccup of spray and his clothes were doused from the shower that spurted from the faceted heads in the ceiling. The door sprang open and he walked painfully and nonchalantly from the conference room wearing the director's tight suit jacket and shoes. Rather than race from the scene like Alice's rabbit, Holden approached one of the frazzled Editors, looked the man in the eyes and said, "We should probably leave the building. Which way is safe?"

Frightened, the man was momentarily mute, as if he had never made a decision of his own at work, and motioned toward the emergency stairs where people were collecting. After following a funnel of frenzied 'coworkers' into the stairwell, Holden followed the group unceremoniously out of the building where they stood and gazed up, wondering what set off the sprinkler system and how their computers were doing and *what about my digital frame and my egg salad sandwich?*

Holden wasn't there to hear the many whispers collecting in the gentle wind of the sidewalk. He was already three blocks

THE BOOK

closer to Wilmette, his feet burning as he raced toward the Lincoln Memorial, tossing the director's expensive jacket at an Unfortunate, who took it gladly, and enjoying the sunshine of unforeseen freedom. He couldn't believe he had escaped. It almost seemed too easy. But Holden knew he had no other choice. And now he had to accept that they would be looking for him and, even worse, they would still be planning to destroy the last library in the world.

He had no identification. He had no wallet or money or anything to pawn. The pain in his toes was unbearable and the face he was wearing would be recognizable to every single person in the world within an hour's time. But still, Holden could breathe. He was free. The Publishing House was behind him. And all he had to do was get home.

Two months had passed since Holden had disappeared and Wilmette seemed to wither in his absence. Trees lost their luster. The green had died and the months of September and October had burnished the leaves to many shades of brown and orange. People who played the game, who read The Book, believed it was the changing of the seasons; but those who missed Holden told themselves something altogether different: The world was dying and Holden may be gone forever.

Carving its way through the flurry of fallen leaves was an old model station wagon with a rack on the top that was overflowing with luggage and plastic containers. Between the boards of wood detailing, the car was painted with a luster of vibrant yellow. It drove slowly through the neighborhoods, winding the streets with its bright hue at an even, almost uncertain, pace. It was searching for something. When the station wagon reached the hauntingly empty driveway of Winston's estate, the car pulled in and navigated its way though the unblemished lawn of leaves. If it weren't for the stones that edged the driveway, they could have very rightly been driving over grass. The place looked abandoned. Obviously, no one had driven over the leaves since they had fallen and there were so many on the ground that the people who had arrived in search of something would, more than likely, be leaving with smiles more withered than the trees. But hope was a powerful thing and evidence of possible disappointment wasn't enough to sway them. They parked near the front entrance and turned off the car.

The passenger door opened and a young woman stepped out with a newborn in her arms. She looked up at the brick and stucco house with smiling eyes, as if it were exactly what she had imagined. From the driver's side came a man in his mid-twenties looking expectantly at the swooping gable roof and the iron plated, diamond glass windows before joining his wife and their child. Dreams were going to be built here. Years of memories they would fondly recall in the decades ahead.

The back door opened from the driver's side and a man stepped out looking haggard and exhausted and beaten. His detached expression was lost behind his beard, humble eyeglasses and dusty brown mop of hair. It was Holden. He had finally made it home after such a long journey. He had done what he could to disguise himself, but it wasn't all that necessary. After what he had experienced, he looked different. He was different. And it was mostly in his eyes. While thin and trodden, they had a new vibrancy to them. There was a mission behind his gaze that was unlike anything they would be expecting from someone who used to be content with a simple, small life.

He had been planning every day. During the long, moonlit walks in the street with his thumb in the air, hoping someone would pull over and save him, to drive him a few more miles before his shoes fell apart. He thought about it every hour. Dreamt of the ramifications. What he was planning to propose to them was something they would not be expecting to hear, but he hoped that the proof of his ability to escape from the hold of the Publishing House would be voice enough. All they needed was to trust in him and trust that his plan, though oddly unbelievable and seemingly against their entire belief system, would work. He just prayed that, in his destabilized condition, he wouldn't appear to be a man that has lost his mind. Because, in truth, the man they would be expecting died somewhere along the road to Washington.

Home again, home again. Jiggety Jig.

"You sure this is it, Holden?" they asked, squinting in the fresh rain at their passenger.

"Yeah, this is it," he replied, nodding.

"You made it seem like there would be a lot of people here."

"Well. I don't know what's going on, but I'm sure we'll find out soon enough." He pulled a cylindrical duffle bag from the roof and dropped it onto his shoulder before limping toward the door. The past eleven weeks had not been kind and he was looking forward to a hot bath and a chance to relax before dropping the bomb on everyone. He led them to the front door. They found it unlocked.

What the three of them were expecting and what actually met their eyes were two very different things. The estate, normally quite serene, was bustling with life. In the foyer alone, there were ten people Holden had never seen before. There was a group of young children in the sitting room listening to a woman as she read from a children's book. In the great room there was another group that seemed to be teaching a class. They were each holding a copy of The Book, except for one, who was steadily reading aloud from an original printing. Holden was so stunned by the complete difference between what he had left and what he now discovered that he didn't see her coming.

THE BOOK

"Oh gosh, I hope you three haven't been standing here too long. Sometimes we don't even hear the door. I'm Marion."

He turned to see her face and there was music.

She looked brilliant and beautiful. Vibrant and alive. Comfortable in her new clothes. All sense of fear and worry gone. In fact, Marion even looked younger. When she reached the foyer, Marion hugged the woman Holden had traveled with before admiring the infant in her arms. "So adorable! I'm sure we'll get down to business and find out how you guys got the address and where you hail from and all, but we always start with hugs. It's just so nice to see new people. And an infant!"

"She's a girl."

"Wonderful. There's another one around here somewhere, so she'll have a play buddy."

"How many of you are there?"

"Uh...just here? About forty-five."

"You're kidding," Holden bellowed, as Marion turned and nodded. She extended a hand to introduce herself. Amused, he held out his own and they shook hands. Holden knew he looked different, but he thought at least Marion would recognize him.

"Well, it's a pleasure to meet you. My name is Alex and this is my wife, Kari. We've just heard so much about this house from our friend here and...well, we really look forward to getting involved any way we can."

Marion turned to Holden again, intrigued. "So, where exactly are you..." She paused and tilted her head. Blinking often, she knit her eyebrows and leaned forward, staring into him. "Holden?"

"Yeah, Marion," he smiled. "It's me."

She released a squeal of unabashed delight and leapt into his arms, only to retract immediately beneath a smile of total shock. "Oh-my-gosh, you stink."

He laughed and nodded, "I know. Shower open anywhere?"

"I've been so...we've been hoping you were okay. We've been watching the news for weeks and you're all over it."

"Why do you think I look the way I do?"

"Well, the beard suits you, but these glasses...ugh..."

"I forgot I had them on." He dragged the glassless frames free and pinched the bridge of his nose. "I could use a haircut, I'm sure."

Marion ran a hand through his hair and ruffled it toward his forehead. "I don't know. I think it works too." They shared a smile. "Holden, I have to tell everyone you're here. They'll be so happy."

"No. No...no...wait," he said, taking her hand. She looked down at it and beamed. "I don't want people to see me like this. But, I would like to kind of...call a meeting. Do we really have forty-five people?"

"Yeah, isn't it amazing!? Most of them are like me...on a watch list or somehow associated with *The Free Thinkers*. Just let me take you around," she pleaded, playfully. "Can I just take you around?"

"Alright, but no introductions."

"Fine. Whatever. Sure." She gripped onto his hand, glanced back at the people he arrived with and said, "I'm sorry. I'll be right back. I just miss him so much. I was so worried."

Alex waved her away. "After what he's been through...go right ahead."

"Yeah, we'll just make ourselves at home," Kari offered, reaching a free hand into the crook of her husband's arm. "Maybe listen to this story with the kids."

Marion gripped his hand and led him gradually through the many rooms where they used to sit and enjoy one another.

THE BOOK

"Holden, I can't even begin to tell you…I don't even know where to start."

He knew where to start.

He stopped and locked eyes with the large wall in the great room where they had begun a list before he was taken. A list of random ideas of where they could find old books or pages or paragraphs. The list had been three lines long when he left. Now, the fine, dark print had bled onto a second wall to the right of the fireplace.

"That man there, and the older couple sitting on the couch, those are two of Winston's neighbors," Marion whispered, pointing them out. One of the older women noticed her and waved. "Their houses are even bigger than this one. It was Jeff's idea to reach out to them because he figured that we would need more space. You wouldn't believe it, Holden. Each of them had a few books in their house. Stuff that their family had hidden for sentimental reasons. They broke the law to keep those books and when Winston showed them the differences…they were keyed up to join. And Holden, I swear you're going to lose your head over this. Without you here, Shane has been amazing. He's really here for himself now. Every time a new person joins the group, Shane forces them to list out their talents, no matter how small, and now he has a construction crew! They remodeled the guest house, built a new bathroom and completely fixed up the attic with bunks and everything. So many people are living here, it's crazy. Oh, and they renovated the basement. Can you believe it! Shane rebuilt all the bookshelves so they're shallow enough to hold as many stories as possible without having to stack books in front of one another."

"Stack them? Since when did we do that?"

"Since we got more books," she chirped. "Must be over three hundred more since you left."

"What?" he sputtered in shock. "You're kidding."

"Nope. We even have some duplicates and almost as many book pages."

"From where?"

"Look at the wall. Everyone comes up with ideas, we follow a few leads and we just...find them. See those people on the couch with The Book. It's their job to read through a new story aloud with four other people. Two of them are following along with the digital version and one is reviewing any possible changes in Winston's log book. Then they take one of the many leaves from the yard," she paused, giddy, "God's paper...remember?" Holden bobbed his head in the memory of little Ronnie. "And then we use our own homemade ink to write out the differences and mark out the page."

"This...this is so great."

Marion turned to agree with him, but she could see so much missing beyond his withered words. Marion saw what Holden had seen in himself every time he passed his reflection. But she didn't ask him that question. "What happened to you Holden? Where have you been all this time?"

"First?" he asked, squinting one eye as the disheartening images were brought to memory. "Hiding out with some Unfortunates until I looked different. Hitchhiking for a while. Staying away from major cities until I met Alex and Kari. After they listened to me about The Book, I drove with them back to their apartment and helped them move. Her favorite novel is *The Catcher in the Rye*. Funny, right?" They shared a laugh, but Holden was embarrassed by his dirty smile and turned away.

Marion's heart was broken for him. She gripped his hand tighter as she spoke. "You don't seem happy."

"I am happy. I just...I'm afraid it may all be for nothing."

THE BOOK

"Holden. If anyone should be happy, it should be you. This is all because of you. If any of these people knew you were here right now..."

"Yeah, well. They're not going to like what I have to say." Marion looked concerned. When he didn't reassure her with his typical shrug of indifference, she grew frightened. There was too much. He needed to avoid the matter, so he changed the subject. "I noticed all those children in the sitting room. Are you teaching classes?"

"We call it *Knights and Bishops*. It was Winston's idea," she noted, walking him back toward the foyer. "He thought that, as a group, we should raise any children we have in the stories of these books and teach them everything we can about the Publishing House with the sole intention of making them as intelligent as possible so that one day they could be placed secretly within any government organization. And then, on the day we strike, they'll all move at the same time."

"The day we strike? Man, you guys have come a long way in only a couple months."

Holden's tired eyes shimmered as he watched the group of seven toddlers listen intently to the young woman who was seated at the piano bench with a tall children's book, its once-saturated cover art now dim and dusty. They weren't just pawns anymore. He had been gone for eleven weeks and they had moved forward without him – to the edge of the board to create their own, much stronger pieces. Marion was so happy to see his response that she began to swing his arm with her own.

"Winston was right, Holden. Every time a new person came in, there was another mind. And it was like we were all one brain that just continued to grow smarter and smarter."

"Is this actually going to work?"

"Holden." A rosy glow twinkled her fresh, strong-featured face and she turned to look deeply into him. "We have a grass roots movement in every state where buildings have been branded. We send people off every week and Moby is constantly out delivering Muckrakers. It's all so –"

"What's a *Muckraker*?"

"Oh, Winston again. I don't know where that word came from, but it's what we call the branding machines now." Holden couldn't help but picture Jane's face. He blinked irregularly and his lined forehead contracted. Marion switched gears without understanding his reaction. "People have quit their jobs to come here...pooled all their life savings into a large fund for groceries and things. Everyone is working. All day long, someone is doing something. I know. It sounds crazy, right? Can I take you to the library? I know you want to clean yourself up, but it'll be quick."

Marion led Holden down the cellar steps so they could keep talking without the constant brewing of people walking around them. Holden noticed the smell before he even reached the cobbled floor and once he noticed the new bookshelves, he was almost sad. The scent had once been musty and unappealing, but that was the cellar. Now, the same, crisp tang that collected in his nose was overwhelmed by the smells of pine and sawdust. Holden knew it was for the better. The shelves looked wonderful and there were so many narrow aisles with plenty of shelf space open for new books. Still, he couldn't help missing the smell.

"It's so empty down here," Holden concluded aloud, as he peeked around the newly-constructed shelves. "You'd think it'd be filled with readers."

"No. Not anymore. One of the men we recruited from the neighborhood was a science teacher and he told us that the moisture we create with our breath isn't good for the books. It makes foxes or foxing or something on the paper. It's mold. So we try to have no more than two people down here at a time."

"Let me guess…"

"That's right," she admitted, spinning in place beneath one of the many new light fixtures. "I'm a Librarian again."

Holden looked admiringly at her for a while without speaking, pleased and impressed with the woman she had become. "You look good, Marion."

"Thanks."

They walked further into the cellar and found a tall man dressed all in black sitting at the desk, reading a book where the letters of the title on the cover were arranged on shelves, leaning and crooked, like a series of books. Holden read the title quickly before the man noticed them. It was called *If On A Winter's Night A Traveller* by someone named Calvino. Holden was amazed at how long it took for the man dressed in black to turn and notice them. He had been so gentle with each page and so engulfed in the writing that when he finally saw them standing nearby, he hastily closed the book and stumbled over his words.

"Sorry, Marion. I'll…give you some privacy."

The man rose, ducked under the pipes along the vaulted cellar ceiling and walked to the stairs. Marion didn't respond as he left. She allowed him to believe that she had brought a newcomer, possibly an Unfortunate, downstairs for their usual eighteen minute ritual. As Holden watched the man's lengthy legs disappear from view, he nodded in the direction of the desk to ask, without a word, who the self-appointedly formal man had been.

"You wouldn't believe me if I told you."

"Try me."

Marion leaned in to whisper, although everyone in the house other than Holden and his new friends already knew. "His name is Finch. About a year ago, that guy came to the bar asking me if he could buy the book pages from the walls."

"Really?"

"Yeah. He gave me his name and number and told me to call him when I was willing to sell. I assumed Finch was a collector or something…but apparently he was involved in some black market for books."

She was right. He couldn't believe it. "How did you find him again?"

"I didn't have to. After you vanished, Ephraim and I were talking and he told me that he used Finch all the time. Sold the stuff he didn't like right out of the antique store. Even went with him to a few estate sales. Finch was the go-to guy for selling and buying anything that had to do with books."

"Wow. You trust him down here?"

"Holden, you don't understand." Marion broke, clearly arriving at the most exciting part of the story. "Finch isn't a reader. Never owned a copy of The Book and never bothered to check out the ones he sold for other people. Not even the more expensive editions. That man feels the most guilt out of all of us. He walks around here ashamed all day, as if he invented The Book. He was the one person who could have figured it all out first and saved books that were close to destruction. And he didn't." Marion tilted her head to look up at the cellar door, still whispering as if he were there. "But although Finch has never read a word, he knows more about the condition of books and how to protect them than all of us combined. That was his livelihood. He cared about the spine, who the author was, the title on the cover, if there were pages dog-eared, torn or missing, but never the content. He couldn't have cared less about the words. He was just concerned with profit. So Ephraim and I reached out and Finch has been here ever since. In fact, he's the reason our list on the wall is so large. The man's a gold mine of information. If there's anyone in this lonely world who would know where to find books, it's Finch."

"Marion, that's so wonderful."

"No, what's even more wonderful is this little green log book he brought with. Inside it are all the people he has ever sold to." She paused, waiting for him to understand the magnitude of it. "A list of people who are looking for books, Holden. People like us. We haven't even reached out to them, yet. But Winston is like a little kid, he's so excited."

"Well, it really seems like you guys have a lot of things going for you. Oh, hey…I could use one of those," he blurted arbitrarily, reaching into a bowl of fingernail clippers.

"No, don't. I'll find you another pair."

"Marion. Check out these bad boys." Holden turned his hand around so she could see how badly he needed them. "One of the many comforts that have been unavailable over the past few months."

She smirked and handed one of the clippers to him. "Flip up the metal handle."

Holden followed her instructions reluctantly, only to understand the purpose of the bowl when the handle spun gently into the light. Engraved into the shiny, metal lip were the words, *Ex Libris*. The bowl was there for the ceremony of it all. The clippers were a right-of-passage for people who were leaving The Book behind. That was why Holden couldn't use them. The one he had reached for was meant for someone else. As Marion took Holden by the hand and led him over to the reading nook, he tried to remember where he had seen those words before and what, at all, they had meant. It came to him when he saw the new art piece that was hanging over the high-backed couch in the corner.

For those raised in a sustainable world, it was hard to break the mindset of reduce, reuse and recycle, but the artist had done so without selling out to the man. The elaborate piece was painted in shades of brown and cream on strips of remnant shelving from Winston's bookcase. Sheathed by a border of painted garland was a man standing in a meadow, gripping a book and holding it triumphantly to the sky. Below him was an open, empty rectangle and guarding the entire image, rising high above the book, were the same two words:

EX LIBRIS

Holden recognized the painting instantly. He had seen that exact image on the day he finally held his favorite book, *The Catcher in the Rye*. In fact, he had been standing in that very spot. The painting was a replica of the bookplate from the inside cover of Winston's copy. And it was beautiful.

"What does it mean?" Holden asked, studying a piece of art for the first time in his life. In such calm curiosity, he repeated himself. "*Ex Libris*. What does it mean, Marion?"

She turned and kissed his cheek before speaking the words with tears in her eyes. "It's Latin. It means: *out of the book*."

"Out of The Book?" he confirmed, hearing the meaning.

"Yeah," Marion turned and gazed up at the painting once more. Smiling proudly, she added, "Whenever anyone sees this painting...they think that man holding the book is you. Holden, don't you realize...this is all because of you. We've only grown strong because we wanted to make you proud."

He didn't know what to say. He had come there ready to lay a harsh reality on them, but the group had grown stronger and they still thought they could win. They believed in what they were doing. They believed in him, of all people. And knowing what he had been preparing to tell them, thinking on it each day as he made his way home, Holden felt a knot of grief engorge his throat.

"I feel so...proud. I just..." he stopped, and gazed up at the victory displayed on the painting before him. He was a statue in oil, immortalized as a hero for something he felt he hadn't even done. "I just hope you guys feel the same way after you hear what I have to say."

"Okay," she hummed, discerning the deep disparity on his face. "What do you want me to do?"

His voice was war-torn and temperate as he laid out a very simple request. "Round people up, Marion. I don't know how, but get them all into one place. As many as you can."

"Alright," she agreed. "But first...you need a bath."

There was a chapel in Wilmette that sat itself within the crooked fingers of several tiny avenues. Most days, it was lonely and empty inside. That afternoon, however, there were nearly fifty people congregating anxiously in expectation of the good news. Among the stillness and between the rows of fugitive readers waiting ardently for their unseen leader to address them, was an unstated atmosphere of sanctity and righteousness that was lost on no one.

At the apse of the small chapel was a sitting room. In the corner of the sitting room sat an ornate wooden chair without a cushion and a table where goblets and other holy paraphernalia were arranged. Holden Clifford had grown accustomed to sitting on the hardened concrete of the world over the past months and he found the cushionless discomfort comforting. He cracked his knuckles and ran a hand over his still-bearded face. It felt good to be clean. Old clothes. Same look. New mind. It also felt good to be alone before giving his proclamation. He didn't have to be alone; he just thought it was smarter. So many people would be vying for his attention to introduce themselves and tell him what they were reading and why they had moved from South Dakota to join his group. Holden wanted to be there for them, but he needed to think.

The people in that room, the courageous *Ex Libris*, were different than what he had been expecting to come home to. More importantly, they didn't really know him. Holden needed time to prepare the exact way he would explain everything so they would understand and not think that he had been brainwashed or recycled or was just plain batty. Of course, he *had* shown up at the house all helter-skelter, but Marion made sure that few people saw him before he cleaned up.

While Holden had been changing in Winston's bedroom, Marion popped in to tell him that the group was thrilled to hear what he had to say and that they would meet down the block at a tiny chapel. One of Winston's neighbors had reached out to the minister there because they knew the man had strong feelings against The Book. Just like every other church in the world, there were small, inexpensive copies of the digital reading device lining the aisles. Simple, small editions that held only enough space for the Bible. The Holy Book, as it was called, was wrapped in green linen and printed with the seal of a golden cross over a recycling icon that, when placed together, resembled an ancient, Celtic headstone.

The minister, Trent Osgood, was eager to join their cause because he had felt betrayed by the government and the publishers of The Book for almost as long as Winston. It was an outlandish thought, but Trent felt that they were trying to change his faith. Again, with subtlety. They weren't so bold as to alter the quotations of Jesus or come up with an alternate ending or remove a commandment. The Bible was the one book in the world that they could never erase. No, instead they decided that new books, a collection called the Apocrypha, would be added to the original text. When the Bible was released digitally as *The Holy Book*, there were twelve letters from completely different authors between the Old Testament and the New. Most of the world believed that they weren't inspired by God. Most did not adhere to the words within them. But when the Publishing House created the single, uniform edition of *The Holy Book*, the Apocryphal books were added. Because, as the story goes, some people believed them to be the word of God.

The minister saw the addition of those books as a way for the church (and apparently the government) to enact more control over their flock because they included rules and laws that couldn't be found in the original books of the Bible. When Trent Osgood arrived to their group with an illegal printed copy, of the Bible, he not only brought a much needed location for them to have large meetings with additional facilities, storage space and more, but he also brought with him a well-cultured wisdom and viewpoint that they hadn't anticipated.

When Holden walked down the stairs to find his way to the church, he noticed another painting on the wall of Winston's estate where, within multiple planes of life, were the words: *The Bereans of Bedlam*. It didn't make much sense at the time, but Marion explained it to him as she walked him to the church.

The first thing the minister had shared with the group upon his arrival was a verse from the Bible – a collection of books that they knew were the most widely read of all time. It didn't matter what religion each of the *Ex Libris* had been, the words Trent read sang of a belief in the discovery of truth that they forever wanted to uphold. The passage was from the Book of Acts.

> "These were more fair-minded than those in Thessalonica, in that they received the word with all

readiness, and searched the Scriptures daily to find out whether these things were so."

The few teenagers of the group began calling themselves *The Bereans of Bedlam* because the Bereans were the 'fair-minded' people from the verse that had taken the time to confirm that what they had been told was the truth. The *Ex Libris* were so fired up about their movement. Each of them was a proclamation of honesty and free speech. And this was the group, with their convictions about fact in the face of fiction, that Holden met at the front of the chapel with the most implausible message.

Clearing his throat, Holden stood from the comfortless chair and stepped into the apse of the chapel. Amid the riotous applause that he attempted to slay with a lower hand, a child said, "That's him, Mom! I know that's him!"

Holden approached the pulpit, emaciated and mild, "Please, you guys." He laughed. "Please, just let me talk. You may not like me very much by the end of this and I just want to make sure that you all have the right outlook on things before I begin." A questioning murmur wound through the group, but it was stunted when he continued.

"Most of you don't know me other than by name. I am a pipe fitter. I am an ex-husband. I'm a dad. I am a reader..." At this, applause erupted and he fought to stifle it by raising his hands in peace. Someone shouted *Ex Libris* from the back and the wave of praise only increased. "Please. This is not a time to be joyful. Our children's children will have that opportunity. Not us. We're in a war. You shouldn't be applauding."

Silence.

Disappointed silence.

Holden took a deep breath.

"This all began because I read the writing on the wall and disagreed. Over the course of the past weeks, I've learned a lot about The Book from people on the road. And you need to know what I know." Holden took a breather before stepping up to something he knew would be taken the wrong way. "The technology itself, although it's corrupted and controlling, is really quite beautiful and when it was created, it was created in love," Holden witnessed the shift toward uncertainty on their faces and he fought hard to remain steadfast in his telling of the story. "See, our planet was in trouble and we were on the verge of technological breakthroughs every day. People longed for something new and a way to save future generations like ours. All that hard work was warped because of The Book. Most of you don't even know how it had gotten so centralized. When this all began, there were libraries and used bookstores scattered throughout the world overstocked with decrepit, rotting reminders of our misused resources. And while I would love to have those back right now, at the time it didn't make sense. I know you don't want to hear any of this, but when The Book came out, it was a good thing. Actually, let me rephrase that," he paused, nodding as he found the right words.

"The digital book was a good thing. Not many people know this, but, at one point, each publishing house came out with their own version of the digital book. There must have been fifteen to twenty versions, each that appealed to a different people group. But the government had a plan that, as I've learned, spans a long time. And it began by using our guilt and our fear. They told our grandparents that selling paper books was wrong. That reading paper books was evil. And if you had any in your library, especially if you weren't reading them, you were just as much to blame for the destruction of our planet as the companies who dumped toxic waste into the water supply. They encouraged the digital book heavily and warned that if we didn't change our viewpoint on things, the world would not survive. The primary solution they endorsed was The Book. The government decided to take technology that already existed and they created something far better using our grandparents' tax dollars. And then they cornered the market on digital reading devices by giving The Book away for free.

As Holden elaborated, gasps wove through the room in warps and wefts. "They gave it away for free because not everyone could afford the new technology. But nothing in the world is free. They had one, uncomplicated stipulation. Our government told people that if they brought in fifty used books, they would be handed a free copy of their new, government-issued digital reading device. The Book was the most functional, most attractive, most convenient version of the electronic book and it easily surpassed every other option on the shelves.

"Trick was, you couldn't just buy The Book and the demand was high. People began raiding used bookstores just so they could get the newest device for free and sell it for an outrageous profit. Eventually, to avoid such pandemonium and theft, which was certainly planned, the government developed *Indivisible Publishing*, a profit-based subsidiary of the Publishing House. This provided them with a way to channel money through The Book as well as a way to create newer editions that would appeal to a large mass, in hopes that it would soon eradicate any of their competition.

Holden took a sip from the glass of water Marion had left on the pulpit and coughed into his fist. "Within eight years...*eight years*...there was only one way you could read without receiving a dirty look from someone else. Through The Book. Within twelve years, you couldn't read from a paper copy without breaking the law and receiving an exorbitant fine of eight hundred dollars. A year later it was jail time. A year after that, the only way anyone could read, was through The Book. It happened that fast. The Great Recycling had removed so many of our freedoms forever.

"To those of you who knew those details, my thanks for remaining patient. To others of you, this knowledge has come as a surprise. The important lesson you should take away is that their primary intent behind manipulating the outlet for reading was motivated by a singular factor. Control. What had once been a marvelous development of technology that reformed our thinking about forestry and paper had quickly been compromised, altered and placed into the hands of people with control at their hearts. Believe me. I completely understand their motivations. And not because of what Winston had shared with me that first day in the cellar," Holden affirmed, raising a hand to greet him, "Missed you, man. The reason is because eleven weeks ago, I was captured by Agents of the Publishing House."

A riot of questioning and frightful noises rumbled like a caravan of horses through the small chapel. Holden grabbed the reins and pulled tight. *"And I think it's safe to say,"* he proclaimed, over the commotion, "that I'm the first person in over a hundred years that has escaped their custody. And all for one simple reason. They underestimated me. Yes, I was captured and, in fact, my daughter was hurt in the process. But there's so much we can learn from what happened. I lived to tell the tale. On top of that, I've drawn a rough layout of the entire building on pieces of fabric and plastic. I know where the *real* Publishing House is located in our nation's capital and I have a rough estimate of how many people work there, since I funneled them out of the building. These are things we can use."

"Did they try to recycle you?" a young woman shouted.

THE BOOK

A roar of other questions barricaded him from continuing and Holden had no choice but to stand and wait for them to subside. In the minutes that passed, he looked around the room for people he knew and noticed Alex and Kari in the front row, smiling. Holden recalled the long journey they'd had across the country together and he smiled back at them and the tiny baby slung between their arms.

"I know you guys have a lot of questions, but you have to accept that they may need to go unanswered." As the murmuring continued, Holden started realizing, all too late, that his attitude of authority was unwelcome in a group of naturally rebellious people. "I was fine and I am fine. When I first got there, they didn't do anything to me. I had been spared, but for a purpose. They wanted to frame me. To use me as they used so many Americans before, to destroy the last remaining copies of books on the planet. At the Library of Congress there is a single copy of every book ever written, except for the ones they've banned entirely. They told me that after using me to destroy the last library in existence, they would kill me and use my crime to incite patriotism throughout the world. From there, who knows? Change laws...change a lot of things. They would be free, once and for all, to alter The Book as they pleased because there would be no originals left in the world to challenge them."

There was a respectful silence in the chapel now. Holden allowed his mind to rest in it before moving on. "I know that our grass roots movement is working. I can see that and I'm proud of you. Shane. Shane, I'm proud of you," Holden hollered out, until he eventually found his friend standing at the back of the room. They shared a smile and he could tell in a glance that they had a lot to discuss. "I just don't think we have a choice. We have to make a big move."

"Well, what do you suggest?" a teenager, one of the *Bereans of Bedlam*, asked from the front row.

"We have to save as many books as possible. I mean, we're lucky that we have such a great library, but there are so many pre-digital stories out there, fiction and non, that we simply don't have. And some of these books, an amount that could fill this church, are worth dying for." Holden recalled what Winston had told him as he raced back to The Library to save Marion. "These pages are worth more than me. Worth more than all of us combined. I know you guys have a lot of ideas of how we can find more, but this whole thing will only work if we stop them from winning. When this is over, and we don't have an original version of a book, we might as well consider it dead. We can never be sure if what we are reading is genuine. We'll never be able to know if another author is on the page or whether our imagination is being forced toward some particular end. How can we preserve our personal freedoms when we can't turn off the propaganda?"

The solutions began to sneak in from the crowd.

"Let's convince the people who work at the Library of Congress."

"Yeah. And every day after work they take home a few books."

A smattering of agreeable noises sprinkled the church.

Someone else shouted. "Yes, specific books that we know will be important in the future."

"No!" Holden disagreed over the racket. "Guys, you're not listening to me. The building and all the books will be destroyed any day now. Hell, they could be gone tomorrow for all we know. We have to move quickly. I got away before they forced me to do it...but they're going through with their plan with or without me."

THE BOOK

He paused to take a breath, stepped back from the pulpit and sat on the carpeted steps before them. He could see in their faces that they were waiting expectantly for his solution. "To be honest, it has been a breath of fresh air, returning here. Your spirit. Your courage. Your hope. It's in the air, guys. I don't mean to diminish that. I truly…I don't. My life over the past eleven weeks has been horrible. There were times I lost hope. Times I thought I wouldn't get through it. But I have. I know we won't be able to beat them overnight. But we still need to try. We need to take risks. Make big moves. It's not a surprise that the rain has come back. Our time of rejoicing in the discovery of their lies and our decision to rebel is over, man. The revolution has to begin today." Holden stood up and raised his voice. "The Book is still updating! I've seen it! I've watched people's faces as they hunger for that machine to turn back on. Their fingers swooping over the page like vultures as they devour the words they trust. Every day it's getting worse!"

Holden, once a simple-minded man, now stood before them a great and powerful mind that could sense their anticipation. As he neared his final statement, he saw them looking up at him with golden eyes of esteem that he knew would not last long.

"These milestones we're making aren't going to matter if we wake up to the bad news. They are still going to win and we can't let that happen. I've had time to think about it and I know what to do. But you have to trust me. We need to take risks. We need to make a single, big move." He paused to clear his throat and said, "So I'm going to set the Library of Congress on fire."

They built their strength upon words, both printed and digital. They determined their calling by what was the same and what was different and deleted. As readers who had been lied to all their lives, seeing their leader and hearing his words for the first time, the members of *Ex Libris* were soon meeting in groups in the gardens of the chapel and in the backyards of the neighborhood to carefully discuss a single, specific concern: whether Holden's mind was the original or if had been altered somehow by the Publishing House.

Eight of them had known Holden before he was taken and one of those eight was an eight-year-old. Their impression of him was limited and their simple acceptance of his reputation struggled to last under such an unexpected atmosphere of distrust and cynicism.

For a few days following, life at Winston's house was unpleasant. People were unimpressed with Holden. And there were some legitimate concerns over his mental condition. A rumor began that he had been brainwashed and that they were no longer safe. Every day, the house woke up to less people roaming the halls. And no one could argue against it. Their leader had arrived looking crazed and at his first opportunity to speak to the group, he told them that The Book was good and then endorsed setting fire to the last library on the planet. Regardless of his reasoning, there weren't many books left and he was willing to burn some of them. Because of that alone, many people didn't believe.

For the others, the most compelling reason to doubt Holden was because he had escaped. Even Winston had difficulty accepting that. Much wiser men had gone before him and only Holden had found his way home. But, as the week carried on, the shock of what he had said subsided and they began to understand his motivation for suggesting such drastic actions. Of course, if Shane hadn't been there it may have all fallen apart.

Holden was given honor as their leader. But they didn't know him and it was hard to trust what he had to say. On the other hand, they did know Shane. And they respected Shane. They listened to him. And when he told them that Holden had the best interest of the *Ex Libris* at heart, they stopped murmuring behind closed doors and started to listen. In less than a day, it made sense. They really didn't have much time. If Holden was right, the Library of Congress might be charred hunks of rubble by dinner. Their leader had spent every day for eleven weeks focused on the singular task of saving as many books as possible and they believed he had more planned than simply starting a fire, grabbing a few books and running. Once Holden was able to speak without dissent, he laid out the plan very clearly for everyone.

The Library of Congress had the most rigorous, most intense fire protection system on the planet. Holden knew that because he and Shane had studied the structure often during their apprenticeship. It was a perfect example of a multiple action protection system. The building integrated three distinct safeguarding methods, all of which General Fire Protection had installed in one or more buildings throughout Chicago.

The first system was the release of flame retardant foam from a hollow sprocket that coated the area and smothered the flames. This was often used in the protection of expensive, non-electronic property. The second, that would kick in if the foam system failed, was a typical, wet piping system. The pipes were filled with water and ready, at a moment's notice, to launch a continuous stream upon the blaze. If the wet system failed, for some unlikely reason, the third and final system would kick in. This option was the most unsafe and widely rejected as a viable alternative. It was incorporated into the most extreme plans when living organisms were unlikely to be present. A ventilation system that extracts all the oxygen from of the room, thus making the fire decay rapidly before having the ability to take down the building. As all of these would be integrated into the fire alarm, the manipulation of the complex system could be done easily by a professional technician like Holden or Shane. Based on their plan of attack, they could either increase or decrease the flames. Even time the burn. Once Holden explained why understanding such a system was beneficial to their goal of extracting the books from the library it was simply a question of when.

If a fire was started at the library and continued to burn at an even pace, the government would have no choice but to keep appearing as if they cared and would need to find an alternate solution for protecting the books. This is because when the government made the decision to recycle all the books on the planet and to bar people from owning paper copies, many rigorous laws were set in motion to ensure the safety of the originals. Holden had learned, through the oddest arrangement

THE BOOK

of wise Unfortunates and ragamuffin book lovers, that there were specific protective measures in place at the Library of Congress if such a tragedy occurred.

The most important books would be channeled from the reading room one shelf at a time and into a holding station before being carted away from the premises in government-issued trucks, while the local fire department would attempt to put out the inferno. At that point, Holden's plan detailed that members of *Ex Libris* would hijack one or two of these trucks. While some books would burn tragically in the fire and others would be ruined by blasts of water from the hydrants outside, they could drive back to Chicago happily because the most prized works of literature would be in their possession. It was an upturned way of thinking, but it was the only hope they had to save the most important literature on the planet.

The following day, after the consensus had been reached to move forward, Moby came home with his band of branders. He was so glad to see Holden was safe that he gave the man a rest and instantly became the voice of the movement. With Jeff's help, Moby developed a plan to 'export' the books from Washington DC while avoiding any satellite tracking systems. Once they knew what had to be done, they slaved over digital maps and crunched the numbers without sleep until they determined precisely where they could separate the books into multiple vehicles outside the capital and ditch the truck.

Helping where he could, Winston posed a suggestion that they would need to send someone to the Library of Congress to scout for help on the inside. They needed to find a well-placed librarian who could guarantee that the books they deemed to be the most important would be funneled into the right trucks and Winston did what he could to secure such a person in the limited time they had available.

Shane became the architect of the fire. He knew more about sprinkler systems than Holden and rallied the group around the plan with his charismatic attitude. Still working at General Fire, he used many of his contacts to gain access to the floor plans and schematic layout of the library, including complete plumbing and sprinkler plans. He even found the exact model of the main protection grid and brought one home so Holden could practice.

Everyone, even the teenagers, had been involved in the planning stage. They worked into the night, every night, until it was done. The only item left to be determined was to choose the four members who would drive east to finish the job. Shane was the first to volunteer, followed quickly by three other strong, confident men, but it didn't take long for everyone to silently agree on a different four. It was only right that the people who threw the first punches were the ones to take the last.

Marion and Holden.

Moby and Winston.

Although the man's body was old, Winston's mind was sharp. Moby was a master of disguise and deception. And while Marion and Holden were wanted terrorists with perhaps the most recognizable faces in the country, neither one would leave without the other. For the four of them, there were no other options. There was a high likelihood that they may not be coming back and they were unwilling to sacrifice a pawn unless it was their own.

The launch date was set and the remaining members of their group decided they needed to throw a party to blow off steam and cut through the obvious tension. Their ambitious plan seemed perfect, but there was no telling what would happen and all of them felt they should send their leaders to the front lines with a bang. Thankfully, although the weather remained gloomy, the rainfall had been kept to the city and they were able to celebrate with a very normal, very relaxed backyard barbecue.

Wearing flip flops and holding a plastic Frisbee, Holden walked out onto the grass feeling content. Little pow-wows of people surrounded the backyard of Winston's estate just as content, having agreed that they weren't going to discuss The Book. No one would utter a word about the Publishing House, or the androidian Agents, or the Library of Congress, or the fact that the four of them may never be coming back. They just had fun.

Fun, Holden thought.

How distant that word felt to him. It was unfamiliar and almost uninvited. The event was already a rousing success and he felt a bittersweetness in his mouth among swigs of beer. He had been able to relax and been able to enjoy himself, but, as every moment passed, he understood ever more that he would not be returning to that house.

Holden knew he would be able to start the fire and that Marion and Winston and Moby would be able to coordinate and bring the books safely home, but he understood his role was different and he accepted it. He was the one who would have to stay inside the building and monitor the sprinkler system to make sure things went according to plan and, if needed, to fight off anyone that tried to stop them. It wouldn't go down easily. He knew that. Men like Martin Trust (the director of Historic Homeland Whatever), would be looking for him. And although that man would not be expecting Holden to play such a risky hand, he would certainly make sure that Holden could not escape the capital after doing so. That was the reason why Holden would not allow Shane to take the role that was meant only for him. Even before stepping out of Alex and Kari's yellow station wagon, Holden had known that he would not be coming back.

But that was not the only thing he had kept from the group. Holden knew that the moment the fire was started and books were destroyed, other laws would be put into place. The government would be forced to treat this as a tragedy in the eyes of the American public and in turn, they would add better protection and perhaps write new laws to keep the books that survived the fire out of harm's way for future generations. It was a risky bet, since books would need to be destroyed for them to succeed, but if there was one thing Holden had learned from Martin Trust, it was that sacrifices were necessary for the greater good.

Winston had been the first one to tell him that books were more important than his own life and Holden believed that now. During so many solitary days sleeping under the watchful, arrogant sun, not knowing if he would ever make it back to them alive, Holden had made that honest distinction and accepted his worth. If he had to sacrifice himself to save all that freedom and change the world, he would do it. But he wasn't supposed to be thinking about that. He was supposed to be trying to relax and enjoy their night. To throw a Frisbee around and mingle. Have a drink or two and work the grill. Just be. Just have fun. Because, more than likely, it would be the last bit of fun he would ever have.

Shane saw Holden standing by himself at the mammoth, gorilla grill and walked over to meet him. A plume of fire launched into his face as he flipped the greasy burgers and he was momentarily lost in the smoke.

"Need some help there, sailor?" Shane asked, throwing an arm around his friend.

"Hey," Holden grinned, hugging him back. "Thanks for everything you did this week. I can't tell you how good it felt to just relax and let you guys close everything out."

"We're not talking about that, remember?" he said, jabbing him in the gut.

Holden nodded and looked away. He could see, across the yard, beyond a group of guys tossing bean bags, that Marion was laughing with another man he didn't know. She threw her head back and clasped her hands together, as he gesticulated wildly and pointed to the dog that was digging up Winston's garden. Marion lowered her head, pulled her hair behind her ears and looked up to see Holden watching her. Her smile faded a bit. And then it changed. Locking eyes with Holden, she smiled for him now. As the man continued speaking, Marion lost herself in Holden's gaze. And that perfect smile told him everything he ever wanted to hear.

He turned back to Shane refreshed and smirking. "Shane, buddy. Old pal of mine," he said in a hokey voice, getting another dig in the gut as he returned to the flame-scorched burgers. "How the Blackhawks doin'?"

"You don't want to know, bro. Let's just say I lost a little cash and Winston gave me a hard time about it. Most of the regulars are using a different bar down the street to watch the game now. It's weird without you there, man."

"Numbskull got you pulling doubles?"

"Aww, bro. You don't realize. We're gettin' hammered over there. This one job on Michigan, got me goin' up five stories and pullin'..."

As his best friend carried on complaining, Holden stood back and handed out burgers to the kids, just listening. Although Shane Dagget was crass and almost always inappropriate, Holden loved him. He was the closest person in Holden's life and it made him sad to think that he'd never see Shane again. He wouldn't say this aloud, of course. No one else needed to know. Most everyone had some hope that they would return unharmed, carrying stacks of books to the cellar. But Holden knew tragedy was coming. And although he would never wish the present away, he would miss Shane. Sitting in their van, tapping their fingers to the music, whistling at girls and just working together. It was stupid, but he would miss the simple act of just looking at blueprints, handing each other tools, bickering over who got to go home early, and just being around each other. The only thing that made it easier for Holden was knowing that Shane, for the first time in his life, had been able to make it on his own. Being apart from his best friend had been hard for him and Holden knew that, but being on the run for two months had been a blessing in disguise. Shane was going to be just fine. In the middle of his best friend's commentary on the over-usage of advertisement space on the ice of the United Center, Holden interrupted him. There was one thing left unsaid between them.

"Shane, I know we're not supposed to talk about this, but I've just gotta say something before I forget."

"Alright, bro...but this is it. We're supposed to be having fun."

"Yeah, I know." Holden unscrewed two beers and handed one off like a baton in a relay race. "In case this goes sour, I need you to look out for Eve and Jane for me, okay?"

"Eve?! That stinkin'..." he broke off, shaking his head, "I'm a monkey's uncle if you think for even a second that I'm taking care of Eve, after what she did to you."

"No, listen to me. She was scared, man. Don't act like you weren't scared when you found that book in my bag. That's what she was dealing with. But she'd been done with me for years. The truth was too hard for her to deal with, coming from someone she didn't trust. And I need you to follow through, alright? I'm just thinkin' that if this doesn't turn out the way it should," Holden tilted his head and carved a sharp look into his friend's eyes. Shane had a name for that look. It was the *last chance* look. Shane had one last chance to listen and agree before he could expect a direct sock to the gut. "There's really no telling how this is going to play out and it's important to me that Jane knows the truth. I don't want you to put her in harm's way and if bringing her into this ain't the right move, don't do it. I just..." Holden was getting worked up and Shane could tell he needed to give his friend a second to get through what had to be said. "Just look out for her, alright?"

"It's done," Shane confirmed with a sip of his beer. "A.D.A.D. bro."

"A.D.A.D." Holden smiled. *Jiggety jig*, it was good to be back. "I told you about that log book I left in her bedroom. By now, I'm sure she's found it and gone through it. And with that mark on her chest..."

"Bro, don't think about that right now."

"Just let me finish," he swallowed, determined to get beyond the thought. "With that mark on her chest, she's gotta be having a lot of questions. And if anyone will be there to answer her, I want it to be you. She trusts you, Shane. She'll listen to you because I won't be there. I know you never wanted to take on this kind of responsibility and I know this is big...but if I ain't here..."

"But you are here. And I heard you already. And I told you. Done."

"Alright," Holden relinquished. They clinked their glasses against one another and swayed a single, decisive nod. A simple gesture that, in some unexplainable way, had the ability to convey the very deep, honest feelings of faith and dependability those two men had for one another.

For most of the remaining evening, Holden relaxed in the comfort of the bench Winston often frequented and watched the groups of people interacting together. Winston found him there, joined him in the tranquility and together they sat and watched, communicating without a word how comforted they were in the knowledge that things would be different. They didn't know how yet, or when, but life would be different soon for all of the people in the backyard and many more to come. Their pace was derailed by Holden's return, but, in time, they would be back on track, heading toward the place where only dreams were possible. And although the two men were able to find such simple joy in the laughter, the wild activity and sounds of fun, there was a regretful sadness in the wind because they knew they wouldn't be around when such an unabashed display of freedom was a permanent fixture in the United States.

As day slid on toward evening, a few of them gathered wood from the trees along Winston's property and built a bonfire near the water. It was technically against the law to burn wood without a permit, especially if it wasn't from a rapidly renewable source, but none of them cared. After taking a few photographs around the billowing flames as one large group, the party moved to abandoned logs and side conversations quickly turned to ghost stories, read from tattered bindings and half-torn pages. They discussed tales, old and current. Even new ideas that sprang forth from the teenagers, feeling too young for the fight and too old for the fight of tomorrow that would be delivered through the *Knights and Bishops*.

And as the discussions carried on and Marion found her way to the log where Holden was sitting, they all began to realize that it was stories that brought them together. There were other obvious pieces to the wide-extending puzzle like freedom from oppression, the fight to restore their rights and the war against censorship, but it all began with books. Oh, how they loved to read. How the characters invoked life that could be felt on the

THE BOOK

page. How stories had the ability to break through the everyday actions of the typical drudgery to show them a world that they would never have been able to enjoy. An adventure of experiences ever beyond their reach. A time in which they were never born. A person they were never born into. An emotion they never knew they had. And a passion that they found they could no longer live without.

As confessions speckled the fire pit and they discussed their favorite stories and how they had come to meet them, Marion interlocked her fingers with Holden's and held his hand delicately in the light of the fire. It was this that made him realize it was love. They all loved books.

Each one of them carried a deep, heavy, profound and unending love for the richness of story and the bountiful eternity of wealth it forever poured upon them. That was something the Publishing House could never take away, no matter how many commas they moved or how many paragraphs they altered. No matter how many names they changed, they could never reach inside someone and stop a story. Could never force someone to retract a revolutionary idea or force their submission. These books were born out of imaginations and experiences. Out of heartache and trials. And those things, while often swimming in a world of fiction and fantasy, were real. Passion and spirit, real.

In a time of such harsh realities, it strengthened them to take a break and remember who they were. To know that they had something within themselves no computer could access. Even if every book on the earth was destroyed, stories would remain alive, inside of them. Unread by others and unedited by greedy, emotionless eyes. Each of them was a book with novels upon novels to tell and no matter what the outcome would be for Holden, Marion, Winston and Moby, they would succeed. Mankind would never lose its imagination. They were a race of scientists and explorers, seekers of truth and players of both comedy and tragedy. They studied for lifetimes and lost themselves in an hour between the wrinkles of velvet fiction. They were lovers and fighters. Soldiers of a war that raged on from the comfort of easy chairs and from below the delicate flicker of candle light. They were bibliophiles. They were the *Bereans of Bedlam*. The *Ex Libris*. And all of them loved the very nature of story.

They had been gone for only a few days, but life on the road was slow. Old men with their old joints didn't do well in tight spaces and they had to find rest stops every hour so Winston could get out and circulate some juice to the veins. It was good that they had planned so many side trips along the way because it meant that Holden and Marion would have practice hiding themselves from the prying eyes of people who watched the news too much.

Traveling incognito was old hat to Holden now. Actually, he wore an old hat during the drive. It was tousled and of the cowboy variety, but what Holden hadn't liked, Marion thought was cute and she constantly pointed out how *cute* he looked as a cowboy. It seemed like a waste of time to him now, choosing the right sunglasses and boots to go with, because although he was still on the 'most wanted' list, with a face that was latched to every media screen on the planet, no one ever expected to see him. At every rest stop, people would look him right in the eyes and not recognize him behind the beard. Holden often wondered if they did recognize, but kept their mouths shut in the interest of self-preservation.

'Cause, let's be honest, Uncle Sam is gonna keep tabs on anyone who keep tabs on others and no one wants to be a hero. Am I right, cowboy?

Marion, who now had short, sable black hair that was sliced erratically around her ears, neck and forehead, looked amazingly unlike the images that were still circulating the Yellow News, the main source for information in the capitol. Holden thought she looked great, but he still took every opportunity to remind her that the bounty on his head was much higher than hers.

It had taken them a dog's age to get to DC, but the conversations they had along the way were surprisingly smooth. There wasn't a need to discuss the plan because it was in the plan not to. All the work was done. Winston, through a series of grapevine phone calls, had discovered someone inside the Library of Congress who was deep and well-connected. They sent a few secure communications over email and were meeting in person once they 'landed' in Washington. Smooth sailing, really. They had their credentials, their blueprints, cash, fake identification and reservations at a swanky hotel. So they did what normal people, those who weren't conspiring to overthrow the government on a Tuesday, would do during a road trip. They spent the passing minutes of passing miles just talking about their lives.

And it was fun. As Moby drove, they shared things that had nothing to do with The Book. Learned things about one another that they hadn't known. Silly, inconsequential things, like the fact that Holden had never eaten coconut until he was in his twenties and that Marion could kill any bug in the world, regardless of its size or its fur-to-shell ratio, but if she saw a spider, of any sort, she would freeze and find herself unable to

THE BOOK

contemplate a solution for taking it from this world and bringing it into the next. They learned that Winston had had a scholarship to play college baseball and that Moby, in another life, had been a photographer for a hotshot clothing magazine, spoke French and had a brother serving proudly in the Marine Corps.

These stories seemed like an adventure into the imagination because, for them, it felt like life began when they learned the truth about The Book. And yet, the real truth was that life had been normal for them once. They had been completely different people, with quests and dreams, passionately opinionated about nonsense and devoted to callings that had little worth in comparison to The Book. But their new life came, and with a family to boot. They were family now, the four of them. Separated by blood but joined by centuries-old ink.

The roads were coming together and they could sense that the drive was nearing an end. As the rickety van rolled ever closer to the openness of Washington DC and further from the safety and seclusion of the home they'd left behind, the interior seemed to grow smaller and the air thinned and it felt as if they were driving up the slope of an endless mountain where the clouds were taking over the windows. Their lungs scratched at the air around them for whatever leftovers of oxygen someone hadn't already stolen. And although the palpable anxiety had seemed to reach its breaking point, it wasn't until they saw the white city along the wet, hazy horizon, with its unspoiled attitude, low to the ground like the teeth of an open and hungry mouth, that they rolled down the windows.

The breath caught in Holden's chest as they entered the city in their scrappy van. The last time he had been anywhere near the spotless buildings that passed leisurely by their vintage, rain-saturated windows, he had been running. In the opposite direction. The most frightening bite of that sandwich was that, from the perspective of the Publishing House, nothing had changed. Right now it tasted good to be back with a plan to take them down, but it could turn stale and soggy real quick if they were seen. Just in case, Holden tipped the brim of his cowboy hat over his eyes and waited for them to reach the hotel.

Minutes later, Marion called from the back seat with the digital map in her palm. "Moby, we're looking for Hotel Tailor. It's supposed to be up here on Independence and New Jersey."

Holden tilted his hat and peeked out the window to see the hotel. The structure had been comprised of an enormous collection of separately built boxes and geometric shapes that pierced one another with erratic intention. The glass windows that looked down on the van with disgust, popped from the ridges of the building at the most irregular, unexplainable intervals.

"Don't you think this is a bit flashy for us?" Holden mused, recalling how important it had been for him to look inconsequential to the world only weeks earlier.

"No, this is perfect," Winston cheered, nodding. "No one would expect that we would be paying eight thousand dollars a night."

Marion wanted to cry out, but she lost her voice. It took an extra moment to react. "What? That's crazy! Do you know how much we could do with that money back at the house?"

"Yes, and we're using it tonight. We are making this happen. And if this is happening tomorrow, it is very crucial that we sleep free and protected this evening. Even if that means we have to spend eight thousand per person."

"I thought you said per night?"

"Per person," he corrected.

"Awhoooo..."

THE BOOK

The van was getting warm.

"Marion, don't worry about it," Moby told her, as he drove the classic mini-van toward the valet. "The guy's loaded."

A young, very chipper valet opened the passenger-side door and greeted them with a smile.

"Be a good man and take this wretched walker away from me."

"Now, now..." Marion declared, suddenly forced to play the character they had decided would work best. "It's my job to look after you and I'm planning to have a good night's sleep. So you grab onto those handlebars and keep chuggin', pilgrim. Lift, one two. Lift, one two. Remember? It's a little dance, all the way to the room." Marion leaned toward the valet and nudged him with her elbow. "Otherwise, I'll be hearing it all night. *My legs. My legs. Why'd you let me walk?*"

The valet giggled, "Can't have that."

"No, we cannot. You guys coming or what? This guy'll park our car for us, ya' know."

"Yeah, I'm coming." The broad, sliding door on the opposite side of the van shot open with an ungreased twang and Holden hopped out wearing his slouched cowboy hat and dark sunglasses. According to Winston, and according to his checking account, Holden's hat and boots were extremely expensive. But, apparently, it was worth the price to achieve the perfect balance of curiosity and disinterest needed to keep the vultures off their backs.

Moby stepped from the driver's seat, flicked the keys to the valet and ambled back to the hatch where he tugged out a few bags almost as large as him and tossed them easily onto the nearby cart. A bellman noticed and skipped forward with a chirpy little grin.

"I'll handle this, kid," Moby warned. A few of the suitcases were empty and he didn't need the whispering of a punky bellman to ruin everything.

"Actually, sir, it's hotel policy that guests not take the..."

"Kid. You hear me now?" Moby snapped two of his fingers out and the boy could see a hundred mixed into the fold of the deliciously green bills.

"Certainly, sir. Right this way." He motioned for them to follow and the unlikely quartet of law-breaking, anarchist book lovers entered the hotel lobby and looked for a place to sit.

They had previously agreed that Moby would keep an eye on the bags, Winston would check them in (because of cameras) and Holden and Marion would keep a low profile somewhere near a coffee machine. As soon as Winston finished paying for their thirty-two thousand dollar (plus twelve percent tax) hotel room, they were ushered through the hallways by the bellman and left to rise to the top floor alone aboard the crystalline elevators.

The ride wasn't very long. It was illegal to construct tall buildings in Washington DC and naughty to even throw shadows on the more important ones. From their viewpoint, through their glass windows that swapped from opaque to clear with a twist of a knob on the wall, they were able to look out upon the white city and see the object of their focus beyond the bustle. Moby, Winston and Marion stared at the Library of Congress and envisioned the many steps each of them would have to take before they'd be on their way home, a success. Holden stared instead at a building to the left of the hotel. It was very average looking. Simple, square structure with stone and glass and steel and stone and glass. And steel. It had a nearly nonexistent entrance and didn't grab much attention from the sidewalk. There was no signage on the building or any feature that was worth noting other than a feathery metal sculpture that could be seen through the lobby windows and an exquisite emergency exit door.

"Is that it, Holden?" Marion asked, as she noticed him staring away at the building. "The Publishing House?"

"First three floors, at least. Simple, isn't it?"

"I would have never known," Winston muttered as he followed their eyes toward the building. "My mother worked there for thirty-seven years. I knew the name of the airport, the street she worked on and the floor, but I never saw an image of the building. I suppose they kept that secret for a reason."

"That's why I sketched out the plans," Holden finished, stepping back from the window. His eyes were done seeing things that only pissed him off. "Who knows, maybe we'll need to access that building one day. Now, at least, you'll know which one it is."

"Doesn't matter though." Marion added, "As long as *you* know which one it is we could always come back."

Holden looked back at her and smiled, reluctantly. "Right. Totally." Holden knew she was fishing. Marion seemed to believe, just as much as he did, that this trip was of the one-way type and she wanted to know why Holden thought the same. He turned toward the room and left her a warm smile instead.

Without talking it through, they unpacked the small amount they had brought with them and walked the open suitcases to the closet as a group. They had brought them along for the ride, hoping that the woman from the Library of Congress would be bringing them some books that evening. There was no guarantee of this, of course, but Winston's contact said the woman was more than eager to save anything she could.

They tried to relax and use the volumetric expanse of their suite to spread out, maybe put their legs up a bit, but the sudden shift from days of focused driving to minutes of waiting around was insufferable. Winston forced them to order something off the room service menu but even *his* stomach, the one that was usually pleased with anything, wasn't agreeing with him. Marion ordered a fruit plate and most of them abandoned the extravagant meals that came up to the room on fine, shiny china for a handful of red grapes and a bite of imported Havarti.

Time passed slowly in that room and they decided it was best to leave the television off and listen to the rain that seemed to follow them to the capital. It was better to avoid hearing any news about Holden, or seeing his face at the bottom of the screen and being reminded of the obstacles ahead and the odds that were stacked higher than the clouds against them.

At nine thirty-one in the evening a knock came at the door.

Wordless, they thought they had imagined it.

At nearly nine thirty-two, it came again.

Moby, being the most oppressive and least recognizable, went to the door and looked through the eyehole. With the distorted viewpoint, the woman appeared very round and, at the same time, very thin. Her eyes darted back and forth and she seemed to be mumbling, as if debating with herself why she hadn't gone home. Moby opened the door and, in quite an ordinary way, to avoid any increase in tension, greeted the woman with a gentle smile.

"You must be Rosemary."

"Yes…yes…" she stammered, rocking in place with two nylon, department store bags held at her sides. Her gray and blonde streaked hair hung in sweaty ropes from her scalp and her thick, librarian eyeglasses hung low on her nose. Moby could tell she was impatient to push them back into place.

"Please come in. We've been expecting you."

THE BOOK

Marion looked across the room at Holden, her cropped black hair swinging over her fretful eyes as her lips folded under each other. There was no going back now. Any opportunity they'd had to turn around had vanished. Gone with the wind.

Winston couldn't have been more thrilled to see her. He was sick of waiting around and had been looking forward to discovering what she had brought with. He hobbled out from one of the side bedrooms and, leading with his left leg, extended a hand as he approached. It took him ten steps to reach Rosemary, but she warmed in the presence of his simple temperament.

"I'm Winston. I am so, *so* overjoyed to see you," he gleamed, releasing her hand. "We have much to talk about."

"Not too much, I hope," she replied, looking jumpy.

"Is there something wrong?" Marion asked, eyeing the canvas bags.

"No. I've just...never been involved in anything like this before. I'm not really the adventurous type."

"Neither are we. Join the club."

"Quite literally...do." Winston chuckled, stupidly. "We have no membership fees and all we ask is that you clip down that flimsy nail on your pointer finger." Rosemary stifled a giggle at Winston's charm and searched for a seat nearby.

"Can we get you anything to drink or eat?" Moby inquired, nervously.

"I'm fine. Thank you. If it's alright...with you...I would like to discuss the matter and head out. It's *not* that I am *not* behind this one hundred percent. I am." She calmed for a moment before repeating, "I am. I simply don't do very well under such...pressure."

"You're doing just fine," Holden said, stepping around Moby to console her. With his hat, glasses and outfit removed, she recognized him instantly from the television and a sudden understanding washed over her.

"That's why you're wanted. Because of this. Because of The Book." She took another look at Marion and began to nod unhurriedly. "Both of you. You aren't involved with *The Free Thinkers* at all."

"No," Winston confirmed, with a curl of his nose. "An untruth that has been thrust upon them."

Rosemary nodded and seemed to relax. Although this was another layer to the cake that unquestionably increased her level of danger, it also added an engaging certainty that she had previously been unable to grasp. That everything Winston had told her friend was entirely true and that, with her job, she had been the literal embodiment of *in the right place at the right time*.

Over coffee (and cake), they discussed the plan for the next day. How Rosemary would begin moving some of the more important books at an earlier hour and how she would leave a few specific doors unlocked for Holden. Since her position at the library was rather elevated, her access was shockingly unlimited and she chose to memorize the list they provided her of the most important books in history, the ones she needed to work the hardest at retrieving, for her own safety.

"They can't search my mind," she noted, timidly. "Not yet, at least."

"I'm sure that's something they're working on," Moby added.

The laugh they shared was much needed because the discussion was about to elevate. About to get serious. And dangerous. Holden needed to talk to her about the fire.

The one detail they had not been sure of was where in the library to actually ignite the blaze. From the plans he and Shane had reviewed, there were nine areas that seemed most likely to stay aflame if all of the fire protection was off. What they needed to know was which of the nine corners had a collection of books that was alright to destroy. The topic was very sensitive to all of them and they had to force themselves to remember what they were doing it for and that their mission made sense and that it was all for the greater good. Some books were sacrificing themselves to save others. The ones that would change things.

Rosemary didn't even hesitate as she scanned the digital blueprints.

"This is the spot. Right here," she said, pointing. "No books. Just a card catalog. That can burn."

Holden circled it with a stylus pen and closed the log book. "Once the fire is set, there won't be much time. This stuff is old. It's going to light up real quick and we have to make sure the fire reaches high enough to react with the sprinkler heads. Once it does, all the sequences in the system will try to exterminate the fire, but I'll have shut those down already. The sprinkler heads will come on. They will sputter and trail off to a dull spray that won't be effective against the blaze. Leaving me enough time to escape," he lied, hoping no one would catch it, "That's when you overreact and begin all those security measures we talked about."

"And there's a lot to that," she breathed, imagining the turmoil. "There's a full team of guards and an office staffed with people that are instructed not to leave in case of a fire. They have to help save the books."

"Well, Uncle Sam must keep up appearances," Winston added.

"After that," Holden continued, "when the first truck is full and sent down the street, the one with as many of the books from that list as possible, you leave the building. At that point, Marion will be standing by to call Winston and tell him that it's left the building. Winston, you will be here at the window watching the truck with binoculars. Once the truck reaches the intersection we discussed, you will call Moby. Then Moby –"

"I take over, man. Like I said, I've got a group of guys on standby. All they know is that it's a heist and that they're well paid."

"By that time, Marion and I meet outside and move to the hotel while the fire department takes care of the building and saves the rest of the books. We arrive in ten minutes and then the three of us check out and drive home where we'll meet up with Moby. That's it." Holden looked around the room and felt the need to prepare them for what was actually going to happen. How they would realize that he hadn't left the building. "All I want to add is that it's very likely we may come upon a few hitches here and there. Some things might not go exactly to plan and when that happens, don't panic. Just take a second. Regroup. And then try to develop a secondary option of what you can do in the moment. If that happens, remind yourself that we have thought out every detail and that the plan is still going to work. Alright?"

They all agreed and Holden agreed with them, knowing that it would not at all go to plan. He was going to stay behind as the fire climbed the walls and he was going to wait until the fire department arrived to make sure that nothing and no one could come and ruin it all.

After working out a few of the minor details, Rosemary took the two canvas bags that she had left near the door and brought them to a table at the center of the room. One by one, she removed the books, like a midwife removing innocent twins from a mother's womb, and laid them out upon the crystal glass surface as gently as her muscles allowed. The four of them circled the table and admired the majestic pieces, each one from the top of their list of importance. A few times Winston stumbled in place, as if he hadn't believed a real copy existed. Once, when Rosemary took out *The Valiance of Raphael Petitto*, he reached for Moby's hand and gripped it tightly, pulling the man's enormous meat cleaver to his chest to stabilize his lungs as raspy, disbelieving breaths escaped his cheeks. Not only were the books on the table some of the most precious in the world, but they were in near mint condition. Their spines. Their bindings. Their covers and pages. Perfect. The four of them had never seen a book in such condition outside of a museum and it was a shock they had not been expecting. If these were the emotions they would feel over two canvas bags, how would their group react when Moby returned to Holden's estate with truck loads?

Rosemary folded the green, reusable canvas bags with the seal of the Library of Congress stamped onto the handles and stuffed them indifferently into the garbage. "This is all I could get...I mean...all I felt safe taking. I could have gotten more. I know I could have. I just felt so nervous."

Holden bellowed a deep laugh and collected himself quickly. "If you even knew what you have done for our cause, you wouldn't be saying that. Just a few of these books are worth the trip down here."

"Just this book," Winston stammered, reaching out for a novel that rested alone at the corner of the table. He almost didn't want to touch it, as if the acid in his fingers would turn it to dust.

Rosemary reached for her purse and jacket. "I'm afraid I must go. We've talked much longer than I was comfortable with and, what with the curfew, I think I shouldn't push my luck."

"Curfew?" Marion questioned. "What are you talking about?"

"Right. You're not from around here. It was the Department of Environmentalism's idea. A way to conserve our energy resources by enacting a curfew every night from eleven o'clock until four. During that time, there's only minimal electricity available and stoplights stay on for safety. That way it will keep people off the streets, generate less crime and the police will be able to monitor while we conserve energy at an outrageous rate."

Winston shook his head. "It's just like you said about The Book, Holden. Instill fear, play on guilt and suddenly people are agreeing to have their freedoms stripped away."

"Well, looks like we should let her go then," Moby suggested, leading her to the door. "Get some rest. Tomorrow is a big day."

"Yes, it is. A big, brand new day." Rosemary shook each of their hands before leaving, outwardly more nervous than when she had arrived.

With the door closed and the smell of old paper dusting the air, Winston returned to the table to admire the books while the three of them walked in different directions. No matter how hard it was to sleep in their private, comfortable bedrooms, they needed their energy. In one swift stroke, they may begin a revolution and regain an ounce of control. Tomorrow could very well be their reckoning.

Holden awoke at four o'clock in the morning. Exactly. He had left the fan on in the shower and when the curfew ended and the power came back on, it burst forth from its slumber to wake him from his. He sat in bed, staring at the white numbers on the face of his alarm clock. Time was an enemy today. It controlled his future and it held him in place. It would keep him impatient, perhaps as a joke. So much time had been needed for the Editors of The Book to make the world what it was. With such patience and diligence. Walking with the tiniest of steps. Holden awoke on the cusp of one large step in the opposite direction and the courage it took for him to rise from the bed, walk to the window, pull back the thick drapes and look out on the moistened monuments of a corrupted country was more than he knew he had.

After a light breakfast (once again their stomachs weren't agreeing with them), they took their time getting ready before reviewing their plans and holding one final meeting. The four of them sat around the table beside eight small towers of the finest literature the world had ever known and found that there wasn't much to say. The purpose for their dangerous mission was stacked in front of them, sharing the gloomy glow from the window, encouraging them to succeed. And that was enough. For they knew they would succeed. As long as they didn't get in their own way.

Winston raised his head slightly, calling attention to himself. "I would like to take this opportunity to thank you all for everything you've done these past months. Marion, what a woman you've become. Your courage to peel those pages from the walls of your family bar. And how you've woken every morning in my home, knowing it could be your last. How wonderful it's been to have you, so often, around me. You are more similar to my mother than I think you realize. And it has been such a treat to have a female presence in my home again. You have placed a new light in my heart. I look forward to us getting back and playing more chess." She smiled and reached a hand for his. He gripped it for a moment and let it go.

"Moby. How related you are to your uncle and yet, how far you have surpassed him. Not a moment's hesitation when I ask something of you or request your opinion. How you work constantly, with such ingenuity, knowing that being steadfast in your pursuits and running toward them may not bring you there when you want, but that it will bring you close. Your positivism and your strong will are two things I have missed from the company I once kept. You have been a gift and I look forward to the inventiveness you will continue to bring to our mission."

Moby bobbed his gargantuan head down for a moment and swooped it back up, again not showing emotion. They knew his gratitude was lingering somewhere inside, but Moby was a quite man with a thick layer of tough skin that took an eye of a dear friend to see through.

THE BOOK

Winston turned to the end of the table and pressed his tired lips together. He removed his glasses for a moment to wipe a tear. He cleaned them off with a handkerchief from his pocket, replaced them and adjusted his bow tie, as if the words he were about to say were important enough to warrant such ceremony.

"Holden Clifford. The son I never had. When you didn't come back with Moby the day you branded the bean and it became clear something had happened to you...how broken my heart was. Inside, I knew you were alright and something told me you would come back with such a story. At our first meeting, when I asked you to install the sprinkler system to protect my books, somewhere, in my heart of hearts, I knew you would protect my books in a much different way, if given the opportunity. I saw it in you. And while I know you do not believe yourself to be what we see...*know* that you *are*. Your fortitude is unparalleled by any man I have ever known. Evidence of such courage could only be witnessed through other people's written words. From books of fiction that were but imagination and hope. Verisimilitude and valiance that has changed my life. You, Holden, have changed my life. And I believe we will be able to witness how you will have changed so many others. What I would like to leave you with is a statement I hope you will carry with you until the day you die. I believe in you, Holden. And while I know you believe you have done nothing to warrant such a comment, know that I am so proud to call you my friend. And when you walk past me as my leader, these weary legs want to stand. I want to hold my head high. For you are a triumph among men in this time of such destitution."

The finality of those words placed a weighty hope in their hearts. It was an honor to know how much that man loved them.

Moby headed out early to get himself in place and contact his men before Marion and Holden left Winston in the room without saying goodbye. There were no goodbyes that day. Marion needed to be near the Library of Congress because she had to call Winston and alert him when one of the trucks was away, so together they walked, Marion and Holden, toward the looming dome of the only official library left standing after The Great (and terrible) Recycling. The rain was light and they walked without an umbrella. When they neared the steps and were prepared to depart, Holden continued walking and Marion grasped for his hand. He had a look on his face that told her not to say what she wanted to say, but he couldn't stop her.

"Holden, something doesn't feel right about this," she began, her eyes darting as if someone was waiting to leap out from any nearby corner and vanish them away.

"No, Marion. This is going to work. It's wonderful. I knew we could change things. I knew we could do something this quickly. It's going to work."

She reached out for him and brought him close.

They were kissing.

As their lips entwined and their warm breath passed and combined in an emotion neither of them thought they could share with one another, Holden released and tottered a step away. When he came forward again, they faced each other with eyes close and moist with affection. Marion wanted to kiss Holden for a second time. To make it more real. More memorable. To keep their first kiss from being abrupt and almost clumsy, but there were too many thoughts passing unspoken between them to make the moment a romantic one. Holden could see that Marion was frightened and knew exactly what she was thinking. Holden had really only met one person at the Publishing House. The director, Martin Trust. How could he be sure that there weren't more people involved? They had gone to such lengths to remove nearly every book on the planet.

How much harder would they fight to remove the remaining few? What they were going up against was so much greater than any of them had realized.

But he wouldn't allow her to say it.

Holden knew the truth. Even if they got a truck load of books, it wouldn't change things. Not in their lifetimes. Yes, it would be worth it. Worth risking his life for. They would have saved great works of literature and perhaps altered a few laws and extended the life of the books that weren't burned or stolen. But none of them were stupid enough to think that the Publishing House wouldn't take advantage of the situation and 'lose' more books in the process. But, at least (what they told themselves, at least), they would save a few.

Marion threw out one final, desperate attempt to keep them together and safe. She latched onto his arm and said, "Holden, we could leave. We can leave. We could...go together...somewhere. We can stop. We don't have to be part of this. We could just live our lives and let it go. I've thought about this so many times and pictured it when you were gone and I wished I would have told you. Then you came back and it...it made me think we could keep going, ya' know? But what if this is too big? Don't you want to just have a normal life?"

He turned to Marion and imagined it himself. In that moment of mere seconds, entire decades of dreams unfolded. How wonderful it would be. Start a new life with her and Jane and just live. Work. Maybe have children one day. Little *Us*'s running around. But it was a lie. Holden knew that dream was from a time he wasn't born into. Those privileges were for the privileged. For people born into a world where those freedoms existed, unthreatened.

Holden kissed her once more before saying, "We can't just let them take away our ability to think what we want. We may be the only ones who can stop them. We are literally walking into the fire they have built to smoke our minds. And if I cannot escape the fire, at least I can douse the flames."

"That was a beautiful thing to say, Holden," she said, understanding what those words meant for them.

"I have to go, Marion."

"I know," she said, "I love you." Marion paused, leaned forward and got his attention with her round and honest eyes. Then she said it again, "I love you, Holden."

"I know you do." He let go of her hand and walked around to the side of the building where he knew Rosemary had left the door open for him, knowing that if he stayed with Marion a minute longer, he would run away with her and leave all that they believed in behind.

Up close, Holden was astonished by the pure white of the building. Its finials. Its detailing. Its molding and perfected architecture. How beautiful it seemed to so many people. And yet, it was a prison. A prison for thoughts and freedom. Its bars were wooden shelves and its punishment was to be barred for the rest of life from so many hungry minds. Holden made his way past the dumpsters and toward the side entrance. The handle turned easily and he entered. No alarm. No problems. No one waiting on the other side to knock him on the head. As the saying goes, *so far so good*.

From his pocket, Holden removed the smart phone they had bought during their drive. It was a one-time-use phone that they loaded with blueprints to the library. He immediately scanned to the correct page and enlarged it to the width of the screen before progressing down the hall toward the staircase that would bring him where he needed to be. According to their plans, Rosemary had told Holden to find the main level and then an alcove where they archived the old card catalog. The space was unused, a fixture of something that had once been constantly busy, and was now the least protected corner of the building. The card catalog could burn. It wasn't as damaging to the rest of the collection, which meant it was less protected. But first, he had a job to do.

After reaching the lower level and navigating a few corners, keeping an eye out for people who could identify him, Holden eventually came to the mechanical closet which had also been left open for him. He checked the hallway again before entering and closed the door swiftly, bolting it in place. He had come this far without being detected and, at the very least, he needed to finish this portion without being bothered.

It was a good thing that Shane had gotten the mainframe from General Fire so Holden could practice on a prototype, because most of the switches and dials had been labeled with odd symbols and a numbering system that didn't match the blueprints. Still, there was an order to all things mechanical and he knew which switches to switch and which to delay. Time was against them right now and they were all waiting for him, the architect of the overthrow, to get the party started. But they would have to keep waiting while he lost two pounds, sweating out his anxieties and triple checking his calculations before moving on. If he was correct, according to the structural overview Shane had included in the floorplans, the foam system and the oxygen depletion system would be offline. Next he had to deal with the water supply.

Leaving the room, Holden trailed back the way he had come before taking another zigzag of staircases to the lowest floor and into the boiler room. The boiler room was the home of an enormous, bright red tank that stored a vast amount of water that was waiting, to be shot to the higher levels to douse the library in old, stagnant, black rain. That is, before it ran out and the main water supply from the city kicked in to finish the job. Although the tank was colossal, it was typically empty in eight minutes. General Fire normally shopped this portion of the job out to a separate company, but Holden knew his way around. He found the correct valve. It was two feet in diameter and it didn't want to move. But with enough pressure, it turned. Three and a half cranks was the right amount to keep the water from pumping steadily enough to beat the fire.

Holden closed the smart phone, put it in his pocket and felt the lighter and the cold can of fluid he knew he was about to use. The metal sparked against his skin in static excitement, as if letting him know that it was ready to play its part. To eat away the words they had so passionately cared for. Words the world may never read again. Holden took a moment to breathe. He put his back against the tank. It was cool and refreshing. He ran a hand through his short mop of hair and closed his eyes. *This is it. There really is no turning back now.* He knew it. Holden pinched the skin of his forehead, pulling out the ache that was beginning to eat his mind, and opened his eyes.

With unadulterated determination, he whispered, "Here we go."

Before the fire began, the activities of the library were as standard as usual. Not many guests beyond the typical group of school students and a few random gentleman and groups of women that seemed to speckle the halls of books like worms with insatiable hunger. People that would be added to a list of the possibly suspicious and the future recyclables. And there was a staff of security guards who were generally bored and spent many of their hours drifting off. The few people that worked the counters, gift area and coat check were often used to seeing so many different types. Life was generally so safe that few of them even noticed Holden. None of the ones that did

THE BOOK

notice Holden even bothered to wonder why he had spent so much time near the card catalog. The guards hadn't recognized the features that had been plastered on so many billboards and news station bulletins. He was just another scholar that faded into the background. One of those who didn't have to work. The ones who had enough money in their bank accounts to take the day off and enjoy a walk through the stale, musty shelves and stare at bindings that no one could open without thick, green rubber gloves.

But the alarm changed a lot of that.

The smoke brought havoc and the flames brought fear and the water brought wetness. Eventually every one of the staff realized that they should have noticed him. *Of course* he would have come to the library. Some of them would even lie and say they had seen him, in order to save their reputations.

But that was after.

Holden felt wrong when he opened the drawers of the catalogs to see the old writing and the many, many paper cards that listed a multitude of books that were housed in the last library. He had to keep reminding himself that he wasn't in a safe place. That the building he was in wore a mask of truth. That it pretended to be a sanctuary for knowledge, when it was actually a bastille, fortified to keep thoughts from escaping and changing things. He had to keep telling himself that he was in the den of the enemy. Because who could ever believe that setting it all on fire was the right thing to do?

As he pulled out the small, rectangular can of lighter fluid and raised the crimson tab, he began to squirt the tart smelling liquid onto the yellowing cards, channeling the self-loathing actions of the fireman, Guy Montag, from a story that no librarian would find. Holden kept replaying the looks he had gotten at the chapel after announcing his mission and how they had simply not believed him. How people were certain there was no way this could work. But it would.

It would, Holden, he thought as he squirted the last dribbles from the can, dropped it to the ground and reached for his lighter. *Another day. Another dollar.*

The hollow clatter from the fallen, empty container of lighter fluid echoed in the frighteningly corrupted silence of the domed building. People would be coming around soon to see where the noise had come from. He had no choice now. Holden felt the gear crack under his thumb, as white sparks of flint ignited a flame from the lighter before he dropped it to the card catalog and spun slowly away.

By the time all those employed by the government to protect the Library of Congress got over their confusion enough to recognize that they had failed in their job and that something horrible was about to happen, they accepted that speed was a necessity. And of course, for some reason, Rosemary, the director of Library Preservation, couldn't be found.

There was a scattering of fright because none of them knew precisely what to do in that situation. The patrons of the library were shuffling toward the large double doors, staring back as the smoke collected into the coffered recesses of the dome, but they were delighted to be a part of whatever was happening. In fact, they would have stayed to watch the books burn, these articles of such great interest, smolder and decay to dust. But when the water came on and doused their clothes with filthy wetness, the escape into the clean rain was swift.

The rest of them, the ones who still seemed unable to recall the correct response methods from their training, scrambled behind the courtesy desk for the emergency manual, because the one thing they did remember was that soon, if the fire didn't go out (and it should have been going out), the doors would shut and seal themselves closed and all the oxygen would be drawn out of the building.

Within two minutes, their hair and clothes were soaked and they quickly retreated to one of the back rooms where the special acquisitions vault should have been funneling books through an automatic emergency system. But the system wasn't running. *It should have been running!* The women looked at one another and realized that only Rosemary had the pass codes. Somewhere, a truck should be filling and preparing to drive away from the flames. *But they didn't have the pass codes and Rosemary was nowhere to be found.* So the women sat in the control center of the Library, their hair and bodies dripping from the smattering of moisture as they flipped frantically through the digital pages of the emergency manual, searching for some clue to a code they would never find.

34

Holden was saturated. His face, his hair, his body, drenched as he hid behind one of the larger bookcases in the corner behind a glass display case that rushed with water. It seemed that everyone had left the main building because the smoke was getting stronger and the smell was consuming. The sprinklers had done their job to keep the flames from overwhelming the nearer shelves. But Holden remained. He had to know that their group had enough time. Once he felt comfortable enough protecting the fire, he would use the single-use phone to call Winston to ensure that the truck was on its way before he left through a side entrance.

Then the water stopped.

All around him, the trusty sprockets in the ceiling ceased sending their failing mist of water onto the flaming shelves below. Holden expected a slight hiccup between the tank and the city's water supply, but he hadn't –

The thought came to him like a hot bullet from the chamber of an enemy's gun and Holden scrambled for the cell phone in his pocket. He called Winston to double check that everything was going to plan, but the response wasn't good. Marion hadn't called him yet. When they hung up, Holden didn't know what to think. According to Rosemary, more than enough time had passed. And with the water no longer reaching the fire sprinkler system, it was only a matter of time before all the books in that building would be destroyed.

Holden ran from the corner and into the flaming inferno. Something was going wrong. The trucks should have been on their way. The water should be running. Things should have been moving in the right direction, but Winston told him to get off the phone and call back in five minutes. Both of them knew that something had either happened to Rosemary or something had happened to Marion. Regardless, it meant that he was no longer safe. Holden did his best not to imagine Marion in pain as he crept along the soggy floor, through the climbing smoke, toward the center of the main reading room.

He knew that the inner circulation desk had the best vantage point. From there, he would be able to see through the doors and assess his safety. But when Holden got there, dodging the crumbling book cases and flames that licked at his limbs, he found more than he expected. Lying behind the counter, unconscious beside a toppled garbage can, was a woman with short, black hair and Japanese floral tattoos lacing her shoulders. It was Marion. Holden froze in the shock of it. Either someone had brought her in from outside or she had come in to find him and someone –

Holden heard a noise behind him and spun on his heels, just long enough to see the man's deformed face through the smoke before an oversized book crashed into his nose and sent him sprawling to the floor. From the man's cheek to his forehead were the words: *Don't Read The Book*, branded and melted into his buckled skin. The man who had silenced Holden as he

THE BOOK

reached out for his daughter had now silenced him as he reached out to the world.

If Holden had ever read the story, *The Steadfast Tin Soldier*, he would have recalled a very specific sentence as his mind drifted in the scorching heat.

"No doubt the little goblin in the snuffbox was to blame for that."

The phone.

Hearing the phone was what startled the two of them awake.

The overtly entertaining jingle that had been preprogrammed into the device burst out in whatever hollow space they found themselves in. Smoke burned their eyes and invaded their nostrils with heat and ash and sulfur. Holden heard someone coughing. He heard the tone in their exasperated voice and he turned, through some dark veil of green haze, to see who it was. But his eyes burned and he had to close them.

"Marion?"

"Holden?" she asked frightened.

"Oh, I'm so glad you're okay."

"I'm trapped. *I can't move!*"

Holden felt the rope around his wrists and struggled in place. "I can't either. I'm tied up."

"Where are we?"

"I'm not sure." He squinted and tried to adapt his eyes to the dark, but it was no use. The only light that streamed in through the foggy smoke came from a green exit sign, with a little white figure running toward an open white door – free to escape and yet ever frozen in that position.

"Marion, we're still at the library."

His eyes adjusted to the dark quickly. He saw the layer of smoke at his ankles which could only be there, and not at his eyes, if it were coming through the floorboards or from below the frame of the door. Holden wrestled again with his binding. It dug caverns of red flesh into his wrists, but the pain and the struggle was a waste of effort. He was practically a part of his chair and the binding was strong. So strong that his hands were cold and tingling.

"Holden, I'm scared. What happened?"

He turned to try and see her. "I was hit in the face by one of the Agents. He must have gotten you too. You came inside to find me, didn't you?"

"Rosemary didn't come out and then the fire was growing and growing. I knew something was wrong. Holden we have to get out of here!"

"Marion. They turned off the water."

"What?"

"The water supply to the building. I hadn't thought of that. Marion, they were expecting us. The whole time I thought they had underestimated me. But I was wrong. They knew we would do this. I played exactly into their hands. Maybe they even arranged my escape from the Publishing House."

"Don't even say something like that."

"Marion, they turned off the water. The entire library is burning and there is nothing we can do to stop it."

"What about the fire department?" she added frantically, "They're trained to handle this."

"Guys like me make their job possible, Marion. They go into the fire assuming that all systems are working. It's too dangerous otherwise. I know fire. It's my job to know. They aren't putting this out."

At that moment, Holden noticed that another figure was in the room with them. It was slumped to an awkward position on the floor. He could tell by her frame that it was a woman. It had to be Rosemary. What frightened him and created gooseflesh along his skin, was that she wasn't tied to a chair. *She wasn't tied to a chair.* That meant that they weren't worried about her helping them escape. From where he could hear Marion's voice, something told him that she wouldn't be able to see Rosemary's body. And he wouldn't tell her.

"Do you think they got the books out?" she coughed. "Or do you think that Rosemary betrayed us?"

"No Marion, I think she did her job the best she could. And if those books don't get out, it's okay."

"*Okay?!* We didn't fix anything and we're going to die in here!"

Holden coughed in the smoke and realized the room was quickly filling with it. "I don't regret anything. If you and I die in here, we die knowing the truth. Free. That's a gift that millions of people in this world don't have and something I wouldn't give up for anything. Die in the truth or live in a lie...today is a good day, Marion. Remember what is happening back at home. People will win."

"Just not today."

"No." He nodded, his eyes burning. "Not today."

"Holden...I love you." She exploded in a fit of coughing and he didn't know what to do to console her. With a raspy voice, she asked, "Can you do me a favor?"

THE BOOK

"Yes." The hot smoke was so thick now that he knew they wouldn't die from the flames. They would already be asleep by the time the fire reached that room. "What is it, Marion?"

She coughed again before saying, "Can you sing me a song?"

Normally he would have laughed at such a request. But it was the end now, wasn't it...?

"What song?"

"I...I don't know." She coughed again. "Just something old."

"Okay."

Holden thought back to all the songs he had ever heard in his entire life. He allowed the digitized mind that had been nurtured in The Book to scroll quickly through them until he reached the perfect song. His voice was meek and gentle. And he began with a hum.

The song was called, *Here comes the sun*. It was written by a man named George Harrison from a band called *The Beatles*. It was the first song on the flipside of their album, *Abbey Road*. He often sang it to Jane when she was an infant and would wake up in the middle of the night to her crying out because the lyrics come from a place in the heart of a loved one. Holden sang with heart to his little darling about how the years had been long and difficult. They had been cold and lonely. But his voice wound smoothly through the lyrics when he came to the line about how the sun was coming. Yes, the sun was coming and everything would be alright. Holden coughed and felt the room getting brighter as he continued.

Before moving into the next verse, Holden noticed that a small flicker of flames had eaten its way through one of the walls. In those tiny seconds, he was able to see more of the space around him and understood that they were in some sort of storage room for old religious artifacts. There were Bibles in glass cases and other books with ornate paintings upon the pages. His eyesight was fading, but through dizzying concentration he could see a large, polished cross on the wall beside him, reflecting the golden flames that mixed eerily with the green glow across the room.

And as he continued singing, Holden noticed a wooden plaque above the door that had been locked against them, that barred them from a freedom that the man in the green, exit-sign world continued to strive toward without success. The plaque of wood had a verse from the Bible carved into it. And as Holden began to grow dizzy, his mind pulling away from life as he strove with effort to stay conscious, he continued to read the verse over and over, picturing Jane and Winston and their group, and how he knew that, regardless of how they failed that day, they would triumph. The sun was coming.

The sun was coming.

The sun was coming.

Holden stopped singing and, with a whisper he said, "I love you Marion." Through the crashing of shelves and fixtures across the library, he waited to hear her respond.

But she didn't.

She was already unconscious. Already asleep.

Holden focused on the plaque as the edges caught fire. And just before his eyes closed for the last time, he read the verse and mouthed the most perfect words from the most famous book.

"Heaven and Earth shall pass away, but my words will remain forever."

36

A squawk came through on the walkie-talkie and it rattled the glass table in the meticulously maintained hotel room. But the old man standing at the window didn't flinch. It seemed as if he had lost his hearing in the shock of what his eyes were absorbing.

Below him, crowds of people gathered along the rain-drizzled streets, curious about the plume of smoke that rose high into the sky above the capital like the darkened twin of the Washington monument. Winston's shaky hand reached out and touched the cold window and he rested his palm against it, bracing himself from falling over as he saw flames between his wrinkled fingers from the dome in the distance. His tottering legs wanted to give out and tumble him through the glass to the ground as the walkie squawked again.

Holden hadn't answered his call.

Marion hadn't answered his call.

The fire department was nowhere to be found.

And the Library of Congress was burning to the ground.

By some cruel joke, the clouds parted above, and the ever-insistent rain stopped trying to put out the fire. It was almost as if the sky had been intimidated by the darkened cloud that formed over the government building, and the sun shot rays of warm light through the smoke to break the darkness with milky beams.

Within an hour, Winston and Moby were miles away from the borders of the nation's capital while every media outlet in the world streamed videos of Holden setting fire to the library from some hidden camera. Bold text of propaganda blazed beside the black and white film. They spliced this brutal act, the dropping of his lighter and the flames bursting from the card catalog, with images of the firemen that never arrived fighting diligently with an inferno that would never cease. Outside, on the respected lawns of the capital, people were on their knees, hugging one another and crying at the horrific scene. An hour after that, a building that the government claimed was the Publishing House for The Book exploded. This act was also blamed on Holden Clifford, the man they all recognized from eleven weeks of television ads, who had now been deemed the leader of *The Free Thinkers*.

Those unfamiliar with the controlling contents of The Book heard this news and were devastated by the fact that so many stories would be lost from the digital corruption and that, almost more importantly, the explosion would take The Book offline for a multitude of weeks. And when it came back on, some things could be different. Pages from their favorite books would be missing. And some of the world's most treasured stories could be gone forever because the last hard copies had burned, thanks to the terrorist, Holden Clifford.

They saw his face constantly in the media and were reminded of his evil deeds week after week. He was vilified and mocked. Children were taught in school about him. And it did not take long for everyone to agree that Holden Clifford was the clearest representation of evil. Within a year, the entire world had grown to hate him.

ADDENDUM

It is time we finished.

Allow me to begin.

The section you are about to read is an addendum to the original version of the story I wrote eleven years ago. We are attaching it to the back of our book and reprinting in full due to the recent outcry for understanding. We apologize for the delay, but the government controls too much and paper is the only technology we can trust. As you have witnessed with your very eyes, there has been success. But I only ask that you remain patient and appreciate what little I am allowed to divulge.

It has been nearly three decades since that day, when the torch burned round the world. I know that Holden's story has spread and that the truth has been delivered to so many of you, but your persistent request's have reached our ears. We realize your need to understand how we are suddenly living in the *happily ever after*. The most important thing I want to say is – *wake up*. The war is not over. You are living in the generation of the privileged. We, the people, thrive off of your support, but we need you to stop asking for updates from the front lines and join us here.

THE BOOK

Including the sentences above, there are a total of 6,860 words in this addendum. Keep track of the word count. Do not allow yourself to forget that a single word can *still* change the world. If the word count is incorrect, the following pages have been compromised. If that is the case, then you won't be reading this sentence. Those who you thought you trusted, those who introduced you to Holden's story, have already condemned you to a certain end. As we have learned, those who carry the misfortune of trust are those who the government will eventually recycle. Do not become one of these. Mind who you put your faith in and stay vigilant. For the end is near.

I know my words are harsh and unforgiving. But you must be fully aware that this is the most important battle our world has ever faced. Stand proud, knowing that you are holding the most powerful weapon society has fashioned. Printed truth. Unedited. Ex Libris.

You, dear reader, must continue on with the surety that you have broken the shackles Uncle Sam had on your thoughts. But this cannot be a celebration. Too many of you have believed the lies printed in The Book by the government controlled publishing house, *Gallantly Streaming*. Propaganda from the desk of Martin Trust. Too many have decided long ago that the war was based on confusion and misguided minds. But that was misinformation. You know that now. And the events of recent months are proof of our success. This is the reason you are still reading. You need to know what events led to our sudden presence upon the world stage.

First, let me remind you of the necessity to be patient. Others could have written this for me. Others with the narrative skill to weave reality through romantic words and creative metaphor. But I began this story and I feel that it is my duty to finish it. Holden gave me his heart and he would have wanted it this way.

So, mold your mind to be like that of an Editor and allow patience to wash over you.

Second, realize that I cannot disclose everything. No matter how hard we try, this story will reach the eyes of those we are attempting to defeat. Not all your questions will be answered.

Lastly, keep reading after you have passed the final page. Keep researching our texts for the truth of science and history. And keep writing. Please, keep writing. As long as we stay strong, they can never delete our minds.

What follows is only a vague description of how our success began. Savor it, because I cannot give more. I will introduce you to him. To the young, average-looking, well-placed chess piece who arrived at our doorstep with the gift of hope.

His name was Moses.

THE ARRIVAL OF THE QUEEN

    The multilevel shopping system that, like many others, had overtaken the downtown of the Chicago suburb, was the most feasible way to enjoy any shopping experience. There were many names for this place. At one time it had been called a market, another time a mall, another time the circuit. Now, it was simply known as the system. Everyone used it. It was much better than shopping at one store that carried everything. At the system, you could find a diversification of style, taste and budget.
    When you arrived at the oversized complex, you usually came prepared to carry many reusable bags as you walked miles from store to store. To get your groceries. Your clothing. Your shoes. Your musical instruments. Many seventeen-year-old boys came to the system with friends and used it as a place to meet young women and spend their inheritance on so many useless items. *This* boy didn't speak to anyone. In fact, he was wearing a baseball cap and sunglasses that shielded his eyes, his head hung low, as he seemed to walk the innocuous balconies of aisles and ride the moving staircases in search of a single store that it could take an hour to find. Shockingly enough, it found him.

A garish voice erupted from the frosted green glass of an enormous shop that rivaled the movie theater. The boy lowered his sunglasses to look at the two triangular windows that broke through the frost to reveal the store beyond. Upon these interactive windows appeared the recycling symbol. It animated slowly and the voice erupted again.

"Hey, there! Why don't you come on in?"

A digitized head of a man with his hair parted down the center poked from the side of the moving triangular icon. He was wearing a goofy grin that looked more devious the longer the boy stared at it.

"I see you there," the voice warned with a chuckle, over the noise of the incoming monorail train. "You've got to come in. Trust me. The glasses are finally in and the sale begins TODAY!" His voice echoed throughout the system and the boy looked around nervously before opening the door and entering the space. This was the shop he'd been looking for. And before he could truly get comfortable, he heard the voice erupt in a greeting once more and turned to see a small square of glass hanging near the front door. Through the smooth, digital surface he could see people walking around the shop. They were too busy admiring items on triple-tiered display counters and shelves of colorful merchandise to notice or recognize him. So he felt comfortable enough to take off the glasses.

"There you are. Couldn't see you behind those," the voice blurted as the man's head moved across the square of glass. "Welcome to the Book store. Where all we sell is THE BOOK!" He announced the title with such forcefulness and compact excitement that the boy was eerily uncomfortable. A few girls crept into the store behind him, but the man on the glass seemed uninterested. Instead a woman's voice erupted from behind him welcoming them in.

THE BOOK

"Ladies, how are you this fine afternoon? How about trying *The Romantic Reader*? Last year's runaway hit." The boy watched in the reflection how the girls ignored the woman's voice and continued on. "With a casing of clear resin and a built-in nano-technological grid of L.E.D. lights that will glow in one of two colors based on the compatibility of the person nearest you with the same book, it's a way to meet your match and yet still have the experience of randomness that we girls don't get from dating sites." The persistence in the advertisement's tactic was working on them. "Green if they're compatible with your book. Red if they aren't. Find your husband TODAY!"

As the boy moved toward the center of the store, the male voice rattled again from a separate square of glass. "Is there something I can help you with today?"

"No thanks," the boy replied, before turning away. He knew what he was there to do and he walked directly to a shelf that was lined with dark green boxes. He reached for one and felt the 100% post-consumer recyclable content texture below his thumb. Its abnormally polished surface was smooth as he pulled it down. And through the cellophane skin, he saw the screen of the newest edition of The Book. On a tiny square of glass that rested like a minuscule photo frame on the shelf flashed the triangle of the recycling icon and the man who was way too thrilled to be the puppet of the publishing world.

"Looks like you got what you came for! Is there anything else I can interest you in? What about our *Optic-eyes*? Buy one TO-DAAAY," he sang, far too loudly, "See The Book the way it was always meant to be seen. Through an enhanced three-dimensional experience."

The boy turned away and searched the store that was lined with graphic images and superior displays with advertisements that pulsed life and energy, and walked directly to the line of people that were checking out. Behind the counter was a screen that stretched to the size of the wall. It showed an average adult with a smile on his face reading on his couch at home from an older edition of The Book. The scene was normal until the man reached for his reading glasses and instead, found himself placing a different pair over his eyes.

Suddenly he was in the middle of a battle where men were racing past him with guns, shooting off into the air as Native Americans with beautiful headdresses and costumes ran toward them with crazed, irregular faces. They were brutally torn down in front of the man on his couch through a hail of bullets and blood. The man with the glasses wore an outrageously wide grin as he removed them, only to find himself back in his living room. He looked down at the glasses in amazement as the goofy man, the voice of the Publishing House, came up to the screen. He began describing the enhancements of the new *Optic-eyes*. How it was an integrated entertainment system that would boost any version of The Book by digitizing a synthetic movie that would stream as you read, by recording your eye movements along the page and assessing where you were at in the story. And as you read each word, multiple images would play out on the glasses between your eyes and the page. A whole new dimensional experience would be awakened.

As the boy brought his package to the front and waited for the sales person to scan the item, he watched the screen illustrate a life-like representation of reading the Book through the new, interactive glasses. What he saw was as a series of images flashing at an amazing rate. They played out as a movie that seemed to flicker with the underlaid text. Words were highlighted on the digital page below the images, as if they were secondary to the experience. He had to turn away from it, but not because he had been overwhelmed. Like most of civilization,

THE BOOK

his digital mind was developed enough to process the data. No. The boy turned away because he felt that if he stared at it much longer he would suddenly buy the *Optic-eyes* instead. That he would turn away from what he was about to do and allow the glasses to absorb him from the comfort of his parent's couch. Unlike most of the people in line purchasing those glasses, the boy was frightened by them. What he had just finished reading that week had made him realize that everything in that store was evil. From the colors to the synthetic, automated images and animated friendliness of the androgynous gate keeper. They were all minor notes in a great composition of wrong.

After purchasing The Book, the boy walked directly to the inventory counter where a young man with spiked blonde hair was waiting with a smile. "Ready to fill up your Book?"

"Uh...yes, thank you," the boy said, masking his face further.

"I'll need to remove it from the box."

"Sure. Go ahead."

The man opened the box with quick, practiced movements and pulled the plastic wrapping from the inside before gently lifting the metal edition of The Book from its resting place. He plugged it into the main computer and began clicking away at a series of keys from below the counter. "So, let me give you the usual spiel. With every purchase of The Book you get fifty stories provided to you by the United States government. These stories come at no charge and are basically provided as a gift. It encourages your reading while expanding your knowledge on subject matter they deem relevant. So, let's talk stories. On the screen to your right, there are collections by category, by author or by random selection. While you take a look at those, I'll work on expanding your capacity. How many stories would you like to fit into your Book?"

"Ninety-seven thousand, seven hundred and seventy-seven."

The man with the spiked blonde hair stopped punching the keys. He pulled his lips together and tilted a curious eye up at the boy, only to swallow in a double take and blink rapidly in surprise before turning away. It wasn't from the number he had said. No. It was him. The boy had seen his face. No surprise there. It was a reaction that the boy had seen often. Strangers knew him. Or, at least, they thought they knew him. The spiky blonde man seemed to catch himself off guard and looked back down at the computer before rubbing his left ear nervously and scratching the back of his neck.

"That is an...irregular number. Are you sure ninety-eight thousand wouldn't just be easier?"

"No. That's the number I want."

The tone of the man's voice was now lower and more direct, after he took a deep breath and continued. "It's important that I tell you, going forth with such a decision may cause your system to crash and for you to...*lose everything*. Are you okay with that?"

"Yes."

"It's also important that I let you know," the man stammered in his usual speech. It seemed that he was unprepared to deal with this moment, as common as it would have appeared to everyone else in the room. "That I *inform* you of the number of people who have decided against such an operation and that you would go forward with such change at your own risk. Is that understood?"

The boy looked directly into the man's eyes, certain of his decision. "Yes. It is."

The man's demeanor shifted. He nodded and said, "This may take me quite a while. If you're willing to come in the back with me, there are a few things I would like to go over with you."

"I'll be a step behind you the whole way."

THE BOOK

The man continued to nod his blonde porcupine head profusely as he led the boy toward the swinging rear door of the shop. The digital screen along the face of the door continued its regurgitation of the reading man and the Indian battle as the door swung into the work room beyond. The people standing and talking and working in the separate spaces were silenced as they watched the boy walk toward the rear of the shop. Their eyes never left him.

Eventually they came to a long, three foot wide hallway that seemed, from all appearances, to be a dead end. Still they continued on. As the boy neared the back, a sliver of darkness became visible in the right corner. There was a gap between the walls, two feet wide. The man sidestepped his way into it and the boy followed without question. After thirty feet, they came to an opening that seemed only wide enough to accommodate the swing space for the massive metal door that stood ominous in the dim light.

Before the boy could respond to the environment, the man said, "This is where I leave you. Just know that even at the bottom of the staircase you still have an opportunity to turn around. It's important that you always recognize your freedom to choose. I may never see you again. So, allow me to be the one to congratulate you on making it through the first door."

The boy named Moses removed his hat and stuffed it into his back pocket, as the man with the spiky blonde hair punched a code into the keypad beside the door, scanned his eye in front of a small glass spoon that seemed a part of the wall and turned away. A gust of treated air escaped the pressurized door as it cracked an inch. The boy was too nervous to notice that the man had already left him alone. But he'd had courage enough to come to the mall and courage enough to find the store. He didn't think twice as he reached for the hefty metal handle, pulled the door wide and walked through.

The store he had been in was on the third floor of quite a wide and vast shopping system. But the staircase that he followed down had no exit for floors and floors. When he reached the single door at the bottom, there was a rectangular opening in the center at eye level and a series of keypads. He glanced up, tired and wondering how deep he had come. Because, without a doubt, he was stories below the main level.

He rapped his knuckles on the door and the rectangular window slid open to reveal a man's eyes. A grungy, deep voice spoke, "The number?"

"Ninety-seven thousand, seven hundred and seventy-seven."

The door opened with a series of beeps and clamping. The African American man standing before him was immense in stature. His face was scarred and war-torn. His arms immense enough to tear the boy in half. And yet, a look of surprise and a tinge of fear took over him and he tripped over his own feet as he stumbled back to allow the boy entrance into the darkened room beyond. Again this was a reaction the boy was used to.

"You're through door number two," the man said before leaving through the staircase.

The door closed with determination and the boy was left alone once more. The space he found himself in was dim with a few florescent lights that glowed faintly from the ceiling. The room wasn't very large. There were counters and rack systems, broken and lying unkempt around the room. Empty shelves lined the walls beside the disturbing presence of antique plasma television screens that flickered occasionally, as if trying desperately to welcome the visitor with advertising. The boy realized in an instant that he was inside a store from the shopping system that had once been the greatest feature in Illinois, before the rest of the world followed the idea.

It had been completely underground, below an enormous park with a small restaurant. After seventy years had passed, it was no longer a novelty and it fell into disrepair like so many other historical buildings. Apparently it had been preserved by someone. Purchased and covered with a new system in the very same spot so as to keep the lower system safe. Whatever the plan had been for the future of that space and whether or not it could be used for tourism, didn't matter. At that moment it was being used by the group Moses was attempting to locate.

Now standing in what had previously been an early edition of the Book store, he realized that the front for the faction he was trying to reach had been surreptitiously hidden behind the very object they had been attempting to overthrow. The boy looked to the walls and saw vintage advertising from generations earlier, when The Book had first been published. The posters had old images of bulky digital devices with cumbersome cords and happy faces. People with stacks of old paper books, handing them over to a government official with a grin. A sign read, *Recycle your books for the sake of your planet.* On a separate poster was an image of the earth with the recycling symbol as a large land mass. Over this, the words said, *Make your Mother proud! Read The Book.*

A fascinating series of posters were rolled together in a cubby hole and wrapped in a rubber band. The boy pulled them out carefully and unfurled the plastic material to find many images of famous movie stars posing by themselves in front of an empty book shelf with a copy of The Book in their perfectly manicured hands. Each of the posters was slightly different, but the subtle smirks on their doctored faces had the same arrogant, yet engaging manner. Along the base of the poster was a single word, running along in wide, bold lettering. A single word that captured all the haunting reality that had recently been revealed to him. The word was:

READ

The most intriguing of all, beside a life size cut out of some early advertising mascot, was a recognizable poster of Uncle Sam pointing to the reader. It was identical to the image he had seen so many times before, only now his clothes were white and green and the words below him said, *I Want YOU to Read The Book!* As the boy took in the rest of the darkened, decaying remnant of a once-glorious champion of technology, he saw a frayed vinyl banner that read, *Save the Environment and Enlarge your Mind* in sans serif green. *ASPHYXIATE* was spray painted in wide swaths of black over the word: *Enlarge*. He was sure that whoever sprayed over the banner found a simple pleasure in editing the Editors.

Still alone, the boy inspected the rest of the room, but there wasn't much to admire. Discarded graphic advertising and once-artistic furniture stacked over remnants of unusable technology. The only item he recognized that was still working was an ancient digital frame resting on the corner of a cobweb-crusted, green acrylic display counter. The boy approached the desk and turned the frame carefully. The screen was cracked and dusty. He wiped at it with the back of his thumb and could see the picture currently on display. It was similar to many he had seen in his lifetime. The photograph of someone standing in front of the bean in Chicago's Millennium Park. The man wore simple clothes that were no longer in style and he stood with his hands down at his sides like a soldier at attention. But there was something odd about him. Different than so many of the

THE BOOK

photographs he had seen over time of friends or family in front of the bean. He was elated. Every pixel the camera captured seemed to confirm this. His smile was stretched from ear to ear and his eyes were bright and wide. The boy wondered what could make the man so overjoyed. And then he remembered the story he had just read, the printed book that was still warm in his jacket pocket. This was the man from the story. Holden Clifford, on the day he had branded the bean. Suddenly the grin made perfect sense. That was before everything had changed. When their group was still simple and Martin Trust hadn't told him about the Library of Congress.

The image darkened under his thumb and a new one arrived. A large group of people were standing around a fire near a lake. There were two rows of them, and many were arm in arm. Along the first row were many children and young adults. They were book ended by a heavy-set Hawaiian man and an elderly gentleman in a bow tie who gripped his walker like a gymnast on a pommel horse. His smile was faint and guarded. It was Winston and Moby.

The second row of friends were standing on a wooden pier that stretched to the faded arches of a distant gazebo. The boy noticed him at once. Holden was standing toward the middle with his arm latched firmly around the shoulder of the man next to him. They carried the smile of old friends and the boy knew it had to be Shane. To Holden's left was a woman with strong features and tattoos on her shoulders. Marion. When the image dissolved to a candid of the same photo, the flames in the bonfire altered from the wind, the boy noticed that Marion had turned to look at Holden. The smile she wore was full of adoration and longing. Of course it was.

The boy heard footsteps and returned the frame to its place on the sleek, green surface.

From behind a half wall came a woman. She was tall and tired, with a face that didn't face him, hidden behind loose curls of stringy, horse hair. The rest was drawn into a long pony tail. The woman wore a visage of conflict and courage. And when the boy could finally see her face, he noticed how the lines that gouged her forehead in asymmetrical streaks resembled a Japanese seascape painting, where thin, delicate waves of wrinkles stretched on toward the setting sun.

She glanced at the boy and took him in for a moment before pulling a chair out from the acrylic counter. Until the moment she showed him the double doors to freedom, there was a cold indifference to everything she did.

"Have a seat."

Her voice was elsewhere.

He walked forward gingerly and took his place at the table. She sat across from him and said, "Give me your book."

The boy reached into his jacket pocket and pulled out a tattered edition of the printed story called *The Book*. The woman took it from him quickly and flipped to the inside cover before releasing an exasperated noise and slid it back to him through the dust, frustrated.

"This is an old copy number, which means you got this book from someone else. If you got it from someone else, that means they chose to remove it from their shelf and give it to you. When you leave here, give it back to them and get your own copy."

"I'm sorry...I..." He didn't know what to say. She had seen his face, hadn't she? He was shocked that she was talking to him that way. No one talked to him that way. Oddly enough, he found it comforting.

"Everyone should have a copy of this book. Don't recycle it. If people lend it to others, they are just as much to blame as those who may eventually destroy it. The more books exist, the

THE BOOK

more the truth I have written remains immortal. If there's one thing we've learned through all of this, it's that choosing to reuse items of power, handing them off to others without care and soon losing them, has been our ruin. We have the paper. We have the means. Everyone needs a copy of my book. The less copies out there, the fewer minds we're reaching."

Had he heard her right?

His words were slow and defenseless to someone who added little weight to them. "It was my brother's."

The woman shook her head and fiddled with the garbage at her feet. "I don't need to know how you heard about us. So many people, when they first come here, want to tell me how they heard about the story. Who gave them *The Book*. How they got here. What they can do to help us. I don't care about any of that. I just need to know that you're ready to do whatever we ask of you and to allow your talents and abilities to be used to further our cause."

"I am."

"You're young, so you must also be willing to accept any job we need to train you for in the real world."

"I will be."

She seemed slightly irritated as she continued. "We are at war. And with war come casualties. You've already walked through the first and second door. There's only one more door…once you go through it…that's it."

"Yes, I know."

"Stop answering so quickly. You're too confident in yourself. Most of us aren't that confident."

He waited. "I apologize. It's just that I…"

"I told you that I don't need to know," she said, rising from her seat. With her back to him, the boy felt a certain confusion coursing through his mind.

Had she said what he thought she had said?

"Excuse me...but did I hear you say that this is *your* book? As in, *you* wrote it?" He lifted the dilapidated stack of printed pages, looked at it for a moment and returned his eyes to her, recalling the introduction. "So you knew him? You knew Holden?" The woman nodded in silence and he couldn't help his need to understand. "How?"

She paced the room for a moment before approaching the boy and, without warning, began unbuttoning her tattered shirt. The boy, not of age to see such things, sat back embarrassed and shocked. What he saw in quick glances careened a flare of understanding through him and his jaw locked. The skin beyond the dirty white bra that hung loose on her flat chest was mangled from the stretching of skin and age, but he could still read the words that were branded across her chest: *Don't Read The Book*. Such sudden realization made her next words unnecessary.

"Holden was my father. He was the greatest man who ever lived. If I hear you say anything different...I'll feed you to the fire myself."

The boy agreed. As he watched her button her shirt and stare down at the digital frame on the desk, he understood her obsessive response. In fact, the first time the boy had learned of Holden Clifford, the terrorist Holden Clifford, was in school, where he had been taught about the destruction of our world's precious storage of printed books. Around his tenth birthday, when he received his first copy of The Book, he stumbled onto the story the government official Martin Trust had written years prior that described, in detail, the story of his friend, Holden Clifford and the anarchy of the misguided *Free Thinkers*. The story was called Propaganda. Even at that age, the boy knew that what he had been reading was a lie. And that this woman before him, Jane Clifford, had written a story that told the truth no one believed.

"You do realize that you're risking your life by being here?"

"I know."

"Who have you told about us?"

"No one."

"That will change," she finished. Jane, now tousled by maturity and a conflict he had only read about, nodded and thumbed flippantly over her shoulder. "Are you ready to go through the final door?"

"Yes," he replied too quickly. He rose from his seat and followed her toward the darkened glass doors of the prehistoric store. Ready for the biggest decision of his life.

With the crank of an angry handle, the doors gave way and the boy was ushered into an entirely new world. A secret world, like nothing he had ever seen. As he stepped out onto the filthied floor, the boy found that he had guessed right. He stood in the lofty expanse of an ancient, underground mall that had been taken over by the *Ex Libris*.

The serpentine pathways, once white and enticing and stretching over a chasm to the floors of shopping below, were now mangy and lined with cracked plastic bins of random shapes and colors. The undulating facades that led high to diamond cut skylights and sharply geometric ceilings were now cracked and boarded over, stripped with garlands of cobwebs and wire that provided electricity to the thousands of hanging light bulbs in the space above and beyond. Jane, looking suddenly more warm and happy to have him beside her, led the boy toward the end of a long shopping strip until they could reach a railing and look down upon the world below.

At the junction of so many pathways, the boy found himself at the main entrance to the mall and facing an immense wall of elevators that were stuck at odd heights and utilized as storage. As he approached the railing and the ramps to go down, he was immediately bombarded by the sounds of systems working all around him. The network of paths and shops, once covered in decorative glass awnings and digital advertisements, were now teeming with machinery and hundreds of grubby people carrying supplies. There were spindles and cranks, plates of metal that somersaulted over one another, gears and coils and rotating platforms that all seemed to be running off of a team of five workers riding stationary bicycles.

Behind this, in an area that appeared to have once served food, groups of people were reading under an enormous green board that was covered in lists of book titles in white, scratchy writing. It was a chalkboard. He had never seen one before. And he gradually came to the conclusion, through the stacks of fresh paper all around them, that the lists were of new books they had been printing like the one he still grasped in his hand. The machines were also running ingeniously off the water from the elderly waterfall to the right of the elevators. One of the water features that had been so popular when his grandfather was a boy. As he studied the massive apparatus, he decided that what he was seeing was a single, manual printing press. They didn't work by scanning or ink jets like The Book had told him. Each letter was chosen very carefully and by a person that loved each word they spelled. The people were printing with blocks and paper that they had made by hand beside a waterfall that left puddles of cool water at their feet and a pleasant mist in the air. It was, perhaps, the most majestic sight he had ever seen.

When he was finished admiring it all, Jane walked him down the next alleyway, to where they passed countless miles of shops that stretched to the stories below and all of which were filled with furniture and families and toddlers. He would never have

THE BOOK

guessed that the mall would have been retrofitted in such a way. But it made sense. They needed to be protected. They needed a home, just like they once had at Winston Pratt's. So all the stores in that wing had been converted into simple, small apartments.

Home again, home again, the boy thought, as they continued on.

At the opposite end of the underground mall, where the clamor of the immense printing presses could never be heard, there came a subtle glow from a wide skylight above. Once he was under its delicate rays, the boy understood where it had come from. In the system above them was a great, rectangular art installation that stretched high, beyond the roof, and was covered in tiles of unreadable black and white script. It must have been hollow and installed only to provide light to that section of the underground.

And as the boy contemplated what could have been so important to warrant such effort, he came to a long string of chalkboards that wove in and out of every shop for a mile in each direction. Up close, he could see that they were all coated in lists of books. Stories that were still missing pages. Looking down excitedly to the four stories of old shopping below, lit delicately by the sun, he saw stacks upon stacks of bookshelves, hiding behind a vast configuration of empty stores. The moment he saw the spray painted genre titles above each of the doors, shadowing the ancient, illuminated signage, the boy's dream was confirmed. An enormous library of printed paper books was directly below his feet. He couldn't believe it. Even after staring for ten minutes and taking in all the hundreds of people who walked the network of roads that threaded across the chasm to the bottom, he still couldn't believe his eyes. Even with the Library of Congress burned to the ground, the *Ex Libris* had found more books than anyone, in their wildest imaginations, could have dreamt possible.

"How?" he asked, his voice breathless.

"Finch," Jane replied, referencing the man from the story who had sold books on the black market. "When they had a funeral service for my father, and they discussed burying his favorite book in his honor, Finch was reminded of something that happened all over the world during The Great Recycling. It was a thought that neither he, nor anyone else, had ever entertained, because it was disrespectful to disturb the deceased. But during that time, people who loved their books too much to see them mulched by the government asked their family to respect their wishes and, at their death, they were cremated and placed in an urn to make room in their coffin for something far more important than their body."

"For books?"

"For love," she corrected. "They loved their characters. Their authors. The writing. What the stories meant to them. And they simply couldn't go to their graves knowing the pages they cried over...the ones that made them who were, would ever be destroyed. We discussed the idea for a long time, with many of the families, and decided to act in the best interest of the stories that were hidden and waiting in every country in the world. And it was almost as if those people, those lovers of words, knew that one day we would need their novels because we discovered that every grave stone with a book etched beside the name of the deceased from that time would be filled with literature. So it was, with deep respect and unending gratitude to those sensible enough to see their worth, that we retrieved this library from the readers that had been protecting it for us and then laid them respectfully back into the ground."

"Where the books had been resting."

THE BOOK

Jane nodded, finished the thought for him. "Resting in peace."

As a few people began to notice the new boy standing beside their famed leader, they stopped and lowered their books. More people noticed the hitch in their pace and stopped as well, turning to see what was so important. And then they saw him also. Whispers spread across the system of ancient stores and the machines slowed until all reading and all speech stopped mid-sentence. Below the boy, and under his smiling face, the librarians stopped shelving. The binders stopped binding. The teachers stopped teaching. Everyone stopped and stood and looked up at the boy that had just entered their home.

Nearby, in a room with many books, there stood an elderly Hawaiian giant with tattoos across his neck and a thin chicken-legged old man who was rambling on to one of the younger children that they were supposed to ask permission before taking one of the books down from the shelves. The kid giggled and scurried back into the mall with the book. When Shane turned to chase him, he noticed the lines of people along the walkway, standing and staring up at the level above. He kicked Moby in the shin and waved him over. Something was going on.

As they approached the door, they noticed the child circling past groups of people who were holding stacks of books and gazing with grins on their tired faces. With even, arthritic steps, the once-great men stepped out onto the walkway and reached for the railing. Finally there, they squinted up at all the fuss.

Moby was the first to recognize him.

"Dagget...is that who I think it is?"

A smile that stretched years into the past, came at long last to rest on his withering face. "Yeah, bro. It is."

In the still silence of the nation of readers, Holden's daughter felt a tear escape her eyes for the first time since she was a child. They were clapping. The riot of applause was so loud; it could have brought the mall to the ground above them. But even if someone had heard them, it would not matter. Their freedom was alive. Jane reached into her pocket and took out a single set of silver fingernail clippers. She handed them to the boy who took them eagerly. He rotated the wing and prepared to cut, under the words *Ex Libris*, but found a different phrase etched into the metal. He pushed down on the sharpened nail of his pointer finger and felt the engraving under his thumb.

Don't read The Book.

Note From The Author

My book is a work of dystopian fiction. I do not presume to know what the ramifications of digital books will be on the future of traditional publishing. I am only, in good, old-fashioned make-believe, assuming what route the next generations will take, based on the current state of recycling, sustainability, the disregard of the typed or printed word, and online information databases like Wikipedia – where anyone can edit the historical truth. I find it apropos that the completion of my story coincides (to the day) with the unfortunate passing of J.D. Salinger, the author of *The Catcher in the Rye*, and the poignant announcement of the *iPad* by Apple. If the progression of the digital music is any indication, handheld electronic media devices (THE BOOK, in my novel) will become popular with the younger generations and reading will be preferred through this new medium. Of course, I do not wish for my e-book to fail. Everyone should rally behind such convenient innovation. My impetus for this story lies in the importance of the printed word and what it used to mean for us as a civilization.

My hope is that not only would my book gain appreciation as a cautionary tale against abandoning the written or printed word, but that it could potentially revolutionize the thinking of readers across the world. Young readers that will one day run this country. That they would feel a duty to themselves and their future children to keep truth and freedom alive by continuing to read from printed books and passing laws to protect their digital content from censorship. And it is never too late to begin.

I'll leave you with a quote from the famous playwright George Bernard Shaw who won the Nobel Prize for Literature in 1925.

"The reasonable man adapts himself to the world; the unreasonable man persists in trying to adapt the world to himself. Therefore all progress depends on the unreasonable man."

Acknowledgments

ROBERT FROST: "The Road Not Taken" from *Mountain Interval* collection (Holt 1916), Public Domain (release date 2009), published by BiblioLife.

LOUISA MAY ALCOTT: from *Little Women* (Roberts Brothers 1868), © 2009 by Simon & Schuster, Inc., published by Signet Classics, a division of Penguin Group (USA) Inc.

J.D. SALINGER: from *The Catcher in the Rye* (Bantam Books 1951), © 1979 by Jerome David Salinger, published by Little Brown and Company, a division of Hachette Book Group USA.

W. SOMERSET MAUGHAM: from *Of Human Bondage* (Modern Library 1915), © 1995 by R. Andrew Boose, authorized agent of Liza Hope a.k.a. Lady Glendevon, sole child of the late author W. Somerset Maugham, published by Signet Classics, a division of Penguin Group (USA) Inc.

HANS CHRISTIAN ANDERSON: "The Steadfast Tin Soldier" from *Fairy Tales Told for Children. New Collection. First Booklet* (C.A. Reitzel 1838), Public Domain.

F. SCOTT FITZGERALD: from *The Great Gatsby* (Charles Scribner's Sons 1925), © 1990 by trustees under agreement dated July 3, 1975 by Francis Scott Fitzgerald Smith, published by Scribner, a division of Simon & Schuster.

J.M. BARRIE: from *Peter Pan* (Scribner 1911), Public Domain as of 2007, published most recently by Ann Arbor Media Group.

LEWIS CARROLL (AKA: CHARLES LUTWIDGE DODGSON): from *Alice's Adventures in Wonderland* (Macmillan 1865), Public Domain, published recently by Signet Classics, a division of Penguin Group (USA) Inc.

L. Frank Baum: from *The Patchwork Girl of Oz* (Reilly & Britton Company 1913), Public Domain, published recently by HarperCollins.

Diane Setterfield: from *The Thirteenth Tale* (Atria Books 2006), © 2006 by Diane Setterfield, published by Washington Square Press, a division of Simon & Schuster.

Abraham Lincoln: from *Letter to Horace Greeley*, Public Domain.

Acts Chapter 17, Verse 11: from *The Bible, New King James Version* (Thomas Nelson Publishers 1982), © 1982 by Thomas Nelson, Inc., Used by permission. All rights reserved.

Luke Chapter 21, Verse 33: from *The Bible, New King James Version* (Thomas Nelson Publishers 1982), © 1982 by Thomas Nelson, Inc., Used by permission. All rights reserved.

*Efforts have been made to trace or contact all copyright holders. The author asks that any omissions be brought to his notice at the earliest opportunity.

God Bless America.
Keep the planet alive.
Recycle your books.
This is not propaganda.

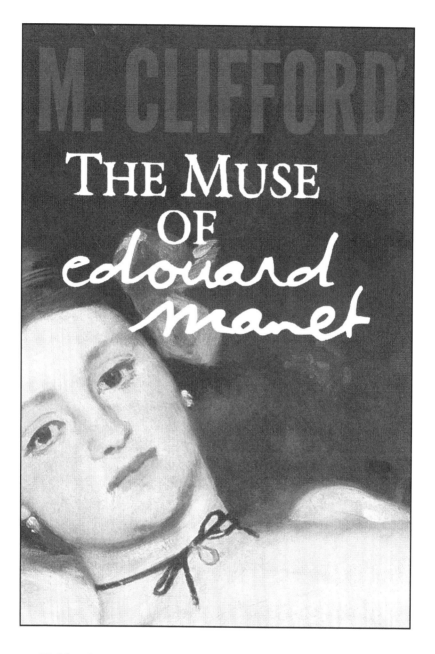

Hidden beneath a painting at the Art Institute of Chicago is a letter in lead white paint that can only be read by x-ray. Emily Porterfield found this letter. And it brought her to Edouard. Across time.

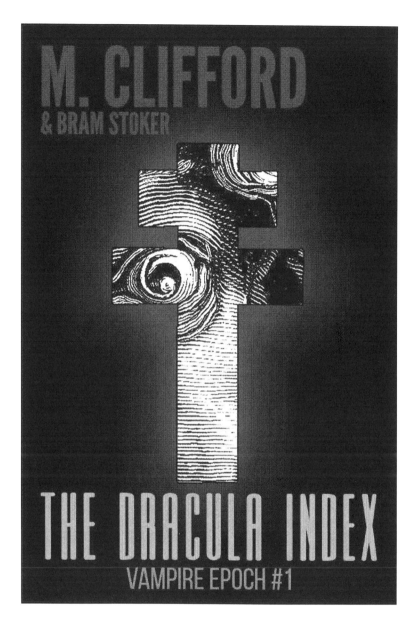

Mell and Bryne are questioning their existence in Encampment R-34, one of the last remaining settlements in the wasteland, circled by tall wooden crosses. Their curiosity turns dangerous when they discover a computer terminal in the ruins of a nearby encampment and a tattered journal outside the protection of their valley.

Made in the USA
Lexington, KY
18 August 2018